TERRIFIED...

It was supposed to be a harmless camping trip. Six wayward teenagers who'd run into trouble with the law, and their court-appointed guardians, Sara and Martin Randhurst. Three nights on a small, deserted island off of Michigan's upper peninsula. A time to bond, to learn, to heal.

Then Martin told a campfire story about the island's history. Of the old civil war prison hidden in there, and the starving confederate soldiers who resorted to cannibalism to stay alive. Everyone thought it was funny. They even laughed when Martin pretended to be dragged off into the woods.

But Martin didn't come back. And neither did Sara when she went in search of him.

Then the laughter stopped.

...TO DEATH

The group soon began to realize that this deserted island wasn't so deserted after all. And perhaps Martin's ridiculous story had more truth to it than anyone thought.

What's the most horrifying thing you can imagine?

This is a hundred times worse...

TRAPPED by Jack Kilborn

It starts where other horror ends

TRAPPED

A novel of terror

JACK KILBORN

Everyone is a moon, and has a dark side which he never shows to anybody.

—MARK TWAIN

There are six books in the Konrath/Kilborn Collective. ORIGIN, THE LIST, AFRAID, TRAPPED, *and* ENDURANCE *are the first five, and can be read in any order. The sixth,* HAUNTED HOUSE, *contains characters from each of the previous books.*

TRAPPED

PROLOGUE

He couldn't move.

The table he lay on was cold against his naked back. There were no ropes binding his arms, no belts securing his legs. But he was immobile, paralyzed.

Yet he was still able to feel.

Panicked thoughts swirled through his brain. *Where am I? Was I in an accident? I can't open my eyes. Am I blind? Am I dead? I can still think, so I must be alive. But I can't move. Can't talk. What's happening to me?*

He concentrated, hard as he could, trying to move his hands and touch his face.

Nothing happened.

Noise, from the right. Footsteps. His body didn't seem to work, but thankfully, his ears did.

Someone's in the room.

He felt a hand touch his face, and then saw painful bright light.

A doctor in a green smock stared down at him.

He just pried my eyelids open.

"Good morning. You're disoriented, I bet. Confused. Probably can't even remember how you got here." The doctor's voice was scratchy, strained, as if he wasn't accustomed to using it.

Please, tell me what's going on...

"You can't move because you've been given a paralytic." He was an older man, bald, his scrubs stained. "Unfortunately, you have to remain conscious for this procedure to work."

The doctor walked off, out of sight. The man's eyes remained open, unblinking, gazing into the light overhead. *Am I in an operating room? What procedure? Who was that doctor?*

It was bright, but it didn't seem bright enough to be a hospital. The light was yellowish, dingy, coming from a naked bulb hanging from the ceiling. And there was a smell. Not an antiseptic, care-facility smell. A smell of rot and decay.

"The drug immobilizes the skeletomuscular system." The doctor was somewhere near his feet. The man couldn't move his eyes to see him. "You're completely helpless. One more dose and you'd stop breathing altogether."

The doctor rested a hand on the man's knee, gave it a pat.

"You've lost your reflexes, your ability to flinch. But other vital functions remain active."

A sudden pressure, between his legs. The doctor was squeezing his testicles. The agony bloomed, white hot and inescapable. His vision went blurry. He tried to pull away, tried with all of his might, but he didn't budge an inch.

"You can still feel pain, as I'm sure you notice. Lacrimation is normal, for now. Your pupils can dilate. And, of course, your pulse and heart rate just shot up considerably. The drug keeps you from moving so I can do the procedure, but it doesn't shut you down completely."

The man felt the tears flow down the sides of his head, the throb still lingering after the doctor released his grip.

This wasn't a hospital. It couldn't be. A doctor wouldn't do that to me. What the hell was going on?

Then he heard the most agonizing scream of his life.

It didn't come from the room, but from someplace else in the building. Nearby, maybe a room or two over. The scream was so shrill it didn't sound human at first. Then it lost pitch and was replaced by shouting.

"NO! PLEASE NO! STOP IT! JESUS NOOOOOO!"

What are they doing to that poor guy?

And what are they going to do to me?

"That's one of Lester's guests," the doctor said. "Lester has been with him for a few hours now. I'm surprised he still has a voice left. I shudder to think what's being done to make him cry out like that. Do you recognize who it is?"

And then, all at once, the man knew who was screaming. He remembered how they got there. The strange noises. Being chased. Hunted. Running terrified. And then being caught. Caught by…

"No need to worry." The doctor leaned over him, smiling. Crumbs wedged in the corners of his thin lips, on his chin, and a small streak of something brown—*blood?*—smeared across his age-spotted forehead. "You won't end up like that. You're being given a gift. An invaluable, extraordinary gift. The world is full of lambs. But very few get to be wolves. Lester's playmate, sadly for him, is a lamb. But you, *you*, my lucky fellow—you're about to become a wolf."

The doctor raised a gigantic syringe.

"This is going to hurt. Quite a bit, in fact."

The man couldn't move, couldn't turn away, and he was forced to watch and feel as the needle descended and plunged into his unblinking eye.

PART I
CAMPFIRE STORIES

Sara Randhurst felt her stomach roll starboard as the boat yawed port, and she put both hands on the railing and took a big gulp of fresh, lake air. She wasn't anywhere near Cindy's level of discomfort—that poor girl had been heaving non-stop since they left land—but she was a long way from feeling her best.

Strangely enough, Jack seemed to be enjoying it. The three-month-old baby in the sling around Sara's chest had a grin on his face and was drooling happily. Sara pulled a tissue from the sling's pocket and wiped off her son's chin, wondering how anyone, especially someone so small and fragile, could actually like this awful motion. Even though she was feeling ill, she smiled at the sight of him. Just like she did every time.

Sara closed her eyes, bending her knees slightly to absorb some of the pitch and roll. The nausea reminded Sara of her honeymoon. She and Martin had booked a Caribbean cruise, and their first full day as a married couple found both of them vomiting veal piccata and wedding cake into the Pacific. Lake Huron was smaller than the ocean, the wave crests not as high and troughs not as low. But they came faster and choppier, which made it almost as bad.

Sara opened her eyes, searching for Martin. The only one on deck was Cindy Welp, still perched over the railing. Sara approached the teen on wobbly footing, then rubbed her back. Cindy's blonde hair looked perpetually greasy, and her eyes were sunken and her skin colorless; more a trait of her addiction to meth than the seasickness.

"How are you doing?" Sara asked.

Cindy wiped her mouth on her sleeve. "Better. I don't think there's anything left in me."

Cindy proved herself a liar a moment later, pulling away and retching once again. Sara gave her one last reassuring pat, then padded her way carefully up to the bow. The charter boat looked deceptively smaller before they'd gotten on. But there was a lot of space onboard; both a foredeck and an aft deck, a raised bow, plus two levels below boasting six rooms. Though they'd been sailing for more than two hours, Sara had only run into four of their eight-person party. Martin wasn't one of them. It was almost like he was hiding.

Which, she supposed, he had reason to do.

A swell slapped the boat sideways, spritzing Sara with water. It tasted clean, just like the air. A seagull cried out overhead, a wide white M against the shocking blue of sky. She wondered, fleetingly, what if be like to feel so free, so alive like that.

In the distance, a green dot against the expanse of dark water, was Rock Island. Even from this far away, Sara noticed its wedge shape, the north side of it several times the height of the south, dropping off at a sharp cliff.

Sara shivered, protectively cupping her hands around Jack.

There was a soft thump, next to her. Sara jumped at the sound.

Another gull. It had hopped onto the deck, and was staring at her with tiny black eyes. Sara touched her chest, feeling her heart bounce against her fingers.

Just a bird. No need to be so jumpy.

Sara squinted west, toward the sun. It was getting low over the lake, turning the clouds pink and orange, hinting at a spectacular sunset to come. A month ago, when she and Martin had planned this trip, staring at such a sun would have made her feel energized. Watching it now made Sara sad. A final bow before the curtain closed for good.

Sara continued to move forward, her gym shoes slippery, the warm summer breeze already drying the spray on her face. At the prow, Sara saw Tom Gransee, bending down like he was trying to touch the water rushing beneath them.

"Tom! Back in the boat please."

Tom spun around, saw Sara, and grinned Then he took three quick steps and skidded across the wet deck like a skateboarder. Tom's medication didn't quite control his ADHD, and the teenager was constantly in motion. He even twitched when he slept.

"No running!" Sara called after him, but he was already on the other side of the cabin, heading below.

Sara peeked at the sun once more, retied the flapping floral print shirttails across her flat belly, and headed after Tom.

She stopped at the top of the stairs. The stairwell was tight, and the sunlight didn't penetrate it.

"Tom?" she called down after him.

He didn't respond. Sara hesitated, adjusted the knit cap on Jack's head, then took the first step down.

As she descended the staircase, the mechanical roar of the engine overtook the calm tempo of the waves. The hallway was dark, cramped. Sara didn't like it, and she picked up her pace, her palms on the walls searching for a light switch and not finding any. Her breath quickened, and her fingers finally grazed some protuberance which she grasped like it was a life preserver. She flipped it up and an overhead light came on.

Sara sighed, then chided herself for feeling so relieved. She tried to remember the Captain's name.

Captain Prendick. A peculiar name, but a familiar one; Sara recalled it used in an old H.G. Wells horror novel.

Prendick was the ninth person on the boat, and Sara hadn't seen him lately either. Her only meeting with the man was during their brief but intense negotiation when they arrived at the dock. He was grizzled, tanned, and wrinkled, with a personality to match, and he argued with Sara about their destination, insisting on taking them someplace closer than Rock Island. He only relented after they agreed to bring his extra handheld marine radio along, in case of emergencies.

Sara wondered where the captain was now. She assumed he was on the bridge, but didn't know where to find it. Maybe Martin was with him. Sara wasn't sure if her desire to speak with Martin was to console him or persuade him. Perhaps both. Or maybe they could simply spend a few moments together without talking. Sara could remember when silence between them was a healthy thing.

A skinny door flew open, and Meadowlark Purcell burst out. Meadow had a pink scar across the bridge of his flattened nose, a disfigurement from when he was *blooded in* to a Detroit street gang. The boy narrowed his dark brown eyes at Sara, then smiled in recognition.

"Hey, Sara. I was you, I wouldn't go in there for a while." He fanned his palm in front of his nose.

"I'm looking for Martin. Seen him?"

Meadow shook his head. "I be hangin' with Laneesha and Tyrone, playin' cards. We gonna be there soon?"

"Captain said two hours, and we're getting near that point."

"True dat?"

"Yes."

"Cool."

Meadow wandered off. Sara closed the bathroom door, made her way up another cramped flight of stairs, and found the bridge. Captain Prendick was at the wheel, his potbelly pressed against it, one hand scratching the stubble on his chin. He noticed Sara and gave her a brief nod.

"Have you seen Martin?" Sara asked.

Prendick motioned with his chin. Sara followed the gesture and saw her husband folded up in a chair, legs crossed out in front of him and his eyes closed, chin touching his chest. Sara momentarily forgot everything she wanted to tell him, everything she wanted to say.

"Martin…"

"I'm not up for talking right now, Sara."

He kept his eyes closed. Jack, hearing his father's voice, wiggled and cooed.

Sara glanced at Prendick.

"I'm running to the head," the captain said to Sara as he flipped a switch on the panel, next to a picture of him and an elderly woman. "We're on autopilot."

Captain Prendick slid past her, his expression dour. Sara moved closer to Martin, put a hand on his shoulder.

"Don't," he said.

"Martin, maybe if we talked about—"

Her husband's eyelids flipped open. They looked unbelievably sad.

"I love you, Sara."

Sara felt her chest get heavy. "Martin…"

"Do you know I love you? That I love you and Jack?"

She nodded, unable to answer because of the lump in her throat.

"Then we don't have anything to talk about."

Martin held her gaze until his eyes became glassy, and then he closed them again.

Sara wanted to touch his cheek, cup his chin and tell him it was all going to be okay even though it wasn't. Then she left the bridge and made her way back into the bowels of the boat. She opened the first door she came to. In the darkness she made out the shape of a chubby girl asleep on a narrow bed. Georgia. Sara tried the next door. Another cabin, this one empty. After a brief hesitation, Sara went into the room, pulled the folding bed away from the wall, and sat down, making sure she left the door open.

The waves weren't as pronounced down here, and the rocking motion was gentler. Sara again thought of her honeymoon with Martin. How, once they got their sea legs, they spent all of their time on the ship, in their tiny little cabin, skipping exotic ports to instead order room service and make love. After a rough beginning, it turned out to be a perfect trip.

Sara checked the door again, rubbed Jack's back, and closed her eyes, wishing it could be like that again.

*   *   *

It was a night exactly like tonight, a few years ago," Martin said. "Late summer. Full moon. Just before midnight. The woods were quiet. Quiet, but not completely silent. It's never completely silent in the woods. It seems like it is, because we're all used to the city. But there are always night sounds. Sounds that only exist when the sun goes down and the dark takes over. Everyone shut your eyes and listen for a moment."

Sara indulged her husband, letting her eyelids close. Gone were the noises so common in Detroit; cars honking, police sirens, arguing drunks and cheering Tigers fans and bursts of live music when bar doors swung open. Instead, here on the island, there were crickets. A breeze whistling through the pines. An owl. The gentle snaps and crackles of the campfire they sat around. Jack's breath on her neck, slow and steady from sleep.

After a few seconds someone belched.

"My bad," Tyrone said, raising his hand.

This prompted laughter from almost everyone, Sara included. Martin kept his expression solemn, not breaking character. Seeing Martin like that made Sara remember why she fell in love with him. Her husband had always been passionate about life, and gave everything his all, whether it was painting the garage, starting a business, or telling silly campfire stories to scare their kids.

Her smile faded. They won't be *their kids* for very much longer.

"It happened on an island," Martin continued. "Just like this one. In fact, now that I think about it, this might actually *be* the island where it all happened."

Tyrone snorted. "This better not be the same island, dog, or my black ass is jumping in that mofo lake 'n swimming back to civilization."

More laughter, but this time it was clipped. Uneasy. These teenagers had never been this far from an urban environment, and weren't sure how to act.

Sara shivered, tucking the blanket in around her baby. All the things she wanted to say to Martin earlier were still bottled up inside because she hadn't had the chance. Since the boat dropped them off, it had been all about hiking and setting up camp and eating dinner, and Sara hadn't been able to catch him alone. He'd been intentionally avoiding her, staying busy, keeping that smile on his face like it had been sculpted there.

"Was it really this island?" Laneesha asked. Her voice was condescending, almost defiant. But there was a bit of edge to it, a tiny hint of fear.

"No, it wasn't," Sara said. "Martin, tell her it wasn't."

Martin didn't say anything, but he did give Laneesha a sly wink.

"So where was it?" Georgia asked, though her face showed zero curiosity.

"It wasn't anywhere, Georgia." Sara slapped at a mosquito that had been biting her neck, then wiped the tiny splot of blood onto her jeans. "This is a campfire story. It's made up, to try to scare you."

"It's fake?" Georgia sneered. "Pretend?"

Sara nodded. "Yes, it's pretend. Right, Martin?"

Martin shrugged, still not looking at Sara.

"So what pretend-happened?" Laneesha asked.

"There were eight people." Martin was sitting on an old log, higher up than everyone else. "Camping just like we are. On a night like tonight. On what might be this very island. They vanished, these eight, never to be seen again. But some folks who live around here claim to know what happened. Some say those unfortunate eight people were subjected to things worse than death."

Meadow folded his arms. "Ain't nothin' worse than death."

Martin stared hard at the teenager. "There are plenty of things worse."

No one spoke for a moment. Sara felt a chill. Maybe it was the cool night breeze, whistling through the woods. Or maybe it was Martin's story, which she had to admit was getting sort of creepy. But Sara knew the chill actually went deeper. As normal as everyone seemed right now, it was only an illusion. Their little family was breaking apart.

But she didn't want to think about that. Now, she wanted to enjoy this final camping trip, to make some good memories.

Sara scooted a tiny bit closer to the campfire and put her arms around Jack. The night sky was clear, the stars bright against the blackness of space, the hunter's moon huge and tinged red. Beyond the smoke Sara could smell the pine trees from the surrounding woods, and the big water of Huron, a few hundred yards to the west. As goodbyes went, this was a lovely setting for one.

She let her eyes wander over the group. Tyrone Morrow, seventeen, abandoned by a mother who could no longer control him, running with one of Motor City's worst street gangs for more than two years. Dressed in a hoodie and jeans so baggy they'd fall around his ankles without the belt.

Meadow was on Tyrone's right. He was from a rival Detroit club. That they were sitting next to each other was a commitment from each on how much they wanted out of the gangsta life.

On Meadow's side, holding his hand, Laneesha Simms. Her hair was cropped almost as short as the boys', but her make-up and curves didn't allow anyone to mistake her for a man.

Georgia Dailey sat beside Laneesha. Sixteen, white, brunette, pudgy. She held a long stick and was poking at something on the ground; a dead frog, belly-up with its legs jutting out. Sara thought about saying something, decided to let it go.

Behind Georgia, Tom Gransee predictably paced around the fire, tugging at his wifebeater T like it was an extra skin he wanted to shed.

These were kids society had given up on, sentenced into their care by the courts. But Martin—and by extension, Sara—hadn't given up on them. That was why they created the Second Chance Center.

Sara finally rested her gaze on Martin. The fire flickered across his handsome features, glinted in his blue eyes. He had aged remarkably well, looking closer to twenty than thirty, as athletic as the day she met him in that graduate psych class. She looked down at her son in the baby sling—a miniature version of Martin—and absently rubbed his back.

"On this dark night six years ago," Martin continued, "this group of eight people took a boat onto Lake Huron. The SS Minnow."

Sara smiled, knowing she was the only one old enough to have caught the *Gilligan's Island* reference, the boat the castaways had taken on their three hour tour.

"They had some beer with them," Martin said. "Some pot..."

"Hells yeah." Tyrone and Meadow bumped fists.

"...and were set to have a big party. But one of the women—there were four men and four women, just like us—got seasick on the lake."

"I hear that." In her oversized jersey and sweatpants, Cindy looked tiny, shapeless. But Sara noted she'd gotten a little bit of her color back.

"So they decided," Martin raised his voice, "to beach the boat on a nearby island, continue the party there. But they didn't know the island's history."

Tom had stopped his pacing and was standing still, rare for him. "What history, Martin?"

Martin smiled. An evil smile, his chin down and his eyes hooded, the shadows drawing out his features and making him look like an angry wolf.

"In 1862, done in secret, Rock Island Prison was built here to house captured Confederate soldiers. Like many civil war prisons, the conditions were horrible. But this one was worse than most. It was run by a war profiteer named Mordecai Plincer. He stole the money that was supposed to be used to feed the prisoners, and ordered his guards to beat them so they wouldn't stage an uprising while they starved to death. He didn't issue blankets, even during the winter months, giving them nothing more to wear than burlap sacks with arm and leg holes cut out, even when temperatures dropped to below freezing."

Sara wasn't a history buff, but she was pretty sure there was never a civil war prison on an island in Lake Huron. She wondered if Martin is using Camp Douglas as the source of this tall tale. It was located in Chicago near Lake Michigan and considered the northern counterpart to the horrors committed at the Confederate prison, Andersonville.

Yes, Martin has to be making this up. Though that name, Plincer, does sound familiar.

Martin tossed one of the branches they'd gathered earlier onto the fire. It made a *whump* sound, throwing sparks and cinders.

"But those starving, tortured prisoners staged a rebellion anyway, killing all of the guards, driving Plincer from the island. The Union, desperate to cover up their mistake, stopped sending supplies. But the strongest and craziest of the prisoners survived. Even though the food ran out."

"How?" Tom asked. "You said there are no animals on this island."

Martin smiled, wickedly. "They survived... *by eating each other.*"

"Oh, snap." Tyrone shook his head. "That shit is sick."

Sara raised an eyebrow at her husband. "Cannibalism, Martin?"

Martin looked at her, for the first time in hours. She searched for some softness, some love, but he was all wrapped up in his menace act.

"Some were cooked. Some were eaten raw. And during the summer months, when meat would spoil, some were kept alive so they could be eaten one piece at a time."

Sara did a quick group check, wondering if this story was getting too intense. Everyone appeared deadly serious, their eyes laser-focused on Martin. No one seemed upset. A little scared, maybe, but these were tough kids. She decided to let Martin keep going.

Martin stood up, spreading out his hands. "Over the last five decades, more than a hundred people have vanished on this part of Lake Huron. Including those eight men and women. What happened to them was truly horrible."

The crickets picked that eerie moment to stop chirping. Sara noticed a brief flash in her peripheral vision. Lightening? No, the weather was fine. Besides, this seemed to have come from the woods. She scanned the woods, waiting for it to happen again. They stayed dark.

Cindy eventually broke the silence. "What happened to them?"

"It's said that these war prisoners became more animal than human, feeding on each other and on those men unlucky enough to visit. Unfortunately for this group of eight partiers, they were all doomed the minute they set foot onto Plincer's Island. When their partying died down, and everyone was drunk and stoned and passing out, the prisoners built a gridiron."

The word *gridiron* hung in the air like a crooked painting, blending into the forest sounds.

Tyrone whispered, "They built a football field?"

Martin shook his head. "The term *gridiron* is used for football these days, but it's a much older word. It was a form of execution in ancient Rome. Coals are spread over the ground, stoked until they're red hot. Then the victim is put in a special iron cage, sort of like a grill, and placed on top of the coals, roasting him alive. Unlike being burned at the stake, which is over in a few minutes, it takes hours to die on the gridiron. They say the liquid in your eyes gets so hot, it boils."

Sara stood up. Martin should have known not to go there with the gore. "I think that's enough, Martin. You've succeeded in freaking everyone out." She forced joviality. "Now who wants to roast some marshmallows?"

"I want to hear what happened to those people," Tom said.

"And I want to be able to sleep tonight," Sara replied.

Sara's eyes met Martin's. She saw intensity there, but also resignation, and something else. Something soft and happy. Eventually his lips curled into a grin.

"But we haven't gotten to the part where I pretend to be dragged off into the woods, kicking and screaming. That's the best part."

Sara placed her hands on her hips, feeling herself smile. "I'm sure we would have all been terrified."

Martin sat back down. "You're the boss. And if the boss wants to do marshmallows, who am I to argue?"

"I thought you're the one who created the Center," Laneesha asked.

Martin glanced at Sara. There was kindness in his eyes, and maybe some resignation, too.

"Sara and I created it together. We wanted to make a difference. The system takes kids who are basically good but made a few mistakes, sticks them into juvee hall, and they come out full blown crooks. The Center is aimed at giving these kids positive direction and helping them to change." Martin smiled sadly. "Well, that *was* its purpose."

"It's bullshit the man cut your program, Martin." Meadow tossed a stick onto the fire.

"It sucks," Cindy added.

There were nods of agreement. Martin shrugged. "Things like this happen all the time. I'm sorry I couldn't do more for you kids. Sara, Jack, and I are a small family, but you guys are like our—"

Martin screamed in mid-sentence, then fell backward off the log, rolling into the bushes and the darkness.

．　　．　　．

Sara, like everyone else, jolted at the sound and violent action. Then laughter broke out, followed by a few of the teens clapping.

"That was awesome, Martin!" Tom yelled into the woods. "I think I wet my freakin' pants."

The applause and giggles died down. Jack slept right through it. Sara caressed his head and waited for Martin to lumber out of the woods and take a bow.

But Martin stayed hidden.

"Martin, you can come out now."

Sara listened. The woods, the whole island, stayed deathly quiet.

"Martin? You okay?"

No answer.

"Come on, Martin. Joke's over."

After a moment the crickets began their song again. But there was no response from Martin.

"Fine," Sara called out. "We're not saving you any marshmallows."

Martin apparently didn't care, keeping silent. Sara picked up the bag of marshmallows and began passing them out, the kids busying themselves with attaching the treats to the sticks they'd picked out earlier. Sara kept glancing at the forest, inwardly annoyed.

"Now what?" Tyrone asked, raising his stick like a sword.

"You put it in the fire," Tom said. "Duh."

"Ain't never roasted marshmallows before, white boy."

"It's like this, Tyrone." Sara held her twig six inches above the flame. "Like we did with the hot dogs. And keep turning it, so it browns evenly on all sides."

Everyone followed her lead. Sara allowed herself a small, private smile. These were the moments they came out here for. Everyone getting along. Criminal pasts momentarily forgotten. Just six kids acting like kids.

"Mine came off," Cindy said. She was sitting so far from the fire it had fallen onto the ground.

"Wouldn't eat it no how. So skinny, oughta change yo name to Annie Rekzic."

"Respect," Sara reminded Meadow.

"Sorry. My bad."

Tyrone pulled his marshmallow out of the fire, blew on it, then offered his stick to Cindy. She took it, plucked off the gooey treat, and popped it into her mouth.

"Georgia. Please stop that."

Georgia had been using her stick to nudge the dead frog into the fire. She gave Sara a blank stare and then jammed a marshmallow onto the tip that had been poking the frog.

There was a comfortable silence. The fire crackled. The crickets chirped. The stars sparkled. Tyrone and Cindy giggled, sharing some private joke.

Sara forced herself to stay in the moment, to not look over her shoulder for Martin. He'd come back when he was ready.

Then she saw another flash in the woods. Tiny and bright, over almost as quick as it began. A flashlight?

"I'm on fire." Georgia held her stick and mouth level and blew hard on the burning marshmallow. Then she bit into it carefully. "Mmm. Gooey."

"Like an eyeball on the gridiron." Tom plucked his off the stick and pretended it was oozing out of his eye socket.

"Awful way to die." Cindy hugged her knees. "Guy I knew, had an ice lab in his basement. He died like that. When he was cooking a batch it blew up in his face. Burned him down to the bone."

"You see it?" Tyrone asked.

Cindy glanced at her hands, then nodded.

Tyrone frowned, his face looking ten years older. "Saw a brother die, once. Drive by. Right next door to me. I was eight years old."

"I saw someone die, too," Tom said.

Meadow sneered. "Man, yo gramma doesn't count."

"Does too. I was there. Does it count, Sara?"

"It counts," Sara said. She gave up trying to find the source of the flash and smiled at Tom. "And let's try to talk about something other than death for a while."

"Damn." Tyrone stuck out his tongue. "My shit is burned. Tastes nasty."

"I'll take it." Cindy held out her hand, and Tyrone passed it over.

Sara bit into hers, careful not to drip any on Jack. The perfect combination of sweet and toasty. She loaded up another, then felt her neck prickle, like she was being watched. Sara turned around, peering into the trees. She saw only blackness.

"When is Martin coming back?" Cindy was drawing in the dirt with her stick, making no attempt to replace her lost marshmallow.

"He's probably just beyond the trees," Sara said. "Waiting to jump out and scare us again."

"What if someone grabbed him?"

"Cindy, no one grabbed him. We're the only ones on this island."

"You sure?"

Sara made an exaggerated motion out of crossing her heart. "And hope to die."

"What if he had an accident?" Cindy persisted. "Maybe hit his head on a rock or something?"

Sara pursed her lips. There was a slight chance, but it could have happened.

"Meadow, can you go check?"

Meadow made a face. "You want me to go in those woods so he can jump out 'n scare the soul outta brother? No way."

Sara sighed, and just for the sake of argument she let her imagination run unchecked. What if Martin's little stunt really had gone wrong and he'd hurt himself? What if he'd fallen into a hole? What if a bear got him? There wasn't supposed to be any bear on this island; according to Google, there wasn't supposed to be any animal here larger than a raccoon. But what if Google was wrong?

She frowned. Her imagination had won. Even if this was a stupid trick on Martin's part, Sara still had to go check.

"Fine. I'll do it." She got up, handed her marshmallow to Cindy, and dusted off her jeans, staring into the darkness of the woods surrounding them.

And the woods were dark. Very dark.

The confidence Sara normally wore like a rain coat fell away, and she realized the very last thing in the world she wanted to do was tread into that darkness.

"Tom, can you help me look?"

Tom shook his head. "He can stay out there. I'm not leaving the fire."

"Ain't got no balls, white boy?"

"Why don't you go then, Meadow?"

"Hells no. At this particular time, Laneesha be holding my balls."

Laneesha rolled her eyes and stood up. "Y'all are cowards. C'mon, Sara. We'll go find him."

Sara blew out the breath she'd been holding, surprised by how grateful she was for the girl's offer. "There's a flashlight in one of the packs. I'll get it."

She walked over to her tent and ducked inside. It was dim, but the fire provided enough illumination to look around. Sara cast a wistful glance at the double sleeping bag. She tugged her eyes away, then located the backpack. While pawing through the contents she removed a canteen, a first aid kit, some wool socks, a bottle of Goniosol medication, a hunting knife, the papers...

Sara squinted at them, staring at the bottom of the last page. Unsigned. Irritated, she shoved them back in. She eventually dug out the Maglite, pressing the button on the handle. The light came on. It was yellowish and weak—which annoyed Sara even more because she had asked Martin to buy new batteries and he'd promised to take care of it.

But he also promised to love, honor, and protect.

Putting the papers out of her mind for the time being, she left the tent and joined Laneesha, who was staring into the woods where Martin disappeared.

"You takin' Jack?" Laneesha asked.

Sara looked down. She was so used to wearing the baby sling she sometimes forgot she had it on.

"He goes where I go."

As a shower gift, Sara and Martin had been given a baby monitor. It was in a closet, unopened. Since giving birth to Jack, Sara hadn't ever been more than fifteen feet away from him. And though putting Jack in his portable crib and letting Cindy or Tyrone watch him was a possibility, it was a far-fetched one.

"Besides," Sara said. "If Martin sees I have Jack, maybe he'll quit screwing around."

They headed for the trees where Martin disappeared.

"If you run into any cannibals," Tom said to their backs, "don't tell them we're here."

"That's weak," Laneesha said.

Sara eyed the girl, normally cocky and busting with attitude, and saw uncertainty all over her young face.

"The story was fake, Laneesha."

"That Plincer cat ain't real?"

"He might be real. The name is familiar. But the way to make campfire stories sound believable is to mix a little truth with the lies."

"How 'bout all them cannibal soldiers, eating people?"

"Even if that was true, and it wasn't, it happened over a hundred and forty years ago. They'd all be long dead."

"So Martin was just joshin'?"

"He's probably just waiting to jump out and scare us," Sara said.

"Probly. That'd suck, but be better than someone grabbing him."

Sara raised an eyebrow. That possibility was so far out she hadn't even considered it. "Did you see someone grab him?"

"It was dark, 'n he was right in front of that bush. Thought maybe I seen somethin', but probly just my mind playing tricks 'n shit."

Now Sara was *really* reluctant to go into the woods. She knew the Confederate story was BS, but wondered if perhaps someone else was on the island. According to Captain Prendick, no one ever came out this far.

"That's crazy," Sara thought. *"There's no one here but us."*

There were over a hundred of these islands on Lake Huron, from the size of a football field up to thousands of acres. This was one of the big ones, a supposed wildlife refuge. But there was no electricity, and it was too far from the mainland for there to be anyone living here.

Other campers?

Sara reminded herself to be rational. Occam's Razor. The simplest solution was usually the right one. Martin joking around made much more sense than unknown habitants, or coincidental campers, or old Warden Plincer and his ghostly gang of southern maniacs.

Still, they did have that radio the boat captain lent them. Sara wondered if her husband goofing off qualified as an emergency, because she was almost ready to contact Prendick and beg him to return.

"Let's do this," Laneesha said.

Sara nodded. Practically hip to hip, the women walked around the bushes and stepped into the thick of the woods.

·   ·   ·

They were watching. They were watching from behind the trees. Listening to words that made no real sense to them.

They smelled things. The woman smelled like soap. The thin girl smelled like mint gum. The thin boy smelled like sweaty feet. The baby smelled like powder and diapers.

There had been other smells, earlier. Better smells. Hot dogs and mustard. Toasted buns. Potato chips. But that had been earlier, when it was still bright out. So they waited. Stayed hidden. Bided their time.

They were hungry. Very hungry. The hunger consumed their thoughts. It was the only thing they cared about. All they cared about.

They had no affection for one another, no idea of how many of them were there. But they hunted as a pack. Hunted raccoon, and birds, and rabbits, and frogs.

Hunted bigger things, too.

When food was scarce, they turned on their own.

None of them remembered how they got to the island. But they knew the island was a bad place. Dangerous.

But they were dangerous too.

They watched. They waited.

Several of them drooled.

Very soon, they would attack.

.   .   .

Sara drew a breath, gasping at the darkness. When they'd hiked to the clearing earlier that afternoon, the woods had been dark. There were so many trees the canopy blocked out most of the sun. Now, at midnight, it was darker than a grave. The blackness enveloped them, thick as ink, and the fading Maglite barely pierced it more than a few yards.

"Be easy getting lost out here," Laneesha said.

Sara played the light across the trees, looking for the neon orange ribbon. They'd tied dozens of ribbons around tree trunks, in a line leading from the campsite to the shore, so anyone who got lost could find their way back. But in this total darkness every tree looked the same, and she couldn't find a single ribbon. Sara had a very real fear that if they traveled too far into the woods, they wouldn't be able to find their way back to the rest of the group. After only a dozen steps she could no longer see the campfire behind them.

"Cindy, Meadow, can you guys hear me?" she called out.

"We hear you! You find any cannibals yet?"

Neither Sara nor Laneesha shared in the ensuing chuckles. They trekked onward, dead leaves and branches crunching underfoot, an owl hooting somewhere in the distance.

Sara had been ambivalent about camping, having only gone a few times in her life. But now she realized she hated it. Hated camping, hated the woods, and hated the dark.

But she had always hated the dark. And with damn good reason.

"Martin," Sara called, projecting into the woods, "this isn't funny. It's stupid, and dangerous."

She waited for a reply.

No reply came.

"I like Martin," Laneesha said, "but screw 'em. I'm a city girl. I don't do creeping 'round the forest at night. This is a total wack idea."

Sara agreed. There was no hole or trench around here he could have fallen into, and if Martin hit his head he'd be lying nearby.

Still, if this was a prank, it was being taken too far. It wasn't funny anymore. It was just plain mean.

And then Sara understood what was happening, and she felt her face flush.

Her husband was doing this because he was angry.

Is this how it's going to be? Sara thought. *Rather than act like the caring adult she fell in love with, he's going to start behaving like a jerk? Was he actually trying to frighten her, knowing what she'd been through?*

Well, Sara could be a jerk, too.

"You can stay out there!" she yelled.

Her voice echoed through the trees, fading and dying. Then…

"*elll…*"

The sound was faint, coming from far ahead of them.

"Was that Martin?" Laneesha asked.

Sara squinted, crinkling her nose. "I'm not sure. Could have been an animal."

"Sounded like *help*. Know any animals that call for help?"

"Martin!" Sara shouted into the trees.

There was no answer. Laneesha moved closer to Sara, so close Sara could feel the girl shivering.

"We should go back."

Sara shook her head. "What if it's Martin? He could need help."

"You the social worker. Y'all good at helping people. I'm a single mom. I gotta take care of myself for my baby's sake. 'Sides, probly just an animal.

"*help...*" The voice was still faint, but there was no mistaking it.

Martin. And he didn't sound angry. He sounded scared.

Sara began to walk toward the voice. "You go back to camp," she said to Laneesha. "Martin! I'm coming!"

The trees were so thick Sara couldn't walk in a straight line for more than a few steps. Even worse, the Maglite was getting dimmer. How far ahead could he be? Fifty yards? A hundred? The woods seemed to be closing in, swallowing her up. There was no orange ribbon anywhere.

She stopped, trying to get her bearings. Sara couldn't even be sure this was the right direction anymore.

A rustling noise, to her left. Sara turned.

"Martin?"

Then something bumped into Sara's side, something strong enough to knock her onto her back. It scared Sara so bad she whimpered, feeling nine-years-old again, helpless and afraid.

Whatever unknown thing had jumped her, it was now strad-dling her legs, wriggling and thrashing.

And Sara had no idea what it was, couldn't see it, because the flashlight had gone flying and winked out.

·   ·   ·

When Cindy was a little girl, she wanted to be a princess. It was partly because princesses were pretty, and had nice clothes, and lived in huge castles. No one ever called Cindy pretty, and her clothes were all her parents could afford, which wasn't much, and she lived in an apartment which was so small you could hear the toilet flush no matter what room you were in. So being pretty, with beautiful gowns, and a house with a hundred rooms, all sounded really good to a seven-year-old.

Meeting a prince would be nice, too. But Cindy didn't really have any interest in boys then, and in fact she was jealous that princes got to do cool stuff like fight dragons and rescue people. Cindy didn't need someone to rescue her. She wanted to fight her own dragons, thank you very much.

The biggest reason, the *real* reason, Cindy wanted to be a princess was because a princess would someday become queen. Queens ruled the country. They were the most powerful women in the world, even more powerful than the President, because there had never been a woman President, but there had been many queens.

Cindy wanted to be a princess who grew up to be a queen so she could take care of herself. She wouldn't have to worry if Daddy made enough money to buy her new clothes, because she would buy her own. She wouldn't care that Mommy wasn't there for her after school, because Queens could take care of themselves, and it didn't matter if their mommies had to work nights.

Yes, Cindy would settle for no less than princess, and then queen. She would be a good queen, too, and treat everyone fairly, and make sure everyone had enough food and toys and clothes and she would make working at nighttime against the law because it made people sleepy and mean.

When she told Daddy, he said regular girls couldn't be princesses, and they'd never be queen, because you had to be born that way. But it was okay to pretend. Sometimes, when you can't get what you really want, the only thing left was to pretend.

*   *   *

"Where's the bathroom?" Cindy stood up, sucked on her lower lip.

"Girl, you kidding, right?"

Cindy looked at Meadow and shook her head.

Tom snorted. "We're in the middle of nowhere. The whole damn island is your toilet. Pick a tree."

Cindy stared into the woods, shifting from one foot to the other. She really had to go. And when she had to go, there was no holding it in. The crystal meth she loved so much had damaged her kidneys, and Cindy knew that if she didn't find a spot in the next minute or two, Meadow would make fun of her for pissing her pants. He was bad enough on the boat when she was throwing up, laughing and making gagging sounds. That guy was a real dick.

She weighed that humiliation against heading into those scary trees alone, and wasn't sure which was worse.

"Go with me, Georgia?"

"I go wit you, baby, help you take off those clothes." Meadow laughed. So did Tom. Tyrone kept quiet.

Cindy looked hard at Georgia. "Please."

Georgia sighed. "Number one or number two?"

This prompted more guffaws from Meadow and Tom.

"Number one. I'll be really quick."

Georgia stared into the blackness of the forest, but didn't get up.

Maybe she was scared, too.

"I'll go with you." Tyrone stood up. He looked sympathetic.

"Jonesin' for some white meat, homes?" Meadow nudged him. "Polly wanna cracker?"

"Be cool, man. The lady needs to go."

Cindy appreciated the gesture, and if it had been another guy she might have taken him up on it. But she liked Tyrone. Earlier on the boat, he stood by her when she was puking her guts out, even holding her hair back. That was embarrassing enough. She didn't want to have to pee in front of him, too.

"Thanks," Cindy said. "But I'd rather have a girl go with me."

She met Tyrone's eyes, saw kindness there. Kindness, and something more. He nodded at her, and sat back down. Cindy turned again to Georgia.

"*Please,*" Cindy begged. "I'm gonna wet my pants."

"I pay money to see that," Meadow snickered.

Cindy looked from Georgia to Meadow and back again. Mercifully, Georgia got up.

Cindy rushed to her, grabbed her hand, and tugged her over to the tree line. Not in the direction Martin went. The opposite direction. That seemed safer.

"Look at those bitches go, holdin' hands 'n shit. That's hot."

Georgia halted, turned around. "Fuck you, Meadow."

"You wish, mama. Maybe when you come back, I give you a chance." He added, "If you come back."

Meadow and Tom laughed. Tyrone stayed silent.

"Come on." Cindy pulled at Georgia. She felt like she was about to burst. "We gotta hurry."

Georgia followed. It became very dark, very fast, but Cindy forced her fear back, her whole body shaking with need. As soon as she was out of the boys' sight she yanked down her sweat pants and underwear and squatted.

"Geez, gimme a little warning," Georgia said, stepping away.

Cindy urinated, her relief so beautiful it was almost as good as getting high. The spray splashed against the leaves, droplets landing on her gym shoes, but she didn't care. She closed her eyes and sighed, deeply, almost enjoying the cool night air on her naked butt.

Less than a dozen feet away, something flashed.

What's that?

Cindy wondered if it was Sara, with the flashlight. Or maybe Martin.

But they'd gone in the other direction.

Cindy continued to watch, waiting for the light to flash again.

"I think I see someone in the woods," Georgia said softly.

Cindy clenched. Her arms and legs broke out in gooseflesh. "That's not funny."

"I'm serious."

Cindy couldn't tell if the girl was kidding or not. Georgia was a strange one, and she had a mean streak.

"Where?" Cindy whispered.

"Oh, God." Georgia's eyes got wide, staring at something over Cindy's shoulder. "He's right behind you."

Cindy jerked upright, cutting off the stream and tugging up her pants. She spun around, looking where Georgia was looking.

Nothing there.

Backing up, Cindy knocked into Georgia, who was quivering with laughter.

It was just a dumb joke.

Cindy made a fist and smacked Georgia on the shoulder. Not hard, but enough to show this wasn't funny. "You ass," she hissed. "You freaking scared me."

Georgia smiled. "Scared the piss out of you?"

Cindy wanted to be mad, but a giggle came out. Aside from Tyrone, Cindy wasn't really friends with anyone at the Center. Georgia wasn't really friend material, and they wouldn't be buddies out in the Real World, but at the moment it felt pretty good to share a laugh.

"Hey," Georgia whispered, leaning closer. "Want to scare those dicks?"

She jerked her thumb in the direction of the camp. Cindy nodded. Frightening the boys was less than they deserved, but it was a good start.

"How?"

Georgia reached into her pocket, and for a fantastic moment Cindy hoped Georgia was carrying, that she was taking out a pipe and they'd smoke some ice right now. But the fantasy died when Georgia pulled some ketchup packets from her jeans. How could she have gotten meth anyway? Cindy'd been at the Center for four months, and security was tighter there than it was in rehab.

Besides, Cindy thought, *I'm done with that shit.*

Cindy had been clean for months, and wanted to stay clean for the rest of her life. Maybe there would even come a day when she didn't think about meth every few minutes. That would be nice.

"We gonna throw ketchup at them?"

Georgia shook her head. "I took these from the fridge, hoping I'd get a chance to use them. I squirt it all over my face and shirt like blood, coming running out of the woods screaming, and fall right in front of those jerks. Then you come up from behind and yell and grab them. They'll shit squirrels."

Cindy nodded, liking this idea. She especially wanted to freak out that tool, Meadow.

"What do I yell?"

Georgia shrugged. "I dunno. Boo?"

"Boo is lame."

"You'll think of something. Help me spread this shit on."

The ketchup was warm, and smelled good. For dinner they cooked hot dogs over the fire, but Cindy declined, saying she was still ill from the boat to avoid admitting the real reason. Now her stomach rumbled at the scent. Cindy smeared some ketchup on Georgia's neck, then licked her finger. Not bad. Maybe there were hotdogs left. Maybe Tyrone was hungry, too, and he could roast one for her.

Stupid. He watched me barf. He's not interested.

But he did give me his marshmallows...

Georgia stopped applying ketchup to her face and stared at Cindy in a funny way.

No, not *at* her. *Behind* her.

"Lemme guess," Cindy said, still sucking her finger. "Some creepy guy behind me again?"

Georgia opened her mouth, but no words came out. She nodded, her head bobbing up and down rapidly.

"I'm not falling for that shit twice, Georgia. It wasn't funny the first time."

Georgia's lips began to tremble, her face crinkling in a prelude to a scream. Cindy had no idea Georgia was such a good actress. She hadn't been this good the previous time.

And for that very reason, Cindy suddenly understood this wasn't acting. Georgia really was seeing something behind her, and she really was terrified.

Cindy didn't want to look. The fear crawled over her like ants, and her legs felt like they weighed a thousand pounds. Georgia had lost all color now, and she was whimpering like a puppy.

Look. You have to look. Just do it.

Eyes wide, mouth dry, knees knocking together, Cindy slowly turned around, expecting to see some horrible ghoul with huge teeth grinning inches from her face.

She looked.

There was nothing. There was nothing there at all.

Cindy spun, pissed off she fell for the same trick twice, ready to give Georgia another cuff on the shoulder.

But Georgia was gone.

•　•　•

Sara frantically pushed against the person pinning her legs. She knew judo. Hell, she taught her kids basic self-defense at the Center. But with a baby strapped to her chest—a baby that was now squirming and crying—all Sara could do was push.

She felt breasts beneath her palms, a neck and chin, and higher up, closely-cropped hair.

"Laneesha?"

"Sara!" The teen's breath was warm on Sara's face, and then she was rolling off. "Couldn't find my way back, so I ran toward the flashlight. What happen to it?"

Sara tried to get her breathing under control. The darkness screamed at her, making her voice sound hollow, far away. "It... flew into the woods."

"Shit. Dark as hell out here. Feels like we got swallowed up by somethin'."

Sara sat up, heart hammering, squinting into the blackness all around them. "It's a Maglite." She forced herself to swallow, her fingers absently digging into one of the sling's pockets and finding the pacifier, which she popped into Jack's mouth. "Those things don't switch off accidentally. It probably rolled under some leaves so we can't see it."

"So how we find it?"

"Couldn't have gone far. You stay where you are, keep talking to me. I'll go around you and feel for it. Can you hold Jack?"

"Yeah."

Sara pulled him out of his sling, handing him carefully over to Laneesha. Without him next to her belly, Sara felt even more frightened.

"You gotta talk to me, or I'm gonna freak out."

Me, too. But I can do this.

Sara crawled off, slowly circling the girl. By judging where Laneesha's voice was coming from, she should be able to cover the area in a widening spiral, without missing any spots or getting lost. In theory, at least.

"If y'all remembered, I voted for horseback riding for our last trip, not camping on some scary ass island. I've never been on a horse before. That will be one of the first things I do when I get out of juvee. Sara, you there?"

"I'm here." The ground was rough under Sara's palms, sticks and rocks poking her, cold dirt wedging beneath her fingernails. She went counter-clockwise, gradually orbiting away from Laneesha.

"I don' wanna go to juvee, Sara. I feel like I been making progress, y'know?"

Sara couldn't hold the darkness back. She had to focus on something else. On finding the light. On finding Martin. On Laneesha.

Focus on Laneesha. Be there for her.

"You're doing great, Laneesha."

Laneesha *was* making progress. Sara had no doubt that when she was allowed back in society, she'd do well. After getting pregnant at sixteen, Laneesha began stealing to make ends meet. When she got arrested at a department store for attempting to steal several thousand dollars worth of jewelry, the state took her daughter. Since coming to the Center, Laneesha had worked hard, studied for her GED, and showed impressive determination to go straight and get her child back.

"You've only got a month left until your next hearing, Laneesha. It will fly by. You just need to stay out of trouble until then."

"Y'all be at court with me?"

Sara touched a bush ahead of her, feeling through the branches, shaking them to see if they were hiding the light. They weren't. The darkness seemed to get thicker.

"Of course I'll be there."

"Martin, too?"

"Martin, too."

"Even though y'all are getting' divorced?"

Sara stopped and looked in Laneesha's direction, even though she couldn't see more than a few inches in front of her. "Divorced? Where did you hear that?"

"Didn't hear it. Takin' a guess. You both don' look at each other like you used to. Figure now the Center is breaking up, y'all will too."

Sara chewed her lower lip. She and Martin had been growing apart for a while, but when the government cut the Center's funding he withdrew completely. That was the definition of ironic; two psychologists specifically trained to understand human nature and communication, unable to save their marriage even though they still loved each other.

The only thing left was for Martin to sign the divorce papers. But he hadn't yet. They arrived yesterday, but instead of getting it over with he chose instead to ignore them, and her.

Sara knew their marriage was over. Once communication failed, so did intimacy. But she still entertained the fantasy of miraculously patching things up over campfire stories and sleeping bag snuggling.

That fantasy faded when Martin pulled this stunt and disappeared into the woods. This trip could have been their chance to really connect, to talk it out, to mend. Instead, she was crawling around on all fours, sorry she ever met the guy.

Scratch that. She could never think that way about Martin. They might not be able to live together any more, but the love was still there. Sara knew the love would always be there.

But right now, she wanted to stab the jerk in the eye. Figuratively, of course.

"Sara? Where you at?"

"I'm here."

"You sound far."

"I'm only a few yards away, Laneesha. The flashlight has to be close. Shit!"

"What? Sara, you okay? Sara!"

"I caught a nail on something. Damn, I think I broke it off."

The pain surged, sharp and hot. Sara parted her lips reflexively, ready to suck her injury. She stopped before her hand reached her mouth, a horrible stench wafting up from the ground. It blanketed her tongue and invaded her nostrils, rank and vile and forcing her to gag.

The unmistakable smell of rot.

"Sara? You okay?"

"I'm fine." Sara coughed, spat. The odor brought back memories of her college years, coming back to her dorm after Christmas break to find her goldfish belly-up in the aquarium. When she lifted up the tank cover, the smell of decay was so bad she gagged and spit up.

That was just from a tiny little fish. This stench was coming from something much bigger.

Sara backed away, and her other hand locked onto a large branch. She gripped it, instinct telling her a weapon would be good. She yanked, but it was wedged in the dirt.

The smell got worse, so bad it was like being immersed in spoiled milk. Sara could feel it in her eyes, her hair, all over her skin and on her clothes.

Another tug and the branch broke free from the ground, her fingers clenching it tight.

And then the same instinct that made her grab it told her to throw it away. But Sara was too frightened to open her hand.

The smell was coming *from* the branch. Because it wasn't a branch at all.

It was a bone.

.   .   .

They waited. They watched. They had the man, but they didn't kill him. Not yet. First they needed to know if the group had weapons. They were many, but they knew that many were no match for guns.

The man moaned. It made their stomachs rumble.

Still they waited.

Not far away, they heard sounds. The woman and the girl, talking to each other. They sounded frightened.

They would be even more frightened, very soon.

They poked the man, made him moan even loader.

He was the bait. He would bring the woman and the girl closer.

And then they would attack.

And then they would eat.

.   .   .

When Tyrone was a little boy, he wanted to be a cop. But not a cop like the cops in his neighborhood. Everyone hated those cops. They hassled kids, and never came fast enough when they were needed, and everyone called them *pigs* and *5-0* and they got no respect at all.

Tyrone wanted to be a cop like the cops on TV. He watched a lot of TV, on account he stayed in a lot. The neighborhood where he grew up had a *bad element*, his moms always said.

"Being poor don't make people bad," she would tell him. "But it makes some people desperate."

He didn't get to play outside very much, because desperate people might try to hurt him, so TV became his best playmate. His favorites were the cop shows. The cops on those shows, they got respect. They actually helped people, and people liked them, and no one on TV had to live in a house with bars on the windows like Tyrone did so the *bad element* couldn't break in and steal his stuff.

When he told his moms he wanted to be a cop, she patted him on the head and gave him a big kiss and said he could be whatever he wanted to be when he grew up, as long as he got out of the neighborhood. And Tyrone promised her he would, and every night, when he said his prayers, he asked God to make him big and strong so he could someday become a cop and take Moms and Grams out of the neighborhood and to someplace really nice, where he got respect, and no one had bars on the windows.

·   ·   ·

Tyrone frowned as he lost another marshmallow to the fire. It plopped onto a burning log and melted down the side, solidifying in the heat. He watched as it went from bubbling white, to brown, to black ash.

"This sucks."

Tom was pacing again, but he paused long enough to ask, "The woods? Or the Center closing?"

"The woods." Tyrone smacked at a mosquito on his arm. "The Center. Shit, both. Don't wanna spend the rest of my sentence in no detention center. An' I don't wanna spend the night on no freaky ass island. I'm street, not woods. Holla back."

Meadow tapped his fist. "Hells yeah."

Tom laughed, but it sounded clipped and forced. "So you guys are scared?"

Tyrone felt the challenge and narrowed his eyes. "Ain't scared of nothin'. You sayin' I am?"

Tom squatted next to Tyrone. He picked a pine cone up from the ground and chucked it into the fire. "You don't have to sell me. I know you're all bad ass. But when you saw that guy get shot when you were eight, did you look into his eyes when he died?"

What is it with white people? Tyrone thought. *Why do they feel the need to talk about stuff like that?*

He shrugged. "Naw, man. My moms hustled me inside soon as the shots were fired."

Tom stared at Tyrone. He had a pretty intense gaze.

"I was holding Gram's hand when she died, looking her right in the eyes. I know this sounds shitty, but we weren't really close. I mean, she was my Grandma. She was always there, for my whole life, giving me money and shit for holidays, babysitting me when I was a kid, going to church with us every Sunday."

Tom seemed to be waiting for a response, so Tyrone said, "Me 'n my gramma are tight. She's a good lady."

"So was mine. But we weren't tight. When she got sick and moved into our house, my parents made me sit with her. I didn't want to. She smelled, you know? Had diapers on and shit. Plus she was on so many drugs she didn't know where she was most of the frickin' time. Or who I was. Or what was going on. But right there, at the very end, she could recognize me. She knew who I was. And she said something."

Tom looked around for another pine cone. Instead he found a small rock and tossed that into the flames.

"What did yo gramma say?" Tyrone asked.

Tom's face pinched. "She said, *'There's nothing, Tommy. Nothing.'* Then, when she was still staring at me, her eyes went blank. I mean, they were still open, still looked exactly the same. But *blank.* Like something was missing. Like she wasn't a person anymore."

Tyrone stared at Tom. The skinny kid got busted for jackin' a car and joy riding. No damn purpose to it. Wasn't to sell it, or strip it for the parts. Just for shits and grins. Tyrone thought it was a real stupid-ass crime. But maybe it made sense. When people were scared on the inside, sometimes they did things to show they weren't scared.

"My moms, and my grams, they say your soul leaves your body."

Tom shook his head. "Naw. There was nothing spiritual at all. One minute she was a person, the next she was just, I dunno, *meat*. There wasn't any soul."

Tyrone didn't like that explanation. He remembered having to say his prayers every night before bed. Soul to keep, and all that. If men didn't have souls, what was the point?

"You can't see a soul, dog."

"It was scary, Tyrone. Like a light turning off. And her saying *there's nothing*. I mean, she went to church every week, never missed it once, and she was about a hundred years old. I thought there was supposed to be a bright light, and clouds, and an angel choir. That's how it is supposed to be, right?"

"Maybe there was," Tyrone said.

"So why'd she frickin' say that?"

"Tom, you said she was on drugs, acting funny. Maybe she saw all the lights 'n clouds n' shit, but her words were all messed up. You don' know for sure."

Meadow guffawed. "Man, this conversation is wack."

Tyrone stared at Meadow. "Don't you believe in God?"

"If there's a God, what he ever done for me? I grew up poor, my moms spendin' the welfare on drugs. I joined a gang just to keep my belly full. God? Bullshit."

"God's up there." Tyrone looked skyward, up at the big orange moon. "He just prefers we work this shit out ourselves."

"Ain't no point in having a god, man, if he's just a slum lord never does nothin'."

Tyrone turned to Meadow. "How do you know? You ever pray for anything before?"

"Naw."

"Maybe you should try it once, see if it—"

The scream cut Tyrone off. High-pitched, piercing, coming from right behind him. The scream of someone in absolute, complete agony, so shrill it seemed to burn into Tyrone's head. Tyrone twisted around, feeling his whole body twitch like he did back in the day when something bad was going down. He automatically reached for his belt, his fingers seeking out a knife, a gun, a bike chain, anything at all to defend himself with. They came up empty. So he stood up and stumbled sideways, bumping into Tom, steadying himself even though his legs were jonesing to run him the hell out of there.

His eyes scanned the tree line, seeing only random shadows flitting across the trunks. Beyond that, a darkness so vast it seemed like the forest was opening its giant mouth to eat them all.

"The fuck was that?"

Meadow was standing next to Tyrone, also slapping his pants in search of a weapon he wasn't going to find. Tom was on Tyrone's other shoulder, holding out his weak-ass marshmallow stick like that would protect them.

Tyrone held his breath. Crickets and silence. This island was too damn quiet. Never got this quiet in Motown. Never got this dark, neither. Tyrone could survive on the street for weeks when he had to, but out here in bumblefuck he knew he wouldn't last a day. Can't B&E for duckets or pop in a homie's crib for food when you're in the middle of the woods. And if something was chasing you, where were you supposed to hide?

"It's one of the girls, messing with us," Tom said.

Tyrone felt a stab of concern for Cindy, then dismissed it. This scream came from the opposite direction. Tyrone didn't know what exactly it was about the girl that he liked, but he just liked her, is all. He never did anything about it. Never even said anything. Both he and Cindy were in the Center to improve themselves. That was a big enough job without adding all that relationship baggage to the mix.

Still, she was a sweet girl. Strong too, in her way. And getting better looking every day since kicking meth. Maybe one day they—

Something flashed, in Tyrone's peripheral vision. He spun toward it, squinting into the dark trees.

"You dudes see that?"

"See what?" Tom said. He looked left, then right, then, comically, up into the sky.

"Some kinda light. Same direction as the scream."

"Someone's gotta be messing with us." Tom rubbed his palm back and forth over his scalp, so quick it looked like he was going to give himself a rug burn. "Lights and bullshit screams. Trying to scare us."

Meadow shook his head. "Didn't sound like no bullshit scream. Sounded real. And close."

"You maybe wanna go check?"

"You go check, white boy. With your little stick."

Tyrone shushed them. "Quiet. I hear somethin'."

He recognized the noise, because they all made the same noise earlier, on the hike to this clearing. It was the sound of people in the woods, trampling over dead leaves and twigs, pushing branches out of the way.

And the sound was moving toward them. Fast.

"Somethin's comin'," Meadow whispered.

The trampling was too noisy for one or two people to make. It sounded like at least half a dozen folks, rushing through the forest, getting closer.

The bushes at the treeline shook like a bear was caught in them. Tyrone couldn't move. He couldn't even swallow. He knew, *knew*, that some crazy Civil War cannibals were going to burst out and start chomping him, and he was too scared to do anything about it.

Then, all at once, the bushes stopped moving. The sound of approaching footsteps ceased. All Tyrone could hear was crickets, and the thumping of his own heart.

"Are they still there?" Tyrone had never heard Tom speak so quietly.

"Dunno." Meadow's voice was just as soft. "Didn't hear them leave. Might still be there, staring at us."

Tyrone's back became really hot—he was standing too close to the fire. But he didn't dare move away. He could feel eyes on him. Predator eyes. Something was in those woods, and it wanted to do him serious harm.

"Hey!"

They all turned to the right, Tom bumping into Tyrone, who backed into Meadow. Walking toward them, arms spread open, was Cindy. She smirked, and Tyrone was surprised how relieved he felt to see her.

"You guys look like you just saw a ghost."

"Were you over there?" Meadow pointed in the direction they'd been facing,

Cindy jerked a thumb over her shoulder. "I came from there. Did you hear Georgia scream?"

Tyrone managed to swallow, find his voice. "Heard someone, that way."

"Georgia was going to try to scare you guys. But she ditched me. She's in the trees there?"

Cindy walked past them, heading for the bushes. Tyrone caught her wrist.

"I don't think that's Georgia."

Cindy's face crinkled up. "Why not?"

"It's more than one person," Tom said, his voice low.

Cindy stepped backward, next to Tyrone. Her hair smelled like shampoo. He relaxed his grip a bit but still kept hold of her wrist.

"Maybe she found the others. Maybe they're all trying to scare us."

"It ain't them."

Tom flinched, bumping into Tyrone, pressing against him. It violated all sorts of personal space, and normally would have resulted in a rough shove and a threat, but Tyrone didn't move because he saw what Tom saw, just beyond the bushes, barely illuminated from the light of the fire.

A person.

Someone was standing in the darkness, watching them. It creeped Tyrone out so bad he finally uprooted his legs, sidestepping the campfire, backpedaling away while tugging Cindy along. Then that fool Tom came up fast, knocking into them, toppling everyone over.

The act of breaking eye contact with whatever was in the woods scared Tyrone even more, as if losing sight of the enemy meant it could suddenly be anywhere. He looked back at the bushes, seeking out the silhouette, barely noticing Cindy's hand moving into his and gripping tight.

The dark figure was still there, features obscured by night. Tall, thin, silent.

The moment stretched to the breaking point. Even the crickets stopped chirping.

"You want some of me, mutha fucka?" Meadow was frontin' now, sticking out his chest and slapping it with his palms. "I'll rip you a new one."

Tyrone watched as Meadow walked toward the figure. He knew he should be backing his boy up. Didn't matter that they rolled with different crews when they were bangin'. Didn't matter that Meadow was a pain in the balls sometimes. At the Center, Meadow was his brother. They were tight there, much as they were rivals on the street.

But this wasn't the Center, and it wasn't the street neither. This place might as well have been the planet Mars. Throwing down in a gang fight was one thing, and Tyrone wasn't scared of that. But scrapping in the woods with some crazy cannibal—that was horror movie bullshit.

So Tyrone stayed put, squeezing Cindy's hand, watching as his friend clenched his fists and stomped toward the darkness.

。　　　。　　　。

The light came on, faint and yellow, shining on the bone Sara clenched in her hand. It was long, over eighteen inches, covered on one side with clumps of dirt. The other side, the side Sara stared at, had strips of dried brown flesh clinging to it.

The smell was an assault, so overpowering and fetid that Sara dropped the bone immediately, violently turning away and retching onto the ground.

"Was that a leg?" Laneesha moved closer to Sara. The girl was clutching the Maglite she'd obviously found.

Sara wiped her mouth with her sleeve, her throat feeling raw, her tongue foul with stomach acid.

"I don't know."

"Looked like a dude's leg."

"I don't know."

"Why is there a dude's leg on the ground? Where's the rest of him?"

Laneesha played the light across the ground. Sara followed the beam as it washed over twigs, dead leaves, chunks of dirt, coming to rest on a single, brown shoe.

"Holy shit! There a foot in that shoe?"

The shoe looked old. Leather decayed and laces gone, flattened by time.

Sara summoned up a bit of strength from some inner well and forced herself to speak calmly. "The light, Laneesha."

Laneesha didn't move.

"Laneesha. Give me the light."

Sara reached for it, and the girl complied. Still on her knees, she hobbled over to the shoe. Using a stick, Sara poked at the tongue, peering inside.

Empty.

"Maybe the cannibals ate the foot," Laneesha said.

Sara spit—the foul taste in her mouth wouldn't go away— then got to her feet. She pushed away all questions and doubts and focused on the facts, fighting not to leap to conclusions. "The shoe is old. Really old. That bone still had meat on it. They aren't related to each other."

"How you know the shoe is old?"

"Look at the laces." Sara captured the shoe in the beam. "They've rotted away. So has some of the leather."

"How long does that take?"

"I don't know, Laneesha. A long time."

"Maybe it takes a long time for meat to rot off the bone, too."

Sara rubbed the hand that grabbed the bone onto her jeans. "No. There are birds on the island. Raccoons. The bone would have been picked clean if it was as old as that shoe."

"So what you sayin'?"

"That probably wasn't a human bone. Could have been from a deer. Or a pig."

"Be a big freakin' pig."

Sara considered looking for the bone again, to prove Laneesha wrong. And to prove herself wrong, that she didn't really see cloth clinging to the bone along with strips of meat. But she decided not to. Some things were better not knowing.

"Maybe the cannibals…"

"Laneesha!" Sara knew she was raising her voice, and silently cursed herself for her tone even as she continued. "There are no cannibals. Got it?"

Laneesha wasn't so easily chided. "Martin said…"

"Martin was trying to scare us. That's all. We're the only people on this island right now."

"So who grabbed Martin?"

"No one grabbed him. He was playing a prank, took it too far, and is now lost in the woods."

"Like us," Laneesha whispered.

Sara opened her mouth to dispute it, but stopped herself. Were they actually lost? She resisted the urge to shine the flashlight in all directions, hoping to find the path back to the campfire. But there was no path, and every direction looked exactly the same. She silently cursed Martin for his stupid tricks, and for bringing them all here.

"Camping," Martin had said, a big grin on his face.

"You want to take a bunch of inner city kids out into the woods?"

"It'll be good for them. We roast some hot dogs, sing some songs. I know the perfect place. I went there before, with my brother. It's beautiful Sara. You and the kids will love it."

"What about Jack?"

"We can bring him with. The fresh air will be good for him."

"He's just a baby."

"He's a hearty little guy, Sara. And I hardly think we're the first parents to ever go camping with a baby."

"You know I'm not good at night time, Martin. And in the woods, in the dark…"

Martin had patted her knee, looked at her like he used to, with love in his eyes. "You're a psychologist. This is the perfect way to get over that fear, don't you think? And besides, I'll be there to protect you. What could possibly go wrong?"

So against her best instincts, Sara agreed. She did it, she knew, out of a need to appease him, make him happy. It had been a while since she'd seen Martin happy. They'd been growing distant for a long time. Sara could even remember the exact moment it began. The precipitating incident was when he lost Joe. Martin took it hard, quitting his private practice to join Sara in social work, coming up with the idea for the Center.

Together—through sheer force of will it seemed—they got the funding and made it happen.

At first, it had been a joy working with her soon-to-be husband. Martin's loss seemed to stir a passion in him for helping others, and Sara didn't mind his long hours, and tolerated his mood swings, because they were making a difference. A huge difference, in the lives of our country's most important people; children.

Then came Chereese.

Chereese Graves was just another confused teenager from a broken family, thrust into their care by the courts. Troubled in the same way so many others had been, before and since. And like others, Chereese preferred to run away rather than deal with Sara and Martin's rules and regulations.

Runaways weren't uncommon. While the Center didn't have the security of even a minimum security prison, it was still a form of incarceration. The windows were shatterproof and didn't open, the doors all had heavy duty locks. But the kids always found a way. Chereese had apparently stolen a set of keys, then left after lights out.

Martin took it personally. Like he'd failed her. That was ridiculous, of course. Martin had a way of reaching kids, of actually being able to rehabilitate them. The recidivism stats for Center graduates were more than seventy percent lower than kids who went to juvee. They were actually helping kids turn their lives around, and part of that meant trusting them to do the right thing, to serve their time, to better themselves.

Of course, that meant greater opportunities to break the rules. While the Center had a greater success rate than any other state-run program, it also had the highest number of runaways.

Martin seemed to regard every lost child as a personal failure. And when they got word the Center had lost funding, he'd become so withdrawn he was almost like a shell of the man she'd met in school.

But Sara didn't want to think about any of that right now. She took the Center's closing as hard as Martin did. It had been his idea, but she'd been there from the beginning, and she felt the loss. Sara hadn't even begun interviewing for another job. She knew she'd be able to find work, either through the state or in the private sector. But even though she'd been headhunted, practically offered other positions, she chose to remain loyal to the Center until the very day it closed.

Now, possibly lost in the woods and growing increasingly frightened, Sara wondered if she shouldn't have detached herself much earlier.

"We're not lost." Sara took Jack back and regained control over her emotions, assuming the role of responsible adult. "This island is only two thousand acres. That's about three square miles. If we walk in one direction, we'll eventually reach the shore. We can follow the shore to the beach where we were dropped off, then follow the orange ribbons back to camp. It might take all night, but we'll find the others."

Laneesha seemed to relax a notch. "So which way we goin'?"

Sara wished she had a compass. Martin had been carrying it earlier, and for all she knew he still had it on him. That would make going in a straight line more difficult, but not impossible.

"You pick."

Laneesha put her hands on her hips, craning her head to and fro, then finally pointed to her right.

"This way. I got a feeling."

Sara nodded, walking next to the teen. "Okay. Let's go."

"What about Martin?

Sara cupped a stinky hand to her face and yelled, "Maaaar-tin!"

They both waited for an answer. Every muscle in Sara's body clenched, hoping she wouldn't hear a reply, hoping Martin had the decency to quit this stupid game.

A few seconds passed. Sara unbunched her shoulders, relaxed her jaw. She was just about ready to release the breath she'd been holding when they heard the scream.

High-pitched. Primal. Definitely not Martin. It was one of the girls, and she sounded like she was in excruciating pain. Cindy, or Georgia.

And she sounded less than twenty yards away.

.   .   .

One of the kids was coming toward them. A boy. He looked strong. Fit. Able to fight.

They could fight, too. And they outnumbered the boy.

They crouched down, blending into the woods, and waited.

.   .   .

When Meadow was a little kid, he wanted to be part of a family. He never knew his dad, and his mama did drugs and kept making him live with cousins and second cousins and neighbors and sometimes complete strangers. She didn't want him, and neither did they. He craved love even more than his little tummy craved food, and he got very little of either.

So when he was thirteen years old, he stood in a circle of Street Disciples—a Folks Nation alliance on Detroit's East Side—and let eight of the biggest members beat on him for twenty full seconds without fighting back.

Meadow had been scared. Of the pain, of course, even though he'd gotten beat on for most of his life. But mostly he'd been afraid of his own reaction. If he tried to defend himself, even in the slightest way, the initiation wouldn't count, and he'd have to do it again later in order to be accepted into the gang.

So he put his hands in his pockets, closed his eyes, and let his homies have at him while he concentrated hard as he could not to follow his instinct and cover up, run away, throw a return punch.

They blooded him in good, breaking his nose and two ribs, kicking him in the kidneys so many times he pissed blood for a week afterward. But Meadow took it all, denying every impulse to save himself, staying on his feet for most of it because he knew if he went down the stomping would be even worse than the kicks and punches. And it was.

When it was over he was given a forty of malt liquor and a blunt the size of a corn cob and he lay on a sofa for ten straight hours, drunk and stoned and bleeding and happy, while his new gang family partied around him all night long.

. . .

Meadow clown-walked into the trees, strutting with a perfect gangsta limp and lean, head bobbing, fists clenched, feeling that same uncertainty he did two years ago when joining the SDs. He knew something was about to happen, and every cell in his body told him it was a bad idea confronting whatever was staring at them, that he should turn around and run away as fast as he could. But he kept denying his instinct, kept moving forward.

Ain't no such thing as having no fear. Best a brother could do was to not project any. Then perception became reality. Act tough, and you were tough. That's what being street was all about.

However, this wasn't the street. And that figure he was heading for wasn't no mark, no rival bopper. Meadow had a really bad feeling he was heading toward some crazy cannibal mutha like Martin was talking about.

But he maintained direction, pimping out his c-walk like he was bangin' in the hood, heading straight for the silhouette. When the bushes were only fifteen feet away he heard that skank Cindy yell, "Meadow, don't!"

But Meadow wasn't going to back down. He hadn't backed down since he was five years old, jumping on a cousin who stole his hot dog, a cousin who was twice as big and mean as spit. You had to fight for everything in life, and standing around waiting for things to happen to you was a sure bet things *would* happen to you.

Better to be the man doin' than the man gettin' done.

"You wanna roll with this?" he challenged the shadow, spreading out his palms in welcome. "Let's roll."

The figure ducked and disappeared.

Meadow braced himself, waiting for the attack. He watched for movement, listened for any sound, still feeling that skin-prickly sensation of being watched but now unsure where it was coming from.

"That how it is?" Meadow opened and closed his fists like he was squeezing tennis balls. "You 'fraid to come out and face me, muthafucka? Then I be bringin' it to you."

"Meadow," Tyrone warned.

Meadow didn't pay his friend no mind, and stepped through the bushes, into the trees.

It got real dark, real fast. Meadow felt his resolve disappear with the campfire light. Five steps into the woods and it was blacker than it was when he closed his eyes.

He stopped, listening hard to the darkness, trying to pinpoint the location of his enemies.

Some time passed, a few seconds at most but they felt much longer, and Meadow was just about ready to turn around and head back to the fire when he heard something.

A clicking sound. Like someone snapping their teeth together.

He turned toward it, momentarily blinded by a bright flash only a few feet away.

"Who's there, muthafucka!"

The clicking sound stopped.

"Come out here and face me!"

More seconds limped by. Meadow could hear his heart beating. This was worse than waiting to be blooded in. At least then he knew what was coming.

Then, barely above a whisper, Meadow heard the most frightening voice of his life. Breathy and somewhat squeaky, but definitely male.

"The boy should run now."

That's when Meadow's nerve ran out. He did run, away from the voice, back in the direction of the camp, and then something lashed out and cracked him in the head, sending him sprawling to the ground.

* * *

Sara shook the Maglite, the sickly yellow beam barely reaching the trees ten feet in front of her. When the light finally burned out—and it was going to very soon—Sara wasn't sure what she'd do. Panic, probably. Even though she had to maintain composure for Laneesha, who stood so close she was practically in Sara's pocket, Sara knew that when the darkness came, she would lose it.

Darkness and Sara were old enemies, going back almost twenty years. Sara had been nine years old, happy and well-adjusted, growing up in a nice neighborhood with loving parents and a decent extended family. In fact, she could truthfully boast that the most traumatic thing that had ever happened to her in early childhood was diaper rash.

Until that day at Aunt Alison's.

Alison was Mom's younger sister, and she had five kids all within a few years of Sara's age. They lived on an apple orchard in North Carolina, and one summer Sara's Mom and Dad took a cruise and left her in Aunt Alison's care.

Sara didn't mind. She liked her cousins, all girls except for a pudgy boy named Timmy who was a few years older. Being on a farm, Aunt Alison was a bit more lax in her childrearing techniques than Sara's mom, and she let Timmy do all sorts of potentially dangerous things, like drive the riding mower and light firecrackers and play with knives.

Timmy had a bunch of knives, mostly small ones, but he had a blade in particular that frightened the heck out of Sara. It was one of those long Army knives with a jagged back. He called it a survival knife, which made no sense to Sara, because anything that got stabbed with that awful thing most certainly wouldn't survive. She refused to go in Timmy's room, because he kept it on his desk on a little stand and it scared her to see it.

For the first few days of Sara's visit, everything had gone well. She had fun playing with her cousins, the food was terrific, and creepy Timmy was told not to handle any knives around Sara.

On the morning of her fourth day there, the girls were gathering wildflowers by the old barn when Timmy came over, his scary knife in his belt, and asked if they wanted to play truth or dare.

Mostly, it was just dare, without any truth. Timmy, being the oldest, tried to show off by performing unimpressive feats of heroism like climbing trees, jumping down hills, and standing on the roof of the old barn.

The barn had a hayloft, which Aunt Alison used for storage. Among boxes of clothes and baby toys was an antique trunk. Made of leather and wood, with a rusty latch and tarnished brass corners and edges.

Timmy dared Sara to get inside and close the lid.

Sara didn't like how the trunk looked, all old and beaten up, and she didn't like how it stunk when Timmy opened it. Musty and moldy.

"That's what a coffin smells like," Timmy said.

"Is not," Sara answered, even though she'd never smelled a coffin before.

"You too chicken to get in?"

"No. But I'm sick of truth or dare."

"This will be the last one. Then we can play something else."

"Let's play something else now."

"Chicken. Bock bock bock."

Sara knew she wasn't a chicken, but she didn't want to get in the trunk. Especially since her other cousins had also gotten tired of the game and were leaving the barn.

"It's a dare," Timmy said. "You have to."

He had his hand resting on the hilt of that scary knife when he said it.

"For how long?" Sara asked.

"Ten seconds. Then you can come out."

Sara decided she was brave enough to do anything for ten seconds, so she got in the trunk, tucking her knees up into her chest so she could fit, and Timmy closed the lid.

It was dark. Dark as the darkest night. It was also tight and stinky and uncomfortably warm.

Sara counted to ten in her head as fast as she could then reached up to open the lid.

The lid wouldn't open.

"Timmy! Open up!"

Timmy didn't answer.

Sara pushed with all of her might. She heaved. She strained. Then she screamed.

The screaming went on for a long time.

Sara had no idea how long she was in that trunk. So long she'd wet her pants. So long she became tired enough to go to sleep, if the fear would have allowed it. But the fear didn't leave. It kept building, and building, each passing minute worse than the last.

And in the silence, the darkness whispered to her. Taunted her. Promised her that she would never get out, that she would die here.

Until Sara reached the point where she wanted to die rather than spend one more second in that horrible trunk.

That's when Timmy came back.

"Sara?" he whispered through the side of the trunk.

"Timmy..." Sara's voice was hoarse, raw, from the hours of screaming.

"Sara, I didn't mean to leave you in there. The latch got stuck. It wasn't my fault."

"Please let me out, Timmy."

"Mom and Dad will whup me if they find out I did this."

The air was so hot and heavy, Sara felt like she was drowning. "Let me out."

"If I let you out, you have to promise you won't tell."

Sara would have promised him anything. "I promise, Timmy."

"You have to swear."

"I swear."

Then the trunk opened, and Timmy was standing there, pointing that awful hunting knife in Sara's face. He looked meaner and scarier than anyone Sara had ever seen.

"If you tell anyone, I'll get you, Sara. I'll cut you into little tiny pieces and bury you in this trunk. I swear I will."

And then Timmy pressed the knife right up to the tip of her nose, and Sara passed out from fear.

Aunt Alison did find out, because when Sara fainted Timmy got scared and told her. And, as he'd predicted, Timmy got whupped.

But Sara's fate was worse. For years she suffered from nightmares and nurtured fears. Fear of enclosed spaces. Fear of knives. Fear of trunks.

But the biggest fear of all was of the dark.

It took Sara ten years of therapy before she could ride in an elevator without having a panic attack, or use a public toilet without leaving the stall door open.

Sara did eventually manage to sleep well, on occasion, but it was always with a nightlight. The thought that the flashlight would go out soon, leaving Sara vulnerable to the smothering darkness, it was too much too—

"*help...*"

The word jolted Sara, making her spin around and hip-bump Laneesha off her feet. *Martin. And he was close.*

Her encroaching dread was overtaken by a sense of hope. Martin, for all his faults, helped Sara through many a fearsome night, holding her close and stroking her hair until she could fall asleep. Finding him would give her a much-needed boost of strength.

"Martin!" she called into the dark. "Where are you?"

"*ara...*"

The voice came from her right, weak but near. Sara grabbed Laneesha's elbow, helping the girl back to her feet, then tugged her toward the pleas.

"Martin. Keep talking."

The sliver of light swept across the trees ahead, seeking out a human shape. Sara stormed forward, underbrush digging at her legs, ducking under a low-hanging bough. Jack didn't seem to like the jostling, and he began to cry softly.

"*elp me ara...*"

He was so close now Sara felt like she could reach out and touch him. She turned in a complete circle, aiming the beam every which way, but her husband still wasn't to be found.

"Martin?"

"*ara...*"

Sara tilted the Maglite, trailing the light up a tree trunk, across the branches, over to...

"Holy shit!" Laneesha's voice was barely above a whisper.

Sara realized that this wasn't some campfire prank, some joke gone wrong. They were all in danger. Very real danger. Because someone had hung Martin by his wrists and hoisted him up a tree, where he twisted slowly like a giant, bloody piñata.

PART II
THE FRYING PAN

Meadow got up on all fours and shook his head. Whatever hit him in the face had hit hard, and his jaw throbbed like he had a toothache. He shifted onto his knees, blinked several times, and tried to brace himself for whatever was coming next.

A twig snapped on Meadow's left. He turned, fist clenched and raised, and then caught the smell. An awful, rancid smell, like body odor and sweaty feet and rancid food.

Then someone tackled Meadow from behind. Meadow twisted, trying to grab his attacker, but he was forced onto the ground face-first, a knee pinning his back. His arms were stretched out, followed by his legs.

How many of them were there?

Meadow opened his mouth to yell for help, but as soon as he did a foul-smelling hand jammed something between his lips, forcing it inside. Something hard and round, like a golf ball, but rougher. Meadow shook his head and pushed at the object with his tongue, wincing as the pain hit. Sharp pain, in his cheeks, his lips, the top of his mouth, like he was chewing on a pin cushion.

Meadows sucked in air and gagged, blood seeping down his chin, comprehending what had been shoved into his mouth while disbelieving it at the same time.

"Meadow?" Tyrone called to him.

Meadow screamed in his throat, screamed for the very first time in his life, as his attackers dragged him off into the woods.

.   .   .

When Tom was a little boy, he wanted to be a race car driver when he grew up. He also wanted to be a pilot, an astronaut, a basketball player, a baseball player, a football player, a sniper, a hockey player, and a boxer, up until he got into a fist fight in fifth grade and another kid showed him how much it hurt to get hit in the face, which made Tom decide boxing wasn't for him.

At first, his parents indulged his interests. Tom's mother constantly shuffled him around from one sporting event to another, and his father bought a $300 flight simulator program for the computer that included NASA-approved specs for landing the space shuttle.

Tom quickly grew bored with the sports. He argued with coaches and teammates, and most of the playing time was spent waiting for something to happen. Tom hated waiting. He also hated the flight simulator. It wasn't fun like his Xbox, It was slow and complicated and boring. Even the crashes were boring, and Tom crashed often.

As for becoming a sniper, the only way to do that was to join the military. The military meant lots of rules and following orders, two things Tom wasn't good at. He'd have to settle for buying a gun when he got old enough, and maybe using it to go hunting or something, even though he didn't know any hunters and had never even held a real gun before.

Driving, however, he loved. He could make his own excitement behind the wheel of a car, and Driver's Ed was the only high school class he ever did well in, the rest resulting in Ds or worse.

But his parents didn't buy Tom a car. Partly because of his bad grades, but mostly because every time he borrowed the family sedan it was always returned with another scrape, ding, or missing part. Tom continuously lied when asked what happened, blaming it on someone hitting him when he was parked, but when a State Trooper showed up at the house with pictures of Tom fleeing an intersection fender-bender that he'd caused, he was completely forbidden to drive. How was Tom supposed to know that some street lights had automatic cameras in them?

The Gransees didn't fully realize their son's obsession with driving, and the lengths he'd go to indulge his obsession. After the courts suspended his license, Tom stole a neighbor's Corvette and led police on a forty minute chase, reaching speeds in excess of 120 miles per hour, appearing live on Detroit TV and as highlights on CNN.

An expensive lawyer, and a sympathetic judge whose son also had ADHD, allowed Tom to get off easy. Rather than doing hard time in juvee, Tom was sent to the Center.

The Center was okay. Sure, it was boring as hell, and Tom missed his freedom as much as he missed driving, but Sara and Martin were teaching him how to stay on task, how to set and reach goals, and how to make better decisions. Also, for the first time in his life, Tom was actually doing okay on his grades. Tests were still a nightmare, but he was allowed to speak his answers instead of having to write them down, and Sara usually helped him study.

Tom liked Sara. She didn't yell at him all the time like other adults, and she seemed to understand a lot about him, things even he didn't understand himself. He even thought she was kinda hot, though she didn't wear hardly any make-up and mostly dressed like a guy.

Martin was cool too. He was pretty straight-laced around Sara, but one-on-one he was more laid back. Like he knew this was all one big joke.

Too bad it was all coming to an end. Unlike the rest of the Center kids who would go into juvee, Tom's father had made arrangements to send him to military school. One of those bullshit boot camps that was supposed to scare teenagers into acting responsible. Tom decided he wasn't going. As soon as they got off the island, he was going to run. Steal a car, drive someplace far away, like California.

That was the plan. But first he had to get off the island.

. . .

Tom stared hard at where Meadow disappeared into the woods, willing him to reappear, to say this all was one big frickin' joke. But deep down Tom knew it wasn't a joke. He'd heard the struggle behind those dark bushes, and something that sounded a lot like muffled screams.

Tom was scared. Scared even worse than when the police caught him after his big chase, twenty cops all pointing guns at him and shouting orders. Every instinct Tom possessed told him to get the hell out of there, to start running and never stop.

But there was nowhere to run. Instead, Tom began to pace, back and forth like a caged tiger, eyes locked on those bushes.

"Yo, Meadow!" Tyrone called. "Stop the bullshit and come out!"

Tom knew Meadow wasn't bullshitting, knew that he wasn't going to come out. Not now. Not ever.

"Something took him, Tyrone."

"Nothing took him, man."

"You saw the bushes shake. You heard the sounds."

"He just messin' with us."

"Something frickin' took him, dragged him away."

"Bullshit."

Tom backed up, toward the campfire, and walked to the other side of the clearing. No escape there. No way out. Just more bushes and trees and darkness. He veered left, began to circle the fire, eyes scanning the woods, neck snapping this way and that way to make sure nothing was sneaking up behind him.

"We need to find Sara." Cindy stood next to Tyrone, and just like the boys she stared into the trees.

"They probably got Sara, too. Like they got Martin, and Laneesha, and Georgia." Tom picked at the dry skin on his upper lip. "They'll come for us next."

Tyrone turned to face Tom. "And who is *they*?"

"I dunno. The ghosts of those war prisoners."

"Ain't no such thing as ghosts."

"You can tell them that, when they're roasting you on hot coals."

Tom really itched to run. He walked the circle even faster, shoving his hands in his pockets, not liking them there, taking them out, clasping them behind his head, then sticking them back into his pockets again.

Cindy made a face at Tom as he passed. "Can you please stop pacing?"

Tom didn't like Cindy, but one of the things Sara taught him was to listen when someone talked to you, to make eye contact and try to understand what was said. Then, after listening, reason out what they want. If you didn't understand what they said, ask for clarification. Sara was big on asking clarification. One of Tom's challenges, Sara constantly told him, was to focus his attention.

So Tom stopped, trying to process Cindy's question. He'd heard her the first time, but hadn't let it take hold in his head. Sara said ADHD was like doing four things at once but not focusing on any of them, sort of like watching TV while talking on the phone while playing a videogame while listening to music. That's how Tom often felt, like everything wanted his attention at once, and because of that he couldn't focus.

"Thank you," Cindy said. "You were making me dizzy."

Tom listened, and processed, and realized he'd unintentionally done what Cindy wanted. That made Tom angry, made him want to grab Cindy and shake her and scream in her face. He might have tried it, but then he noticed that she and Tyrone were holding hands. Tom wasn't afraid of Tyrone. Tom was taller, and probably stronger. But Tyrone knew how to fight, and Tom didn't.

Maybe if I had some sort of weapon to even the odds...

Tom cast a quick glance at the fire, seeking out a flaming branch or a log or something. Why the hell was Tyrone getting all lovey-dovey with that meth-head skank anyway? Maybe some firewood upside the head would knock some sense into him.

"Just calm down," Tyrone said. "We need to figure this shit out. And you look like you're ready to lose it, Tom. Remember group? Working out your anger issues? Remember what Sara said about keeping cool?"

Tom made a fist, his anger nearing the boiling point, and a little voice in his head told him to exercise some control, reminded him he had problems controlling anger when off his meds.

Which made Tom remember he hadn't taken his nightly medicine.

Tom took two pills a day for his Attention Deficit Hyperactive Disorder. The first was Adderall, which helped him focus even though it was a stimulant and should have made him even more hyper. He took those in the morning. At night, he took Risperdol, an anti-psychotic which helped him calm down.

Tom didn't know what time it was, but he knew he needed his Risperdol. When he missed a dose he just got more and more agitated until he wound up in big trouble. He was already close to freaking out, and without his meds he might wind up running off into the woods, which would be big trouble for sure.

Tom walked toward Sara and Martin's tent.

"You're not allowed in there."

"Mind your own frickin' business, Cindy."

Tom knew he wasn't supposed to go in the tent. He also knew he was supposed to treat everyone with respect. But Sara and Martin weren't there, and he needed his meds, and they were probably in Sara's backpack because she was the one who gave Tom his pills. How else was he supposed to frickin' get them?

He ducked through the entry flap, using a Velcro strap to hold it open so the fire from behind lit up the enclosed space. On the left were a sleeping bag, a small cooler, and a stack of canned goods. That would teach Tyrone to mind his own business—bouncing a can of creamed corn off his dome. On the opposite side of the tent were two backpacks. One was already open, some things lying beside it.

Tom knelt next to the open pack. It was dark, but he noticed a walkie-talkie, a first aid box, and a prescription bottle. He picked up the bottle, but it was Martin's, not his. He tossed it aside and began to paw through the bag, finding clothing and some papers and nothing else.

Getting even more annoyed, Tom unzipped the second pack. Sara better not have forgotten his meds. If she did, whatever happened was her fault, and Tom couldn't be blamed for acting—

"Holy shit."

A big smile crossed Tom's face, and without even thinking he picked up what he was staring at, holding it and extending his arm. It was heavy, heavier than he would have guessed.

But that was because the only guns Tom had ever held before were toys. This was a real one, big and black wicked-looking. He fussed with the switches on the side, finding the button for the clip and the safety next to the trigger. Tom pulled the top part back—the slide—like he saw on TV, jacking a round into the chamber. Immediately, he felt alive. Even more alive than when he was joy-riding.

Tom cocked the hammer back.

Who's the frickin' man now, Tyrone?

* * *

They watched as the woman and the girl found the bait. But they didn't attack yet.

Lester was too close.

They feared Lester, almost as much as they feared The Doctor. So they left the woman and the girl and the man they'd hung up.

Their stomachs growled, but it was okay. They had found a boy. He would be enough for the moment. They could come back for the others when Lester was gone.

There was no rush. No hurry. They had time. Days, if they needed it.

No one who came to the island ever left. Ever.

There was a flash of light in the trees.

Lester.

They began to back up, but they didn't have to.

Lester was leaving.

They waited. As soon as Lester was gone, they would attack.

.   .   .

Sara reached her hands up over her head and touched Martin's shoes, making him twist slowly.

"We'll get you down. Just hold on."

Sara knew that was redundant—bordering on moronic—thing to say, but she didn't stop to dwell on it, already shining the weakening Maglite up past her husband's bound wrists. She followed the rope to where it looped over a high bough and stretched taut on an angle through the branches, all the way down to its end, tied around the base of a tree trunk a few meters to their right. Sara hurried over, sticking the flashlight in her mouth, attacking the knot with her fingers.

The rope was thin, nylon, the knots small and hard as acorns. She tried to pry at it with her fingernails, wincing as she bent one backward. The Center didn't allow weapons or anything that could be used as a weapon. Matches, lighters, aerosol sprays, tools, and even the plastic cutlery they used for eating; all was kept under lock and key. This rule was retained for the camping trip; the sharpest thing they'd brought along was some fingernail clippers, but those were back at the campsite.

Another nail bent and cracked, and Sara felt like screaming. The agony Martin was in must have been unbearable, and if he'd been strung up there for as long as they'd been searching for him chances were good his hands had lost all circulation. No blood flow meant tissue death. Sara felt like whimpering. If they didn't get him down fast...

"Try this."

Laneesha stood next to Sara, and held a dirty rock about the size of a softball.

"It's got a sharp edge," Laneesha said, pointing.

Sara traded Jack and the flashlight for the rock, took a deep breath, and tried to keep her emotions under control.

"Good work, Laneesha. Hold this on the rope for me."

Sara raised the rock up and struck the rope where it wound around the trunk. She hit it again, and again, and again, the bark slowly chipping away but the rope seemingly unmarred. Cramps built in her hands and shoulders, but Sara had to save Martin and she wouldn't relent, gritting her teeth against the pain, willing the rope to break, not daring to stop until—

The *twang* sounded like a bass string being plucked, the rope whipping past Sara's face as it shot upward. Martin fell to earth. He made an *umph* sound when he hit, tumbling onto his side, his back to her.

Sara ditched the rock and scrambled over, awash with concern. Laneesha came up from behind with the Maglite, shining it onto Martin's shoulders, then around to his face.

"Oh, shit."

Laneesha dropped the light, and Sara wasn't sure what she'd seen. She picked it up off the dead leaves and knelt next to Martin, focusing the weak beam on his face.

Jammed into her husband's mouth and protruding from his lips was a ball of nails. They jutted out of his cheeks like cat whiskers, dark with dirt and blood.

"Oh, jesus, oh baby…"

Sara's first instinct was to help, to nurture, which she would have done with anyone in this situation. She worked soup kitchens every Thanksgiving. She spent a summer in Peru with the World Health Organization, helping to care for a TB epidemic. Sara had endless resources of empathy, and equal measures of strength to keep from breaking down. But seeing Martin—her Martin—like this, hit her right in the heart, and the tears came so quick and fast she wondered how she could have been so resolved to divorce this man if she still cared this deeply.

Sara put a hand on his forehead, her touch gentle so as not to hurt him any further. Her husband's eyes found hers, locked on.

"*ara...*"

Sara handed Jack off to Laneesha. "Shhhh. It's all going to be okay. Are you hurt anywhere else?"

He made the slightest of nods, then brought up his bound hands, tied together at the wrists. They were swollen, and the color of ripe plums.

Sara wasn't able to hide her wince. She examined the rope, saw it was a simple slip knot.

"Okay, I'm going to count to three, then free your hands. When your circulation returns, it's going to hurt really bad. You ready?"

Another nod. And Sara saw something in his eyes, something beyond the fear and pain. Trust. Trust, and unconditional love.

"*Do you know I love you?*"

She nodded, unable to answer because of the lump in her throat.

"*Then we don't have anything to talk about.*"

Sara blinked away her tears, clamped the light under her armpit, and held his wrists.

"One...two..."

Sara went on two, pulling at the rope with one hand and pulling his right arm with the other. The rope resisted at first, then slipped off.

Martin's eyes went glassy, then rolled up into his head as he let out the most chilling, agonized howl Sara had ever heard in her life. Sara bit her lower lip and kept her own cry inside, patting Martin's chest, wishing she could bear some of the pain for him.

His back arched, bending at an almost impossible angle, and then, mercifully, he passed out.

Sara seized the opportunity. She worked fast, digging a finger into the corner of his mouth and touching the horrible gag stuck inside. It was a wood, roughly golf-ball sized, and Sara counted eight nails protruding out of it, each two inches long. Two skewered his right cheek, one his lower lip, and three his left cheek. The other two jutted from his mouth like tusks.

She stretched his left cheek back, forcing the gag further to the right, making the wounds on that side bleed fresh.

Martin's eyes popped open and he lashed out, smacking Sara on the side of the head, sending her sprawling.

Sara opened her eyes and stared up at the forest canopy, a small opening allowing a few stars to shine through. She'd once again lost the flashlight, but little bright motes swam through her vision like sparks. Her head was ringing.

It was the first time Martin had ever hit her. Not his fault, of course. He'd been unconscious. But it was as good a blow as she'd ever sustained, especially since she hadn't been on guard to block it.

She sat up, squinting as the light hit her eyes.

"You okay?" Laneesha asked. "He clocked you pretty good."

"Shine it on Martin, Laneesha, and kneel next to him."

When the beam rested on Martin's face he was looking Sara's way.

"*orry,*" he said around the gag.

Sara blinked a few times. "We need to get that out of your mouth. I know your hands hurt, but I need you to keep them behind your back for me. I have to put the rope on again."

Martin's red eyes went wide with panic.

"Not tight," Sara assured him. "But I don't want you lashing out and hurting me or Jack or Laneesha. Okay?"

He hesitated, then nodded. Sara located the rope and again tied the slip knot, this time higher up on his arms, near the elbows. Then she ran her palm across Martin's sweat-soaked hair.

"This is really going to hurt. But I need you to keep still. If you thrash, it could tear your cheeks off. Understand?"

Martin squeezed his eyes shut. "*urry...oo it.*"

"I...I really don't want to be here," Laneesha said.

"I need to you hold the light for me."

"This is awful. Just awful. What if the people that did this to him come back?"

"You're jiggling the light. Hold it still."

"If someone put one of those things in my mouth...shit...I can't..."

"Goddamnit, Laneesha! Act like an adult and hold the goddamn light steady!"

Sara never yelled, never swore, at the kids. And perhaps this shocked Laneesha so much that she shut up, keeping the light perfectly centered on Martin's ruined mouth.

Sara again stuck a finger into the hinge of his lips, peeling back the cheek, trying to free the left side while forcing the nails on the right in deeper.

Martin's head twitched and he screamed again. Sara felt the wood and nails vibrate from the sound, making her even more determined to free her husband from this horrible thing, pulling back as hard as she could, stretching the skin to an almost ridiculous length, then, with one quick motion, she tugged fast and firm.

The nail gag came out so fast it jabbed Sara's palm, and Martin twisted violently to the side, pressing his bleeding face into the leaves, his whole body wracking with sobs.

"Honey." Sara crawled over to him and put a hand on his back. "We've got to get going. Laneesha's right. Whoever did this to you was planning on coming back for you. You need to get up."

Martin continued to cry. Jack joined him. Sara took Jack back, and tried to comfort both of her men at the same time.

"Sara..." Laneesha was whispering.

"Laneesha, help me with Martin."

"Sara..."

"I know. The sooner we get him up, the sooner we can get out of here. We'll find the orange ribbon on the trees, follow it back to camp, then use the radio to—"

"*SARA!*"

Laneesha's scream trumped Martin's in volume, and Sara turned and watched as something filthy and foul-smelling grabbed Laneesha around the waist and dragged her off into the darkness, taking the flashlight with her.

. . .

When Georgia was a little girl, she wanted to have a friend. It didn't matter if it was a boy or a girl. Just someone to play with. To talk to. To understand.

Her parents divorced when she was a baby. Georgia only saw her father on weekends, and on those weekends he ignored her. During the weekdays, Georgia's mom worked most of the time, leaving Georgia in the care of an assortment of uncaring babysitters.

While the adults in Georgia's life were indifferent, the children were downright cruel.

Part of it was her looks, she knew. Georgia used to have a lazy eye before she learned a vision exercise on her own in order to correct it. She'd also been overweight since birth. The combination of the two made her a joke among her peers, and a constant target for ridicule and torment.

So, instead of friends, Georgia had pets at both households. Puppies and kittens and fish and birds and hamsters and gerbils and even an iguana.

Had her parents been paying more attention, they might have realized that the continuous deaths and disappearances of the animals they bought her were a warning sign that their daughter was severely disturbed. But they were busy with their own lives, and when one of Georgia's pets met with a dubious accident, it was easier to buy a new one than question why.

Georgia pretended her pets were people. Usually her parents or schoolmates. In her fantasies, they would do something bad, and Georgia would be forced to punish them. Soon, her own steady stream of pets wasn't enough to satisfy her urges, so the neighborhood dogs and cats began to disappear.

No one ever suspected anything, until Georgia turned fourteen and began babysitting kids in her mom's apartment building.

At first, the job thrilled Georgia. These weren't dumb animals she was dealing with. These were actual human beings, who depended on her. Maybe these children would be the friends she so desperately craved.

But it turned out the kids were needy, a lot of work, and just plain annoying. Georgia was smart enough to not hurt any of them—microwaving a gerbil was one thing, but Georgia knew that hurting a child would bring big trouble. But one of those brats she watched was just so freaking irritating, crying non-stop all the time no matter what Georgia did.

Georgia only stuck the child in the clothes dryer because she needed just a moment of peace. It's not like she turned the dryer on or anything.

Then Georgia took a little nap because she was really worn out, and the baby's parents came home earlier than expected. The baby didn't die, but the lack of oxygen in the dryer did some sort of damage to its stupid little brain and Georgia went to jail.

In truth, she felt zero remorse. But she played it up big for the shrinks and the lawyers and the judge, crying like a drama queen and begging for forgiveness. The ploy worked. Instead of jail, she was sent to the Center.

Georgia fully expected to be let out early for good behavior. She figured she could con Sara and Martin the same way she conned everyone else, and they'd sign off on her mental well-being, and she'd be able to return to her so-called life.

But every time there was a court hearing, Sara said Georgia wasn't ready to be released yet. Georgia had no idea how the bitch knew, but Sara knew, and it pissed Georgia off to the nth degree. So for the last two years, Georgia had been a guest of Mr. and Mrs. Do-Gooder, enduring countless bullshit therapy sessions, sticking to her story of mistake and regret even though it apparently wasn't working.

Often, Georgia thought of running away. It was difficult, but not impossible. Since it opened, nine girls and two boys had run away from the Center, and ten of them were never ever caught. Georgia figured she was smart enough to get away with it. Certainly smarter than some of the rejects who succeeded. But if she did get caught, that would work against her at her next court hearing, blowing two years of acting and effort. Georgia had been tried as an adult, sentenced to seven years, and she didn't want to be sent to an adult detention center when she turned eighteen. The smarter plan was to wait it out.

It finally looked like the plan would work. The stupid Center was closing, and Georgia would be sent to juvee. She could snow those dumb, overworked shrinks at juvee, no problem. Then she'd get released, and be sent back home.

She had business at home. Business she'd been planning for a while. The parents of that little retarded brat had taken away two years of Georgia's life, and they needed to be taught a lesson. Them and their brain dead kid.

Georgia read a lot. She knew what she was. The American Psychiatric Association's Diagnostic and Statistical Manual called it *antisocial personality disorder.*

Georgia was a sociopath, and sociopaths couldn't be cured. And why should they be?

Being one was so much fun.

. . .

Georgia ducked under a branch, pine needles tangling in her hair, and smirked once again at how she'd scared the shit out of that loser, Cindy. She wished it wasn't so dark so she could have seen her expression better.

Frightening others was a pleasant sadistic thrill. Scaring the little brats she used to babysit was especially rewarding. It was easy, and satisfying, to reduce a five-year-old to hysterics. But since being trapped at the Center, playing the role of Good Georgia to the hilt, she hadn't had any opportunities to let loose.

Tonight, she would do more than just let loose.

Georgia had been planning this for weeks, and had secretly smuggled all the supplies needed to do the deed. In her front pocket

was an envelope containing five ounces of powder, a combination of four different materials. Powdered sugar, that she snagged
while helping Sara make some insipid cookies. Iron oxide, in the
form of rust particles, that Georgia meticulously scraped off a
pipe behind the toilet at the Center. Saltpeter, which Martin had
poured on an old tree stump out back to dissolve it. And non-
dairy creamer.

The creamer by itself was flammable, as were most powders
because of their high surface ratio. The other three ingredients
combined to make a primitive form of black powder, a propellant
used in bullets and fireworks. Georgia wished she could check the
recipe on the Internet, but Center residents weren't allowed un-
supervised access, so she had to make do from the descriptions in
old Civil War history books. She also wished she could test it first,
but that hadn't been possible due to the Center's anal retentive
lockdown on matches. It should work, though.

The plan was to wait for everyone to go to sleep, then sneak
next to Sara's tent, lift up the side, pour the powder in her hair, and
set that bitch on fire. Georgia didn't have matches, but the campfire was the perfect substitute. Maybe Sara would live. Maybe
not. While killing her would be cool, leaving her horribly crippled
and disfigured had its appeal. And with five other dysfunctional
kids there, it couldn't be conclusively blamed on Georgia.

Now all she had to do was get back to camp and wait for Sara
to return and fall asleep. But that was becoming problematic.

Georgia had ducked into the woods to freak out Cindy, and
had only gone maybe a dozen steps, but that was enough for her
to be having some trouble finding her way back.

She thought about calling out to the others, but that wasn't a
real option. Georgia hated all of them. Hated them passionately.
She preferred to stay lost than ask for help from those idiots.

So she began to wander around, which wasn't working out
too well. The darkness, coupled with too many damn trees that
all looked alike, led Georgia on a meandering half-hour hike all
the way to shore. When she saw Lake Huron, spreading out into
infinity like a pool of black blood, she knew her only way back

was to circle the shoreline and find the orange ribbons they'd dutifully tied to the trees. That would lead her to camp. Unfortunately, the island was a few miles in circumference, which meant a long, boring hike.

Georgia stared up at the stars and the bright orange moon, and tried to decide whether to go left or right. She chose left, walking along the sandy beach, holding her arms tight across her chest as the cool waterfront breeze raised chills.

After a hundred yards or so, Georgia realized she was being followed. She sensed it at first, then spun around in time to see a figure scuttle off the sand and into the tree line, less than a stone's throw away.

She felt the tiny hairs on her arms stand at attention, then quickly shook off the fear. It was probably one of those jerks back at camp, playing games. Georgia didn't believe any of Martin's silly campfire stories. Besides, if there was anything to be afraid of in the dark, it was Georgia. She was the one with the propellant in her pocket. She was the one with murder on her mind. Everyone else better stay the hell out of—

A twig snapped on her left. Georgia jerked her head toward the sound, and in the moonlight spotted a man-shaped figure leaning against a tree. It was too dark to make out any details beyond a shadow, but he looked thin and very tall, about the size of a pro basketball player.

Definitely no one from the Center.

Georgia wondered what to do. If the man intended to harm her, he was too big to stop. There was nowhere to run, and if she tried he would easily catch her. Hiding might be an option, if she could get back into the woods, but the trees were a good twenty feet away.

She filled her lungs with cool air and stood as straight as possible.

"What do you want?" she said, making her voice strong.

The figure didn't answer. One arm hung limply at his side. The other seemed to be holding something.

"You deaf?" Georgia forced herself to take a step toward the man. "I'm asking you a question."

A light flashed, followed by a familiar clicking sound.

He just took my picture.

Georgia stopped cold. She could feel her heart thumping, and her palms getting wet while her mouth went dry.

"Who are you!" Georgia screamed at him.

Instead of answering, the man began to walk to her. Slow, languid, with long, easy strides. Georgia stood her ground, having to crane her neck upward as he got within an arm's reach. He had to be close to seven feet tall. Thin, but with thick wrists and a broad chest.

The moon was bright enough for Georgia to make out his features. He was white, and his face had a lot of sharp angles. High cheekbones, a long pointed nose, a chin that jutted out in a V. He wore denim overalls, like a farmer, and a dark sweater. A smiley face button was pinned to a bib strap.

"Lester," he said, his voice soft and pitched too high for such a big man. He took her picture again, causing her to startle at the flash.

Georgia never wanted to run away so badly before. She had to clench to keep from pissing herself.

"That's rude, Lester," she managed to say without stuttering. "You should ask permission before you take someone's picture."

Lester cocked his head to the side, like a confused dog.

"Lester takes what Lester wants."

"Not from me, he doesn't. If you snap my picture again I'm going to shove that camera up your ass."

Lester leaned down, close enough for Georgia to smell his breath. It smelled like a dog's.

"Isn't the girl afraid of Lester?" he purred.

Georgia's knees knocked together. "N...no," she stammered. "I'm not afraid of you."

Lester smiled. Instead of flat teeth, his had all been filed to sharp points.

"The girl will be."

.   .   .

Meadow counted four men dragging him off, two holding his arms, and two gripping his legs. They worked silently, in unison, binding his limbs to two long poles, then carrying him on their shoulders. They navigated the trees and underbrush at a quick clip. Meadow struggled like crazy, wore himself out, and eventually went limp, the nail gag in his mouth forcing him to twist his head sideways so the blood didn't run down his throat. He began to shiver, from the cold, and from fear.

It was dark, real dark, but every few hundred yards a space opened up in the tree canopy, letting in the moonlight, and Meadow caught glimpses of his abductors.

They looked like cavemen, with long hair, beards, rags and furs for clothes, dirt smeared on their faces. And they stank of piss and sweat and blood. They were also hella strong, Meadow knew, from experience, how hard it was to carry somebody, even with three other guys helping. But these dudes didn't stop to rest or change positions. They didn't talk, neither. That scared Meadows most of all. Brothers talked when they threw down. If they were gonna pop a cap, they let you know why, let you know how they felt about it. Meadow had no idea what these men wanted, and he wasn't able to ask. Not knowing was worse than the pain.

After five minutes of running, they stopped and dropped Meadow onto the ground, causing instant agony in both his tail bone and his mouth. He tried to tug at his bonds, but his arms and shoulders didn't want to follow orders—they'd been stretched out for too long.

Meadow managed to roll onto his side. Strangely, the dirt seemed warm. In fact, this entire area seemed a lot warmer than the run through the woods. It seemed brighter, too, but he couldn't tell where the light was coming from. He craned his neck, trying to see beyond a thick patch of bushes, when an old lady came out of nowhere and knelt down in front of him.

She was rail thin, and her white hair was scraggly and all knotted up. She wore a tattered sweater with more holes in it than threads. The lady grinned insanely at Meadow. He tried to say, "help me," but it came out as more of a moan.

Then the crazy bitch stabbed him in the arm with something.

Meadow howled, trying to twist away. She pulled her weapon back, then held it in front of her face.

It's a fork.

Meadow watched a line of spit snake down her chin, then she stuck out a drooly tongue and licked the blood off the tines. Just as she was raising the fork for seconds, one of the men batted her across the side of the head, knocking her over.

"Dinner... not... ready... yet."

He reached for Meadow, who flinched away. The man, and a partner, grabbed the poles and dragged Meadow uphill, around the bushes.

Meadow now understood the source of the fire and the light. In a small clearing, they'd covered the ground with a bed of white-hot coals. On top of them was some kind of metal cage, big enough for a person.

"Grid... iron," the man said.

Meadow, a devout atheist, prayed for the first time in his life. He prayed for forgiveness for all of his sins, prayed that there was an afterlife, and most of all prayed with all his might that these crazy fuckers would kill him before they put him on the fire.

His prayers were not answered.

*   *   *

Sara didn't think, she reacted, thrusting Jack into her husband's arms and lunging after Laneesha as the girl disappeared into the woods.

Sara had always wanted to have children, a desire that eclipsed all others in her life, compounded because she and Martin had such a hard time getting pregnant. When they founded the Center, the kids they cared for became Sara's surrogate children, each one as dear to her as Jack. Losing them was the hardest part of the job.

In some cases, the losses were happy ones, with the teens being released back into society, the majority of them going on to live fulfilling, productive lives. But several—the runaways—proved particularly painful for Sara. Like Martin, Sara felt like she failed those children, and grieved for the loss, both hers and theirs.

So having Laneesha snatched away right under her nose was something Sara just couldn't allow, even if she had to fight to the death to prevent it.

Sara was no stranger to fights.

Following the sounds of Laneesha's cries, Sara navigated through the trees and underbrush, moving faster than safety allowed. Laneesha wasn't a tiny girl, and whoever grabbed her was obviously struggling to carry her off, because in only a few dozen steps Sara saw the bouncing yellow beam of the Maglite. Sara poured on the speed, bursting through an elderberry bush into a small, rocky clearing, and found herself facing Laneesha's abductors.

At first Sara thought they were homeless people, like she was used to seeing on the streets of Detroit; dirty and hairy with tattered clothes. But their snarls, and the crude tree clubs they brandished, made them look more like savages; some crazed prehistoric tribe of headhunters from an epoch long passed. Both of them were thin, bare arms rippled with muscles, wearing insane, malevolent expressions, and it took Sara a moment to realize one of them was a woman—the only way to distinguish her from her partner was the lack of facial hair.

The man snarled, spit flecking his filthy lips, and then charged.

He kept his arm high, ready to bring down his weapon in a clubbing motion. Textbook attack, even if he wasn't a textbook assailant. Sara went in under the arc of his arm, pivoted her body while grabbing him, and flipped him over her hip, hard, using leverage and momentum to her advantage. She turned on him quickly, kneeling on his ribcage, and cocked her hand back.

She'd thrown the killing blow a thousand times in judo practice, but always pulled the punch. This time she didn't, giving it all she had, her fist connecting with his bulging Adam's apple. She both felt and heard something crack beneath her knuckles.

Without pausing to reflect on what she'd just done, Sara whirled on the second attacker, who now stood behind Laneesha, a rusty kitchen knife pressed to the teen's throat.

"Instep!" Sara yelled.

A small spark of recognition registered in Laneesha's eyes, the intended result of the many self-defense classes Sara taught at the Center, and she lifted up her right foot and ground the heel down onto the woman's.

The woman howled, stumbling backwards, and then limped off into the night. Sara didn't pursue her, instead running to Laneesha for an embrace.

"Are you okay" and "I was so scared" came out at the same time, and then Laneesha began to cry. Sara held the girl, but it didn't take long for her to calm down. Laneesha was made of strong stuff.

"I thought…I thought I was dead."

"I know."

"Why'd they grab me? What'd they want?"

"I don't know."

First they went for Martin, and now Laneesha. What the hell was going on?

Sara turned and looked at the man. He was still on his back, hands clawing at his throat. Sara knew she'd broken his trachea, cut off his airway. There was nothing she could do to help him. Sara watched him struggle, even though it was excruciating to see someone suffer so. Mercifully, he stopped moving after a very long minute, and the weight of her actions pressed on Sara like a crate of falling bricks.

I took a human life. I'm a murderer.

"He dead?"

Sara watched his chest, didn't notice it moving. "Yes."

She patted the girl's back, then took a step toward the dead man. Laneesha grabbed her wrist.

"Whatchoo doin'?"

Part of Sara wanted, needed, to touch him, just so she could persuade herself this was all real, that she'd really done what she knew she'd done. Since high school Sara had been involved in the martial arts and self-defense—a textbook case of empowerment and a way to gain mastery over her many fears. Every teacher she ever had, and even Sara herself when she began to teach, repeated time and again the importance of not holding back when in a real fight.

But none of her instructors told her how it actually felt to hurt—to kill—another human being. Part of Sara was exhilarated that she survived. But a larger part, the part that recognized how every human life was precious, made her feel like she'd just committed an unpardonable sin.

"I need to search him," Sara heard herself say, "try to figure out who he is. I have to call the authorities, tell them what I did."

"You saved me."

Sara's veneer cracked even further. "I... I just killed a man, Laneesha."

"It was self-defense. You save my life."

Sara managed a nod, then tried to pull away. Laneesha held her tight.

"Don't go over there."

"I have to check him for ID. This man might have a family somewhere."

"Look at him, Sara. Any family he got won't give a shit he's dead."

Sara stared hard at the corpse, his open mouth exposing a jungle of missing and rotten teeth, eyes bloodshot and staring into infinity. The shoes on his feet were battered old Nikes with the toes exposed, and his pants were held up with a length of rope.

Even in death he looked fearsome. But still, he was someone's son, and maybe someone's brother, husband, father. Sara often felt she was put on this earth to help those in need, and here she'd just murdered one of them.

"You have to let go of my arm, Laneesha."

"I'm afraid you go over there, he gonna jump up and grab you."

"That isn't going to happen."

"I seen the movies. He gonna jump up."

Sara tugged her arm away, a move both sudden and angry. "He's not going to jump up! He's not going to do anything ever again except rot! I killed him, Laneesha!"

Then the trembling started, and the tears came. Sara stood there for a moment, feeling alone and impotent and dangerous, and then she felt Laneesha hugging her, giving her comfort, and Sara regained control.

"There..." Sara cleared her throat, "there may be more of them, out there. Let me check the body and then we'll get back to Martin, and the camp. Cell phones don't work out here, but we have that radio the captain gave us. We can call for help."

Laneesha released her. Sara approached the body reverently, kneeling next to it and placing two fingers on its neck to feel for a pulse she knew wouldn't be there. She jerked her hand back when she felt the broken windpipe beneath the skin.

Stay focused, get this over with.

Sara crinkled her nose against his odor and began to pat him down. His pockets were empty except for a rusty fork and a length of balled up twine.

The poor bastard.

She was putting the twine into her pocket when the man jerked up into a sitting position and lunged at her.

* * *

Tyrone wasn't sure how they'd gone from being friends to holding hands, but he didn't mind. He'd been with girls before, but never anything more than a quick lay at the club house. To bangers, girls were like liquor and drugs; a way to have some fun and kill some time. While Tyrone indulged, he was never really okay with the whole hooking-up thing. Not just because of diseases and babies and stuff like that, but because two of the people he respected most in the world were his moms and grams, and if they deserved respect then other women did too.

So Tyrone never actually had what he could call a girlfriend. For him, joining a gang was a financial opportunity, a better way to make some cash than some dead-end fast food job. His family needed money, and Tyrone took on that responsibility. He lived the thug life, but didn't breathe it like some of the other dogs in the club, and certainly wasn't going to do it forever. Getting arrested for hitting a liquor store was probably the best thing that could have happened to him. It gave him a chance to reevaluate things.

Holding Cindy's hand, simple act that it was, felt better and more real than anything he'd done while rolling with the People's Nation. It didn't matter that Cindy was white, or a drug addict. She radiated an inner strength, and had plans for what she'd do when she was released. Cindy was going to get a job waiting tables and save up money to go back to school. A simple ambition, but Tyrone had been without ambition for so long it made him realize the simple things in life were the ones worth doing. He'd always been good at math. Maybe he should try to do something with it. Become an accountant, or some shit like that.

"We should check on Tom," Cindy glanced at the tent. "He shouldn't be in there."

"I think he's lookin' for his meds. Sara didn't give him none tonight."

"Still, he could be messing things up. Or stealing stuff."

"True that, but we know what Tommy Boy is like when he's off his pills. You wanna have to deal with him running around, trippin' out on everything, 'specially when things are falling apart?"

Cindy shook her head. Tyrone gently rubbed his thumb over her knuckles. Too many people would rather fight to the death to defend their bullheaded positions. Tyrone was impressed whenever someone changed their mind. It meant acting on reason, and with reason came self-improvement, as Sara often said.

"Where do you think everyone else is?" Cindy asked.

"Dunno."

"What happened to Meadow?"

"Dunno. Sounded like someone dragged him off."

"How about Sara and Laneesha? And Georgia? And what about Martin?"

"Don't do no good to speculate on what we don't know. They either all okay, or they ain't. We find out when we find out."

"Wassup, bitches?"

Tyrone turned toward Sara's tent, and saw Tom posing there. What Tom was holding made Tyrone's neck muscles bunch up.

Where did he get a gun?

The first time Tyrone ever held a piece was at age thirteen. An old Saturday night special, thirty-eight caliber, with a history going back dozens of crimes. It was put in his hands by Stony, a cold-as-ice muthafucker who ran the local club like it was the Marines. To Stony, guns weren't toys to play with or bling to flash. They were tools. Like any tool, it was only as good as the person who held it.

Tyrone learned to shoot in a slumhouse basement, plinking empty soda cans propped onto a stacked pile of dead sod from fifty feet away. There wasn't no gangsta-style double gun shooting, and certainly no holding a weapon sideways, like Tom was doing now.

Aiming right at Tyrone.

"You never point a weapon at somethin' you don' intend to kill," Tyrone said, keeping his voice even.

Tom laughed. "What's wrong, brutha? Making you nervous?"

"Tom! Put that down!"

"You gonna make me, skank?"

Tyrone gave Cindy's hand a tight squeeze, told her under his breath to be cool, then gave her a little shove to the side and took a step toward Tom. Tom switched his aim to Cindy, which wasn't Tyrone's intent. He wanted Cindy out of the line of fire.

"Tommy boy, put that shit down before you hurt yourself."

Tom swung back to Tyrone. "You think you're so badass, Tyrone. You and Meadow. Bangin' and jackin' and doin' drive-bys and shit. Don't look so tough now."

Tyrone took another step forward. Tom's aim was twitching back and forth. That sideways grip looked cool in the movies, but unless you were point blank it was real tough to hit anything. It was tough enough to hit anything with both hands on the weapon and a steady target. Aiming a gun was a lot harder than it looked. Tyrone had been in one firefight, him and a brother named Maurice against two boppers from a rival outfit. It went down in an alley, and they were twenty yards away from each other with no cover. Sixteen shots fired, no one hitting anything except for bricks and asphalt before both cliques ran off.

Still, Tyrone didn't want to get ventilated by a lucky shot, and having a gun pointed anywhere close to him was a sobering situation. Time was moving so slow that Tyrone felt like he could sense each blood cell inchworming through his veins. He desperately wanted to get his life back on track, to live up to his potential, to make his mama and grandmamma proud. Dying out in the woods because some loony kid was off his meds was not the way he wanted to go out.

"You ever shot a gun before, Tom?"

Tom sneered. "Plenty of times."

He was lying. Tyrone was good at spotting lies, but with Tom it was easy. Every third thing out of that kid's mouth was BS.

"I bet you a ten-spot you can't hit that log Martin been sittin' on."

Tom glanced sideways. "I can hit that, no problem."

Tyrone put his hands in his pockets, all cool and casual, and walked two steps closer. He was fifteen feet away from Tom. As soon as the boy gave him a chance, he was going to bum rush the fool. No use trying to talk down a head case.

"I give you three tries to nail it."

"You really don't think I can hit that log?"

Tyrone took another step. "I'm puttin' my money on it."

"Log's too easy." Tom grinned, his eyes glinting in the fire-light, and then he switched his aim. "How about I try for Cindy instead?"

*   *   *

Georgia walked alongside Lester, through the woods, barely able to see because of the darkness. The tall man had his hand under her armpit, gripping her biceps, and his fingers were so long they completely encircled her arm. It wasn't a powerful hold, and Georgia probably could have twisted away, but to what end? She had nowhere to run to.

"Where are we going?"

"Lester is taking the girl to his playroom."

"It sounds fun." Actually, it didn't sound fun at all. Georgia felt her whole body shudder, conjuring up images of what horrible things this man had in his playroom.

"It is fun. For Lester."

"Maybe I'll have fun too."

He stopped and looked down at her. The moon peeked through the trees, silhouetting his massive form.

"No, the girl won't. No one ever does. The girl will beg to die, like all the others."

Georgia didn't hesitate. She reached up her free hand and put it behind Lester's neck—it was like hanging onto a tree—and then she leaned up and kissed him.

She'd never kissed a boy before, let alone a man, let alone a maniac. But she knew everything in life was about control. So far, he'd been calling the shots. But maybe she could confuse him a little bit.

Lester did seem confused, and when her mouth locked on his he pulled slightly back, lifting her up off her feet, her body press-ing into his.

Georgia held on for a moment, couldn't sustain her own weight, then dropped to the ground.

The rejection was almost as painful as the thought of what this psycho was going to do to her. She knew she wasn't attractive. And even though she was seventeen, a year past the age of consent in Michigan, she often wondered if she'd die a virgin. Georgia preferred to remain asexual, and her fantasies were more about hurting others than getting laid.

But, still, her first kiss, and the creep pulled away.

"Don't you like me?" she asked, trying to keep the disappointment out of her voice.

Lester didn't reply.

"I like you." Georgia reached for his pants, her hand brushing against him. When she touched his fly she lit up. He was hard.

Were men really that easy to manipulate?

"You do like me. So why can't you kiss me?"

Lester bent down again. "Lester can kiss. But he might chew on the girl's lips and bite off the girl's pretty little tongue."

"The girl's name is Georgia," she said, tilting up her chin and kissing him again before she lost her nerve. At first, his mouth was closed, his lips cool and still. Then he opened his mouth, just a bit, and she probed inside with her tongue.

His teeth were sharp, sharp enough to draw blood if she pressed against them too hard. If he actually tried to bite he could probably tear off her lower jaw.

She forced her tongue in deeper, touching his, poking against it. Lester's tongue was wet and slimy like raw liver, but not wholly unpleasant. Then his mouth closed a bit, the pointy teeth trapping her, exerting just enough pressure for it to just begin to hurt, for blood just to begin flowing.

Georgia didn't pull away. Instead, she stuck her hand down the front of Lester's pants.

Lester's whole body went rigid, and Georgia thought she'd screwed up, that he was going to munch on her with those terrible teeth, gnaw every bit of flesh off of her face.

And then, unexpectedly, he moaned.

I actually made a man moan.

She felt almost giddy with power, kissing him even deeper, beginning to work her hand in a way she guessed a man would like.

Maybe it didn't matter, and Lester would still take her back to his playroom and torture her to death. But at that moment, Georgia felt wonderfully normal, like those braindead cheerleaders she used to go to school with, or the old couple who lived in her mom's apartment building that were always holding hands. She thought about returning to the campsite, and when those losers asked her where she'd been, she could them that she was in the woods, making out.

Georgia gripped him hard as she could, and then his huge hands were around her waist, making her feel dainty, and she might have even moaned a little too, and then she tasted something tangy and realized it was blood and that it was hers.

*   *   *

Sara jumped back so fast she fell onto her ass. The corpse of the man she'd killed flopped over onto its side. Then it was still.

Reflex action, Sara thought. *Like a chicken still running around after its head has been cut off.*

Sara had a pre-med roomie in college who told her all sorts of stories about dead bodies twitching, opening their eyes, even making sounds.

"I just had like fifteen heart attacks." Laneesha had both hands clasped to her chest. "He really dead?"

Sara nodded. "Let's go back, find Martin."

"How many more of these crazies you think are in the woods?"

"I don't know. That's why we need to get back to the camp."

They moved slowly, the flashlight so pathetically weak now that a match would have been brighter. Sara knew they hadn't run far from Martin, and she felt they were going in the right direction, but the trees all looked the same and it was so easy to get disoriented. She considered calling out to him, but as badly as she wanted to find her husband she didn't want to announce their presence to whatever else might be lurking in the woods.

Movement, to their left. Something was rustling a bush.

Sara aimed the beam in that direction, and that's the moment the Maglight finally went dead.

She held her breath, Laneesha clinging to her arm so hard it hurt, listening to the rustling as it faded out. For a bad moment Sara felt like she was locked in that awful trunk again. The darkness was too big, too heavy, pressing on her from all sides and making it impossible to move.

"Sara?"

Martin.

"Are you and Laneesha okay?"

His voice broke the spell, and Sara tore away from Laneesha and ran to him, throwing her arms around his familiar form, Jack cooing and wiggling between them, the hug feeling so good and right that it made the desperation of their predicament fade just a little bit.

Then the relief was replaced by confusion, and anger. She took Jack and pushed Martin away, keeping him at arm's length.

"Martin, what the hell is going on?"

Sara felt his shoulders slump. His voice was thick, pained, and he winced when he spoke. "I don't know."

"That whole campfire story. That civil war prison. You made that up. Right?"

"No. I mean…it's just a story. A story that I remember from camp when I was a kid in Boy Scouts. Scared the wits out of me and my little brother. But it's not true. It can't be true."

"What happened back at the campsite? Were you dragged off?"

"That was supposed to be a joke. I was going to pop out and scare everyone. But before I could, some people grabbed me, strung me up."

"So you don't know what's going on?"

His face sank, his red eyes looking desperate. "Honey, I swear, I'm just as freaked out as you are. I picked this island because I've been here before. I didn't know there was anyone else here; Sara. Jesus, I would never do anything to hurt you or the kids. You know that."

Sara did know that. Martin got moody sometimes, but he was one of the gentlest people she had ever met. This man would catch and release spiders he found in the house rather than kill them. Sara knew he'd gladly die to defend her.

"What about Plincer? You said this was Plincer's island. That name sounds familiar."

"That's just what we've always called this island. Sara, we need to get out of here. When they grabbed me—I counted at least five of those people. Maybe more. We need to get back to the campsite. Do you have the flashlight?"

"It died."

"Give it here."

Sara handed the flashlight over. Her husband moaned when he took it.

"Help me, we need to open it."

Her fingers grazed his swollen hands, then grasped them gently. Together they unscrewed the back off the Maglite. Martin dumped the batteries onto his palm.

"Do you have an emery board?"

"No. Laneesha? You have a nail file?"

"I don' go nowhere without one. Y'all don' allow no acrylics, so I gotta make do with what God gave me."

"Let me borrow it," Martin said.

Laneesha handed Sara the thin strip of cardboard, the size of a popsicle stick. Martin pressed the batteries between his palms.

"Sand the tops and bottoms. Really rough them up. And then dab the ends in the blood on my wrists. This'll make them more conductive, suck a bit more energy out of them."

Sara followed instructions, then popped the Ds back into the flashlight. Light trickled out, faint yellow but better than nothing.

She swept it over the trees. If she just found a single orange ribbon, they could get their bearings and get back to the campsite. Then they could use the radio, call for help, and get off this crazy island.

Sara spotted orange, but it was dead leaves, not a ribbon. The strips were phosphorescent, and glowed like reflectors when light hit them. Why couldn't they find any?

"Where the hell are those ribbons?"

Martin put a hand on her shoulder. "We'll find them."

She flicked the beam from one trunk, to another, to another. Nothing.

"We must have tied a few dozen."

"We'll find them."

Sara spun around, tried the other direction. All the trees looked the same. Every damn tree looked the same. They just needed to find one, dammit. This island wasn't that big. How hard could it be to find a single goddamn...

Then Sara heard something horrible.

"Oh, god, no..."

In the distance. Faint, but obvious.

Screaming.

"Can you hear that?"

"What, hon?"

"Someone screaming."

Martin looked around. "That's the wind."

"It's not the wind. It's one of the kids. Do you hear it Laneesha?"

The teen cocked her head. "I don' hear nothin'."

Sara began to walk faster. "Which direction is it coming from? We have to help."

"Sara...you need to calm down."

"Don't tell me to calm down, Martin. That's one of our kids out there."

The screams seemed to get louder, more frantic. What was happening to that poor child? What could cause someone to scream like that? The thought of somebody hurting one of her kids was—

Sara felt herself get grabbed from behind. She went on automatic, widening her stance, shifting her body to flip the attacker. But he got his leg between hers, preventing her leverage, one hand snaking over her mouth and the other reaching for the flashlight.

Sara bared her teeth, ready to chew the bastard's fingers off, when Martin's voice whispered in her ear.

"Kill the light. They've found us."

Sara tapped the Maglite button just as she noticed three… four…six…no, at least *eight* people—filthy and ragged and obviously insane—walk into the clearing just ten yards ahead of them.

·　　·　　·

Cindy watched Tom turn the gun on her, so clear and precise that it seemed like slow-motion. He aimed it at her chest. She could feel a cold spot where the bullet would enter, right next to her heart. It made her knees shake.

Growing up in northern Michigan, Cindy knew guns. Her dad had several, and when money was tight—and it usually was—he would supplement groceries with fresh rabbit, possum, and deer.

Knowing the damage guns could do, and the respect they demanded, made her understand the depths of Tom's stupidity. Even at this distance she could see the pistol was cocked, which meant the slightest touch of the trigger, or even dropping the gun, could cause it to fire.

It made Cindy realize, with a combination of both fear and relief, that she didn't want to die.

Being in rehab before, and being around other addicts, showed Cindy how deadly meth was. It killed you three times. First, it killed your will, making you a slave to another fix. Then it killed your looks, turning you into a toothless, underweight skeleton. Then it finally snuffed out your life, but by that point the end was welcome.

Cindy had begged, borrowed, and stolen to get high, giving up everything she cared about. She even had meth mouth, her teeth starting to rot in her head, losing three molars before being put into the Center. Her first few months at the Center, Cindy didn't care if she lived or died. She thought she wanted to straighten out her life, but she was unsure if that was just the therapy talking.

But now she knew. Staring down the barrel of the gun, Cindy wanted to live.

"Tom. Don't point that at me. It's not funny."

Tom stuck out his chest. "Who's trying to be funny? I know what you—what all of you—think of me. You think I'm some kind of joke. You laughing at me now?"

Cindy cast a quick glance at Tyrone, his knees bent and his head slightly lowered, and figured he was getting ready to rush Tom. Tyrone was fast, but bullets were faster.

"I never thought you were a joke, Tom. I always liked you."

"Is that why you were holding hands with Tyrone? You pretending he was me?"

Cindy forced a smile, tried her best to make it look genuine. "If you wanted to hold my hand, all you had to do was ask. But how much do you think pointing a gun at me will make me like you?"

"I don't care who likes me."

"Sure you do, Tom. Isn't that why you stole that car? For attention? But there's good attention and bad attention. This is just more bad attention."

"Give me a break, Cindy. I'm not the loser here. How many guys you suck off to get a fix? Is that why you're playing Tyrone? You think he's got some ice?"

Cindy let the smile fall away, and anger replaced some of her fear.

"Do you like it here, Tom? Because if you shoot me, the place you're going will be a lot worse, and for a much longer time. No juvee hall. You'll be tried as an adult, stuck in general pop. Then we'll see how many guys you suck off to stay alive."

Tom lowered the gun, just a fraction. Then Tyrone lunged, crossing the distance between him and Tom in two steps, driving a shoulder into the kid's chest while stiff-arming Tom's gun hand up and away from Cindy.

Tom toppled like he was on hinges, the gun arcing out of his hand and plopping into the campfire with a puff of sparks.

Cindy's automatic instinct was to reach for it, but she stopped. She'd gotten burned before. Second degree on both hands. That's why she didn't roast a hotdog or marshmallows earlier. Fire scared the crap out of Cindy.

She often had nightmares about it. The meth lab, her friend cooking a batch, the flask of chemicals exploding and setting him ablaze. He ran at her, screaming, and she had to push him away to keep from dying herself, scorching her hands in the process. They healed, with minimal scarring, but the pain wasn't anything she'd ever forget.

Badly as she wanted the gun, Cindy knew there was no way she'd reach into fire to get it.

Instead, she ran toward Tyrone and Tom. Tyrone was straddling him, one hand on Tom's neck, the other raised to punch him in the face.

Cindy caught Tyrone's fist, held it back.

"Don't."

"Fool needs to be taught."

"He's off his medicine, Tyrone. Beating him up won't teach him anything."

Tom looked small, terrified, a big difference from the swaggering macho dipshit he'd been seconds ago.

"Apologize to the lady," Tyrone told him.

Tom wheezed out, "I'm sorry."

"You ever gonna try that shit again?"

Tom shook his head, much as he could with his throat being squeezed.

"We're all on the same side, fool. We gotta watch each other's backs. And y'all are trippin' on Clint Eastwood. Be cool."

Tom nodded, and Tyrone got off him. Cindy still held Tyrone's fist, which opened and then clasped her hand, and then he turned and looked at her, his face soft and his pupils wide. His free hand slid around her waist, pulling her a little closer, and Cindy felt her legs get weak again.

Tom had been wrong. She hadn't ever done anything sexual for drugs. When she was so far gone she was willing to, the boys she hung out with her too far gone to want any. So her experience was limited to a few French kisses, and a freshman year groping session on a couch that felt more like wrestling than foreplay.

But looking up at Tyrone, she felt her knees start to shake for the second time in only a few minutes, and as his lips moved slightly closer she tilted her chin up and began to close her eyes.

"Jesus!"

Tom's outburst was followed by him tearing ass into the woods, disappearing into the dark.

Both Cindy and Tyrone looked in the opposite direction, at what had made Tom run.

Three men stood along the tree line. They were each tall and thin, dressed in dirty, ripped clothes. Cindy knew Martin had made up that Civil War cannibal story, but that's exactly what these men looked like. Like crazed cannibals out of an old horror movie.

"What do you want?" Tyrone barked at the men, moving Cindy behind him.

Astonishingly, the one in the middle stepped forward, and out of his pockets he pulled a rusty knife and fork.

* * *

Meadow had gone insane with pain, sometime shortly after his eyes boiled and burst. But now, even though a thin thread of consciousness remained, he was at peace. The agony was gone. He had no way of knowing it was because most of the nerves on the front side of his body had burned away, but had he known, he wouldn't have cared. All that mattered was he didn't hurt anymore. His throat was too swollen to scream anyway.

Then they flipped him over onto his uncooked side, and the screaming began again.

. . .

When Georgia felt Lester's horrible teeth begin to pierce her tongue, she squeezed his testicles. Not hard enough to cause damage, but as a warning; if he didn't let up, neither would she.

Lester's jaw clenched, and Georgia realized she'd judged him wrong. He was going to bite off her tongue, and her lips, and her face, and that would just be the beginning. The first man she'd ever kissed was going to make headcheese out of her.

But then his mouth opened, his own tongue snaking out of her mouth and across her lips in a way that made her chest feel heavy and her breath quicken. He stuck the tip into her ear, sending sparks throughout her body. His tongue flicked across her chin, down her neck.

This was all happening fast. Too fast. She'd never done anything like this before, and she didn't know this guy at all. Plus he was psychotic. Georgia knew she should be scared, and maybe she was. Her heart was beating so fast she couldn't differentiate between fear and exhilaration.

Then he reached down, for the front of her jeans.

That was too fast for Georgia. As exciting and dangerous as this all was, she wasn't going to let this psycho fuck her.

On the other hand, she didn't want to be taken back to his playroom either.

So she compromised and jerked him off.

It wasn't erotic, at least not for Georgia. In fact, she found the whole process strangely mechanical, and more than a little tiring. But she did feel a tremendous sense of control. The same kind of control she felt when cutting the feet off a gerbil. Lester was moaning and helpless in her hands, and even though it made her feel powerful Georgia wondered what the hell he was going to do to her when she was finished.

. . .

When Martin was a little boy, he wanted to be a doctor. He didn't really have an interest in medicine, and got woozy at the sight of blood. But he had an inner drive to care for people who needed help.

At fifteen years old he and his older brother Joe went on a camping trip, a tradition that began when both boys were younger and would continue on into adulthood. This particular excursion was in Michigan's Upper Peninsula. Three days in the woods, no adult supervision. Martin and Joe didn't suffer from the sibling rivalry that plagued most brothers born a year apart, and they were the best of friends. Camping with Joe was Martin's favorite time of the year.

The second day into their hike, Joe slipped and broke his leg—a nasty compound fracture that swelled up to the size of a melon. It was a decade before cell phones and GPS became commonplace, and a compass miscalculation put them two miles from the spot they told their parents they would be. Worst of all, it had happened in gray wolf territory. Joe was hurt so bad he couldn't move, drifting in and out of consciousness. If Martin left him, chances were high the wolves would kill Joe before he could return with help.

So Martin stayed with his brother, gathering food and water, keeping the fire going. And most importantly, talking.

Martin hadn't understood the true power of words before that fateful trip. How talking about the future, of dreams and hopes, of fears and failures, could sustain a person in an increasingly hopeless situation. Martin learned more about Joe than he ever could have imagined. He also learned about himself. As sure as man needed to eat, sleep, and breathe, he needed to communicate.

The boys were rescued after four days. In a way, Martin was almost sad to see it end. He had bonded with, and helped save, a human being, and that was rewarding on a level he'd never dreamed possible.

Ironic how, so many years later, Joe would wind up in even worse trouble.

As for Martin, this incident led him from an interest in medicine to an interest in social science and psychology. Human nature, and the way people interact, never ceased to fascinate Martin. He thought he was unique in that curiosity, until he met Sara.

Sara's desire to help others was only matched by her desire to learn. Unlike Martin, who believed that certain psychological problems could inhibit socialization, Sara was convinced that actions, not thoughts, dictated a person's social potential. They were a perfect match for getting wayward youth back on track, Martin working on healing their psyches, Sara teaching them how to integrate into society.

And now, with the funding for the Center being cut, Martin was cut off from Sara as well. He'd hoped, on Plincer's Island, to bond with Sara in a way they'd never bonded before.

But being attacked and hunted like animals hadn't been part of the plan.

·　　·　　·

Martin hurt. His swollen hands throbbed in time with his pulse, and his face felt like it had been pulled off and sewn back on off-center. But these aches disappeared when he saw the tribe of crazies cross his path only a few dozen feet ahead.

Being caught by them once was enough for a lifetime, and the thought that they might get Sara or Laneesha was unacceptable. Because of this, his pain was surpassed by a surge of adrenalin that made him grab both women and drag them and Jack to the ground so they wouldn't be seen. The trio collectively held their breath. Martin's imagination boiled with images of horrific tortures and screaming victims, and he squeezed his eyes shut and decided, if need be, he'd fight to the death right here rather than let those bastards take him again.

The tribe moved closer, not bothering with stealth, marching single file and slapping wayward branches out of their way. Martin felt Laneesha squirm, and he kept hard pressure on her shoulder, preventing her from bolting and giving away their position.

Laneesha whimpered, a single sharp vowel, brief but unmistakably human. And loud enough to be heard by the hunters.

Martin watched as one of the feral people fell out of line, cocking a head in their direction. He took two steps toward them and stopped again, sniffing the air like a dog. This man was fatter than the others, his shoulders broad and powerful looking.

Again Laneesha squirmed, kicking some dead leaves, making a shuffling sound.

Dark as it was, Martin could see the hunter raise his arm. He was holding an ax.

Martin felt the tension in his legs, wondering how he could spring up from a prone position. He adjusted his toes, silently digging them into the ground for traction, forcing his crippled hands to grasp some loose dirt to throw in their attacker's face.

Then there came a scream.

Not from Martin or the women, and not from any of the hunters. This came from deep in the forest, shrill and agonized, a sharp note that went on and on.

The axman turned toward the scream, then lumbered back into the woods.

Martin let out his breath. "Let's wait a minute," he whispered, his jaw throbbing and his tongue and cheeks feeling like he'd just gargled acid. "Make sure they're gone."

"Who's screaming?" Laneesha said.

"I don't know."

"Martin." He felt his wife's hand grip his shoulder. "That's one of our kids."

Martin placed a thumb and forefinger on his eyes, rubbed them gently. "We don't know that."

The scream returned, a high-pitched chord that Martin could feel in his molars.

"That's Meadow," Laneesha said.

"We don't know it's Meadow, Laneesha."

"Jesus, what are they doin' to him?"

"Laneesha, you have to stay calm."

"It's Meadow. I know his voice. What could make him scream like that?"

Sara clutched Martin's arm. "We have to help him, Martin."

"Sara, I counted eight, *eight*, of those people. And even if it is Meadow, and it might not be, someone is making him scream like that. We have no idea how many of them there are on this island."

Sara got up onto her knees. Their son was in his sling, asleep. Martin admired the child's resilience.

"We still have to try," his wife said.

Martin put his hand on the small of her back. "We will. I promise. But we need to get back to the campsite first."

Another scream, weaker this time, ending in a horrible sob.

"We don't have time," Sara said, standing up.

Martin debated whether or not to tell her, and decided he had no choice. He painfully got to his feet and caught up with Sara, who was already heading toward the scream.

"Sara, I have something at the campsite we can use." He paused. "A gun."

Though he couldn't see it, he could imagine the shocked look on his wife's face.

"A gun, Martin?" Her voice was sharp. Sara didn't like weapons of any sort. Knives especially, but guns were high on her list too. "Why the hell do you have a gun?"

"I took it as a precaution. Camping can be dangerous."

"Do you know how dangerous it is to bring one along, especially with our kids? What if one of them found it?"

"It's hidden."

"Jesus, Martin, I didn't even know you owned a gun."

"Look, hon, I understand you're angry, but this isn't the time for righteous indignation. If that is Meadow out there, we need to find our camp, get the gun. That's the only way we'll have a chance against those people."

Martin held Sara's elbow, felt her tense up.

"Look," he said, keeping the edge out of his voice, "I was a Boy Scout, remember? My brother and I both got our shooting merit badges. I know how to use weapons, Sara. Safely. And this could be Meadow's only hope."

He heard her sigh, and she stopped tugging against him. "How do we find camp?"

"The orange ribbons."

"I've been looking for those for more than an hour."

"I'm pretty sure I know where one is. Come on." He walked back toward Laneesha, spoke quietly. "You doing okay?"

"This is one fucked up trip, Martin."

Martin kept the smile off his face because it would have hurt too much. "That it is. Sara? The flashlight?"

She handed it over. Martin walked past, through a patch of dogwood, and found the large elm tree he remembered tying a ribbon to earlier. Sure enough, the reflective orange strip was wound proudly around the trunk.

"The next one should only be a few yards away," he said. "Let's all stick together, and try to stay quiet."

Something touched Martin's hand, and he flinched at both the surprise and the jolt of pain. He spun, saw Sara at his side.

Her touch was gentle but firm.

Much as it hurt, he grasped her hand back.

* * *

Tyrone pushed Cindy behind him, standing between her and the three men. He'd never seen cannibals before, but this trio looked just like he pictured they would. The dirt on their tattered clothing wasn't dirt at all, but dried blood. Their beards and hair were tangled with burrs and twigs. Their eyes were crazy, darting every which way. The one in the middle—the one with the knife and fork—was actually drooling.

Tyrone reflexively reached for his hip, but there was no weapon. The only weapon nearby was currently roasting on a burning log in the campfire. On the one hand, Tyrone had no idea what the heat had done to the mechanisms and the bullets. He didn't want to depend on a pistol and have it jam on him, or worse, blow up in his grasp.

On the other hand, he didn't want to be eaten.

He quickly picked up one of the sticks they'd used for marsh-mallows and nudged the pistol off the log and through the ash, to cool ground, one eye on the cannibals. They just stood there, staring. Then the one with the cutlery spoke, his voice dry and raspy.

"Give...the... girl... and...we... let... you... go."

He smiled when he said it, revealing a witch's mouth of blackened and missing teeth.

Tyrone felt Cindy press against him.

"That ain't gonna happen."

The drool dribbled down the man's beard. "Then... you... both... die."

Tyrone shook his head. "That ain't happenin' neither."

The cutlery man grunted at his two companions, and they each walked off in a different direction. Circling the campfire, moving toward Tyrone and Cindy.

Tyrone dug a hand in his pocket, pulled out the lining, and ripped. It tore away.

"Y'all don' wanna do this."

"Yes... we... do." The cutlery man reached into his pants and pulled out...

No *fucking way*, Tyrone thought. *It's a salt shaker.*

The two men flanking them came in low and slow, stalking like lions. The cutlery man stood his ground, cutting off that escape route. In just a few moments, Tyrone and Cindy would be surrounded in a tightening triangle.

Go time.

Wearing the ripped pocket like a sock puppet, he bent down and grabbed the pistol.

The cloth offered some protection from the heat, but in the time it took Tyrone to raise the gun and seek the trigger, the pain became overpowering and he dropped it between his feet.

None of the cannibals reacted to Tyrone's attempt, not even pausing in their approach.

"Shit," Tyrone said. Again he reached for the gun.

It felt like holding a hot coal, and every instinct, every nerve in his body, screamed at him to drop it, to pull away from the pain.

Tyrone grimaced, aimed, fighting to hold on, his finger frantically seeking the trigger, trying to get it inside the trigger guard—

And he dropped it again.

His hand was definitely burned, and he felt that sick dizzy feeling of being badly injured. He chanced a look. The cloth of the pocket had burned away in spots, revealing bloody blisters.

The cannibals now had them surrounded.

Tyrone stared down at the gun, gritting his teeth, his hand twitching. He needed to pick that son of a bitch up, but his brain and his body were deadlocked. Even as he bent for it a third time, his hand refused to go near it.

So Tyrone grabbed it lefty.

This time his finger got inside the trigger guard on the first try, and the gun was already cocked, making the pull easy. He raised, aimed, and fired in less than two seconds. The weapon kicked in his hand, and he let go again, it falling to the ground beside him.

His target, the cannibal approaching on their right, jerked his head back. The bullet hit him just above his right eye. He stood there for a moment, then dropped like his strings had been cut, flopping onto his knees, then his side.

Tyrone had both hands to his face, blowing on them, eyeing the next immediate threat while psyching himself up to reach for the gun again.

But there was no next threat. Rather than continue their attack, the cutlery man and his companion slunk over to their fallen comrade.

The knife and fork flashed in the firelight. Tyrone refused to watch, pulling his shirt up over his head, backing up, and wrapping the hot gun in the fabric.

He heard Cindy gag. "Oh...my god..."

"Don' look at them."

"They're *eating* him."

Tyrone kept his eyes averted. "We gotta get outta here. When I say run, we run."

"He's still wiggling. Tyrone, he's not even dead yet."

Tyrone stared into the woods. They were dark. Too dark. Without light they'd be walking around in circles. He needed a torch.

"Gimme your shirt," Tyrone said. He turned and stared at Cindy. She was watching the cannibals, her face a mask of horror and revulsion. He gently touched her chin, turning her face toward his.

"Cindy. I need your shirt."

She nodded, lifting it up over her head. In just her bra she looked smaller and younger, and she automatically folded her arms, either out of cold or shame.

Tyrone located the half-full bag of marshmallows near the fire. He had no idea if this idea would work, but he knew from recent experience these things burned nice and slow. He wrapped Cindy's shirt around the bag, then tied that to the end of a two foot branch from their firewood pile.

When he placed the branch in the flames to ignite it, he chanced another look at the cannibals, just to make sure they weren't planning another attack.

The cutlery man's mouth was full, his cheeks distended. Blood dribbled down his face, mingling with the drool. He noticed Tyrone's gaze, and while watching him, shook some salt onto something red and shiny he held in his hand.

Tyrone felt the bile churn in his stomach. He picked up the torch, tucked the shirt and gun under his armpit, and told Cindy it was time to go.

Twenty yards into the forest, Tyrone dropped the gun, dropped the torch, and fell to his knees and vomited.

Cindy knelt next to Tyrone, patting his back, comforting him until he was ready to go on.

* * *

When Lester Paks was a little boy, he was diagnosed with Stereotypic Movement Disorder. Rather than the more common repetitive behaviors associated with SMD, such as hand waving, rocking, or fiddling with fingers, Lester's affliction was more severe.

He could not stop biting himself.

While SMD was often associated with mental retardation, Lester had a higher than average IQ. But something wrong in his brain compelled him to stick his fingers, hands, arms, and even feet, into his mouth and gnaw.

Medications and behavior modification therapy had little effect. In the first grade, his disorder escalated sharply. Instead of limiting his bites to himself, he began biting other things. Furniture. Appliances. Pets.

It culminated when he locked his jaws onto a classmate named Jesse Sloan, and it took six people to pull him off.

Lester went into an institution after that. They kept him drugged up, and when that didn't stop the biting, they removed his baby teeth.

When his adult teeth grew in, he was given an orthodontic device that prevented him from opening his mouth more than a centimeter. After more drugs, and therapy, and nine years in the institution, he was finally able to get his disorder under enough control to be released. By then puberty had arrived, and blessed Lester with a large stature. At age fifteen, he stood a foot taller than most adults.

Lester celebrated his release by running away from home, removing the orthodontic block with a hammer and pliers, and abducting a forty-year-old woman at a gas station. During his two days with her, he learned about the joys of sex, of causing fear and pain, and of biting without any restraint at all. Her cause of death was listed as exsanguination—blood loss resulting from over three hundred of his special little kisses.

Lester was caught, tried as an adult, and caught an incredible break. A brilliant doctor testified in his defense, and got him free. Later, the doctor was able to cure him of his SMD. Lester still had the compulsion to bite, but he no longer desired to bite himself. This meant he could finally live out a lifelong dream without fear of self-mutilation.

It took countless sessions, sitting in front of a mirror with a power drill and a nail file. But when he was finished, twelve of Lester's front teeth had been sharpened into points that rivaled any predator in the animal kingdom.

The biting became much more fulfilling after that.

*　　*　　*

Lester's hips spasmed and he came, moaning deep in his throat.

Then he smiled and took a picture.

Prior to this, Lester never had any sexual experience that was consensual. This Georgia girl was the first person to ever come on to him. And though, like the others, she seemed afraid, she also seemed very willing.

Because of that, Lester had no immediate desire to chew her into little pieces. The idea of an active participant was so exciting that he was able to keep the biting urge in check.

He bent down to kiss her, and she didn't pull away. She opened her mouth to him fully, jabbing at his tongue with hers, even grinding her hips up against him.

Yes indeed, this Georgia girl was something special.

"Lester is taking Georgia girl home."

Her eyes got big, and she sucked on her lower lip. "To your playroom?"

"Yes. But Lester won't hurt Georgia girl. He likes her. He wants to show her something."

Her hands moved down, grabbing him again. "Lester already showed Georgia girl something. And she really liked it."

Lester blushed, and then felt the stirrings of a second arousal. But this wasn't a good place for sex. The feral people were around. They feared Lester, but there were too many, so he had to stay on guard.

He zipped up the fly in his overalls. "Lester wants to show Georgia girl the pet. Lester thinks Georgia girl will like it."

The girl tugged up her pants and stood, and for a brief moment she looked scared and Lester thought she was going to run. That would be bad. Lester would have to chase her, and then he'd take her to the playroom and tie her up and hurt her very badly.

But she didn't run. Georgia girl reached out and took his arm, resting her cheek against his elbow.

Yes, she would like meeting the pet. And afterward, Lester would introduce her to Doctor. But Doctor wouldn't give this one to Subject 33. Not this one.

This one, Lester was going to keep.

*　　*　　*

Sara found the next ribbon in the direction Martin said it would be. After hours of fruitlessly searching for the damn things, her relief was palpable. But so was her fear. Every moment they remained undiscovered seemed like borrowed time.

The trio moved slowly, stopping often to listen if they were being followed.

All they heard was screaming. Meadow's screaming.

Sara walked with her shoulders rigid, her fists clenched, tucking Jack's blanket up around his ears so he wouldn't have to hear it.

Please, stop screaming.

Every wail was worse than a slap. As a psychologist, she knew about the mental processes involved in certain instances of child abuse—research she boned up on to better understand Georgia, who put a child in a clothes dryer. The trigger of Shaken Baby Syndrome was usually a frustrated caregiver who couldn't take the crying, and began to resent the very life they were supposed to protect.

For God's sake, just stop.

Then Sara had her son. She was in labor for eight and a half hours with Jack. Toward the end she was exhausted, wracked by pain, and just wanted the whole damn "miracle of birth" thing to be over with so she could get some sleep.

But then Jack finally entered the world, and when she was holding him in her arms and looking into his tiny eyes the implication of it all hit her harder than the labor did. Sara felt love like it was a physical force, and she swore she would do everything in her power to make this little person happy. It was an absolute joy she hadn't ever experienced, before or since.

The idea that anyone could lose control and hurt a child was monstrous.

But after listening to Meadow's screams for more than ten minutes, Sara began to lose control. She recognized it happening, knew the reason why, and still couldn't stop it. Rage coursed through her, and it wasn't directed at whoever was hurting Meadow.

It was directed *at* Meadow.

Just shut up, please just shut up. Why won't you fucking shut…

And then the screaming stopped. Sara stood still, listening.

Crickets and nothing else.

The silence came with a real measure of relief. But at the same time, Sara feared it meant Meadow's death. The fear trumped the relief, the weight of the realization threatening to sink Sara into the ground. Having one of her kids run away was bad enough. But Meadow actually dying? Dying when it was her job to protect him?

Oh no. Oh no no no.

Sara fell apart.

Laneesha sidled up to her. She'd been walking with her fingers in her ears, and in the moonlight her face glistened like a wet plum. Sara hugged the teen, who hugged back, and they spent a moment sobbing.

Martin touched Sara's hair.

"We have to keep going, hon."

"But Meadow… he's…"

Martin pulled Sara in close, and she felt herself melt into him. "I know. But we have other kids that need our help. We have to be strong for them."

Sara nodded, wiped a fist across her face, rubbing away tears, and began searching for the next ribbon. As she walked, she raged against the conflict going on inside of her. One part, grateful the screaming had ended. The other, angry at herself for being grateful. Add this shame to the horror of murdering a man, and Sara questioned her capabilities to counsel children, or anyone else for that matter. Her job description required empathy, along with the ability to dispassionately disconnect. Sara seemed unable to do either.

That made Sara even more disgusted. On top of everything going on, she had to throw herself a pity party.

"We should be there soon," Martin said, coming up behind her. He spoke deliberately, a measure of pain in his voice.

Sara knew this was a completely inappropriate time to bring it up, but she did anyway.

"Martin. You haven't signed the divorce papers yet."

He was silent for a moment, then said. "I was hoping I wouldn't have to. But if that's what you really want…"

"What I really want is you."

In the darkness, his hand found hers.

"Then let's not give up on us yet," he said, giving her fingers a gentle squeeze. "Can I hold Jack? That screaming…well…it got to me."

Sara understood completely. She gave her sleeping son a kiss on his head and passed him, sling and all, over to his father. Martin slipped the straps over his shoulders and patted Jack's back. It was something she'd seen dozens of times before, and the thought of never seeing it again was devastating.

If—no—when they got out of here, she would do everything she could to make their marriage, and their family, work.

"How many ribbons have you counted?" Martin asked.

"Ten or eleven."

"If we're going in the right direction, the campsite should be very close."

"Or we're heading toward the lake, and will have to retrace all of our steps. We need to pick up the pace, Martin. If there's any chance Meadow is—"

Laneesha's scream cut Sara off. She rushed over to the teen, flashlight bobbling, and aimed the beam at the large hill of rubble the girl was facing.

The hill was well over ten feet high, and stretched on for dozens of yards. It was pale gray, made up of what appeared to be stones and branches.

Laneesha clutched Sara's shoulder, hard enough to make her wince. It pushed Sara closer to the mound, and in a moment that seemed utterly surreal, Sara realized that those weren't stones and branches.

It was a gigantic pile of human bones.

* * *

The boy wasn't quite dead yet, but his meat was so tender it practically fell off the bone. They feasted, filling their bellies to bursting, fighting among themselves for the juiciest parts.

Though they hunted as a pack, they had no bonds with each other. Their broken minds reduced them to something less than human, driving them to fulfill their base needs at any cost. Higher mental functioning was gone, leaving only a compulsion to kill, to feed, to kill again.

If there were no strangers on the island, they showed no reluctance in attacking one another. For food. And for something just as primal; the unquenchable desire to hunt and kill.

This was a compulsion buried deep within all creature's brains, as primitive as the first vertebrates to inhabit the planet, eons ago.

In most human beings, this compulsion was repressed.

In them, it had been liberated.

When the urge came upon them, they couldn't control it. And if there was no fresh meat to hunt, they hunted each other.

But now there was fresh meat on the island. Plenty of it.

And though their hunger for food was momentarily sated, their hunger for death was not.

.   .   .

When Laneesha was a little girl, she wanted to be a big girl. Or more precisely, an adult. She found children her own age boring, much preferring the company of grown-ups. Dolls and games of tag weren't nearly as stimulating to her as learning to cook, sew, and knit from her mother, change the oil on the car and spackle drywall like her father, bake like grandma, and repair appliances like Uncle Ralph.

Uncle Ralph wasn't actually her uncle. He was a friend of Dad's. He was also the nicest adult Laneesha knew, treating her as an equal even when she was as young as six. He never talked down to her, never reprimanded her, never was anything but 100% cool.

When Laneesha turned sixteen, she realized the next step in adulthood was motherhood. She babysat all the neighborhood kids, and wanted one of her own. So she decided to get pregnant. To accomplish this she sought out the one person who she knew would make an excellent father, and after riding with him to a house to install a satellite TV system, she seduced Uncle Ralph in the back seat of his repair van.

He resisted, at first. But she was legal, and insistent, and Ralph didn't have a girlfriend at the time. The affair was short lived—a guilt-ridden Uncle Ralph broke it off after only three trysts. But three was enough. Laneesha, now pregnant, assumed that stand-up Uncle Ralph would do the right thing. She was mature enough to know he wasn't going to marry her, but expected child support and shared custody.

Instead, her father beat the hell out of Uncle Ralph, ordering him to never see her again, and then insisted she terminate the pregnancy. Laneesha refused, and her father kicked her out. Uncle Ralph also refused to see her again, offering her the money for an abortion and nothing else.

Laneesha had no friends because she'd never bothered to make any. She was forced to live in shelters, and eventually gave birth to her beautiful daughter, Brianna. But welfare checks didn't stretch very far for a young mother. Without a babysitter she couldn't get a job, and without a job she couldn't get a babysitter, so she took to shoplifting to survive.

Chicago had many chain department stores, and Laneesha kept her strategy simple. She'd steal something at one store, then return it at another store for the cash. If they refused to give her cash, as they sometimes did without a receipt, she traded the item for something she needed, or something she could pawn.

It worked for several months. Laneesha began looking for a place of her own, and was planning on getting a job and a nanny once she saved up a thousand dollars. She was only sixty bucks short of her goal when a dumb department store clerk became distracted and left a pair of expensive diamond earrings on the counter unattended. It was only for a few seconds, but Laneesha couldn't resist the temptation. She grabbed them, shoved them in Brianna's diaper, and beat a hasty retreat.

But she was caught. Even worse, the store had tapes of her stealing four other items over the course of several months. It had been a trap. They pressed charges for grand theft, social services took Brianna, and Laneesha wound up at the Center.

The Center made her realize two things. First, people her own age weren't so bad. Meadow, for all his frontin', was actually a pretty good guy. Not daddy material, but they developed a bond that Laneesha could honestly say was love. Second, Laneesha was more determined than ever to get released and get Brianna back. And she was on track to do so. A hearing was coming up, and Sara was going to recommend parole, and once she had a job she was going to begin the steps to reclaim her child. Maybe Meadow would even be in the picture.

But staring at that huge pile of bones after half an hour of listening to Meadow's tortured screams made Laneesha doubt she'd ever get off the island alive.

*   *   *

Laneesha clung to Sara, digging her carefully manicured nails into the psychologist's arm, staring at the most horrifying thing she'd ever seen.

"How...how many you think?" she asked.

"Thousands," Sara whispered.

Martin took the light from Sara, moved closer to the pile. "These bones are old. Really old."

"Who are they?" Laneesha asked.

Martin shook his head. "I don't know."

Sara began to back up, pulling Laneesha along with her. "Martin, those... *wild people*. They must have retied the ribbons. To lead us to this place. They're probably coming right now."

Martin went rigid, then whispered. "I think they're already here."

Laneesha felt like she stuck her finger in a socket, electricity jolting through her and prompting her to run somewhere, anywhere. She broke away from Sara and dashed into the field of bones.

There were no trees here, and the moon was bright, so Laneesha could move much faster than she had in the woods. Part of her brain registered Sara yelling her name, but Laneesha wasn't going to stop. Not for Sara. Not for anybody. While Laneesha feared those crazy cannibal people, she had more to think about than just her life. If she died, Brianna would be motherless.

Not a day, not an hour, went by when Laneesha didn't long for her beautiful daughter. Being separated from Brianna was a physical ache that dominated Laneesha's every action, every thought. She would see her daughter again, and love and protect and raise her, and nothing was going to stop that. Not now. Not ever.

Laneesha turned a quick corner around the mound, kicking something that she realized was a skull, switching directions again and seeking out the woods. She could hide in the trees, wait until morning. Then she would find the camp, radio that boat guy, and live to be with Brianna again. Hopefully, Sara and Martin and the rest of them would make it too. But a part of Laneesha, a large part, also made her understand that if those cannibals were busy eating the others, they would have full bellies and be less inclined to track her down.

It's all for Brianna, she told herself.

But stupid as it was, she couldn't find the trees. Earlier, she thought she'd be stuck in the woods forever, never seeing the clear sky again. Now all she saw was sky and bones.

The bones were everywhere, a giant garbage dump of various-sized mounds, some only as high as her hip, others too tall to see over. There was no real path, no real direction, and Laneesha took another turn and found herself standing on top of an unstable pile. She stopped, turned, and her foot got stuck. Lanessha looked down, saw she was caught in some sort of trap.

No, not a trap. A man's ribcage.

Another spark of panic made her cry out, kicking the foul thing off her foot, pushing onward through the bone field. There was no ground any more, no dirt. She waded, calf-deep, through bones. When she tried to get on top of them, they wouldn't support her completely. Laneesha had a ridiculous thought about Chuck E Cheese, that children's pizza slash arcade with the room filled with thousands of plastic balls. It was impossible to stand up in that room, and almost as difficult standing here.

Laneesha attempted to backtrack, feeling bones snap under her weight—*bones, Jesus, these were once inside human beings*—and she tripped, falling face first into the pile.

The pain was sharp and made her draw a breath. She turned onto her side, tried to sit up, her hands fluttering around the knife embedded in her shoulder.

But, of course, it wasn't a knife at all.

I've got someone's bone sticking in me.

Laneesha felt the blood drain from her head, the whole world start to spin. But she couldn't pass out, for Brianna's sake, so she twisted onto all fours and began to crawl, determined to get away, determined to survive.

Then the smell hit her. A musty, rotten stench, moist and cloying. It reminded Laneesha of food gone bad. But this wasn't food, this was *people*. People who once breathed and loved and laughed and feared just like her. Laneesha shut her eyes and crunched up her face so her lips blocked her nostrils, and moved even faster while she tried not to puke.

The throb in her shoulder stabbed deeper, hurting ten times worse, and Laneesha cried out. She tried to move, but couldn't.

The bone had caught on something.

Laneesha didn't want to touch it, and she tried to ease back, but she felt like she'd been staked to the spot. Eyes still closed, she raised a hesitant hand to her shoulder, felt the object she was stuck to.

The bone had caught on something large and bumpy, shaped sort of like a big pretzel.

Someone's pelvis.

Laneesha pushed, but the pelvis held firm. Then she tried to pull the bone from her shoulder and almost passed out. While the bone was no bigger than a hot dog, it was old and brittle. When Laneesha tried to remove it, the bone splintered, digging in like a fishhook barb,

Laneesha had to take a breath, becoming dangerously lightheaded, her gorge rising fast. She cradled the pelvis in her hand and tried to lift. It was attached to something. Not having any choice, she looked down.

Legs. Bits of sinew still connected the pelvis to two decimated leg bones.

Laneesha jerked up, and the hip joints pulled free of their sockets with a cracking sound. Then she crawled, one hand pressing the pelvis to her chest, crawled through the bones until she could stand up again.

Only a few yards away, silhouetted by the moonlight, a man rushed at her.

Laneesha got to her feet, stumbling away from the man, ignoring the pain and dashing through two large mounds of bones. The trees had to be close. The bone piles seemed to end just ahead. If she could just make it, just get away long enough to—

She stopped abruptly. The bone field did end, but instead of the forest Laneesha found herself facing a large stone building. It looked like a fortress, two stories high, stretching out a hundred feet in each direction.

Laneesha heard a creaking sound, looked up, saw an arch above her. Hanging on chains was an ancient wooden sign.

Rock Island Prison.

Then something hit her on the head and everything went black.

. . .

Cindy felt her heart sink when the screaming stopped. It was awful to hear, the most awful thing she'd ever heard. When it ended she had a very real feeling that Meadow—and it sure sounded like Meadow—was dead.

Still, she and Tyrone headed in the direction the cries had been coming from. Cindy didn't like Meadow. But if there was a chance to help him, she would take that chance. One thing the Center had taught her was the value of life. Every life.

She held the torch, grateful for both the light and the warmth it emitted. In only her bra, the night air gave her goosebumps. Tyrone walked at her side. He held the gun, now cool enough to touch, in his left hand. His right hand was wrapped in his T-shirt. After fleeing the campsite, Cindy had insisted on examining his injuries. His left only had a few small blisters. His right looked like raw hamburger.

Still, Tyrone didn't complain. He marched onward, just as determined to save Meadow as she was.

Neither of them talked about what they'd seen at the camp. But Cindy couldn't help but think the same thing had happened to Meadow. She shivered. In the past, she'd thought a lot about death, and always expected it would be with a needle in her arm. But death by cannibals? Who could have ever conceived of such a thing?

And yet, it might actually happen to her. But instead of fleeing from it, she was heading toward it.

"Smell that?" Tyrone asked.

Cindy stopped, sniffed the air.

Her mouth watered.

Barbecue. Smoke and meat, reminding her of the venison steaks her dad would cook over an open fire.

Then Cindy's brain caught up with her salivary glands, and she realized what she was probably smelling.

"Tyrone...could that be...?"

She saw him stiffen. "I'm gonna kill 'em. I'm gonna kill every one of those fuckers."

Tyrone stormed forward, rushing through the woods, Cindy unable to keep up. Running with a torch wasn't easy, It threw sparks, and if she moved too quickly the wind shrank the flame, threatening to snuff it out. Cindy feared Tyrone would get too far ahead and she'd lose him, feared not only for herself, but for him as well. They'd counted six bullets still in the gun, but that may not be enough, and he was already injured and—

Cindy stopped abruptly before she tripped over Tyrone, who was on all fours, wheezing like he'd been punched in the gut. Beyond him she saw a faint light, coming through a gap in the trees. The roasted meat smell was overwhelming. Awful as it was, Cindy's stomach rumbled, and she cursed herself for missing dinner.

"Don' look," Tyrone said.

At first, Cindy thought he meant *don't look at me.* She turned away, and Tyrone caught her ankle, even though squeezing it must have caused him pain.

Tyrone meant don't look at where the smell was coming from.

She was fine with that. Cindy already had enough images seared onto her brain for a lifetime of nightmares, and had no desire to add to them.

"How many are there?" she asked, crouching next to Tyrone.

"I dunno. Five or six. I'm gonna take 'em down, soon as I catch my breath."

Cindy didn't bother to argue. Every human life was indeed sacred, but when someone was trying to eat you, the best defense was a good offense.

"Can you shoot lefty?"

"Did okay back at camp."

"My dad taught me about guns. Used to take me hunting."

"You ain't doin' it, Cindy."

"I'm not afraid."

Which was a lie. She was terrified. But even scarier than shooting some cannibals was thinking about what would happen if they caught her and Tyrone.

"You don' want this on your head, girl."

"Let me see you hold the gun."

"I ain't playin'"

"Neither am I. Hold it."

Tyrone picked the gun up off the ground, held it in his left hand. He winced, unable to keep it steady.

"Give me the gun, Tyrone."

"No way."

"Your hands are ruined, and you won't be able to aim. Not at six people. After the first shot, they'll scatter, be moving targets. One of them might even run at us. So either give me the gun, or we get the hell out of here."

Tyrone narrowed his eyes. "You can really shoot?"

"I can hit a rabbit at a hundred yards."

She didn't tell him that she'd never actually hit a rabbit, only rabbit-sized targets, and that was with a rifle, not a pistol. Cindy didn't like hunting. While she had no problem eating meat, doing the killing herself was a little too personal, and after several attempts her father stopped taking her on his hunting trips because she would never pull the trigger when the moment of truth arrived.

Thinking of that, she questioned her own commitment here. How could she shoot a person when she couldn't shoot a deer?

But it was too late. Tyrone was nodding, passing the gun to her, butt-first. She took it, handing him the torch.

"We gotta do this. For Meadow. For ourselves. But Cindy..."
Tyrone paused. She waited.

"...try not to look at what's on the fire."

Cindy nodded. The gun felt warm in her hand, and she automatically checked the clip, the safety, the round in the chamber, just like her father taught her.

Don't think about it. Just do it.

She crouched, creeping toward a nearby bush. The pistol seemed to get heavier with each step. When she reached the thicket she planted her feet a shoulder's width apart, gripped the gun in two hands, and sighted down the length of the barrel.

It was an image straight out of hell.

A gridiron.

Meadow.

Fire.

A circle of cannibals.

Eating.

Cindy froze. The smell of roasted pork didn't jibe with the parts they were putting in their mouths. Her finger was on the trigger, but she couldn't shoot. She couldn't so much as breathe.

The largest of the tribe—a wide, hairy man with an ax propped against his leg—was chewing on...

Jesus, that's Meadow's—

The man looked up, his eyes meeting Cindy's. He bellowed like a bull, raising the ax.

The other cannibals turned to look.

Cindy experienced fear so visceral it hit her like a punch. She staggered back, unable to support her own weight, screaming as loud as she could, the gun dropping from her hand and disappearing into the underbrush.

.   .   .

Clutching Lester's hand as he led her through the forest both frightened and exhilarated Georgia. She attributed her survival so far to her cunning and determination, but she also knew that

Lester might not be as smitten as he seemed, and he still had every intention of taking her to his "playroom."

During the walk, Lester made what he must have thought was small talk, mentioning some of the horrifying things he'd done to previous playroom guests.

Georgia had a strong stomach, but some of his descriptions made it do flip flops. She did not want to wind up at this psycho's mercy.

That meant coming up with some kind of plan.

"Lester is home."

Georgia was lost in her thoughts she hadn't noticed they'd arrived at a building. The façade was gray stone, old-looking, sort of like a medieval castle. Lester released Georgia's hand to pull a key out of his pocket and fuss with a very big and heavy iron door. After unlocking it he needed to tug hard to get the rusty thing open. It squealed like a tortured pig.

"It's strong," Lester grunted, "so the ferals can't get in."

"Ferals?"

"On the island. Ferals run free and eat people. People like Georgia girl."

Georgia peered into the unlit building and hesitated. She had the same feeling she did when her parents took her to that haunted house on Halloween, on one of their rare family outings. Georgia knew there were scary things inside, and while she liked scaring others she didn't like being on the receiving end.

Lester seemed to sense her hesitation, and if he mistook it as reluctance, she lost her edge. Mustering her courage, Georgia marched inside, a hand stretched out in front of her so she didn't bump into anything in the dark.

The room was cold, damp, and smelled like mildew. Georgia sensed it was large. The floor beneath her was hard, possibly cement. She took a few more tentative steps and then touched something cold. Feeling around, she realized it was a rusty iron bar.

The lights came on, accompanied by a buzzy, electric sound. Even though there were only bare low-watt bulbs hanging from the ceiling every ten feet, Georgia still squinted against the sudden brightness. It took her a moment for her eyes to adjust, and then she realized what sort of building this was.

A prison. The iron bar she grasped was part of a cell, one of hundreds, stretching out in all directions in a wide open space almost as big as a football field. Except, upon closer examination, she wondered if it was perhaps a kennel instead. Or some sort of barn for livestock. The cells were so small that there wasn't enough space for even a child to lie down.

"Each cell held four Confederate prisoners," Lester told her. "They shared half a loaf of bread and a single bucket of water each day. The bucket was also their toilet. Many died from scurvy, dysentery, and smallpox. But starvation took the majority. Others murdered to get more of the bread. The dead were stacked in piles and left to rot. Thousands of them. It drove many of the prisoners mad. All that fresh meat, spoiling, just out of reach. They broke out of here just to get to the meat."

It sounded like Lester was reciting something he memorized.

"This is Plincer's prison?" Georgia asked.

"Rock Island Prison. Warden Plincer was Doctor's great great grandfather."

Georgia couldn't believe that Martin's stupid story was actually true. "So those...ferals...those are civil war cannibals?"

Lester smiled at her, his teeth making him look like a shark. Seeing him in the light brought color to his face. His complexion was pale, teeth yellowish, the whites of his eyes bright pink. "Don't be silly, Georgia girl. Those Confederate soldiers died a hundred years ago."

"Their descendants?"

"No descendants. They were men. It takes a man and a woman to have descendants." He took her hand and rubbed his finger along her knuckles, the intimate gesture making her shiver. "Georgia girl knows that."

Lester led her through the ranks and files of cages, their footsteps echoing off the iron and stone, making the space seem even emptier. Georgia tried to picture it filled to capacity with starving, desperate men, men who killed each other for a crust of bread or to feast on their flesh.

The image was kind of exciting.

"How did you get here?" Georgia asked. "On this island?"

"Doctor brought Lester here."

"Why?"

Lester stopped, then looked down at her. "Doctor is Lester's friend."

"Georgia girl is Lester's girlfriend, too," she said, giving his hand an extra squeeze.

They walked out of the cell room, up a barely lit stone staircase. Unlike the first floor, which was all open space except for the bars, there were walls up here. Lester took her down a hallway, passing several closed doors.

"This is where the prisoners were punished. Beaten. Whipped. Branded. This is where Lester's playroom is." They stopped before an ancient wooden door. "Is Georgia girl ready to meet Lester's pet?"

Georgia nodded. He opened the door and they went inside.

The smell hit her first. Like a public bathroom, but worse. On one side of the small room was a long metal table. There were shackles at the head and foot. Next to the table, a workbench, on top of which were various tools and devices, many of them rusty from blood. Near a small dresser, on the far wall, was a box spring with a stained mattress on top. Behind it, covering the wall, were dozens of photographs, many of them close-ups of people screaming.

On the other side of the room was a large wooden crate, the top off.

"The pet is in the box," Lester said.

Georgia couldn't see what was in the crate from where she stood, and she got that same haunted house vibe. On one hand, it might be something harmless in there, like a dog or cat, or maybe some animal indigenous to the island, like a raccoon. On the other hand, Lester was a psychopath, and he might be expecting her to nuzzle a rotting corpse.

Either way, Lester was watching her, judging her. She had to make a good impression.

Besides, what's the worst thing that could be in there?

She chewed on her lower lip and approached the crate cautiously, the foul smell getting stronger. At first, all she noticed were clumps of hay. And then she saw it.

"Georgia girl can touch the pet," Lester said. "The pet is tame."

Georgia clamped both of her hands to her mouth and tried not to throw up.

.   .   .

Sara ran. Not from their pursuers—she didn't even see their pursuers. Sara ran after Laneesha, determined to catch her and bring her back. They needed to stay together. Sara couldn't handle losing any more kids.

But the teen was fast, and it was dark, and after two quick turns Sara lost her among the piles of bones.

Sara stopped, turning in a full circle, looking and listening for any movement.

Laneesha was gone. So were Martin and Jack.

Sara tried to backtrack, weaving her way through the bonefield, fighting the urge to yell out either of their names. She didn't want Laneesha to be alone. Martin either, especially with his injuries.

She ran, frantic, thinking only of them and not her personal neuroses, rounding a particularly large mound of the dead, coming face to face with the forest, the darkness. From the darkness, came a cry.

It wasn't Meadow. It was a girl, high-pitched, a scream of fright rather than pain.

Laneesha?

If so, she'd gotten pretty far pretty fast. The sound came from deep in the woods. Without thinking, Sara ran into the trees.

When the forest surrounded her, she froze.

Martin had the flashlight.

Sara whirled around. Trees. Shadows. Darkness. Looking up, the dark had even swallowed the sky.

She felt it in her chest first, a tightening that made her pant. Her palms got wet. Her mouth went dry. Sara was nine years old again, back in the trunk, waiting for someone to free her. She tried to get her feet to move, tried to battle the weight of the darkness pressing upon her. But she remained locked in place, a statue, too frightened to even blink.

Sounds, to her left. Someone coming.

No, more than just someone. A lot of people.

Move! Dammit, Sara, move!

But she stayed rooted to the spot, even when they burst through the bushes and rushed at her.

PART III
THE FIRE

Laneesha startled herself awake, freaked out by a crazy dream she had about running through mountains of human bones.

She didn't know why her head and chest both hurt, or why she was sitting down rather than lying in her bed, or why she couldn't move her arms.

Then she saw the old man standing in front of her, an old man she'd never seen before, and it all came back to her in a horrible rush.

"Hello, child. I gave you a little something to help you wake up. I also took the liberty of removing that nasty bone from your shoulder. It was a fibula, if you're curious. Very old. About a hundred and forty years old, to be more exact. I even stitched you up. No need to thank me. I am a doctor, after all."

The old man tucked an empty syringe into his coat pocket. It was a white coat, the kind doctors wear. But this one was covered with ugly brown stains and peach-colored smears.

The man himself was also ugly. He had a bald head, freckled with liver spots, and a long neck with a lot of wrinkled loose skin hanging from it. His face was unusually dull, as if he had make-up on. He wore glasses, which were coated with a layer of dirt and grease so thick Laneesha wondered how he could see through them, and he stood in a stooped way, his back bending like a question mark.

Laneesha tried to stand, and realized her arms and legs were strapped to a wheelchair. She fought against the bonds, the leather digging into her wrists, and succeeded only in causing abrasions.

"My name is Doctor Plincer. You're about to become part of a very important scientific study. An epic one, in fact. Unfortunately, you'll be part of the control group. Sort of. Well, not really, but it sounds better."

Laneesha looked hard at the doctor, more angry than afraid. "You better let me go, you dirty ol' man. Or I am gonna kick yo ass."

Doctor Pincer scratched at his chin and something flaked off his face.

"You see, my dear, there are wolves, and there are sheep. While I admire your spunk, I'm out of sheep at the moment, and I don't want Subject 33 mad at me. So I'm giving you to him."

"What the fuck you talkin' about?"

"Hmm. Yes. Well, no harm in telling you, and truth told, I don't have many people to talk to these days. The ferals are, well, *feral*, and they would prefer eating you to good conversation. Lester, dear Lester, he listens, but he's heard all of my stories before, and I worry I bore him sometimes. And Subject 33, well, frankly, he frightens me. He frightens the piss out of me. Which is why I've kept him locked up. He hasn't been out in over a year."

Laneesha looked away from the doctor, taking in her surroundings. She was in some sort of hallway. The walls were brick. The only light was a bulb hanging from the ceiling. Her wheelchair was next to a large iron door with a slot in it at waist-level. Laneesha recognized it as a solitary confinement door. The slot was for food, and it was open. She peered through and it seemed to lead to another room, with another identical door and slot.

Through this second slot, a pair of bloodshot eyes stared at her.

"He's watching you, I see. I think he likes you. If he doesn't like what I'm giving him, he doesn't keep looking. He's one of my greatest successes, Subject 33. Too much of a success, really. The procedure worked like it was supposed to. Worked perfectly. But afterward he wouldn't follow orders, couldn't be trusted. Tried to kill me on several occasions. Once he even dragged me into that horrible room of his. If Lester hadn't been there to help, I shudder at the things he would have done to me."

Subject 33 blinked. Then his head moved up and he stuck his nose in the slot. Well, part of a nose. Even at this distance Laneesha could see the disfigurement. His nose twitched, and Subject 33 snorted.

He's trying to sniff me, Laneesha thought. And that freaked her out even more than his scars and creepy stares.

"I don't even remember his name," Doctor Plincer said. "Isn't that funny? My second greatest success. He was a soldier, I think. In bad shape when I got him. Broken back. And animals—wolves or coyotes or some other such apex carnivore—had been snacking on him. Bad shape, nearly dead. I can relate, let me tell you. But I patched him up. Even better than that. I *enhanced* him."

Subject 33 stuck his tongue through the slot and licked the air.

"But he doesn't follow orders," Doctor Plincer continued. "Not at all. He hasn't even spoken a word since the procedure. He writes me notes. That's how he tells me what he needs. The last few have been, well, rather odd."

Subject 33's tongue disappeared, and then those red eyes were back. Wide and staring. Laneesha wanted to turn away, but couldn't.

"He's building something in there. I'll be damned if I know what it is. Here I am, a future candidate for the Nobel Prize, and I can't figure it out. Besides enhancing his appetites, the procedure also seemed to amplify his intelligence. So he leaves me notes, I order the parts, and give them to him when the supply boat comes. I'm curious to know what he's building, but I'm too frightened to look. Some sort of pain machine, I suspect. The lambs I bring to him scream like I've never heard screams before. And, believe me, I've heard screams. Lester is very good at making people scream.

I know this firsthand. But Subject 33... well, whatever he's doing to those people, it's *inhuman*."

The doctor knocked twice on the iron door.

"I'm bringing her to you. Please assume the position."

The eyes disappeared, and Laneesha watched Subject 33 turn around and stick his hands through the slot, palms up. They were bent and twisted and covered with gnarly scars, like the fingers had been cut off, broken, and sewn back on in the wrong places.

Laneesha shrank into her chair. "Old man, please don' put me in there."

Doctor Plincer reached into his pocket, removed a dart pistol. He winked at Laneesha. "He's my greatest triumph, but he's difficult to control. The second door in the antechamber isn't locked. He can open it any time. But he stays in there, because he knows if he doesn't I won't give him food. Or any parts for his infernal machine. So he behaves, but I still can't trust him. That makes me proud, in a way. I created an evil so powerful it only answers to itself."

The doctor lifted the iron bar off the door, then opened it, keeping his pistol aimed at the inner room, at the slot in the second door.

"Keep your hands where I can see them, please. You should enjoy this one. Plenty of fire in her. Maybe she'll last you two weeks. That's your record, isn't it? For keeping one alive? Two weeks, isn't it?"

Still facing the inner door, the doctor backed up, walking carefully around Laneesha. Then he began to push her wheelchair into the small room, toward that second door. Laneesha's eyes were locked on Subject 33's ruined hands. On top of their deformities they were filthy, fingernails cracked, blood caked under them.

"No." Laneesha shook her head. "No no no no no..."

"Please leave the wheelchair in the antechamber. I'll pick it up when I bring breakfast in the morning. I'll assume breakfast for two, unless you leave me a note stating otherwise. I know sometimes the lambs don't have the strength to eat. Especially after the first night. I'm making French toast." The doctor stared down at Laneesha. "Do you like French toast, dear?"

"You can't leave me with him. Please. I'll do anything you want. Anything at all." Laneesha couldn't stop the tears. "I have a daughter. Her name is Brianna. Please don't put me in there with him."

Doctor Plincer patted her head. "I won't likely see you again. Or more to the point, you won't see me. I'll see you when he discards the remains. But, truth told, there haven't been very many remains lately. The machine has something to do with it, I suspect. What can he be building in there? I don't know. But *you*...you'll soon find out, my dear, dear girl."

The doctor backed away, and Laneesha heard the iron door slam closed behind her, the crossbar falling into place. She strained against her bonds, strained so hard she saw stars.

Subject 33 removed his hands from the slot, then he opened his door.

Laneesha's scream would be the first of many.

.   .   .

Tom walked along the beach. He was still a little out of breath from his sprint. One moment he was holding a gun—an actual gun—then the next moment Tyrone was on top of him, and the next moment...

What the hell were those things?

Tom knew they were people. No duh. But they looked more like wildmen. All they needed were leather undies and some spears, and Tom could picture them hunting dinosaurs.

For about a zillionth of a second he felt bad for leaving Cindy and Tyrone there. He wasn't really gonna shoot either of them. But those frickin' wildmen looked crazy, and Tom knew when to fight and when to run, so he ran. Through the forest, through the trees, all the way to shore. And now he didn't know what to do next.

So he began to walk around the island. It wasn't a big island; Sara said it was only a few miles across. Tom figured he would keep walking until someone found him. It's not like Sara and Martin were going to leave him here. They were responsible adults. Even if Tyrone told them about the gun, they still had to take him back to Michigan.

Tom tried not to think about the wildmen.

He walked, and walked some more, and then the beach sort of ended and rose up, becoming kind of a cliff with trees on it. Tom climbed, staying away from the edge, and kept heading in the same direction. The night was cool, but he was sweating and really thirsty and kind of hungry too. He thought about drinking lake water, but heard that all the water in the great lakes was dirty and could make you sick.

That's when he smelled it. *Barbecue.*

He paused, trying to figure out where it was coming from. Obviously, Sara and Martin had come back to camp, and now they were cooking something. And then Tom shook his head, wondering how he could have been so gullible.

The wildmen. They were fake.

It must have been part of Martin's stupid plan to scare them all. In fact, one of them might have even been Martin, all dressed up to look like a wildman. And Tom took it for the real thing, like a dummy.

No, not like a dummy. It wasn't Tom's fault he was scared. He was off his meds. He always acted stupid off his meds.

Which was a perfect excuse for why he pointed the gun at Tyrone and Cindy. It wasn't Tom's fault. It was Sara's fault, for not giving him his Risperdol. Which meant they couldn't punish him for anything.

Tom headed into the woods, toward the barbecue smell. He couldn't wait to dig in.

*   *   *

Georgia stared at Lester's pet, her hands over her mouth, the odor so bad it made her stomach roil. At first, she wasn't sure what she was looking at. It looked like a giant, pale worm. But then she noticed the buttocks, the shoulder blades, the bumps of the spine beneath the dirty flesh.

It was a torso. No arms. No legs. Just a body with a head attached. And it smelled awful.

"Go on, Georgia girl," Lester said. "Touch the pet."

She wrinkled her nose. "Is it dead?"

"The pet is not dead."

Lester kicked the crate, and Georgia watched in awe as the head swiveled up and faced them.

"Uhhhhhnnnnnn," it said.

Georgia dropped her hands. "Holy shit. This thing is freaking alive?"

The man's face was a ruin. Eyes gone. Ears gone. A big scar across the scalp. When he opened his mouth to make that hideous sound, Georgia noted the tongue was also missing.

"The pet Lester's best friend," Lester said. "Except for Doctor." He glanced sideways at her, showing his fangs as he smirked. "And Georgia girl."

"Did you do this to him, Lester?"

He nodded. "It took a long time. Lots of cutting."

Georgia stared, fascinated. It was at once the most horrible and most amazing thing she'd ever seen.

"Want to see the pet do the funny dance?" Lester asked.

She nodded.

Lester walked over to the tool cabinet and grabbed something. He brought it over to the crate. It was a broomstick, with a nail sticking out the end.

When Lester poked his pet in the butt with it, the thing flopped around, rocking back and forth. When it rolled onto its back, Georgia noted that its genitals were also gone.

"Does Georgia girl want to make the pet do the funny dance?"

The next thing Georgia knew, the broomstick had been pressed into her hands. She stared down at this poor pathetic creature, rolling around in its own mess on a pile of dirty hay, and searched for any semblance of humanity. She didn't see any. This wasn't a person anymore. Just a mindless thing.

The thing began to roll again, making a moaning sound, and Georgia realized that without even being aware of it she'd given it a poke.

So she poked it again. And again.

The fourth time, she began to laugh.

"So I see you have a new guest for your playroom, Lester. But why isn't she strapped onto your play table?"

Georgia turned, surprised at the voice, and saw an old man in a lab coat standing in the doorway. She instinctively backed away, bumping into Lester.

"This is Georgia girl. Georgia girl is Lester's girlfriend. Georgia girl and Lester are going to make babies."

Georgia looked up at Lester, then unconsciously rubbed her belly. She decided that now wasn't the best time to tell him how she got along with babies.

The old man clucked his tongue. "You tried to make babies before, Lester. Do you remember? But whenever you get a new girlfriend you always wind up biting her too much. How many times have we been through this?"

"Georgia girl is different."

The old man glanced at the stick she held, and then nodded. "Yes. Yes she certainly seems to be, doesn't she?"

"You must be the doctor," Georgia said, finding her voice. "Lester's friend."

"Indeed, indeed I am. Doctor Plincer, and it's a pleasure to make your acquaintance, young lady." Georgia shook the dry, bony hand he extended toward her. "You like playing with Lester's pet, I see."

"He's funny," Georgia said.

"Funny? Hmm. Yes, I suppose he is. No real brain activity anymore. Delta waves. More like delta bumps. Full frontal lobotomy. Had him for years, kept trying to escape, even without limbs. And the begging, all the time, non-stop. We finally did a little work on his prefrontal cortex, just to calm him down. Not much for conversation anymore. But he is kind of funny, isn't he? Especially when you stick him with the nail. Yes?"

Georgia wondered if this was some sort of test. She responded by giving Lester's pet a few more pokes.

The doctor stroked his dirty chin. "Interesting. Very interesting. Sadistic personality. No remorse. Obvious sociopathic tendencies. And I don't see a single bite mark on you. For one of Lester's girlfriends, that's remarkable. Did he happen to tell you what kind of doctor I am?"

Georgia shook her head. She couldn't tell if she passed this old coot's stupid test or not.

"I'm a brain specialist. Perhaps the foremost in the world. And I think, I think that you would be perfect for my experiments."

"Lester is keeping Georgia girl." Lester draped his long arms over her.

Doctor Plincer nodded. "But of course, Lester, of course. But perhaps your little girlfriend could be," he smacked his lips, "*enhanced*. By the procedure."

Georgia didn't like the sound of that at all.

"Lester doesn't want Georgia girl to be like the ferals," Lester said. "Lester and Georgia girl are going to make babies."

"This one won't go feral, Lester. This one has all the traits I'm looking for. Plus she's young. Strong."

Ferals? Lobotomies? Procedures? Georgia didn't like the way this conversation was heading.

From somewhere else in the prison, Georgia heard screaming. A girl. It sounded like Laneesha. She held her breath, resisting the urge to run away, making sure her face was calm even when she was close to freaking out.

"Lester won't let Doctor take Georgia girl."

"You hear that, Frankenstein?" Georgia said. "Back the fuck off."

The doctor nodded again. "I see. I see. But I think, Lester my boy, that this is the best for all concerned. For me, for you, and for her. So I'm going to ask you, very nicely, to bring her to my lab. I promise no harm will come to her."

Lester's protective hug turned into a grab, seizing Georgia in his gigantic hands.

"Lester!" she cried, squirming to get away. She might as well have been bound with steel cable.

Doctor Plincer came closer, smiling. He was bent over with age, and Georgia could see straight down his collar. He wore no shirt beneath his lab coat, and his hairless pink chest was covered with shiny, puckered scars.

"Don't you worry, my dear. I'm going to take very good care of you. You may even thank me for this later. Thank me, or…God forbid…try to eat me. Let's all hope it's the former."

Georgia tried very hard not to scream as Lester dragged her off to the lab.

She almost succeeded.

° ° °

Martin closed his eyes. The throb in his jaw was finally going away. He wondered how this had all gone so horribly wrong, and questioned his decision to bring everyone to this island.

He rubbed his eyes and dismissed the thought; regretting the past was a fool's game. The thing to do now was think ahead. But was that even possible? What could he do to save Sara, the one-time love of his life, from the horrors in the woods?

The key to saving her was predicting her next move. What would she do next? Where would she go?

He stared down at his son, asleep in the sling, and an idea came to him.

Martin began to plan.

° ° °

Moments after Cindy dropped the gun, Tyrone was dragging her away from the scene. It had been a mistake to try and shoot the cannibals. No one could have looked at that horrible feast and still been able to act. Tyrone would never be able to forget that image, even if he scrubbed his mind with steel wool.

He winced at the pain—he'd stuck his burned right hand under Cindy's armpit to pull her, while his less-injured left held the torch. The extra illumination allowed them to move fast, side-stepping obstacles, minding their footing. Unfortunately, it was also like a beacon to those cannibals. From the sounds of it, they had no problems moving quickly in the dark. Tyrone guessed they were less than twenty yards behind them.

Seeing he had no choice, Tyrone ditched the torch, tossing it into a clump of bushes and then tugging Cindy to the immediate left, breaking their current trajectory. Without the light it was like swimming in ink. Tyrone was forced to slow down to a quick walk, moving with one hand in front of him so he didn't knock himself out on a tree. Gradually his night vision adjusted, and the trees thinned a bit to let occasional moonlight in, and the pair moved at a jog, Cindy in step beside Tyrone.

The figure stood in front of them, so still it almost looked like a tree. But the outline was definitely human, and there was only one, and rather than change directions yet again Tyrone lowered his head and charged.

His aim was good, and he prepared for impact, bunching up his neck and shoulder in a driving tackle.

But then, as if by magic, he was ass over head, flipping through the air, landing on his back so hard it knocked the wind out of him.

Tyrone had heard the term before, and knew what it meant, but he'd never had the wind knocked out of him before. It felt like a car was parked on his chest, and he couldn't draw a breath, couldn't make a sound.

This brought instant panic, and he began to flail around. Not at the figure. Just random, spastic movements, as if that could somehow fill him with the oxygen he so desperately craved. Little sparkly motes began to float through his vision. He felt close to passing out.

Then something dropped on his stomach. A person. Miraculously, the pressure forced his diaphragm to work again, and Tyrone wheezed in air like a vacuum. He tried to raise his arms, to defend himself against whoever had thrown him, and then he heard Cindy yell, "Sara!"

"Tyrone?"

It was Sara sitting on him. She was the one who flipped him. Maybe there was more to that judo shit than Tyrone had thought.

"You beat on all yo kids like this, Sara?" he whispered.

She immediately got off him, and Tyrone felt her hand grab his, pulling to help him up. He flinched away, her touch on his raw palm making him swear.

"Are you okay, Tyrone?" Sara asked. She sounded pretty frazzled.

"Hands are messed up, 'n my pride just took a beatin', but I'm okay."

Sara tried again to help him stand, this time lifting by the elbow. When he was vertical, he had to endure a hug. Then Cindy came by and also hugged him, which Tyrone found much easier to endure.

"Girl, I know this ain't the time, but, *damn*, if you don't look good in nothin' but that bra."

"Thanks," Cindy said. "Look, Tyrone, about—"

"Not your fault." He rubbed his fingertips along the small of her back. "I couldn't do it neither. That's why I gave you the gun."

"You found the gun?" Sara asked.

"I dropped it."

Tyrone pulled Cindy closer, "It's not her fault."

"Where are the others? Are they okay?"

Tyrone and Cindy spent the next few minutes filling Sara in on everything that had happened, eventually asking her where Jack was. Sara, in turn, told them about all she'd been through.

"Mountains of bones?" Tyrone still had his left hand on Cindy's back. It hurt, but he could deal with it. "How many damn cannibals are on this island?"

"These bones were old. Real old. I think Martin's legend about there being a civil war prison here may have been right. There were thousands of soldiers missing after the war, soldiers that have never been accounted for. Thirteen thousand men died at the Confederate prison, Andersonville. Six thousand at its Union counterpart, Camp Douglas. It's possible the Union army also had another, secret prison. A place they'd kept hidden, off the record books, in case the South won the war."

Tyrone didn't get it. "Those cannibals move damn fast for bein' over a hundred years old."

Sara shook her head. "Those people, the ones after us, they aren't from the prison. They're something else."

"What are they?"

"Martin called this Plincer's Island, and the name has been nagging at me." Sara paused, then said, "But I think I finally remembered who he is."

*   *   *

Laneesha tried to think about Brianna, tried to cling to sanity by picturing her daughter's sweet little face. But she couldn't concentrate over the sounds of her own agonized screams.

*   *   *

Georgia couldn't move. She thought she might be strapped down, but she didn't feel any straps. In fact, she felt naked. Naked and lying on a cold table.

Lester's play table? Isn't that what the crazy doctor called it?

No. That had shackles, and was wooden. This table felt like metal.

She tried to open her eyes and, amazingly, she couldn't. Nor could she turn her head, clench her fist, or so much as moan. Nothing seemed to work at all.

Georgia remembered Lester holding her tight, then the doctor sticking her with some kind of needle. Must have knocked her out. But she wasn't knocked out any more. She was awake, and aware, and could feel. But she couldn't move any of her muscles.

Then, abruptly, light.

It took a moment to focus, and then Georgia found herself staring up at Lester, who was leaning over her. She realized he'd opened her eyelids with his fingers.

"Don't worry, Georgia girl. It only hurts for a little while."

She stared hard at Lester, imploring him to stop this, to help her get away. He smiled at her, then brought something in front of her eyes.

His camera.

The flash made Georgia's pupils painfully constrict. Then Lester stepped back, and Doctor Plincer's face came into view.

"I can't express, my dear, how excited I am by the opportunity to try my procedure out on you. I've experimented on dozens of people over the last decade. Not nearly enough, considering the importance of my work. Only about ten a year, average. I'm limited, you see. Not many people visit the island. And those that do, well, I usually don't have the opportunity to work with them. My, *failures*, I suppose you can call them, are quite hostile toward strangers. And quite hungry too, I'm afraid. I'm an old man, on a fixed income. I really can't afford to feed so many."

She felt the doctor's hand touch her neck, then smooth her hair behind her ear. From deep within the bowels of the prison, Georgia heard screaming.

"Pardon the bluntness," Dr. Plincer said, "but you really aren't much to look at. You do have something about you, however. Something extraordinary. You see, most of the people I've had the pleasure to experiment on, they're *normal* people. I've only had one success with a normal person. True, I've only had two successes with sadistic personality types, but the overall percentage is much greater."

Doctor Plincer kept his hand on Georgia's ear. Then he began to squeeze the lobe. Hard. Digging his nails in. Georgia's eyes teared up, but she couldn't flinch away from the pain, not even a millimeter.

"The drug used to paralyze you is called succinocholine. It renders you completely immobile. This is necessary, as I'm working with a very precise area of the brain. If you moved, even slightly, you could end up being lobotomized, or having your language center damaged, or your neuron clusters regressed. That would be a waste. Unfortunately, for you, I have to keep you awake for the procedure. The brain is an amazing organ, and it has many different states of consciousness. For this experiment to be successful, you need to be in a beta wave state. Fully awake."

He moved in closer, smiling. Georgia could smell his sour body odor.

"I'm using a serum. A special serum. It contains, among other things, pluriopotent stem cells. You've heard of stem cell research, I'm sure. The bans. The controversy. The ethical dilemma."

The doctor scratched his chin, and a bit of dried skin flaked off. Georgia felt the crumb land on her lower lip.

"The reason stem cells are so important in research is that they are, in layman's terms, *blank*. A stem cell can develop into any sort of cell at all, if properly coerced. Skin cells. Bone cells. Nerve cells. *Brain cells.*" Plincer shrugged. "Alas, the only continuous and plentiful source for stem cells is unborn babies. Hence the banning and the controversy. But I have an arrangement with a doctor on the mainland, one who specializes in terminating pregnancies. He supplies me with all the stem cells I require."

Georgia willed herself to move. She had to get away from the maniac. But no matter how hard she tried, how much she concentrated, her muscles refused to obey her commands.

"Lester is right. This is going to hurt. The only way I can inject my experimental serum to the correct area of your brain is through your tear ducts. My colleagues, the fools, didn't think it could be done. But it can. I'm going to enhance certain portions of your brain. Make them grow larger. With a little bit of luck, you may soon join my other successes."

Doctor Plincer held something in front of Georgia's line of vision. A syringe. A big fucking syringe, with the longest needle Georgia had ever seen.

He can't plunge that into my eye. Dear god sweet jesus oh no he can't...

"From what I've been told, the first injection is the worst." The doctor smacked his lips. "The five after that aren't as bad."

He raised the needle above her eye, leaning in even closer, the point coming down slowly, methodically, until it rested on her tear duct. It was a minor sting, like a piece of grit caught in her eye. But Georgia couldn't rub it away. She couldn't even blink.

Then Doctor Plincer shoved.

The pain was preternatural. Blinding. Explosive. Like her eyeball had burst and her brain was boiling and it went on and on and ON...

Plincer extracted the needle, sighed, and used his dirty coat sleeve to wipe away some sweat that had beaded up on his bald head. Georgia's head still throbbed. Somehow, each thought, each sense, had taken on an almost physical manifestation. Words that she cognated felt like stab wounds, each syllable a twist of a knife. Doctor Plincer's BO smelled like Georgia's nose was on fire. His hand on her face was a jumper cable attached to her nerves, roasting her alive. Every single sensation, every single thought, brought agony she couldn't escape from.

Then her vision turned red.

"Good girl. I'll give you a lollipop later. Let me suction off some of this blood."

Dr. Plincer held a tube to her tear duct. It hurt worse than a hornet stinging her eyeball, and the sound made her ache like her teeth were being drilled.

"What you're feeling now is called synesthesia. It's when each of our senses mixes up its signals on the way to the brain. It's how someone taking LSD thinks he can smell the color red, or taste a

Led Zeppelin song. But in your case, every sense you experience is activating your pain receptors. And because of that, I'm ashamed to admit I've lied to you."

Doctor Plincer raised another syringe. "These next five injections are going to hurt quite a bit more."

* * *

Tom's stomach was really making noise now, loud enough for it to be heard above his stomping and crashing through the forest. The smell of cooked meat was intoxicating. The faster he got there, the faster he could stuff his face. Then he could take his meds, go to sleep, and try to enjoy the rest of this mini-vacation before his dumb-ass father sent him to that dumb-ass military academy.

He wasn't worried about getting in trouble for the gun incident. A large component of his ADHD was an inability to take responsibility for his actions. Tom didn't feel empathy, or remorse, especially since everything that went wrong in his life was someone else's fault.

Tom was getting close now, because he saw the flickering orange light of the campfire through the trees. He was so intent on reaching it, and the food, that he didn't watch his footing and tripped over an exposed tree root. Right into a burr bush.

"Aw...shit."

The burrs clung to his shirt like little Velcro jelly beans. He got on his knees, fussing to tug them off, then on impulse he reached up and checked his hair.

More burrs.

"God damn it!"

They were stuck good, too. The last time Tom encountered burrs he was a kid, maybe six or seven. The only way to remove them was with a haircut. A drastic haircut that made him look like frickin' Homer Simpson. He yanked at one stuck in his bangs, pulling until his eyes watered.

Frickin' great.

Tom didn't like being laughed at, and he was sure everyone else would think this was the funniest thing ever. It wasn't even his fault. Stupid root. Stupid burr bush. Stupid Martin and Sara for taking him on this stupid trip. He debated whether he even wanted to go back to camp. Maybe if he went back to the lake, went swimming, the burrs would loosen up.

No. Bad idea. It was too easy to get lost.

He sucked in air through his teeth, seriously annoyed, and decided he would punch anyone who made fun of him. Ten steps later, he was at the campsite.

Except this wasn't the right campsite. First of all, there were no tents. Second, what he thought was a fire wasn't really a fire. It was a big patch of glowing orange sticks and what looked like charcoal. And there was some kind of broken swing-set sitting in the middle of the fire.

Tom walked around the fit pit, searching for people. No one was around. But the cooked meat smell was definitely coming from here. In fact, it was coming from that swing-set thingy.

He gave it his full attention. There was some kind of meat roasting there, a large hunk between the metal bars. Maybe half a cow. No, not big enough for a cow. A pig, maybe. Or a big turkey. Hard to tell by looking at it. The meat was really scorched, and there weren't any features to identify it.

Whatever it was, it smelled awesome. And no one appeared to be nearby, so no one could protest if Tom helped himself. The burrs in his hair were forgotten. Another symptom of ADHD was a severe lack of memory retention, coupled with an ultra-short attention span. Tom had been told this many times, but for some reason it never stuck with him.

He took a quick look around for some sort of barbecue fork or tongs that he could use to grab some of the meat, then figured he could probably just stick his hand between the bars and grab a hunk from the top part. So he did just that.

It was hot, almost too hot to touch. But Tom was quick, and the meat was so tender it fell off the bone. He brought back a nice, long strip, and played hot potato, tossing it from hand to hand, blowing on it. When it was finally cool enough, Tom raised the greasy morsel to his lips.

Hmm. Tastes like chicken.

Damn good, though. Needed some sauce, and some salt, but as far as mystery meat went it sure beat the frickin' meatloaf Sara cooked every frickin' Sunday.

Tom licked his fingers clean and reached for seconds.

.   .   .

Sara squatted on her haunches, and she instructed Tyrone and Cindy to do the same. They listened to the night, straining to hear the distinctive sounds of pursuit. The night only offered crickets, and the whistling wind.

Sara had calmed down a bit, but still wished she had a light. If Tyrone hadn't run into her, Sara knew she would still be standing in that same spot, freaking out. But slipping into the role of responsible adult had forced her to push back her fear of the darkness, at least for the moment. Plus Sara surprised herself by being able to flip Tyrone, even in her semi-catatonic state. Maybe she wasn't as helpless as she thought.

Her mind once again flitted to Martin and Jack, and she absently touched her chest, missing her son's weight. She hoped like hell they were both okay.

"So who was Plincer?" Cindy whispered.

The question took Sara back to college, more than a decade ago. "A footnote in abnormal psychology. I learned about him in school, in an advanced psych class. In the 90s, he made waves as an expert witness in serial killer trials. For the defense. If I remember right, Plincer thought evil was a genetic physical trait."

Cindy leaned in closer. "You mean like hair color? Or height?"

"Exactly. He believed some people's brains were different, that they were born that way. If it was their brain that made them evil, it wasn't really their fault, so they couldn't be blamed for their crimes."

Tyrone snorted. "That's crazy."

"It's far out, but it does have some basis in fact. The amygdale, thalamus, hypothalamus, and the cingulate gyrus—these are all parts of the brain responsible for forming emotions. Studies in animals have shown if these parts are damaged or removed, it has radical effects on behavior. They can be made more aggressive, more violent. There have also been cases in humans where injury or aneurism completely changed someone's personality. I heard of a recent murder trial in Chicago where a brain tumor allegedly contributed to a police officer going on a killing spree."

Sara also recalled the famous case of Phineas P. Gage. She had written a report on him in school, as had every other aspiring psychologist. Gage was a railroad worker in the 1800s. He was blasting rock and the explosion drove a three foot long iron bar through his head. Incredibly, he survived. He was even coherent, and could speak moments after the accident. But after the bar was removed, Gage's personality changed dramatically. He'd become more impulsive and violent, prone to risk-taking. Friends said that he was unrecognizable, a completely different person.

This incident proved revolutionary. Science hadn't previously known that specific regions of the brain effected behavior.

"Whether or not we want to think about it," Sara continued, "who we are as people is very much tied into a bunch of cells, chemicals, and electrical changes in our brains. Tampering with this delicate balance can turn someone into someone else."

The wind died down, and the crickets stopped. Sara listened for the sounds of approaching footsteps. There was something in the distance, a branch snapping.

Then, nothing.

"So this Plincer cat," Tyrone said, startling Sara. "He believed people could be born evil?"

As a psychologist herself, Sara didn't believe in evil. Morality was dictated by the majority in any given society. In Roman times, it wasn't considered evil to throw Christians to the lions. The Nazis didn't consider themselves evil, they were judged so by the victors. Human beings throughout history did terrible things to each other, but whether or not these things were evil remained subjective. To some, the death penalty was evil. To some, not going to church every Sunday was evil.

Sara preferred to believe that human beings were inherently selfish, and when this selfishness infringed upon the well-being or lives of others, a psychological problem was usually at play. Evil had no place in psychology.

"I don't believe evil exists, Tyrone."

"You do know we hidin' from some folks tryin' to eat us, right?"

"That could be because of many different psychological and physiological factors, including hunger."

"But Plincer thought people were evil because they had evil brains?"

"Plincer thought people could be born with brain irregularities that made them evil. Irregularities that were so extreme, it was impossible to stop violent impulses."

"Was he right?" Tyrone asked.

"Tough to say. Morality, free will, personality, impulse and action, even consciousness itself, still aren't completely understood. The brain holds a lot of secrets science hasn't figured out yet. But Plincer bragged he knew the exact parts of the brain that made people evil. He even said he could prove it, that he could make a person evil with drugs and surgery."

"Could he?"

Sara closed her eyes. She couldn't even remember her professor's name from that class, let alone anything he specifically said about Plincer. The only reason she remembered Plincer at all was his 15 seconds of news coverage after his last trial.

"I might be wrong, but I remember some newspaper printing something about an orangutan Plincer experimented on. He did something to his brain, and basically turned the orangutan into a psychopath. It killed six other research animals."

"So what happened to Plincer?" Cindy asked. She was whispering.

"Some would call it karma. One of the criminals Plincer was called to defend..." *What the hell was his name?* "Parks. No, Paks. Lester Paks. He killed a woman by biting her to death. Doctor Plincer testified Lester wasn't responsible for his actions, and he also said that if the court released Lester into his care, he would be able to cure him. The court allowed it."

"Did Plincer cure him?"

Sara shrugged. "No. Lester almost killed him. Soon after, both Doctor Plincer and Lester disappeared. Neither have been seen in years."

"So you think Plincer came here?"

"I don't know, Tyrone."

Cindy spoke so softly that Sara had to strain to hear her. "Maybe he came here and kept doing his research. Only instead of monkeys, he did it on people."

"If so, Cindy, we're in a lot more trouble than I thought."

Another branch broke, this one so close it made Sara flinch. She squinted into the dark, saw something move. Then something else.

"We need to run," she told the kids. "Right now."

*   *   *

When Archibald Mordecai Plincer was a child, he was picked on a lot. He didn't understand why. He was thin, and a little small for his age, but otherwise relatively happy and well adjusted. But, for whatever reason, he was a magnet for bullies.

The abuse got so bad that Plincer's parents finally plucked him out of public school and enrolled him in a private academy. This new school also had bullies, and one of the worst was the headmaster, who seemed to delight in doling out punishment.

Plincer eventually had a growth spurt, bringing him up to average height and making him a less desirable target for his peers. Since he did what he was supposed to, Plincer also managed to keep away from the headmaster for the most part. But he remained fascinated by *schadenfreude*—the act of taking joy in the misery of others. He decided to become a doctor and specialize in psychiatry, just to figure out what made sadistic personalities tick.

But where others in the psychiatric field gravitated toward drug therapy and talking sessions and their effect on the conscious and subconscious, Plincer was fascinated by the physical nature of the brain itself. If the heart was malfunctioning, you didn't use a couch trip to cure it; you went in with a scalpel. Why should the brain be any different?

His early research was done on animals. Plincer used psychosurgery and implanted electrodes to perform what he termed *reverse lobotomies*. While his predecessors used frontal lobotomies to neutralize aggressive behavior—like what happened to Jack Nicholson at the end of *One Flew Over the Cuckoo's Nest*—Plincer was able to stimulate parts of the brain to make the subject more aggressive.

Unfortunately, there proved to be little research money available for doctors interested in making meaner animals. Because Plincer was more curious about the brain's physiology than psychology, and there were laws against tampering with people's gray matter, human experiments were impossible. So he drifted into criminal psychology with the intent to study anti-social behavior.

He met with criminals in prison, got them to donate their bodies to his research after they died, but they weren't dying fast enough or in large enough numbers for Plincer to conclusively prove the link between brain deformity and evil. So he began to testify in criminal trials, pushing for the courts to entrust a psychopathic criminal into his care.

Lester Paks was that criminal. By that time, Plincer was sure he knew which parts of the mind controlled violent behavior, and if he could cure Lester it would usher in a whole new era of psychiatry.

But he wasn't as careful with Lester as he should have been. Lester managed to escape his room.

What happened next still gave Plincer nightmares.

Though he survived Lester's attack, it effectively ended Plincer's career. No one would give a job to a doctor proven so dramatically wrong. They turned their back on him, and his research. He became an outcast, unable to publish in the journals, unable to work at even a community college.

Luckily, Plincer's family had some money. Old money, earned in blood, going back to the Civil War and his great-great grandfather. Plincer secretly set up shop on Rock Island, and he brought Lester with him, committed to revealing the true physical nature of evil.

But Plincer did more than reveal it. He discovered he could enhance the part of the brain to make people even *more* evil.

The scientific community might not care, but Plincer found out that others did. He wound up in bed with some powerful people who found this result intriguing. Since then, Plincer was supplied with money and prisoners to experiment on, along with a guarantee that his island would be left alone.

Unfortunately, Plincer couldn't repeat the results he had with Lester. He managed to come close with Subject 33. But Subject 33 proved impossible to control. The procedure drove the other subjects insane, making them regress to the point that they were more animal than human. The ferals.

Plincer kept working, kept revising his procedure. He has one more success, and many more failures. But only a few weeks ago he had overcome the final hurdle and perfected his enhancement technique. It was not only 100% effective, but it was repeatable.

They'd laughed at his theories.

Soon, no one would be laughing.

If the world wouldn't give him the recognition he deserved, it would make him disgustingly rich instead.

That it also might bring about the end of civilization didn't bother Plincer in the least.

*   *   *

Dr. Plincer sat behind his desk, applied more putty to his chin, and frowned at the letter once more. Plincer didn't get much mail, but he maintained a PO Box in Traverse City, and his delivery man checked it once a month and brought it along with the rest of his supplies.

The doctor read it again, as if the words were going to say something different from the other thirty times he'd read it.

The letter was from his accountant, and described several recent events in the news which Plincer knew nothing about because he didn't follow the news—there was no phone, cable television, newspaper delivery, or Internet service to the island. The letter went on to say the market had taken a beating, the economy was in ruins, and Plincer was very close to broke.

Plincer wondered, not for the first time, if his accountant was crooked and stealing funds. The doctor could easily send Lester to his house and get the truth out of him. But if the country really was at war in the Middle East, and the Dow Jones had really crashed, torturing the man wouldn't provide anything more than the empty thrill of vengeance.

Still, an hour with Lester might teach that idiot the importance of diversification in a portfolio.

It was all water under the bridge. Plincer's only chance at funding now hinged on how his meeting tomorrow would go. He checked another letter from the pile on his desk, and rechecked the arrival time. The helicopter would be arriving at nine A.M. Plincer had instructed them to land on the east side of the prison, where there was a clearing.

While the doctor rather enjoyed the isolation the island provided, he did wish he could confirm this meeting again by phone or email. So much was riding on this venture. If they were a no-show, it would take weeks to contact them again to find out why. By that time, he'd be broke, and perhaps forced to scrounge for food alongside the unfortunate cannibals he'd inadvertently created.

Doctor Plincer closed his eyes. There was still much to do before the meeting. He'd given that black girl to Subject 33 on the understanding that there would be other volunteers to use in his demonstration tomorrow. And while performing the procedure on that Georgia person was an unprecedented opportunity, the doctor wondered if he hadn't been too eager, too hasty. But the prospect of another success was impossible to pass up.

Unfortunately, that currently left Plincer with a deficit of victims.

According to his intel, there were still five likely candidates on the island. Though the ferals had surprised the doctor by proving themselves able to work together, he doubted they would be able to grab all of the new arrivals. Some would survive.

Plincer glanced at the clock. He had less than eight hours to get his hands on them. It would make for a much more effective presentation if he were able to grab all five. But all he needed was a single volunteer.

It was time to send Lester back out to find one.

⁕　　⁕　　⁕

Martin stared below him, through the leaves of the bough he perched upon. His swollen hands had resisted his efforts to climb the tree, and his ruined cheek resting against the rough bark of the oak's branch made his injury light up every time he swallowed. But he felt lucky to have gotten up in time.

A few moments earlier, in a semi-frantic search for Sara, he'd come upon a group of feral people. He fled before they saw him. Or so he thought. Within ten minutes, the ferals were on his trail, closing fast. Martin ran as hard as he could, not daring to use the flashlight, fearing he'd give his position away. Only moments into the chase, something surprising happened; he bumped into another group.

After his third right turn, Martin's gut burned with realization. They had him trapped. These insane, witless cannibals had somehow managed to surround him.

With no choices left, he shifted Jack's sling from his chest to his back, picked a large tree, and hoped for the best. The ferals closed the circle and converged, twelve of them total, right beneath his perch. More than expected, too many to be able to handle, less than ten feet beneath him.

The largest man in the group, the one with the ax, grunted orders at the others, pointing in various directions. Then he leaned up against the tree and reached into the sack he had hanging over his shoulder.

Martin couldn't make out any details, but the axman pulled out a dark round object the size of a football. He brought it to his face and took a bite. The scent of cooked pork wafted up to Martin. But Martin knew whatever this guy was eating, it wasn't pork.

The axman sat down. He began to really gnaw on the thing, shaking his hairy head from side to side like a dog worrying a bone. Martin's leg began to fall asleep. The pins and needles sensation grew from a minor discomfort to a spreading numbness. He shifted slightly, anxious to stay quiet, twisting his pelvis so the blood flow could return.

Then Jack shifted on Martin's back, throwing off his precarious balance. Martin's adrenaline spiked, flushing his body with heat, causing every muscle to contract as Martin lost his grip and began to fall.

. . .

Cindy knew she was hurting Tyrone—clenching his left hand so tight—but she was too frightened to let go. They ran as fast as safety allowed, heads down to keep from getting lashed in the face by wayward twigs and branches, arms swinging like walking sticks for the blind, so no one head-butted a tree. Cindy had no clue how many pursuers there were, or how close they'd gotten, and she was ready to circle the island ten times before she slowed down to find out.

But her lungs and legs and stamina were casualties of meth, and though she'd been off the drug for a while her body still hadn't fully recovered. After only a few minutes of running, Tyrone practically had to drag her, and Cindy's panting was becoming increasingly labored and loud.

When Sara finally stopped, Cindy fell to her knees, pressing a hand hard against the stitch in her side and gasping for air.

Sara came over, and whispered, "Shh."

Cindy's face pinched as she tried to get her breathing under control. Sara crawled ahead, up to a bush, and stuck her head inside. It was still dark, but Cindy could see pretty well. She moved her head to the side, so Sara's shadow didn't block her vision.

Wait... shadow?

On all fours, Cindy crept closer to Sara. All at once she understood where the light was coming from, and the importance of being quiet.

Somehow, they'd gotten back to their campsite.

Their fire was smaller, the few logs left burning slow and steady. The last time Cindy was here there were two cannibals, eating their fallen friend. Only one remained. The one with the knife and fork and salt shaker. His head was resting on the chest of the dead one, using it like a gory pillow.

Cindy turned her head away before viewing any details.

"He asleep?" Tyrone whispered.

"Can't tell." Sara withdrew her head from the bush. "But he's right next to the tent. That's where the radio is."

"I'll go," Tyrone said. "I'll be real careful, won't wake him up."

Sara shook her head. "No. I'll go. You both stay here."

"You be better off watchin' my back. If I'm in that tent, lookin' for the radio, I won't know if this crazy dude wakes up. But you know that judo shit, can stop him better than I can."

Sara shook her head. "You stay here, guard Cindy."

"How'm I supposed to guard Cindy when I can't even make a fist?"

Cindy touched Tyrone's shoulder. "The best way to do this is to crawl. You can't crawl with your burns." She looked deep inside herself, and was surprised by what she found there. "But I can."

"Hells no."

"No way, Cindy."

Cindy's mind was made up. She looked at Sara. "Tyrone is right. If that man gets up, you're the only one who can stop him."

Sara looked away. "I...I don't think I could do that again."

"Yes you can. You're strong enough."

And so am I.

Before she lost her nerve, Cindy scrambled through the bush and into the clearing. She rested her belly on the ground and craned her neck. The cannibal was to her right, five yards away, lying down in front of the tent. His chest rose and fell slowly, rhythmically.

You can do this. You can prove you're more than just some selfish meth addict.

Cindy crept forward, slow and easy and quiet as a mouse wearing slippers. That was what her father used to say when he took her hunting. The image would make her laugh, which of course wasn't quiet at all.

God, she missed him. Missed him and Mom so bad. They hadn't visited her at the Center, and she couldn't blame them—Cindy had stolen everything of value in the house, pawning it to get more meth. But now more than ever she wanted to see them again, to tell them how sorry she was, to promise she'd pay back every cent. She would too, if she lived through this.

Cindy kept low, eyes darting back and forth between the tent entrance and the sleeping killer. She was so focused on her destination that she didn't see whatever it was she rested her extended palm on.

But Cindy didn't have to see it. She knew without looking. It was warm, and wet, and squishy, and she'd helped Mom prepare it enough times that the smell normally evoked pleasant, homey feelings.

This time it didn't.

Her stomach clenched, and she felt ready to hurl. In fact, she was eighty percent there, mouth already open, the gagging sound working her way up her throat, glancing anxiously at the cannibal to see if he could hear her.

She squeezed her eyes shut and repressed it, forced the reflex down. Vomiting was noisy, noise would draw attention, and that could kill her.

The moment passed. Cindy breathed through her mouth, slow and deep, relaxing her abdomen. Then she carefully lifted her hand off and wiped it on the dirt. Gravel and ash stuck to the moisture on her palm, and she vowed that she would never, under any circumstances, eat liver again.

She adjusted her direction to avoid encountering anything else, and continued forward. But it didn't matter. The cannibals had been messy eaters, and Cindy's fingers kept brushing against various bits and parts strewn all over the ground. The knees of her jeans soaked through, and her hands glistened in the flickering campfire. She pressed forward, getting to within ten feet of the tent.

At eight feet away, her mouth went completely dry, making swallowing impossible.

When she was within six feet, her breath was coming out in pants.

Four feet from the tent, her head began to feel strange and hollow.

Two feet away, hyperventilation made her dizzy to the point where she was going to pass out. She paused, trying to suck in air through her nose and slow down her heartbeat.

Just a few more inches, Cindy. You can do it...

Then the cannibal grunted, shifting his body. The knife and fork, resting crisscross on his chest, shifted, sliding off and making a clanging sound that to Cindy felt like a shotgun blast. He was now on his side, facing her.

She froze, staring at his still-closed eyes. His cheeks were wet with blood, and little stringy things were caught in his beard. If he opened his eyes it was over. Sara and Tyrone wouldn't be able to save her in time. Here was a man who ate what seemed to be his friend. What would he do to someone he considered an enemy?

Cindy glanced right, her shallow breathing causing her vision to blur. The entrance to the tent was tantalizingly close, but she was too scared to move. She thought she'd hit rock bottom when she'd passed out in a disgusting gas station toilet, a needle stuck in her arm, lying in a puddle of someone else's urine for hours until the owner discovered her and called the police. But this—an arm's length from a crazy man who wanted to snack on her—this was the all time low.

Quiet as a mouse in slippers, little girl. Move like you live in the woods.

Cindy tore her eyes away from the killer, locking them onto the tent. Moving oh so slowly she forced herself toward it, hand, knee, hand, knee, ignoring the horrible, slippery things she crawled over, and then, all at once, her head and shoulders were inside the tent, relief coursing through her like the meth she was so intent on quitting.

That's when Cindy heard the snoring.

The other cannibal was in the sleeping bag.

· · ·

Tom patted his full stomach and yawned. He was dog-ass tired, and had eaten waaaaay too much. All he wanted was to curl up someplace and go to sleep. He was even considering doing so right there, in front of the coals. It was warm, and comfortable, and whosever camp this was hadn't been around for over an hour. If they did come back and get mad that he ate their food, it was their own frickin' fault for leaving it here.

Sara and Martin would be frantic, of course, if he stayed out all night. But it was their frickin' fault for playing that stupid trick and trying to scare him. Screw those two anyway. It wasn't like anything Tom did mattered at this point. The Center was closing and Tom was going off to some frickin' boot camp. Let them worry themselves to death.

He yawned again, stretched out his arms, and stood, looking for something that would serve as a pillow. There was some sort of cloth near the coals, and he bent down and picked it up, immediately recognizing it.

Meadow's shirt.

Huh. Weird. But then, Meadow was probably in on the prank too, pretending to get grabbed in the woods. Maybe he was in the trees right now, waiting to jump out.

Tom turned in a full circle, scanning the treeline. It looked just as dark and quiet as ever.

Then Tom did something he almost never did. He doubted himself.

For just a fraction of a second, he wondered if maybe this wasn't all some big joke, and that there actually were cannibals in the woods. Hell, that mystery meat he just stuffed himself with could have even been a person.

Tom was all about impulse, forging ahead, not looking back. Doubt and guilt existed only as fleeting thoughts. Without his ADHD medication, Tom couldn't stand still long enough to spell the word *worried*, let alone act worried.

So he dismissed the doubt as soon as it came, rolled Meadow's shirt into a ball, and propped it behind his neck as he stretched out onto the ground, facing a severed human hand.

Tom jerked back into a sitting position, unable to believe what he just saw. He looked again.

A hand. Cooked and fleshy, except for three skeletal fingers that had no meat on them.

Never one to pay attention to his surroundings, Tom twisted around quickly, his eyes scanning the ground for the first time. In short order he found four rib bones, a burned lump that looked like a kidney, and a partially eaten leg that still had the foot attached.

"No way. No frickin' way."

He reached out, touched the leg bone.

It wasn't a plastic prop. It was the real thing. And the blackened, melted shoe still attached had a green Nike swoosh on it, just like Meadow wore.

Tom threw up so hard and fast it felt like his throat was being torn out. That's when the tall thin man with the camera stepped out of the woods and snapped his picture.

. . .

Martin's lower body slipped off the branch, then his chest followed the lead. He hung in a chin-up position, his feet dangling within reach of the axman sitting beneath him. Martin held this position, his fingers screaming at him, knowing he'd be unable to swing his body back up, and knowing what dropping down meant.

Then Jack began to shift. Martin only had one shoulder strap around him, having moved too quickly to buckle the second strap or the waist belt. Jack moved along Martin's back, under his armpit, and hung over his belly. He opened his tiny eyes, looked up at Dad, and gurgled happily.

Martin's arms began to burn, then tremble, then unbend slowly, like the air being let out of a pneumatic jack. Below him, the axman continued to gnaw on that large round object. But it was only a matter of seconds until he looked up. Martin knew his best chance was to move closer to the trunk, find a toe hold. But he wasn't sure his hands would hold out.

Jack gurgled again, blowing a tiny baby spit bubble that burst against his father's neck.

Martin reached out an aching hand for a grip near the trunk.

His fingers missed the branch.

Jack's sling slid right off his shoulder.

Martin frantically reached down, catching the strap, tangling Jack only a foot above the cannibal. The hand still holding the tree felt like it had been set on fire. He let out an involuntary grunt.

The cannibal kept his attention focused on his snack, and didn't see the baby swinging over his head.

Martin summoned up his last bit of strength, swung Jack's sling in a wide arc, and the strap hooked onto a broken twig.

Jack apparently enjoyed the quick motion, because he squealed with joy.

The cannibal looked up.

The tug was sudden and violent, ripping Martin's hands from the bough. He slammed into the ground on his side, the shock of the impact making him bite his already injured tongue. Inches from his nose was a severed, cooked head, much of its face eaten away.

Martin instinctively rolled left, just as the ax struck where he'd been lying. Martin continued the roll until he had room to get his hands and knees up under him. A moment later he was on his feet, dizzy and hurting, but with his fists raised. He looked up, saw Jack hanging precariously from the tree branch. Then he took another quick look at the head.

Meadow.

"That was one of my kids," Martin said softly. "*My* kids. You think you can kill one of mine?"

The axman was large, powerful, with thick arms and a neck like a tree stump. But when he swung the ax again, aiming at Martin's chest, he showed his weakness. The bigger man was slow.

Martin side-stepped the swing and kicked out his foot, connecting between the axman's legs. Then he grabbed the ax handle and twisted it sideways, trying to tug it from its owner's thick fingers.

Leverage and momentum were on his side. The axman grunted, stumbling forward, and Martin did a quick spin, propelling the weapon around, burying the head into his adversary's shoulder. The axman howled, dropping to his knees.

"My kids, asshole."

It took six more whacks before the creature was dead. Martin surveyed the carnage, breathing heavily, and then reached up to pull his son from the tree.

Jack was blowing more spit bubbles.

"Let's go get Mommy."

Martin adjusted Jack so the sling was in front, made sure both straps and the belt were secure, and then went to go find his wife.

.   .   .

General Alton Tope was career Army, and those under his command joked that when he nicked himself shaving he not only bled red, but white and blue as well. For more than thirty years he practiced keeping his face unreadable, his thoughts invisible, but anyone looking at him in his bedroom would have noticed obvious signs of worry creasing his weathered features.

He loosened his tie and undid his top collar button, poured himself the last finger of twenty-one-year-old Dalwhinnie single malt, recapped the bottle and placed it in the empty waste can next to his desk, and took the glass over to the bureau. General Tope set the scotch on top and used both hands to open the cabinet doors, then took a moment to frown at the OSST monitor. He tapped the flatscreen with his left hand and retrieved the liquor with his right, bringing the rocks glass to his mouth and smelling notes of heather and honey amid the ethanol vapors.

The monitor flickered on, showing an orbital view of a familiar green planet in perfect high-definition color. He touched the familiar mitten shape of Michigan, and took a sip while waiting for the Orbiting Strand Satellite Telescope to track his command. The whiskey was warm and smooth, and he finished it too quickly.

Self control, Alton. Always. Get a hold of yourself.

He went back to his desk and opened the drawer where he kept his spare bottle. It wasn't there. His maid knew he was to always have a spare on hand, and the lack of one meant she'd either forgotten to stock it, or taken it for herself.

General Tope shook off his annoyance. It was a forgivable mistake, and he was a forgivable leader. In the morning, he'd write her a brief note as a reminder. He set the empty glass on his desk and returned to OSST.

The image got bigger and bigger, zooming in to Lake Michigan, and ultimately Rock Island, at a viewing distance equivalent to three hundred feet above it. The picture was too dark to make out anything, so he pressed the top corner of the monitor and opened the onscreen operations panel. He switched the view to infrared and had the telescope software calculate a body count.

The number surprised him.

Twenty-seven.

According to the read out, there were twenty-seven people on the island.

But that shouldn't be. That had to be wrong.

He had the program recalculate.

"Twenty-seven," he said, reading the reconfigured total.

General Tope's brow creased even further. Certain key military personnel knew about Rock Island. It had been on their radar for quite some time. He pondered what this new development meant, and realized he should have acted sooner.

"Tomorrow," General Tope said. "I'll take care of it all tomorrow."

Then he picked up the phone, apologized to his secretary for the late hour, but instructed her to find him a bottle of single malt scotch, even if they had to send a platoon to break into the nearest liquor store to do so.

The interior of the tent was warm and sour, smelling of fresh blood and old sweat. Though the light was low, on her left Cindy could make out the shape of a person wrapped in a sleeping bag—the dirty, hairy man she'd seen earlier, the one who tried to grab her and Tyrone. He snored wetly, making the hair on Cindy's arms stand on edge.

Cindy's first reaction was to back up, get the hell out of there, and she went so far as to lean toward the exit. But her limbs stayed put. The radio was in that tent, and it was their only chance to get off this island alive. So she ignored all the voices in her brain screaming at her to leave, and instead inched forward.

There were backpacks to her right, their contents strewn about, probably by Tom. Cindy squinched her eyes, not even sure what the radio in question looked like. Before she rushed bravely in, possibly to her own death, she should have at least asked how big it was. In the dimness she could make out some clothing, Jack's crib, a stack of cans, and something square-shaped. Were radios square? She crawled closer to the square thing, keeping the instinct to flee at bay.

The snoring cannibal kept a steady rhythm, every snort a reminder that death was less than three feet away. As Cindy got closer she saw a familiar red cross on the box.

A first aid kit. Tyrone needs this for his hands.

She picked it up and carefully placed it on the ground behind her, near the entrance. Then she began to paw through the discarded clothing.

After carefully setting aside one of Martin's shirts, Cindy noticed a tiny red light, no larger than a BB. She reached for it, touching something hard and rectangular. Her fingers brushed over an antenna. It was either a very old model cell phone, or...

A walkie-talkie.

Cindy seized it, snugging it to her chest, and it let go with a loud burst of static hiss when she accidentally pressed a button.

She froze, holding her breath, waiting for the inevitable; the cannibal waking up and reaching for her.

It didn't happen. There was only stillness, and silence.

Cindy paused, her hands shaking, her kidneys aching. If attacked, she needed to scream to alert Sara and Tyrone. She also needed to find a weapon. The radio had some heft, but she couldn't risk damage by throwing or swinging it. The first aid kit was in a metal box. Heavier and stronger.

If he wakes up, scream first, then go for the kit.

Still no sound. Cindy hadn't exhaled yet.

If she had to defend herself, she needed her hands free. Carefully feeling around the walkie-talkie, she discovered what she sought; a belt clip. Ever so slowly she hooked it onto the top of her pants.

Silence continued to pervade the tent. The cannibal wasn't moving at all.

Cindy let her air out slowly, through her teeth, in an extended, soft hiss. She wanted to take another breath—her heart was thumping like mad—but she was too frightened.

Just get out of there. Get the hell out.

She began to back up, nice and easy, the quiet pressing down on her like a weight, when the obvious hit her.

Why isn't he snoring anymore? Could he be awake?

That's when the cannibal sprung up, winding his filthy arm around Cindy's mouth before she had a chance to scream.

·   ·   ·

Sara felt ready to explode. She wasn't sure how long it had been since Cindy crawled into the tent, but each second seemed like a little stretch of eternity in hell. Not being able to see her, not knowing what was happening to one of her kids, made Sara's imagination run riot with atrocities.

She forced herself to count the seconds. A minute was more than enough time for Cindy to find the radio. After a minute, Sara was determined to go in after her.

Sara began a slow count to sixty.

"How long Cindy been in there?" Tyrone nudged her.

"Not long," she whispered back.

The numbers ticked through Sara's mind, and she pictured them as she thought of them, each one big and red and sounding like a gong.

By the time she reached number twenty, it felt like a year had passed.

"I'm going after her."

Sara held Tyrone back. "Give her a minute."

"Been more than a minute."

The number thirty shone like a spotlight in Sara's head. "He's still asleep. She's okay."

"There were two of those cannibals," Tyrone said.

Number thirty-four hung in the air, then disintegrated. "Two?"

"I just had a bad thought. Maybe the other guy is in the tent."

"Oh... shit."

Sara abandoned the count, springing up from the crouching position, making her way through the thicket to the campsite.

It's murder, Sara. You can't murder another human being. Not while he's asleep.

She crept over to him, crossing the damp ground where blood had mixed with the dirt, making mud. Bits of sinew clung to her hiking boots, and organ meat squished beneath her feet. On the ground, next to him, were some filthy eating utensils, dried bits of gore stuck to them.

This is cold-blooded. It's not even self-defense.

Sara stood next to the sleeping cannibal, raising up her foot, ready to stomp down on his neck.

He's asleep for chrissakes. You're killing a defenseless, sleeping man.

The cannibal opened his eyes.

He's not asleep anymore.

Sara brought her heel down as hard as she could. She put her weight into it, twisting her hips, trying to separate his head from his body.

But he moved at the last moment, and her foot hit his shoulder.

Then Sara was stumbling backward, thrown off balance, and the cannibal was on his feet and eyeing her malevolently, crouching in an attack position. He'd picked up his cutlery, the blood-stained fork in his right hand, a rusty steak knife in his left. Sara found her center, spread her feet, and waited for the charge.

Behind her, in the tent, Cindy screamed.

That distracted Sara long enough for the cannibal to slip inside Sara's defenses, feinting with his left, jabbing the right at Sara's thigh.

The fork penetrated her jeans, her skin, her muscle, and stuck firmly in the bone.

Sara spun, whipping her elbow around, hitting her attacker squarely in the nose. The cannibal staggered back, arms pinwheeling, and then tripped and fell onto his ass, right in the middle of the campfire.

He laid there for a second, then began to flap his limbs, almost like he was making a snow angel in the burning ashes. He cried out—trying to turn over—his legs getting tangled in some of the firewood—getting to his feet—slipping and falling face-first—getting to his feet again with his hair and beard on fire—and finally running into the woods, screaming like a police siren as he retreated into the night.

That's when the pain hit. Sara doubled over, her hands fluttering around the utensil sticking out of her leg, afraid to touch it. This was worse than a charley horse, reducing Sara's world to nothing but an agonizing throb. She whimpered, saw Tyrone in her peripheral vision. He was streaking out of the woods and heading for the tent.

Now there are two of my kids in danger.

Sara slammed her eyelids closed, clenched her fingers around the fork handle, and yanked.

She staggered sideways, her balance, her stomach, her mind all going wavy. Jerking her eyes open, Sara oriented herself and limped to the tent, ducking inside, seeing Tyrone struggling with a man, a man who was growling and biting Cindy on her shoulder. Cindy beat at his head and whined like a kicked dog.

Sara made a fist, pressing her thumb down hard across the top of her index finger knuckle, and threw the punch.

Her thumbnail jabbed into the cannibal's eye. He opened his teeth and howled, allowing Tyrone to snake his arm across his neck. Sara grabbed his torn, filthy shirt, and she and Tyrone manhandled him out of the tent, forcing him to his knees. The eye she'd poked was bleeding. The other one was bloodshot and... crying.

He ceased struggling, his arms limp at his sides.

"I... am... bad... man." His voice was odd, somewhere between a croak and a hiccup.

Sara paused. She was hurt, and sick to her stomach, and part of her knew she needed to end this monster's life, but another, bigger part saw he was not only docile, but quite possible in need of help himself.

"Who are you?" Sara asked.

"My... name ...John."

Cindy crawled out of the tent, crying. She held a white gym sock to her bleeding shoulder.

"What's your last name, John?"

He blinked. His body shook with sobs, but there were no tears. "Don't... know."

"How many of, uh, *your group*, are on this island?"

"Many." The wildness in his red eyes was still there, but behind it was a tinge of sanity. "Like... animals. We... hunt. We... kill. We... eat."

Sara bent down, wincing at the pain in her leg. "What happened to you, John?"

"Brought... here..." He swallowed, and moaned. "Doctor... did... something... to... brain."

"Dr. Plincer?" Sara asked.

John made a nodding motion, restricted by Tyrone's grip.

"Maybe we can get you help, John."

"I've...done... *things*."

By his tone, Sara could assume what those things were.

"Maybe that's not all your fault, John." She felt revulsion, and pity. Sara was a big proponent of free will, but she also knew that decision-making, morals, values, and even personality could all be altered with drugs or damage to the brain. But the fact that he was aware of his actions meant he had a choice.

His breath came faster. "I... want..."

Sara looked into his eyes. They seemed to implore her.

"What is it, John?"

"Want... to..."

"Want to get help?"

Sara wondered if she could get him help. They would have to restrain him somehow, maybe tie him up. Then, when the Coast Guard arrived, maybe he could be taken somewhere and treated. Sara had no clue what Plincer had done to this poor man, but perhaps it could be reversed.

"...to..."

"Maybe we can get you help, John. Maybe you don't have to be like this."

The corners of his mouth turned up in a smile.

"Want... to... *EAT!*"

He grabbed Sara's hair, pulling her close, his ugly mouth opening to bite her face. His breath was hot and the few teeth he had left were tinged red.

Tyrone pulled him back, muscling him to the ground. They wrestled for a moment, and then everyone heard the *crack*.

Both Tyrone and John stopped moving. Then, slowly, Tyrone disentangled himself, letting John slump onto his face, unmoving.

John blinked. "Can't... feel... body."

Tyrone scooted further away on his butt and elbows. "I think I broke his neck, man. I think I broke his fuckin' neck."

John let out a breath, blowing dirt away from his mouth. His eyes darted around, frantic.

"Kill... me."

Sara went to Cindy, peeled the sock back. The bite was ragged, ugly, but not very deep. She limped over to the tent and almost stepped on the first aid kit. She picked the box up and opened it. Inside were bandages, hydrogen peroxide, acetaminophen, and—thank God—a mini flashlight.

John began to wail. "They... will... eat... me! Kill... me!"

"Tyrone. Come here."

After pouring peroxide on Cindy's shoulder, Sara had Tyrone hold out his hands. She dumped half the bottle into his palms, the blisters foaming pink and gray from blood and dirt.

"KILLMEKILLMEKILLME!"

"There are bottles of water inthe tent. Get a few, and each of you take some painkillers." She handed him the acetaminophen, which he gingerly took using two fingers. "Don't come out until I say so."

Sara and Tyrone exchanged a knowing look, and he nodded, putting his arm around Cindy and leading her away. Sara moved over to John. He looked pathetic, sad, terrified. Human.

"Please! They... will... cook... me... alive."

Sara chewed on her lower lip. She knew what the right thing to do was, and it made her stomach churn. With effort, she sat down next to him.

"Chi... children..."

"Are you a father, John?"

He blinked. "Yes..."

She didn't want to do this. She really didn't want to do this.

"Do you remember their names, John?"

"Greg... Jen..."

"Do you want me to," Sara swallowed the lump in her throat, "give a message to your children?"

"You... can't..."

Sara closed her eyes, the tears rolling down her cheeks.

"Yes I can, John. When I get off the island, I'll make sure I find out who you are. I promise I will, John."

She looked at him, and he was smiling again. Sara placed her other hand under John's chin, winding her fingers in his hair.

"Tell me, John. What should I say to your kids?"

His eyes opened really wide. "I... ATE... THEM!"

Human beings always had a choice. If you knew the difference between good and evil, you could choose good. If you knew the difference between mercy and vengeance, you could choose mercy.

Sare looked deep inside herself, and found mercy.

The *crack* when John's neck hyper-extended wasn't as loud this time. It was more like a *pop*.

.　　.　　.

Lester peered at the vomiting boy through the viewfinder, then pressed the button again. The flash went off, and he looked at the screen on his digital camera to see how the picture came out.

Very nice. He glanced up at the boy, who was looking around, wondering what was happening.

Time for Lester to show him.

Lester tucked the camera into the bib pocket of his overalls and walked out of the scrub brush. He smiled at the boy's reaction, a mixture of fear and awe.

"The boy shouldn't try to run. It will just make Lester mad."

Lester strolled over, appearing casual but ready to bolt if the boy took off. But the boy stayed on his knees, mouth hanging open, some barf on his chin.

Lester stood next to the boy and peered down at him. He reached down, and with his index finger, caressed the lad's cheek.

"What is the boy's name?"

"T…Tom."

"Lester."

Lester glanced down at the mess Tom made, locking his eyes onto one of the bigger chunks. He tried to remember all the things he'd ever put in his mouth, but knew he'd never be able to remember them all. If Lester could bite it, he had. But he didn't think he'd ever eaten something that had already been eaten by someone else.

Unable to control the impulse, Lester snagged the piece of meat from the puddle of stomach acid. He opened his jaws and tossed it in like popcorn.

Tangy.

"Lester has a girlfriend," Lester said, chewing.

"That's…uh…cool."

Lester nodded. "Does Tom have a girlfriend?"

Tom's eyes were very wide. He shook his head. "No."

"That's sad. Does Tom have a boyfriend?" Lester asked.

The boy shook his head again.

"That's good." Lester got on his knees. He still towered over the boy, and had to lean down.

"Lester doesn't have a boyfriend either. What a lucky day for Tom and Lester."

Lester felt Tom scream in his mouth as he kissed the boy's deliciously tangy lips.

◦　　◦　　◦

Doctor Plincer got under the bed covers, then reached onto the nightstand for his earplugs. Subject 33 was really coaxing some screams out of his new playmate, and Plincer needed to get some sleep before the meeting tomorrow.

He found the two foam plugs by the base of the lamp, and spent a minute taking off his prosthetic ears and shoving the plugs into the holes. When the cries were dulled to a whisper, Plincer placed his glasses where the earplugs had been, switched off the light, and rested his head back on the pillow.

Oops. Almost forgot.

Plincer flicked the lamp back on, sat up, and spent a minute picking the facial putty out of the divots in his nose, chin and cheeks. Specifically made for burn victims, this make-up was used to smooth out scar tissue. It didn't hold up to close scrutiny, giving his complexion an artificial dullness, and when it dried it would flake off, making him look like he had crumbs on his face. Still, it was preferable to looking like a loaf of headcheese.

When he had a decent sized ball of it, he set that next to his glasses and again killed the light.

The doctor actually did sympathize with the poor suffering girl. Sympathize, and empathize.

Plincer rested his hands on his bare chest and ran his fingers over the rubbery scars. There were several dozen gnarled, shiny bumps, in precise, even rows. It felt like touching a truck tire.

The plastic surgeons weren't able to do skin grafts, because there was no place on the doctor's body where skin could be harvested. His arms, legs, back, and even buttocks had the same scars.

Scars from Lester.

Doctor Plincer knew, firsthand, what it was like to be completely at the mercy of a psychopath. After the court ordered Lester into Plincer's care, the doctor had been so intent on curing the teenager he hadn't given enough thought to precautions. Lester was smart, and managed to escape his room one night and sneak into the doctor's.

For two days, Doctor Plincer had been victimized by the boy. Lester stripped him naked, tied him up, and began the methodical process of biting him over his entire body.

Human beings can clench their teeth with a hundred and fifty pounds of force. It hurt worse than being pinched with pliers. Not to mention the obscene intimacy of it. Plincer often imagined he could still feel Lester's lips, his warm breath, his slick tongue, on his skin. Followed by the piercing, tearing pain.

Plincer had screamed during the ordeal. Screamed until his throat went numb. And when Lester finished, when he'd covered almost every bitable square inch on the Doctor's body, he started over. Nibbling off the scabs. Reopening the wounds. Ramping the agony up to surreal levels.

The maid saved Plincer's life. Coming in for the weekly cleaning, she heard the doctor's whimpering and called the police.

Doctor Plincer needed over two hundred stitches and staples, and three pints of blood. The most extensive reconstruction work was done on his face and genitals, to little effect. It took him weeks to recover, and Plincer knew that perhaps he never truly did get over the psychological aspects of the attack.

But he didn't blame Lester, any more than he could blame a shark for following its nature. When Plincer healed, he resumed his experiments with Lester. But instead of curing him, he enhanced him, making the boy even more evil.

The world didn't care about him curing psychotics. But it turned out people were willing to pay big bucks to Plincer to create psychotics.

So strange how life works out.

Plincer sighed, digging another bit of putty out of the gap in the bridge of his nose and flicking it off into the dark. Funny, that he'd still have so much vanity he had to put on his face before the new arrivals saw him. He had no reason to care if they saw his disfigurement or not. Even if one of the female visitors on the island took a liking to Plincer, there wasn't much he could do about it. Lester had bitten off those parts of him.

Chalk it up to an old man's pride, Plincer thought. *We're all entitled to our little idiosyncrasies.*

He sighed deeply and burrowed his head into his pillow. If all went as planned, by this time tomorrow he would no longer have money troubles.

Plincer allowed himself a small smile. Perhaps he should write a letter to his accountant, have him invest in a company that made ear plugs.

If the meeting went as well as Plincer anticipated, there would soon be a lot of screaming, all around the world.

. . .

The flashlight from the first aid kit was small, but it had a nice bright LED bulb. Sara clenched it between her teeth and bit down, hard, as she peeled off her jeans. The wound didn't look too bad when she cleansed it; just four tiny punctures and a growing oval bruise. But it bled like hell and wouldn't stop. Sara knew that a vein, or maybe an artery, was torn beneath the sin, and wasn't sure what to do about it. She settled for wrapping it as tight as she could, then putting on a fresh pair of jeans and a sweater.

While Sara chugged a bottle of water she went through the backpacks, searching for anything useful. She pocketed some fingernail clippers, a lighter, and a compass when something caught her attention. Resting unfolded on the ground, like a dead dove, were the divorce papers.

Seeing them brought a lump to her throat.

Martin, *her* Martin, was out there, in the woods, with their son. So were Tom and Laneesha and Georgia. Of course she worried about Jack, and the others, who were like surrogate children.

But I'm worried sick about him, too.

The thought surprised her. Here they were, a signature away from never seeing each other again, which was something Sara initiated. Yet the thought of Martin being killed—it scared her down to the marrow.

Sara reached down, picked up the papers, and crumpled them into a ball.

If we get out of here, Martin, we're going to find a way to make it work between us. I swear.

Then she left the tent to check on the kids. Both Tyrone and Cindy had put on shirts. Cindy had opted for something less baggy and a bit more flattering, a gray button-down top that showed she had a waist. Tyrone was in a familiar red and blue plaid shirt, but it wasn't familiar on him.

"Meadow's," he said, noticing Sara's stare.

She nodded at him. They'd told her about Meadow, and Sara had compartmentalized that particular horror, sealing it away until she had time to deal with it.

"I'm going to use the radio." She knew she didn't need to add anything else, but she said it anyway. "Stay on guard. There are twenty more of them out there."

Sara studied the walkie-talkie, a Core-Sea VHF One Way Radio. On its face were an LCD screen, which was empty gray, a tiny red light near the base, and half a dozen buttons including *wx band, 16/9, band, hi/lo,* and *mem.* She had no idea what any of that meant. There were two equally confusing dials on the top, and a large black *call* button on the side. Sara hoped Captain Prendick already had it set to his unique channel or frequency, so she pressed *call.*

"Um, I'm calling for Captain Prendick, or the Coast Guard, or anyone who can hear me. This is Sara Randhurst. I'm stranded on Rock Island in Lake Huron with my husband, baby, and five children. We're under attack, and one of my children was…" The words wouldn't come out. "We need immediate help."

She released the button and waited for a response. There was only silence.

"Please, we're fighting for our lives. Can anyone hear me?"

More silence. Sara stared at the buttons, wondering which one to try, and then the radio squelched at her.

"*Mrs. Randhurst, this is Captain Prendick, I read you, over.*"

Sara felt like crying in relief.

"Captain, thank God, there are people on this island. They're trying to kill us. You have to call for help."

"*Did I hear you correctly, Mrs. Randhurst? Someone is trying to kill you? That's an uninhabited island, over.*"

"Not anymore. Please. You have to hurry."

"*Is this some kind of joke, Mrs. Randhurst. There are stiff penalties for using a marine radio for pranks.*"

"This isn't a joke, Captain. I swear. We're under attack. You have to believe me."

Sara waited, hoping he would believe her.

"*Do you know how to work the radio? Can you call the coast guard?*"

"No. I don't understand what any of these buttons mean."

"*I'll call them right now. I'm in the area, only a few miles away, so I should be able to get there quickest. Can you make it to the spot where I dropped you off?*"

Sara glanced into the black void of the woods, her hands shaking. "I don't think so. We're lost."

"*Do you have a compass?*"

"Yes."

"*Follow it north-east. That's where the beach is. If you reach the cliffs, you went too far north, so go further east. I'll meet you there in an hour, maybe less.*"

"Thank you, Captain. Please hurry."

"*I will. Over and out, Mrs. Randhurst.*"

Sara held the walkie-talkie, wondering what to do next. Though she had a responsibility to Cindy and Tyrone, and a duty to get them to safety as soon as possible, Sara wasn't going to leave without the others. But she couldn't go after Martin and the kids by herself. She needed the Coast Guard, or the police, or a whole Army platoon to do that. And she certainly couldn't do it dragging Cindy and Tyrone along. She had to get them on the boat before she searched for anyone else.

Hopefully, Captain Prendick would arrive with the cavalry.

Sara considered turning the dials, pressing a few buttons, to see if she might be able to raise the Coast Guard herself, but she was afraid she would change the setting and no longer be able to contact Prendick. Besides, there wasn't time to play with the radio. Three cannibals had already found their campsite. Sara didn't want to spend any more time here than necessary.

Just in case any of the others showed up, she found a notebook and left a message.

We went north-east, to the beach, to wait for the boat. Captain Prendick is coming with help. Hide nearby and wait for us to return. Sara, Tyrone, and Cindy.

She left the notebook open to that page, sitting on the ground near the fire. For a few seconds she wondered if maybe she should use a stick to point north-east, but her time in the woods had shown Sara how easy it was to lose your sense of direction.

Sara took a last, lingering look at John, his head askew and his red eyes staring off into infinity, and told the kids it was time to go.

·   ·   ·

Captain Edward Prendick got off the radio with the Coast Guard, and wondered if everything was going to work out okay.

Prendick considered himself a good man. He loved his mother, and visited her on every holiday, Labor Day and Valentine's Day included, even though she lived out of state and it cost a fortune. He treated other people with decency and respect. He had an aquarium on board his boat, which contained a single goldfish, named Goldie, which he'd dutifully taken care of for more than five years.

That's why the distress call from Mrs. Randhurst was, well, so *distressing*.

Rock Island was a bad place. It even had an aura about it. An evil vibe. And something shady was definitely going on there.

He'd tried to warn them, to get them to camp elsewhere. But they'd been insistent.

Now he was forced to head back there. Something he didn't relish at all.

"Mama told me not to become a sailor, Goldie."

Goldie was asleep in his tank. Or *her* tank. Prendick didn't know if it was a boy fish or a girl fish. Actually, he didn't know if Goldie actually slept, either. She certainly didn't close her eyes and start snoring. But sometimes she'd stay in one place for an extended period of time, not even moving when he fed her, and Prendick assumed she (or he) was sleeping.

He glanced from the tank to the locked cabinet next to it. A gun cabinet, containing two revolvers and a rifle. Prendick checked the GPS and turned the wheel, silently praying he wouldn't have to use them.

Tom didn't think he could possibly be more frightened, and then the giant kissed him.

His first reaction was shock. Not only was the act totally un-expected, but it was so frickin' gross, so frickin' sick, that Tom didn't know what the hell to do.

The obvious answer—push the freak away—scared Tom even more. This guy was so big and scary that rejecting him didn't seem like an option.

So Tom closed his eyes as the psycho explored his mouth with his tongue, nibbling on his lips with those horrible needle teeth and making an awful, moaning sound in his throat.

Worst of all, this was technically Tom's first French kiss. Yuck.

It was almost as bad as realizing he'd eaten Meadow.

Tom endured it, staying stock-still, praying for it to end. Eventually it did, and this crazy Lester person looked down at Tom and patted him on the head.

"Mmm," Lester said. "Tom tastes yummy."

Lester moved in closer, like he was going for another kiss. Tom leaned away and quickly said, "Uh, are you the one that cooked my buddy?"

The giant shook his head. "Lester doesn't cook people. He likes to eat his raw."

That was enough for Tom. He shoved Lester as hard as he could, then broke the land-speed record for sixteen-year-old boys and ran the hell out of there. It was too dark to see, and the trees were everywhere, so he stuck his hands out ahead of him to avoid busting open his head. When he did finally hit the tree, he was spared a concussion, but it hyper-extended his pinky, which hurt worse than just about anything Tom ever felt before.

He was cradling his injured finger, wondering how to get it to stop throbbing, when someone grabbed his shirt from behind.

"Tom shouldn't have run from Lester," the giant whispered in his ear. "Now Lester is taking Tom back to his playroom."

"My finger," Tom said, whining. "I think I broke my finger."

Lester grabbed both of Tom's wrists, encircling them like handcuffs. He raised them to his lips, and then—*oh god no*—he put the jutting pinky into his mouth.

Tom felt like throwing up again. Lester swished the finger back and forth in his mouth, causing such incredible waves of pain that it made the darkness come alive with orange and blue flashes. Tom began to beg, and when that didn't stop the manipulation he fell to his knees and alternated between crying and screaming. There was no possible way the pain could get any worse.

Then the biting began.

. . .

General Alton Tope slugged down his fourth shot of scotch. It was a single malt, but a young one, and the alcohol burned his throat. The private who brought him the liquor needed a lesson in the selection of fine spirits, but he was grateful to the lad nonetheless.

He glanced at the OSST monitor again, frowning at the new population count.

Twenty-six.

Jesus, they're dropping like flies.

General Tope understood the chain of command. He lived by it. Orders were orders, and the soonest he could get to Rock Island was tomorrow. There was no leeway.

He hoped he wouldn't be too late.

.   .   .

Tyrone hurried through the woods alongside Cindy, three steps behind Sara. His palms were slathered in burn cream, which contained a topical anesthetic. It didn't really kill the pain, just sort of turned some of the throbbing into tingling. He could manage.

Cindy had a finger stuck in his belt loop, which was a poor substitute for holding hands. But the persistent tug made him feel closer, connected. After they'd dressed, Cindy had been the one to apply the burn cream. It hurt, and the ointment smelled foul, but her tenderness and dedication touched Tyrone. For a moment, he actually felt like a kid again, way back when safety was taken for granted, and love was given freely, and life had possibilities.

"Do you think we'll get out of here?" Cindy had asked, not meeting his eyes.

"We will."

"How do you know?"

"Because I won' let nuthin' happen to you."

Then she looked at him and all at once Tyrone felt nervous. Because he knew what he wanted to do, and the risks involved. Funny, there they were, surrounded by cannibals, and the thing that scared him most at that moment was leaning in for a kiss and being rejected.

But he did lean in. Cindy's eyes got wide, then closed, and his lips lightly touched hers.

For ten beautiful seconds, all was right with the world.

Now they were trekking through the forest, heading for shore. That kiss had felt so right, but it had raised the stakes. Tyrone had spent so long just caring about himself, he'd forgotten all the pressure that came with caring about someone else. He couldn't let anything happen to Cindy. Not now. He'd die first.

Sara got slightly ahead of them, even while limping, so Tyrone picked up the pace. She kept the light cupped in her hand, only flashing the beam occasionally to check the compass.

Tyrone always liked Sara. She was one of those people who actually wanted to help. She didn't pretend to understand all the things the kids at the Center were going through. She didn't make the mistake most adults did, trying to relate. Unless you were bangin' and jackin' and scoring drugs and hootchie mamas and livin' day by day, how the hell were you supposed to know what the thug life was like? But Sara never fronted like that. She just showed the kids how they could change their lives if they tried, and that was cool.

But Tyrone hadn't known how strong Sara actually was. He watched when she broke that guy's neck. That was some tough as hell shit. Tyrone felt better knowing she had his back.

Sara stopped again. When she shined the light on the compass, Tyrone saw a face behind her. A crazed, snarling, charred and bloody face, the long hair and beard half-melted away, the burned lips and swollen to twice their size.

The cutlery man.

He lunged at Sara, his knife and fork raised. Tyrone shot forward, pulling Cindy off her feet, straight-arming the cannibal in the shoulder. The shock of the impact made Tyrone stagger back, and it knocked the cutlery man sideways. Then the pain came, starting off slow like a distant train, speeding in to become huge and loud and unstoppable.

Tyrone fell to his knees, staring at his right hand. The skin on his palm, already blistered and loose, had sloughed off.

A roar, almost like an animal, drew Tyrone's attention upward, and he watched the cutlery man's attack, the knife slicing down through the air, a perfect angle to bury itself into his neck.

Then, just as fast, the cutlery man was knocked to the side, the knife spinning harmlessly in the air and dropping to the ground.

Sara pivoted and brought her other foot around, landing this second kick on the cannibal's face. Another inhuman roar escaped the burned man's ruined lips, and even though his face looked like one of those Picassos in the art book Martin made them read, he continued to come at them.

The cutlery man dashed forward, and Sara turned slightly, bumping out her hip, flipping the cannibal over. She immediately followed up by dropping her knees onto his chest, and raising her fist back.

But she paused.

Why wouldn't she hit him? Why didn't she kill the fucker?

The cutlery man used the advantage, flailing at Sara's bad leg, stabbing it with his fork.

Sara cried out, knocking his hand away. She hit him twice more. First in the nose, snapping his head back. Then in his bare neck.

The cutlery man's eyes rolled up. He clutched at his throat, bucking Sara off and rolling onto his knees. Tyrone saw that the cannibal couldn't breathe, that Sara must have broken something in his neck.

Cindy crouched next to Tyrone, her arm around his back, burying her face in his shoulder. Sara got to her feet, limping worse than before, then touched Tyrone's head.

"We need to keep going."

Tyrone didn't move. The pain wasn't what immobilized him. It was the terrible spectacle of watching the cutlery man desperately try to gasp for breath. The madness and evil in his eyes had been replaced by a very human look of raw panic. Seeing that made Tyrone understand why Sara had hesitated.

This wasn't a monster. It was a human being. A suffering, dying, human being. And it was horrible to watch.

Then the cutlery man brought his rusty fork up to his own throat, dug it in, and tore a big hunk out.

The blood sprayed in Tyrone's face, accompanied by a sound not unlike the *whoosh* of a fire extinguisher. Then the cannibal raised the fork again, a piece of him still hanging from it, and leapt to stab Sara, who was turned away.

Again Tyrone reacted, both hands up, blocking the cannibal's attack. Again Tyrone's raw palm hit the cutlery man's filthy shirt, making his vision go red with pain.

Sara noticed the movement and spun around, dodging the thrust, striking at the cutlery man's throat and temporarily losing her fist in the hole. She pulled away with a sucking noise, and the cutlery man fell to his knees, then onto his side, convulsing.

The pain built, getting stronger and stronger, and when the train finally hit him Tyrone couldn't handle it and everything went blurry, then black.

·　　·　　·

Conflicting feelings assailed Sara so quickly she felt like she was playing emotional ping-pong. Rage and pity, fear and triumph, disgust and elation, concern and regret. She wasn't sure whether to scream, weep, or laugh. Sara held everything back, including the pain in her thigh, and went to Tyrone, lying on his back. She sat next to him, stretching her leg out, and checked his pulse.

Tyrone's eyelids fluttered, then opened, his wince expanding into a rictus of pain.

"Cindy, the med kit is in my backpack. We need to wrap his hand up."

Cindy dug into the bag. Sara held up Tyrone's wrist.

The boy's palm looked like he'd dipped it in red paint. His whole arm was shaking, and he had a far-off look that made Sara question his connection with reality. She touched his forehead. Cool and clammy.

"Tyrone, can you hear me?"

"Huh?"

"It's Sara. You need to stay awake. Cindy, when you've got the kit, put the pack under his feet to elevate his legs. Also, give me that vial of ammonia."

Cindy handed over the bottle. Sara avoided looking at the cannibal, who was still twitching. She pulled the stopper and waved it under Tyrone's nostrils. He tried to turn his head, but she kept it close until he lifted up his good hand to push the ammonia away.

"We have to get going," Sara said. "Can you understand me?"

"Hand hurts bad," he mumbled.

"Can you understand me, Tyrone?"

"Yeah."

Cindy raised Tyrone's feet, increasing the blood flow to his brain.

"Can you wrap his hand?" Sara asked.

Cindy nodded and got to work. Sara took the time to examine her new injury. It was just a few inches below the previous one, and not bleeding as badly. Sara found an Ace bandage in the kit and wound it tight around both her wounds. Then she checked her watch.

Half an hour until the boat arrived. Hopefully the Coast Guard was en route as well. Sara pulled the radio off her belt and pressed the button.

"Captain Prendick, this is Sara Randhurst. Can you hear me?"

A few seconds of quiet, then, "*I hear you, Mrs. Randhurst. I should be there soon.*"

"How about the police?"

"*I contacted the Coast Guard. They're on their way. Over.*"

Sara pressed the call button, but didn't speak. She wasn't sure how to say what she was thinking without sounding paranoid.

Not that she didn't have good reason to be paranoid.

Captain Prendick must have guessed her intent, because when she released the button he was in mid-sentence. "*...try it for yourself. Emergency frequency is on channel A, one, five, six, point, eight, zero, zero. Use the word* mayday. *The Coast Guard will respond. Over.*"

"Say that again. What do I press?"

"*Hit the 16/9 button two times. That resets it to the emergency channel. Then hit it two more times to be able to reach me again. Over and out.*"

Sara followed instructions, then pressed the *call* button again.

"Mayday, mayday, this is Sara Randhurst. I'm on Rock Island with several children and we need help."

After a pause, a nasally voice said, "*Mrs. Randhurst, this is the Coast Guard. We have been informed of your situation. Estimated time of arrival is nineteen minutes. We'll be coming ashore on the north-east beach, over.*"

"Thank you so much," Sara said. She took a quick glance at the still-twitching cannibal and added, "Bring guns. Lots of guns."

"*Roger that, Mrs. Randhurst. Coast Guard over and out.*"

Sara clipped the walkie-talkie to her belt and let out a long breath. They needed to get moving. Not only because of the danger, but because Sara didn't want to sit still long enough to deal with everything on her mind. She and Cindy helped Tyrone to his feet, Sara shouldered the backpack, and the trio got on their way.

The woods were dark. Quiet. Scary. Sara stopped often to check the compass and scan the outlying foliage for pursuers. Tyrone was moaning softly, but not soft enough. Sara was afraid he might be heard.

Cindy whispered, "How much farther?"

"I don't know."

"Tyrone is really cold."

"I think he's going into shock, Cindy."

"What do we do?"

"We keep going. Help is on the way. They'll take care of him."

A few steps later, Tyrone couldn't walk anymore. Sara sat him down and handed Cindy a bottle of water.

"Make sure he drinks this."

"Where are you going?" The teen looked panicked.

"I think I can hear waves. I'm only going a few yards ahead."

"Please don't leave us, Sara."

Sara drilled her eyes into Cindy. "I won't. You have my word. I'll be back in a minute."

Leaving Tyrone in Cindy's capable hands, Sara pressed ahead. In just a few steps she found something. Not Lake Huron, but something that indicated the water was close.

A boat.

It was on its side, the hull split wide open, vines and overgrowth obscuring the outline. Sara guessed it had been here for years. She played the tiny flashlight beam across the bottom, up the side, to the stern, and read the fading name painted there.

SS MINNOW

That was the boat from the TV show *Gilligan's Island*. But it was also the name Martin had used in his campfire story, when he talked about the party of eight who had come to the island and were attacked.

It couldn't be a coincidence. This must have been the boat he was talking about. But how could he have known? Unless...

Sara crept around to the other side of the boat, a growing feeling of dread creeping up her back. She had to fight the thicket, and branches poked at her hair and caught on her clothing. The cabin was setting on the ground, partially crushed like a stepped-on soda can. Two of the bridge windows were broken out. Sara shone the light through one, peering into the cabin interior.

The inside was filled with mud and dead leaves. Pieces of a deck chair, part of a life preserver, and various other detritus vied for space with an abandoned raccoon nest. Amid the mess, resting on a pile of disintegrating magazines, was a hardcover book that looked disturbingly familiar. The silver embossing on the cover was faded and dirty, but it clearly said, LOG.

Sara reached through the window, brushing the book with her fingertips. She leaned in further, snagged it, and then something screeched. Before she could pull back, it pounced, scrambling up her arm, over her shoulder, and racing into the forest.

Guess that raccoon nest wasn't abandoned after all, Sara thought, leaning against the wreckage, clutching the book to her hammering heart. When her pulse returned to something resembling normal, she took a closer look at the log.

Please don't let this be what I think it is.

The book was damp and smelled of mildew. The cardboard cover wilted as she opened it up. There, on the first page, Sara's fears were confirmed. Handwritten on the first blank line was:

SS MINNOW, CAPTAIN JOSEPH RANDHURST
Joe. Martin's brother.

Sara had always liked her brother-in-law. Joe was sort of like a more playful, less serious version of her husband. Rather than dedicating his life to making a difference, Joe preferred the life of leisure, day trading and blowing his money on travel and toys. Sara could remember the day Joe talked about buying a boat. He'd come over for Thanksgiving dinner before she and Martin had gotten married, extolling the many virtues of living on the open water. The three of them killed four bottles of wine, and afterward Martin and Sara disregarded Joe's plans. Joe always talked about doing silly things like that, but never did.

For Christmas that year, Sara had bought Joe the captain's log book as a gag gift, a goofy nod to that memorable night.

That spring, Joe disappeared.

Martin had taken some time off to search for him. He still continued to take occasional weekends to follow down some old lead or ancient hearsay, refusing to believe his brother was dead.

It seemed Joe had bought that boat after all. He'd apparently named it the SS Minnow, and taken it here.

Which meant Martin knew Joe had come here. After all these years, he'd followed his brother's trail to Plincer's island.

Sara shook her head, not wanting to believe it. How could her husband bring the children here? How could he risk all of their lives?

"*I didn't know there was anyone here, Sara. Jesus, I would never do anything to hurt you or the kids. You know that.*"

But was that the truth? Was he so anxious to find his brother that he had jeopardized all of them?

No, not Martin. Martin couldn't have brought them here if he thought it could do them harm. Especially Jack. Martin wouldn't ever willingly put their child in danger.

Yet Sara couldn't help but wonder. If Martin had kept this secret from her, what other secrets had he kept?

Sara was dwelling on that when she heard someone scream.

.   .   .

Martin followed the cries, hurrying through the woods as fast as he could, one hand protectively covering his sleeping child.

Meticulous a planner as Martin was, he couldn't have predicted all of the misfortunes that occurred on this trip. It was all his fault, he knew. Hopefully the consequences wouldn't be as dire as they were shaping up to be.

He hurdled a cluster of Hawthorn shrubs and stopped dead, his flashlight focusing on Tom.

Tom wasn't alone. A large man with sharp teeth was munching on his finger.

Martin's first reaction was surprise. Then came disbelief, swiftly followed by anger.

"Hey! Freakshow! Get your goddamn hands off my kid!"

"Martin…" Tom whimpered.

The tall psychotic opened his mouth, releasing Tom's finger; the bone was still attached, but the flesh had pretty much been stripped off. The giant smiled at Martin, flashing his vampire teeth.

"Martin. Tom hurt his finger. Lester is making it all better."

Martin clenched his fists. "Lester better back the fuck off."

Lester stuck his hands in his overalls, winked, and then quickly backed into the woods. Good thing, too. Seven feet or not, Martin was so angry he had been ready to throw himself at the larger man.

"Martin…"

Tom was on his knees, his body wracked by sobs. Martin went over, placed his hand on the teen's shoulder.

"Easy, Tom. Easy."

"That guy…that guy Lester…he was…"

"Lester is gone." Martin's eyes darted around the forest to make sure. "He won't hurt you anymore. I promise. I've got you, now."

He patted Tom's back, then eased his hands under his armpits, gently guiding him to his feet. The kid looked shattered, and with good reason.

"We've got to find the others, Tom. Do you have any idea where they are?"

Tom sniffled, seemingly getting his control back. Then he looked at his hand and began bawling again. Martin could appreciate the pain and fear, but they didn't have any time to waste.

"Tom, do you know where Sara is?"

"That's my bone… *Jesus Christ*… my bone is sticking out."

"Your finger can be fixed," Martin lied. "Now do you know where Sara is?"

"How can it be fixed?" Tom whined, drawing out his vowels. "Theeeere's nooooo skiiiiiiiiin leeeeeeeft."

Martin put his hand on Tom's chin, forcing the boy to look at him. "Focus, Tom. Sara. Where is she?"

"I dunno."

"How about the kids? Cindy?"

"She's with Tyrone. I think they're still at the camp."

"Meadow?"

"Oh, God."

"Where's Meadow, Tom?"

"I aaaaaaaate Meeeaaaadooooow…"

Martin grimaced. This had gone from bad to horribly worse. But this wasn't the time to dwell on the loss. Martin needed to keep a clear head, needed to figure out what to do next.

"He tasted like chicken!" Tom wailed.

Martin realized he wasn't going to get anything out of Tom. He stared off into the woods, thinking of Sara, and felt like putting his fist through a tree.

Calm down. This island isn't that big. You'll find her.

Martin knew he would. He swore on it.

He just hoped Sara would still be alive when he did.

. . .

They approached the giant iron door, the only entrance to the prison.

There were people inside, they knew. They could smell them. Practically taste them.

The doctor was in there too. The doctor who had made them like this.

They hated the doctor.

Two of them yanked on the door, trying desperately to open it.

They strained and groaned, but it wouldn't budge.

It never budged.

But they kept trying. Every day, they kept trying.

Waiting for the day when it wouldn't be locked.

Their efforts were interrupted by screams, coming from the woods. Several of them peered into the forest. Then, as one, they headed for whoever was screaming.

They would try the door again later.

. . .

Cindy used the last of the burn ointment on Tyrone's hand, then wrapped it in gauze. Her shoulder hurt like crazy, so she couldn't imagine the pain he must have been in.

"Sara said you need to drink this. When she comes back, I'll ask if you can have more aspirin."

Cindy tilted the water bottle up to Tyrone's lips. Some spilled down his chin, but he managed to swallow a few gulps. She cupped his cheek, feeling such a flood of affection for him she was ready to start crying.

"Thanks," he mumbled.

Cindy wanted to hug him, to comfort him, to take his pain away. Almost as badly, she wanted him to comfort her, to tell her it was all going to be okay, that they'd live to see the morning. But she didn't want to seem clingy or needy. She cast her nervous eyes over Tyrone's shoulder, scanning the woods, knowing what was hiding in there, knowing they could pop out at any time and attack.

"Sara will be back soon," Tyrone said. "The boat is coming. We're gonna be safe."

He didn't sound convinced. Neither was she.

"You're in a lot of pain, huh?" she asked. After she said it, Cindy looked around for a hole to bury her head. Of course he was in a lot of pain. He was probably thinking she was an idiot.

"Ain' so bad," Tyrone said. His eyes softened. "Cuz you're here."

Cindy felt nervous again. Not because people were trying to kill them. But because she was suddenly overcome with the oldest insecurity known to teens. The abrupt change from one kind of apprehension to another was silly, but at that moment she couldn't help it. Staring at Tyrone, one thought blocked out all others.

Does he like me?

A totally inappropriate question, considering they were in a life-or-death situation. But right then, Cindy's silly, girlish anxiety mattered more than the pain and the fear. She'd spent her last few years either doing drugs or trying to get drugs, so this completely normal emotion took her by surprise. Especially since she'd never actually had one like it before.

Does he like me?

On one hand, Tyrone has always been nice to her. When he kissed Cindy, it made her heart feel like it would pop like a birthday balloon. But Tyrone probably kissed a lot of girls. It might have been the stress of their current predicament. Or—God forbid—it could have been a pity kiss.

Does he like me?

And what if he did? What did it mean? Cindy liked Tyrone. A lot. But how did this relationship thing work? Did that kiss mean they were going out? Were they exclusive? Was she Tyrone's girlfriend?

"You look kinda freaked out," Tyrone said. He reached out and stroked her cheek with his knuckles. "I don't want my girl to be freaked out."

Cindy didn't know how to read that. But she knew how to find out. The girl who had the courage to crawl into that tent could certainly find the courage to ask him.

"So, uh, I'm your girl?"

He gave her a sly grin. "Yeah. I mean, if you wanna be."

Cindy lit up. "I wanna be. So we're going out together?"

"Yeah. I won't be no good at holding hands for a while, though."

"I know." Cindy moved a little closer. "But maybe we should, you know, kiss to make it official."

He nodded. "That would probly be best."

She put her hands on his chest and leaned into him.

The kiss made her toes curl.

Cindy held the embrace until she realized how exposed they were. With neither of them paying attention, those wild people could sneak up.

She moved back, just a millimeter. "We should, um, watch the trees. Make sure no one is coming."

"Yeah." Tyrone learned backward. He looked quickly over her shoulder, then back at her. "One helluva first date, huh?"

Cindy smiled shyly. "Best I ever had."

"Me too."

Cindy watched one side, Tyrone the other. The woods were quiet and dark, and though a sliver of moonlight broke through the tree tops, it was hard to see more than a few yards. Her eyes swept back and forth, like a security camera.

When she heard the scream it made her feel like she needed to pee again.

"That's Tom," Tyrone said.

"He doesn't sound too far away."

They listened, and the sound made Cindy want to claw her ears off. She didn't like Tom, especially after he acted all crazy with the gun. But he didn't deserve whatever horror was happening to him.

"You think they're cooking him?" Her tone was hushed. "Like Meadow?"

"Dunno."

"What should we do?"

"We have to wait here for Sara. That's what she told us to do."

Tom was begging now, screaming, "No!" and "Stop!"

What could they be doing to that poor kid? Something even worse than burning?

"It's awful." Cindy wanted to cover up her ears, but was afraid if she did she would miss the sounds of someone coming.

"Be strong, girl. I know you strong."

Cindy nodded, trying to stay strong. Being strong didn't make it any less horrible.

Then, after a very long minute, the screaming stopped.

Now what?

They waited. Cindy's imagination went into overdrive. *Is he dead? Are they eating him? Or did they gag him with a spiked ball, like Sara said they gagged Martin?*

Cindy stood perfectly still, staring into the woods, waiting, *hoping*, to hear Tom scream again.

Then something flashed. Bright and quick, temporarily blinding her.

Cindy took a step back. "Tyrone…"

"I saw it too."

"What was it?"

"Maybe Sara's comin' back. She got a light."

Another flash, lasting only a few milliseconds. From the thicket to their right. Cindy realized with a shock what it was.

"It's a camera," she whispered. "Someone is taking our picture."

Tyrone stepped in front of Cindy. "Who's there? Answer me."

Another flash. Cindy doubted the cannibals had a camera; they seemed too primitive and animalistic.

So who is it? And why don't they say anything? This is seriously freaking me out. Where is Sara?

"Maybe we should go," Tyrone said.

"What about Sara? We have to wait for her."

The bushes shook. Whoever had the camera was coming toward them. Cindy decided that Tyrone was right. The smartest thing to do was get the hell out of here, fast.

Tyrone apparently wasn't waiting for her to approve, because he had his left arm around her waist and was already leading her away. The pair had only taken three steps when they heard:

"The boy and girl are Martin's kids."

The voice was soft, almost effeminate, but definitely male. Whoever it was, he knew Martin. Cindy stopped and swung around to face him.

The man was ridiculously tall and thin. He wore blue denim farmer's overalls, and even in the low light Cindy could see a smiley face button pinned to one of the straps.

Tyrone had also turned to look. "Who the hell are you?"

"Lester."

Lester raised his camera and took another picture, causing Cindy to blink. She was still scared, and this guy totally qualified as creepy. But he seemed extremely relaxed. So far, his appearance was more menacing than actually threatening.

"Do you know Martin, Lester?"

"Martin is Lester's friend."

Cindy didn't know if she bought that. But Martin was a psychologist, and he did work with all types of people.

"How do you know Martin, Lester?" she asked.

"Martin is Lester's friend." He paused, cocking his head to the side. "Would the boy and the girl like to follow Lester to Martin?"

God, did she ever. Martin was smart, and strong, and Cindy trusted him like she trusted Sara. Unlike most teens, Cindy liked adults. During her drug years, Cindy had begged for money from hundreds of adults, and the overwhelming majority were either indifferent or somewhat caring. But as much as she wanted to trust this tall man, he had a strange vibe to him.

She came out from behind Tyrone and took a tentative step closer. "Do you know where Martin is, Lester?"

"Lester knows. The boy and the girl should come with Lester."

Lester smiled. Cindy was shocked to see fangs in the big man's mouth.

Tyrone shook his head. "I don't think so." He backed up, pulling Cindy with him.

"Lester won't hurt the boy and the girl. That would make Martin angry. They should come with Lester."

"Where's Martin?" Cindy asked.

Lester took another picture.

"Stop taking pictures and tell me where Martin is!"

The strength in her voice surprised her. It must have surprised Lester too, because his smile became a deep frown.

"The girl yelled at Lester. Lester doesn't like that."

Tyrone pulled her closer. "You know where Martin is, man? Then tell us."

It hit Cindy all at once, like a physical blow. *Lester.* Lester *Paks.* This was the serial killer Sarah had told them about, the one that crazy doctor had experimented on.

"Lester will take the boy and girl to Martin." The giant moved toward them, spreading out his arms. His reach was so wide he looked like he could hug a truck. "Martin will be so happy."

When Lester got within five yards he'd officially gone from menacing, to threatening, to terrifying. She and Tyrone continued to back up, but Lester's strides were so big he'd be on them in only a few seconds.

"The boy and the girl shouldn't try to run. Lester gets angry when they run."

That's when Cindy was grabbed from behind.

*　　*　　*

Sara couldn't find the kids.

After hearing Tom's screams, she quickly stuck her head back through the window and into the cabin to grab something she saw inside. By the time she had it, the screaming had stopped.

Her first intention was to go after Tom, to protect him, to save him, and without considering anything else she'd impulsively headed in the direction of his cries.

But Sara wasn't sure where he was, or even how far away, without the sound cues. Even worse, once she lost sight of the boat she became lost, unable to find her way back.

Oh God, I've abandoned Cindy and Tyrone...

She spent a good minute studying the compass, panicking to the point of hysteria, and then decided to follow a south-west direction, keeping as quiet as possible, listening for their voices.

Luckily, she found them, coming up from behind and placing a hand on Cindy's shoulder so she didn't get trampled by their quick pace.

Unluckily, they weren't alone.

The man chasing them was so grotesquely tall it was almost funny. But unlike the cannibals, he had short hair and was clean shaven, and his clothes, though odd, looked relatively new.

Sara raised the weapon in her hand, pointing it at the tall man.

"Stop," she said, Not loud enough to attract undesired attention, but hard enough to show it wasn't a request, but rather an order.

The tall man stood still, his arms still outstretched. "The woman has a flare gun."

Sara had hoped it would be mistaken for the real thing, but she rolled with it. "And if you come any closer, I'm going to shoot it at you. It doesn't shoot bullets, but I'm pretty sure it can set you on fire."

He lowered his arms and titled his head at an angle, like a confused dog.

"Is the woman Martin's wife?"

She wasn't prepared for the question, but she answered. "Yes. I'm Sara."

"Lester will take the Sara woman to Martin."

"Where is Martin?"

"Martin is at the prison. With Tom boy, and Georgia girl."

"Is Jack there?"

Lester smiled, baring teeth that looked like they belonged to an alligator. "Baby Jack is there. Doctor is taking care of baby Jack."

"Doctor Plincer." Sara felt the lump in her throat. "And you're Lester Paks."

"Lester is Lester Paks. Doctor Plincer is Lester's friend. Martin is Lester's friend. The Sara woman should come with Lester."

Sara's hand was shaking now. She believed, *hoped,* he was lying, and desperately wanted this man to get the hell away from her and the kids. But first...

"How about Joseph? Joe? Joe Randhurst? Is he at the prison, too?"

Lester's eyes got wide, and his angular head bobbed up and down in a nod. "Of course Joe is there."

Sara limped in front of Cindy and Tyrone, putting herself between them and the serial killer. Her gun hand was shaking, but she made sure her words were strong.

"Thank you for talking with us, Lester. But we aren't going to go with you right now." She tried to swallow, but her mouth was dry. "We'd like you to go away."

Lester pulled something out of his pocket, and Sara cringed, trying to shield the kids. But Lester didn't have a weapon. It was only a camera.

He snapped a picture, the flash momentarily blinding her.

"The Sara woman is pretty."

Sara blinked a few times, tried to focus.

"Thank you for the compliment, Lester. Now you really do have to go. I don't want to have to shoot you."

Lester took another picture.

"I'm serious, Lester. It's time for you to leave."

A tongue flicked out of Lester's mouth, running across his bottom lip. He seemed to come to some sort of conclusion. "Lester is going to ask Martin."

"We want you to leave us alone, Lester."

"Lester will ask. Lester wants permission first."

"You need to go. Now."

"Lester wants permission to bite the Sara woman's pretty face off."

He opened and closed his jaw several times, his sharp teeth making clicking sounds.

"Get. The fuck. Back." Sara said.

Lester raised the camera, took one more picture, and then advanced on them.

Sara didn't think. She reacted. Planting one foot, pivoting her hips, swiveling them around and kicked Lester as hard as she could, throwing her bad leg into his stomach.

The pain was otherworldly, making her vision burn orange.

But the blow had its desired effect, doubling the tall man over, making him fall onto his ass.

Lester stared up at Sara, his face a mask of disbelief. Blood tricked from the corner of his mouth.

"Lester bit his tongue." The aforementioned tongue darted out, licking at the line of blood, making an even bigger line of blood.

Lester's eyes got a glassy look, and he smiled, his vampire teeth streaked with red. He held up his hand and stared at it, as if in a trance. Then he opened his jaws wide, and began to gnaw on his fingers.

The blood really started to flow after that.

"We need to leave," Sara said.

Tyrone nodded. "No shit."

Lester moaned, then locked eyes with Sara. She saw depths of hatred there that she didn't think possible in a fellow human being. He tugged his bleeding hand from his mouth, spat at her, and then rolled over, scurrying on all fours off into the woods.

Sara stood guard for a moment, listened to the woods. All she heard were crickets.

"That was seriously effed up," Tyrone said. "I would have shot his ugly ass."

Sara nodded. "Me too. But the flare gun is empty. I couldn't find any cartridges."

"He dropped something." Cindy began to move toward the spot where Lester was sitting. "It's his camera."

She brought it over to Cindy. It was a digital model, with a large LCD screen on the back. Dread perched on Sara's shoulders like a gargoyle, weighing her down. Even though she didn't want to look at any of the pictures, her finger hit the play button, beginning a slideshow.

A photo of Sara appeared on the screen, the one Lester had taken a few moments ago.

A second later, a photo of Cindy and Tyrone came on.

Then a photo of everyone sitting around the campfire, Martin telling his story.

Then a photo of Georgia, alone on the beach.

Then a photo of Tom, looking terrified.

Then a photo of Sara and Laneesha, walking in the woods.

Then a photo of Meadow, locked into the gridiron...

Sara put a hand over her face, stifling the cry. The image was the single most horrible thing she'd ever seen.

But the next picture shook her even more. Sara let loose with a cry that was half sob, half scream, and she fell to her knees, her whole body trembling.

It was a picture of Jack, being held by an old, bald man in a white lab coat.

.   .   .

Tom hurt. Physically, and emotionally. As he walked the tightrope between hysteria and unconsciousness, he knew he was going to die.

A weighty realization. Tom's ADHD meant he took self-interest to a whole new level, and the thought of him no longer existing was almost too much to grasp.

And yet, having spent his whole life not caring about anyone but himself, Tom was somewhat surprised that another thought entered his head. A sympathetic thought, for someone other than himself.

That poor baby. Jack never hurt anyone. How can something this awful happen to him?

Tom prayed to God, asking for an answer.

God didn't reply.

.   .   .

Martin rubbed his eyes, then extended the motion into probing the puncture wounds on his face.

This had all gone so terribly wrong.

He thought about Sara, and the kids, and his brother Joe, and how this simple trip had become a horrifying clusterfuck.

Martin took a deep breath, let it out slow, and hoped for some miracle to make everything right again.

.   .   .

The OB/GYN rubs the transducer over Sara's distended belly. The conducting jelly it glides across is cold and wet, and Sara shivers.

Martin grips her hand tighter. They're both focused on the ultrasound monitor, staring at a triangular cone that is revealing their baby's head.

"Did you want to know the sex?" the doctor asks.

Sara and Martin had discussed it, ultimately deciding not to know. But seeing her child's perfect little face on that blue screen, eyes closed and actually sucking his tiny thumb, Sara changes her mind.

"Let's find out," she says, looking at Martin.

"Are you sure?"

They had already bought paint for the nursery—a sexless, neutral green—and crib blankets and sheets to match, and enough onesies to last the child until Kindergarten. But the prospect of exchanging everything for pink or blue is so tantalizing that Sara can't resist.

"I'm sure," she says.

The doctor slides the transducer around, revealing the baby's right leg. Sara thinks back to Martin's promise when they got pregnant, of letting her name their child.

Sara had bought baby books, scoured the Internet, and even kept a dictionary next to the bed to leaf through in case some random word lent itself to the perfect name. But her choices ultimately came down to the obvious ones, and she decides to share them with Martin for the first time.

"If it's a girl, let's name her Laura," Sara says. "After my mother. And if it's a boy, how about Joe?"

Martin smiles, but it's painful. "I appreciate the gesture, but I'm not sure I want to think of my lost brother every time I hold my kid."

Sara knew he might act that way, so she has a back-up.

"Jack." After Martin and Joe's father.

Martin's smile is genuine this time. He holds Sara's hand so hard it almost hurts.

"Mr. and Mrs. Randhurst," the doctor says, keeping the transducer steady. "Meet your son, Jack."

Sara starts to cry. "I want him to be like you, Martin. I want him to grow up to be just like you."

Her husband bends over and kisses away her tears.

*   *   *

Sara's tears fell on the camera screen, onto her baby's face.

She flinched when someone placed a hand on her shoulder. Cindy.

"I'm sure he's okay, Sara. The doctor has him, not the cannibals."

Sara wanted to scream *that's even worse!* but she kept it reigned in.

"Sara," Tyrone also put his hand on her, even though it must have been painful. "We have to get to the beach."

Sara stared up at her kids. She had to find Jack. But she also had to make sure they get to safety. Prendick and the Coast Guard would be here soon. As soon as Cindy and Tyrone were okay, they could go in search of Jack and the others.

An image of Martin appeared in Sara's mind. If the doctor had Jack, what had he done to her husband?

"Please, Sara." Cindy looked ready to cry. "We need to go."

Sara nodded, allowing the teens to help her to her feet. She took a last look at the picture of her beautiful baby boy, then tucked the camera into her pocket, digging out the compass.

After a big breath she said, "This way."

Sara led them through the woods, heading north-east. The water noises were faint at first, almost imaginary. But they grew stronger, the unmistakable sound of waves lapping at the shore. Then the trees finally parted, revealing...

"It's the beach," Cindy said, her enthusiasm making her sound ten years younger.

Sara was relieved as well. That relief became excitement when she saw the running lights of a boat moored offshore. She headed for the boat, her leg hurting a little bit less, her energy level kicking up several degrees.

"Do we have to swim to it?"

"No, Cindy. The Captain will use the dinghy again."

The dinghy was a sixteen foot inflatable, shaped like a large U. It sat five. When they'd arrived at the island, it took two trips to get everyone from the boat to the shore. Sara listened for the outboard motor, but the lake was quiet.

"Maybe he just got here," Tyrone said.

"Or maybe he's already here."

Sara spun around. Captain Prendick stood on the sand. Sara's joy in seeing him was immediately dampened when she saw the pistol in his hand.

It was pointed at her.

PART IV
SOWING

When Edward Prendick was a little boy, he wanted to be rich. He didn't want it for himself, though better clothes and new toys would have been nice. He wanted the money for his mother.

His father died in a car accident three days after he was born. Since the day Prendick learned to crawl he'd listened to his mother talk about *making ends meet* and *pinching pennies* and *buying happiness* and *the root of all evil.* Money made the world go around, and the Prendicks never seemed to have any.

Mom worked in a snack cake factory. She made barely enough to get by, so when Prendick was old enough he helped supplement her income by taking whatever work he could get. Supermarkets, fast food, construction, retail, delivery, landscaping—Prendick had done it all. Most of the money went to Mom. The rest went into a savings account.

When he was in his thirties, he had enough for a down payment on a boat. Finally self-employed after a lifetime of working for others, he was able to earn enough to help Mom even more, and she retired to Social Security, a decent pension, and regular checks from her son.

Then the economy tanked. Mom's former employer went bankrupt, taking her pension with it. Prendick's business also took a hit, and he was barely able to make payments on his boat, let alone help Mom.

Two weeks after Medicare dropped her for missing a payment, Mom was diagnosed with cancer. Prendick had no way to pay for her treatment. Even if he sold his boat, it wouldn't be enough to cover the surgery, let alone the chemotherapy and radiation.

Prendick vowed to do whatever he could to help his mother. He let the word get out that he would use his boat for any purpose at all, no questions asked.

That's how he got hooked up with Dr. Plincer. And now Prendick was in so deep, he didn't see how he could ever get unhooked.

Captain Prendick hated doing this, but the thought of Mom at home, needing her next chemo treatment, steeled his resolve.

"Drop the flare gun, Mrs. Randhurst."

"Captain, what are—"

He fired. The bullet went high over Sara's head, but the sound was so loud she staggered backward.

"Drop it. I have orders to take you to the prison. If you don't want to come willingly, I was told to shoot you in the leg and leave you for the ferals."

Sara dropped the flare gun. "You work for Dr. Plincer."

Prendick tried to sound tougher than he felt. "I'm his supply man. He needs something, he pays me to get it for him. Now start heading up the shore. Anyone tries to run, they're a cannibal snack."

"What do we do?" Cindy whispered.

Sara, whom Prendrick recalled was so lovely on the trip over, now looked like she'd been chewed on and spat out. "Do what he says, Cindy."

They began to march back the way they came. Again, Prendick felt a pang of remorse. Again, he thought about his mother and pushed the remorse down.

"You know you're taking us to our deaths," Sara said, over her shoulder.

"Maybe. Of maybe you'll just wind up crazy with a taste for other people."

"If it's money you want..."

Prendick hesitated. They always wound up trying to bribe him. If only they could.

"I'll listen to any offer, but the problem is the pay-off. You can promise me money, but then go to the police when we get back to the mainland."

"I could make a bank transfer. All I need is a working phone."

"Again, what's to stop you from going to the authorities? I'd love to take your money, really I would, Mrs. Randhurst. But I can't figure out how to make it work."

Even if he somehow managed to take it after she died, it could still be traced back to him. And with Prendick in jail, what would happen to Mom?

Sara stopped walking and stared at Prendick. She pushed her hair behind her ear.

"Maybe, maybe I can offer you something else."

He sighed, feeling bad for her. "I get that offer a lot, too. But there's still the law thing. If I let you go, I'll get in trouble. Plus, I really do need the money." He paused, not expecting sympathy, but feeling the need to unburden himself. "It's for my mother. She needs cancer treatment."

Sara took another look at the water, then began to walk slowly toward Prendick.

"I'm sorry about your mother, Captain. Maybe I can convince you I won't say anything."

Prendick shook his head. "You're an attractive lady, Mrs. Randhurst. But I wouldn't feel right about it. Besides, having to hold a gun on a woman while I make love to her isn't exactly a turn on."

"I'll hold it for you," Tyrone said.

"Nice try, kid. But the answer is no. Besides, I don't want you thinking that you just need to stall me until the Coast guard gets here." Prendick pinched his nostrils together. "*Mrs. Randhurst, this is the Coast Guard. We have been informed of your situation. Estimated time of arrival is nineteen minutes."*

Prendick watched Sara deflate.

"Don't blame yourself," Prendick said. "The radio I gave you was broken. Only worked on my frequency. If it matters any, I'm sorry. I wish there was some other way."

In a burst of anger, Sara unclipped the walkie-talkie from her belt and pitched it at him. She missed by two feet. He bent down and picked it up, keeping the gun on her the whole time.

"I told you to pick another island, Mrs. Randhurst. I tried to insist. But you wanted to come here. Now turn around and get to walking. Please."

"You're a bastard," Sara said, her words dripping venom.

"True. But I love my mother, and I promised I'd do anything for her."

"You think this is what she'd want?" Sara said. "You killing people?"

"I don't do any of the killing. I'm just a delivery man, and I think, deep down, I'm a good person. But I will shoot you and leave you here if you don't keep walking. Point the flashlight forward, and keep your mouth shut."

They were pretty much quiet after that. Prendick had walked this route enough times that he didn't need a compass, even at night. But he did keep his eyes and ears peeled for the feral people. Those primitives seemed to respect his guns, but they'd been getting bolder lately, sometimes even following him from only a few yards away. They scared the crap out of Prendick. He'd seen the aftermath of some of their feasts. The nightmares were so bad he had to borrow Mom's prescription sleep medication.

But from what Prendick could gather, the things that went on at Doctor Plincer's prison were a thousand times worse.

When they arrived at the entrance to the prison, Prendick tossed the girl his key, instructing her to put it in the lock. It took both women, and the boy, to tug the heavy iron door open.

The hinges squealed, the equivalent of a lunch bell for the cannibals. Prendick quickly scanned the forest for movement, then ushered the group inside. It was dark, quiet.

"Point the flashlight to your right, Mrs. Randhurst. See those first three cells? Each of you get in one."

They followed orders. Prendick wondered why the people he took here were always so docile. None of them ever fought back, or tried to run. Maybe because they truly didn't believe this was going to be the end. Or maybe because the prison was old and scary, and the cells seemed like a safer alternative to running off alone into the darkness. Or perhaps they were just tired of fighting and had accepted their fate. Like cows marching into the slaughterhouse.

Prendick checked each cell door, made sure they were locked.

"Can't you at least let the kids go?" Sara said, barely whispering.

"I'm sorry, Mrs. Randhurst."

"You're a monster. Your mother would be so ashamed of you."

Prendick didn't have a reply to that. He tucked the gun into his pants and left the prison, tugging the huge door closed behind him.

A monster? Me? No. I'm just an average guy, doing the best I can.

Those things in the woods? They're the monsters.

Halfway back to the beach, Prendick heard something in the woods. He stopped, listening, and there was only the sound of crickets. But when he started to walk again, the sound repeated.

Those damn wild people?

Last time he'd dropped off supplies, two of them had come right up to him, waving sticks and hooting like monkeys. He shot at them a few times, scared them off.

If they were following him now, he'd do the same thing. Or something even more serious. Prendick had never taken a life, but he would if he had to. He wasn't some rube, unable to defend himself. If cornered, he knew he could fight back.

He gripped his pistol and dared those bastards to try something.

There was no way in hell any cannibals were going to get the jump on him. Guaranteed.

* * *

Tyrone kicked the iron bars again. That made fifty-eight times. Each impact made his right hand throb. He lifted his leg once more, going for fifty-nine.

He'd never seen a prison like this before, and Tyrone had some jail experience. These cells were the size of his walk-in shower at his mom's house. There were dozens of them, all lined up next to each other, in a large room that smelled like a basement where the sewer line backed up.

Cindy was in the cage to his right. Sara to his immediate left. There was also someone else locked up, a few rows back. Tyrone could hear rough breathing, see the outline of a person curled up on the floor of the cell, but it was too dark to see who it was, and Sara's mini-flashlight beam didn't reach that far. Repeated calls to the mystery figure provoked no response.

The bars, and the locks, looked older than hell. This was probably the civil war prison Martin had talked about in his campfire story. Regardless of age, the iron was still solid, and the bars didn't budge an inch, even after kicking on them for half an hour.

And if this place wasn't dank and scary enough, somewhere else in the building, someone was screaming like mad. He was pretty sure it was Laneesha.

Tyrone tried hard not to think about what was happening to Laneesha, what they were doing to her. But as bad as Tyrone felt for his friend, what terrified him even more was the thought that he and Cindy would be next in line for the same treatment.

He kicked the door again, feeling the shock run up his leg and jar his burned hand, the clang reverberating across the room and fading away.

"It'll be dawn soon," Cindy said. "It's getting brighter."

Tyrone stared through the bars to a window in the brick wall. It was open to the outside, and had more iron bars set in it, like an old-fashioned Wild West jail. Still looked pretty dark out, but he could make out the barest glimmer of pink.

Sara hadn't said anything since the captain left. Before then she was all spit and fire, ready to throw down. Now she looked like a beat dog. Tyrone wondered if his court-appointed caregiver had finally reached the limits of her endurance.

He used the mini-flashlight to check the bars again. No progress.

All things considered, this was turning out to be a pretty shitty camping trip.

Tyrone reared back to kick again when someone mumbled, "Lester..."

It was a male voice, coming from across the room. The person in the cell.

"Hey!" Cindy shouted. "Who are you?"

Tyrone shushed her. While he was curious who this guy was, he didn't want to attract any unwanted attention. And this island seemed to be full of folks looking to pay unwanted attention.

"Martin..." the man said again.

That single word seemed to rouse Sara from her stupor. She stood up and gripped the bars.

"Martin? Is that you, Martin?"

"Sara? Frick...where am I?"

Tyrone recognized the voice. *Tom.*

"Tom, we're in a civil war prison. Are you okay?"

"I'm...sleepy. Everything is all weird looking. Tilted-like."

"Can you remember how you got here? You mentioned Martin. Was he with you?" Sara's voice sounded awfully desperate.

"I don't know. It's fuzzy. I remember...I was with Lester...aw, frick! My frickin' finger!"

Tom began to whimper. Tyrone had no idea what Tom had been through, but he didn't feel much sympathy for him. That kid needed to man up.

"Tom, please, tell me what happened. Do you know where Martin and Jack are?"

"Martin." Sniffle. "Martin saved me." Sniffle. "From Lester. Poor little Jack."

"Where's Jack, Tom?"

"I dunno."

"How did you get here, Tom?"

"We were... we were looking for you. Followed those orange thingies—the ribbons—on the trees. To get back to camp. But then we found these huge piles of bones."

The lights went on, surprising Tyrone and making him flinch. Footsteps echoed across the concrete floors, and Tyrone followed the sound, his eyes finally landing on—

"Martin!" Sara made a happy, squealing noise, reaching through her bars for her husband. Martin rushed to her, holding her arms.

"Sara!" Tom yelled.

Tyrone watched, unable to do anything, as Martin dug a syringe out of his pocket, jabbed it into Sara's arm, and pressed the plunger.

"Martin? Wha..."

Sara fell to her knees, then onto her side.

Cindy said, "Martin? What are you doing?"

But Tyrone knew. He knew in his gut.

"You one of the bad guys, ain't you?"

Martin smiled at Tyrone, walked over to him. "Bad as they come, *brutha*."

Tyrone lunged at Martin, his left hand slipping through the bars, trying to grab the man's neck. Martin stood just out of reach.

"You need to save your strength, Tyrone. Trust me. You'll need it."

"You son of a bitch."

Martin turned away, taking a key from his pocket and unlocking Sara's cell.

"He did that to me, too," Tom whined. "Jabbed me with a needle and knocked me out."

"Too little too late, dumb ass," Tyrone said.

Martin crouched down, pulled Sara's arm over his shoulder, then hefted her up in a fireman's carry.

"Martin?" Cindy's voice was meek, disbelieving.

Martin glanced at her. "Let me say what a distinct displeasure it has been working with you pathetic little fuck-ups. You're going to die today. Die in more pain than you can possibly imagine. And you know what, Cindy? Not a single person in the world is going to care."

Martin winked, then carried Sara out of the room.

Cindy began to cry. Tyrone had no idea what to do. So he reached through the bars with his left hand, held Cindy's, and squeezed.

"I care," he said.

But for some reason that made her cry even harder.

. . .

Sara opened her eyes. Her head was muddled, thoughts groggy, her brain floating in a state between sleep and awareness.

Then she remembered Martin stabbing her with that needle, and all at once she was on full alert, processing her situation. She was on her side, on an old cot that smelled like mildew and dried sweat. Sara tried to sit up, but discovered she was hogtied; hands behind her back, the same rope snaking down her legs and securing her ankles.

Sara looked around. She was in a room, well lit and relatively warm, with a lingering scent of lemon air freshener masking something rank. The gray stone walls told her she was still in the prison, and the nearest wall had shackles hanging from it by a large metal bolt.

The wall was covered with reddish-brown stains.

Near the far wall was a wooden dresser with eight drawers. Next to that was a table. Sara craned her neck to see what was on top, and saw a variety of power tools, including a portable drill with a large bit.

On the other side of the room, there was a wheelchair, and a pegboard, on which a wicked assortment of knives and saws hung. Next to that…

An old wooden chest, with Jack's baby sling resting on top.

"Good morning, sunshine."

Martin walked into view. He looked happier than he had in a long time.

"Martin, where's Jack? What's going—"

His hand lashed out, hard and fast, slapping Sara on her right cheek and rocking her head back. Sara felt the blood rush to her face, then the inevitable sting.

"Don't be stupid, Sara. You must have figured it out by now."

Sara took a moment, until she was sure she could speak without breaking down. The betrayal was so unexpected, so absolute, she felt she had to make sense of it.

It hit her all at once, and she understood.

"I see it in your eyes," Martin said. "You finally get it. Please. Enlighten me."

Her voice was soft, and sounded hollow. "When Joe went missing. You were with him, on his boat. You came here. Martin… where's our son?"

"Finish the story, then I'll tell you."

Sara felt like she was listening to someone else talk, even though the words came from her mouth. "Plincer must have gotten you both. The cannibals brought you to him."

"Lester got us, actually. Back then there weren't nearly as many of the ferals, and they weren't organized."

Martin pulled up a folding chair, set it up near the bed.

"Did you know it was Plincer's Island?" Sara felt like she was teeter-tottering between depression and hysteria.

"No. What I said in my campfire story was true. Joe and I and six others. You were actually supposed to come with, do you remember? We were dating at the time, but you were under the weather. But I swear, I *do* hold that against you."

He sat down. Sara said nothing. This was too much, too fast.

"One of the women actually did get seasick. And we did beach the boat. And the cannibals did attack. Joe and I got away, but Lester found us. Took us back to the Doc."

Martin rubbed his eyes. They were tinged with red, like they always got without his Goniosol medication. The holes in his cheeks had stitches in them.

"Plincer made you evil," she whispered.

"That's not quite how it works. The procedure enhances the parts of the brain that process aggression. The doctor simply enlarged these portions, making violent acts not only more appealing, but necessary. Sort of like the sex drive, except this is the violence drive."

Martin lashed out again, slapping her harder this time. Sara's cheek burned.

"Doing that to you, it gave me a huge rush. I can feel the serotonin spike, my dopamine receptors feasting on it. Better than any high I've ever known. And especially sweet, since I've wanted to do that to you since the day we married."

Sara couldn't help the tears now, but she managed to keep from sobbing.

"The orange ribbons on the trees…"

Martin nodded. "That was me. After I did my disappearing act at the campsite, I changed the ribbons to lead us to the prison. The next morning, I was going to lead everyone there, and we'd be met by Lester and Prendick. It was supposed to be nice and easy. No running around in the dark. Nobody dying until they had to. But those feral fuckers got the jump on me. I was so caught up in playing Mr. Nice Guy Martin, telling scary stories, I forgot to take the gun in my backpack. You really did save my life, Sara. Allow me to thank you for that."

He hit her again, this time with a closed fist. Sara had been expecting it, though, and turned her head in time, so his knuckles met the top of her skull.

"Bitch," he said, shaking his hand and then blowing on his knuckles. Then he laughed. "I'd feel that if I wasn't on painkillers. You're going to pay for that."

Sara's eyes blurred with tears, her nose ran like a faucet, and her voice was a pitiful wail. Even though she didn't want to, she glanced again at the trunk, Jack's sling draped across the lid.

"Where's Jack, Martin? What have you done with our son?"

"Our precious little Jack? Are you worried you'll never hold him again? Never gaze into his adorable little face and tickle him to make him laugh?"

Martin leaned over, his face inches from hers.

"Maybe later I'll let you hold his tiny little corpse."

Sara looked for the lie in his eyes. All she saw was malice and glee.

Something inside her shattered.

"You didn't... Martin... no..."

"You want to hear what happened to the others? Plincer gave Laneesha to Subject 33. He's had her for a while now. I doubt there's very much left of her. He's got some sort of device he uses on them. Personally, it gives me the creeps. And Georgia? Bad girl, that one. We both knew she was faking her remorse. I think she was hiding more than that. We're taking good care of her."

"Martin," Sara was only mouthing her words now, without any sound coming out. "Why?"

"Why do you think I married you so soon after Joe's disappearance? Love? I never loved you. I used you as a cover. Marrying you was the perfect way to indulge in my particular tastes without being detected." He winked. "Plus, I couldn't have opened the Center without you."

Sara realized where this was going, and she shook her head. "No..."

Martin smiled. "Do you really think we've had eleven runaways? Wasn't that statistically high?"

He stood, walking over to the dresser. Keeping his eyes on Sara, he opened the top drawer.

"Remember Chereese Graves? One of our first court-appointed cases at the Center. Also our first runaway."

Martin reached into the drawer. Sara didn't want to watch, but she couldn't turn away. He pulled out what looked like a brown shirt. But then he held it up, letting it unroll to full length.

Sara gagged, throwing up on the cot mattress.

"Not my best work," Martin said. "Skinning isn't easy. Especially when the person is still alive. All that flinching and bleeding. That's why there are all the holes on this one. Take a look."

Martin tossed the skin across the room. It glided, almost like a kite, then landed on Sara.

The hair was still attached, and it fell on Sara's chest. She shook it away, and it slid across her neck. The texture was stiff, rough, not unlike burlap, and it carried an odor of salt and beef jerky. Gravity took the hide over the edge of the bed, and Sara tried to twist away from it, watching as the legs and feet—complete with toenails—fell onto the floor.

"Poorly done. I know. But I got better, as time went on. Here's Jenna Hamilton."

Martin tossed another skin at her. "And Rich Ardmore." He threw that too.

Sara managed to dodge the first, squirming backward on the cot, but Rich landed directly on her face. She screamed, shaking her head back and forth, able to see Martin through a hole that was actually Rich's mouth.

Martin tossed another at her.

"Here's Miranda Walker." The skin landed on Sara's legs. "And remember Henry Perez, liked to start fires? I gave him a nice, charred finish."

Sara freed herself of Rich, only to have Henry smack her in the head. He smelled like burned bacon. She managed to scootch back into the corner of the bed and get onto her knees. The skins piled up around her like tangled sheets.

"Here's one you were particularly fond of, from just last month. Tonya Johnson. All set to straighten out her life, start fresh. Then I brought her here. She doesn't smell so fresh now."

Tonya's skin hit Sara hard, with a slapping sound. It was still moist, and left a pink, wet splotch on Sara's sweater.

"Martin... no more..."

"No more? But we're just getting started, Sara honey. I've been forced to live a lie with you these past few years. Ever since the procedure, do you know how difficult it has been to restrain myself? To push down my urges? I had to pretend to be a responsible, upstanding adult, a caring psychologist, and a decent husband, while all the time *thirsting* for my next opportunity to cut someone apart."

Martin rushed at her, making Sara cringe.

"I... I love you, Martin."

His smile was demonic. "And I hate you, Sara. Hate you with every fiber in my body. Hate you so much, in fact, that I've got something really special planned for you. Remember your summer at Aunt Alison's?"

The memories came hurtling back. Being nine years old, locked in that horrible trunk.

"It took a while to find the right one, but you told me the details of the story so many times I think I found a pretty good approximation."

Martin grabbed her with both hands, one tangling up in her hair, the other tugging on her sweater. He yanked her off the bed, and she hit the floor on her knees, hard. Then he began to drag her toward—

"Martin... oh no... please don't..."

"It'll be just like old times, Sara. A blast from the past."

He pulled her to the old chest in the corner of the room, and popped open the top.

Sara didn't want to look, afraid to see her child dead inside. The trunk was empty.

And for her, that was just as terrifying.

"Nice and dark in there. Dark and cramped."

Sara struggled, contorting her body, not letting him get a firm grip. But he did, yanking the rope so hard her shoulders felt like they were about to pop out of their sockets, lifting her up, and—*oh jesus, oh god no*—dumping her face-first into the trunk.

The lid closed, catapulting Sara into absolute darkness.

She screamed; a muffled, constricted sound that was so intimately familiar to her.

Martin knocked on the top of the trunk.

"So here's what's going to happen, Sara. I'm going to leave you in there. I don't know for how long. Maybe a few days. I'm going to make you wait for so long that you'll be happy when I finally open it up to kill you. That's what you used to tell me, those nights when you couldn't get to sleep. You told me you were so scared you wanted to die rather than stay in there any longer. How fucked up is that?"

Sara looked all around, seeking a crack in the chest, a seam, something that might allow a sliver of light in. But there was only darkness.

"I'm going to make you wait even longer, Sara."

No. Please not that.

"Then when I finally take you out, I'm going to show you my knife collection. Do you remember Cousin Timmy?"

Sara felt like the world was spinning. She found it hard to breathe.

"Remember the knife he had? The hunting knife, with the jagged back? I've got one of those, too. Can you picture it, Sara? You used to get woozy when you saw a steak knife whenever we went out to eat. Can you imagine Timmy's big ole survival knife?"

Sara could imagine it. It was the only thing in her head, blocking out everything else.

"Well, no need to answer me right now. You've got plenty of time to think about it. And then, later, much later, you can tell me how it feels when I try it on you."

"Please," Sara whispered.

"Did you say something, hon?"

"Please. Martin. Don't leave me in here."

"Would you prefer I let you out, get started on you right now?"

Sara couldn't believe her response, but the word left her mouth. "Yes."

She waited for Martin to answer. The seconds ticked away.

"Martin?"

There was only silence. Silence, and smothering darkness.

"Martin!"

But just like Cousin Timmy, he was gone.

Georgia opened her eyes. They were dry, raw, like someone had rubbed sand into her tear ducts. She closed them again, touching her eyelids, and that made her realize the paralysis had worn off.

She was in a warm bed, beneath a thick blanket. With a yawn she sat up, the blanket falling away, exposing her bare breasts. Georgia saw she was naked. It didn't bother her at all, and she wondered why. Much as she tried to delude herself, Georgia knew she had body image problems. She didn't want anyone to see her without clothes on.

But her appearance no longer mattered to her. In fact, for the first time ever, she felt proud of her body. She slipped out from under the covers and padded over to the window. Dawn had come, flooding the outdoors with light. Georgia walked past, coming to a dresser with a mirror on top. She stopped, stared at her saggy belly, her large hips.

But instead of shame, Georgia felt strangely proud. More than proud. She felt strong, powerful. Like a completely new person, one who could conquer the world. It was as if something dormant inside her had opened its eyes and awoken. She let the fantasy take hold, Georgia sitting on a throne perched up on top of a mountain, and beneath her on all sides, crosses. Crosses with people nailed to them, screaming and begging for mercy. Crucifixions as far as she could see. Hundreds. Thousands. Millions.

Then the fantasy switched. The crucified morphed into the impaled. Georgia remembered reading about Vlad the Impaler, how he would place people on tall wooden stakes. Gravity, and strug-gling, would cause his victims to slide down the pole, piercing organs and tissue until it eventually came out of their mouths.

The image made her tingle all over.

Power was something she'd always aspired to. She had mas-tered its younger sibling, control. Georgia's whole life had been about control. Controlling her emotions, manipulating others, keeping secrets.

But power felt better than control. A million times better. While control was about maintaining order, power was about being in-vincible. The old Georgia was a weakling. This new Georgia was unstoppable.

She rubbed her eyes again, considered the procedure Doctor Plincer had performed on her. Not a pleasant memory, but the pain was gone, replaced by an overwhelming sense of self. With this newfound feeling of absolute power came an overwhelming urge to hurt somebody. Anybody. Hurt them horribly.

Georgia walked to the metal door. Locked. She scowled, irri-tated that she was stuck there, unable to indulge in her newfound desire. Then she noticed the package next to the door.

It was the size of a shoe box, wrapped like a birthday present in bright red paper with a big white bow on top. Next to it was a smaller box, wrapped in the same paper. A card taped to the top of the larger present read:

TO GEORGIA GIRL
FROM LESTER

Georgia plucked off the bow and tore into the large package first, revealing a steel cage. Inside, complete with matted gray fur and tiny black eyes, was the biggest rat she'd ever seen.

Rather than flinch, which is something the old Georgia would have done, the new Georgia eyed the creature with something akin to hunger. It was so weak. So vulnerable.

She opened the slim package next. Inside were a roll of duct tape and a pair of long, sharp scissors. There was another note at the bottom of the box.

Georgia smiled.

How did Lester know this was just what I needed? What a thoughtful man.

A rat this large wouldn't die right away. If Georgia restrained herself, it would be good for a few hours of entertainment.

"Hello, little friend," Georgia told the rat, reaching for the latch with greedy fingers. "Would you like to play?"

Cindy opened her eyes. She hadn't been asleep. Just sitting with her back against the bars, resting, conserving her energy. Exhausted as she was, Cindy didn't know if she would ever be able to sleep again.

Or if she'd have the chance to.

There was light coming in through the window, enough to illuminate the cells. She glanced over at Tyrone, who was staring at her. They were still holding hands.

"How you doin'?" he asked.

"This motel sucks. No room service. No cable TV. And the bathroom is seriously lacking."

"You need to pee, I can turn away."

She shifted her bad shoulder and gave his left hand a squeeze, regretting it when she saw him grimace.

"I'm okay. You wanna hear something funny?"

"Hells yeah. Could use somethin' funny right about now."

"I haven't thought about meth in hours. This is the first time, for as long as I can remember, that I haven't had any urge to get high."

"Cool. Sounds like you beat it."

"You think?"

"Yeah. You're strong. I always knew that about you."

Cindy felt herself blush, but it was a good feeling, not an embarrassing one.

"How's your other hand?"

"Hurts. It started to scab over, but now every time I move it, starts to bleed again."

"I'm sorry."

"Won't stop me from beatin' the fuck out of whoever opens my cell door."

Cindy smiled, gave his hand a much gentler squeeze.

"We gonna get outta here, Cindy. I promise."

"Good morning."

Cindy and Tyrone looked toward the staircase at the far end of the room, following the sound of that familiar, effeminate voice.

Tom noticed too, and began to make a high pitched, keening sound.

Lester strolled up to them slowly, casually. He was holding a broomstick in his left hand. His right hand—the one he'd bitten earlier—was wrapped in a bandage.

"Today is a big day. The meeting with the important people. Lester needs the boys and the girl to behave."

He reached into his bib overalls and removed a pair of handcuffs.

"Lester wants to know the black boy's name."

Tyrone said nothing. Lester raised up his broomstick, and Cindy saw it had a nail sticking out of the end. He aimed it at Tyrone.

"His name is Tyrone," she quickly said. "He's Tyrone, I'm Cindy."

Lester tossed the handcuffs into Tyrone's cell. They made a jingling sound when they hit the floor.

"The Tyrone boy needs to put the handcuffs on, behind his back."

"Fuck you, you ugly, rat-toothed mutha fucker."

Before Cindy had a chance to yell, "No!" Lester had jabbed Tyrone on the hip with the nail. Tyrone recoiled, making a small grunting noise.

"The Tyrone boy will put on the handcuffs."

"You hear me the first time?" Tyrone said through his teeth. "Fuck. You."

Lester jabbed him again, this time aiming for Tyrone's crotch. The teen shifted and managed to deflect the strike, instead getting pierced in the thigh.

"Tyrone, baby, honey, please put them on." Cindy ran her hand over his head, willing him to listen. "Please, Tyrone, for me, just do it."

Lester raised the stick again. Tyrone scowled at him, then reached for the handcuffs.

"I'll help you." Cindy put her arms through the bars, cinching the cuffs loosely on his wrists.

"Now the Cindy girl will put on the handcuffs."

Lester tossed her a pair, and she dutifully snicked them on behind her back.

"Let Lester see."

She scooted over, showing him. Lester walked off, moving to Tom's cell.

"The Tom boy puts on the handcuffs."

The cuffs jangled the concrete floor.

"My finger, it's, it's all messed up," Tom said. He had the hiccups. "I can't put them on."

Lester thrust out the broomstick, poking Tom in the stomach.

"The Tom boy puts on the handcuffs."

"Jesus! Stop it! I can't do it!"

Lester jabbed him again, this time in the leg.

"The Tom boy puts on the handcuffs."

Tom reached for the cuffs, then moaned. "I can't get them open."

Lester hit him in the ribs this time.

"The Tom boy puts on the handcuffs."

"Tom!" Cindy had her face pressed to the bars. "Tom, just put them on!"

"I'm trying." *Hic.* "I... I can't."

Lester stabbed Tom in the ribs, and he made a sound like tires screeching.

"The Tom boy puts on the handcuffs."

"Tom, for God's sake!" Cindy yelled. "Put on the goddamn cuffs!"

Slowly, painfully slowly, Tom managed to lock one bracelet across his left wrist, and get his hands behind his back. Cindy watched, intent but also repulsed at the site of his damaged finger.

"You can do it, Tom," she urged. "Don't give up."

Tom was shaking like mad, still hiccupping, but he managed to finesse the second cuff on.

"Show Lester."

Tom got to his knees, letting the man see his hands. Lester raised the stick again.

"No!" Cindy cried.

In rapid succession, Lester jabbed Tom four more times. He was raising back for a fifth when Cindy said, "Lester."

Lester turned to look at her. He was grinning, a thin streak of drool running down his chin.

"Don't," Tyrone told Cindy under his breath.

But it was too late. Lester was coming over.

"Is the Cindy girl jealous that the Tom boy is getting all the attention?"

Cindy looked at Lester, then at the nail on the stick, which was glistening with Tom's blood.

"I just, uh, had a question, Lester. You said we're meeting important people today. Who are we meeting?"

"It's a surprise," Lester said.

"But these people are important?"

"Very important."

"And you said we need to behave. But if you keep poking us with that stick, we won't be able to behave. We won't even be able to move. Is that what you want?"

Lester seemed to think about it, then slowly shook his head.

"No. That wouldn't be good."

Then, lightening quick, he thrust out the stick, stabbing Cindy in the arm.

"But one little poke can't hurt," Lester said.

Then the giant walked away, across the room, back up the stairs.

Cindy clutched her arm, which felt like she'd been kicked by a mule, and stared out the window fully believing that this was going to be the last sunrise she ever saw.

. . .

Dr. Plincer opened his eyes. He stretched, yawned, removed his earplugs, put on his glasses, and then forced himself out of bed and into the bathroom, where he sat down on the toilet to urinate. Running water and electricity were the only two utilities on the island, and both were limited. There were only three toilets and four sinks in the entire prison, and the water they used was rust-colored and tasted muddy.

It was a big day today, so he showered. The electric generator used a lot of gasoline, and one of the biggest power hogs was the water heater, which Plincer kept on the lowest setting. The doctor stoically braved the lukewarm water, toweled off quickly, and then stood in front of the mirror to put on his face.

First he shaved, never an easy task because of the extra bumps and divots. Then he spent ten minutes building up layers of scar putty, filling in holes and smoothing over rough edges. When he was finished, a bit of pancake make-up to blend. He checked his profile, found it to be suitable, and then dressed in slacks, a fresh shirt, and a clean lab coat.

The dart gun was a pistol model, not accurate more than five feet, but able to be fired using just one hand. Plincer made sure it was loaded, and he put in a fresh CO_2 cartridge. Then it was off to make breakfast.

The prison hallway was scream-free. Either Subject 33 had been unable to restrain himself and had killed his playmate too soon, or he was having a rest. Plincer was grateful for the silence.

There was no better way to start a day than a cup of hot coffee and some quiet contemplation.

He used bottled water for the coffee, and while it brewed he scrambled ten eggs in a large bowl. Plincer then took a loaf of bread out of the freezer, microwaved it until thawed, and dumped the slices into the eggs. As the bread soaked, he heated up the large cast iron skillet on the stove top.

The secret to perfect French toast was timing. Timing, and just a dash of cinnamon and sugar. When the skillet was hot enough, he gave it a spritz of non-stick spray, then arranged the first four slices on the pan using a spatula. He flipped them at the exact right time, and took them off the heat when both sides were golden brown but the insides still soft. Plincer repeated this process, sipping coffee and musing about a neighbor he once had, a bitter old man who used to yell whenever anyone stepped on his lawn. Perhaps if the neighbor had taken pleasure from the simple things in life, such as making a nice breakfast, he wouldn't have been so unpleasant.

Doctor Plincer stocked the cart with the tray of toast, plates, glasses, a carton of orange juice, napkins, some plastic knives and forks, tiny carafes of maple syrup, and some dog biscuits.

Getting it up the spiral staircase was a slow affair, one step at a time, making sure nothing fell off, but Plincer looked forward to it. Frankly, it was the only exercise he got during the day.

He pushed the cart to Subject 33's room at the end of the hallway, checked the slot to make sure he wasn't in the antechamber, and took the dart pistol out of his lab coat.

"Good morning. Breakfast is here."

Plincer waited, and as the seconds ticked away he tried to recall Subject 33's name. It would have been on the tip of Plincer's tongue, if Lester hadn't bitten that off. Something beginning with the letter T...

Thomspson, maybe? No, that was the neighbor's name, the one so overprotective of his lawn.

After a minute or so, Subject 33 put his hands through the slot in the second door. They were caked with dried blood.

"One plate or two?"

Subject 33 held out two fingers.

"Excellent."

Doctor Plincer filled two plates with French toast, and set them on the floor of the antechamber, along with two glasses of OJ, forks, and syrup.

Taylor! That's his name. Some sort of former special op soldier.

Plincer chuckled, pleased to have remembered. After locking up, he pushed the cart down the hall to Martin's room.

Neither Martin, nor his guest, was in. Scratch that—Plincer heard someone whimpering inside the chest. A part of him wanted to open the chest, because he so rarely prepared meals for guests and a small part of him wanted to hear a bit of praise for his cooking. But whatever Martin was doing to her was Martin's business, and the doctor wasn't going to interfere.

Subject 33 was enhanced to the point where he was impossible to control. Plincer was able to control Lester somewhat since his enhancement, but the alterations he'd made to his teeth, along with his freakish height, made it difficult for him to blend in to the general populace. But Martin; Martin was the embodiment of everything Plincer was trying to do.

The doctor had taken a normal man and made him into a psychopath. Martin was truly evil, but also able to keep his tastes hidden and function within society. Function at a very high level. He'd been successful in maintaining both a job and a marriage, while keeping his killing secret.

Plincer didn't want to do anything to annoy Martin, so he moved along.

Next it was on to Lester's room. The tall man was sleeping, as was his pet.

"Lester, my friend. It's time to start your day. We've got a big one ahead of us."

In one fluid motion Lester levered himself out of bed and picked up the box of dog biscuits. He threw two into the pet crate, and popped one into his own mouth.

"Lester, I made French toast. I wish you wouldn't ruin your appetite with those things."

"The biscuits help support healthy teeth and bones," Lester said, quoting the line on the box. "Lester likes healthy teeth."

"Do you have any idea where Martin is?"

Lester shook his head.

"After breakfast, meet me in the lab. We have to go over a few last minute things. And perhaps it's time to change your pet's hay. I believe it's getting a bit stinky in here."

Doctor Plincer rolled the cart further down the hallway, to Georgia's room. He paused, fearful that he'd set his hopes too high. If the procedure had been successful, Plincer could brag that he'd finally perfected the formula. If not, the afternoon meeting would require a bit more finesse.

Time to find out.

He placed his ear to the door, and heard a high-pitched screeching. A good sign, or perhaps not. If Georgia was tormenting the rat Lester had given her, she'd been properly enhanced. If, however, she was eating the rat, she would have to be tranquilized and left out with the feral people.

Plincer didn't knock. He unlocked the metal security door and pushed it open with one hand, aiming the gun with the other.

Georgia was naked. The squirming, duct-taped rat in one hand. The scissors in the other. Blood was spattered on her bare breasts.

The procedure had been a success.

He pocketed the key and pulled the cart inside, the door closing behind him and locking automatically.

"Good morning. I made French toast."

Georgia stared at him, neither hostile nor fearful.

"Thank you," she said. "And thanks for what you've done to me."

If Plincer could still blush, he might have. "Yes, well, you were a perfect candidate for it, and an excellent subject. What you're doing right now, with the rodent there, do you think you might enjoy doing that same thing to a person?"

Georgia's eyes lit up. "When?"

"Sometime after breakfast. I'll come to collect you. I'm assuming it doesn't matter that you'd be doing it to one of your friends that you came to the island with."

"Those aren't my friends."

"Yes, excellent, it's a date then. Might I ask, do you like orange juice?"

"Sure."

Georgia moved slowly toward him, swaying her hips. Rather than be embarrassed by her nudity, she seemed to flaunt it. One of the added benefits of the procedure. Grandiose narcissism. Plincer raised the dart gun.

"I must ask you, tell you, to stay back. We need to establish some mutual trust first. You understand. The metaphorical roadblocks have been taken off your morals, which can lead to episodes of, overindulgence. Until I see you're able to control the appetites my procedure has enhanced, you need to keep your distance."

She nodded, running her tongue across her upper lip. "My eyes itch."

"There is a bottle of artificial tears in the bathroom, above the sink. That should relieve the redness. Let me set down your food."

He quickly made a plate for her, placing everything on the dresser.

"The door is locked," Georgia said. "Am I a prisoner?"

"It's for your own protection," Plincer said, adding *and mine too* in his head. "Once we're sure you've been successfully enhanced, you'll be able to roam freely."

Georgia made an exaggerated pout. "Don't you trust me, Dr. Plincer?"

Plincer didn't go there. "Enjoy the meal. I'll be back later."

He fumbled to put the key in the lock, glancing back at Georgia several times to make sure she wasn't sneaking up. When he finally got the door open, the girl was standing right next to him.

The doctor yelped, surprised, and tried to aim the dart gun. But Georgia had already caught his wrist, and she was strong for her size.

"Relax, Doctor. I was just going to hold open the door while you pushed out the cart."

She stood next to him, her palm on the door. Plincer thanked her and quickly hustled out of there, the door closing and locking behind him.

Doctor Plincer again faced the staircase, but going down was always easier, and the cart was considerably lighter. Then it was back to the kitchen where he set a plate for himself.

Eating was an arduous process that took some time, but Plincer enjoyed it as best he could. Food, and thumbing his nose at the scientific community with his experiments, were the only pleasures he had in life.

He cut the toast into very tiny squares, but still needed to manipulate his jaw with the hand to get it chewed enough to swallow. As he ate, he reflected on his life. Doctor Plincer believed creating psychotics was an appropriate way of saying *fuck you* to the world that had abandoned him. Money, too, played a part. Pure research was the most rewarding part of science, and his enhancement procedures were going to keep him well-heeled for the rest of his life.

But Plincer was a man of science, and he couldn't discount the possibility that vengeance, monetary concerns, and a thirst for knowledge were his only motivators. He knew, after his ordeal with Lester, that something had snapped inside of him.

At the end of the day, Plincer mused, *it might just come down to the fact that I'm insane.*

Not that it really mattered.

There were many pieces of French toast left, but no one on hand to eat them. He supposed he could toss them out a window, let the ferals find them. Or maybe give them to the children in the cells downstairs.

No. Bad idea. He didn't want them throwing up in front of the company.

In Dr. Plincer's experience, people in terrible pain sometimes threw up.

Since French toast didn't reheat well, he went with the simplest solution and tossed the leftovers into the garbage.

Such a shame, such a waste.

When the last slice hit the can, he changed his mind and fished out all the food he'd thrown away. Piling it onto a paper plate, he went to the window and tossed it through the bars.

Throwing perfectly good food away was wrong, and Plincer didn't want that on his conscience.

. . .

Captain Prendick opened his eyes. For a moment he thought he was asleep on his boat, but then the headache hit, followed swiftly by the memory of how he received it.

He'd just locked up the Randhurst woman and the two kids in Doc Plincer's prison; something he would be getting a large bonus for. Martin had asked him to stay close and ready, just in case. Prendick understood why. He hated coming to the island. When he did his monthly supply drop-off, it was during the day. Being here at night really upped the danger quotient.

He hadn't seen a single feral on his walk back to the beach. He'd heard things, but figured they feared him too much to try anything.

Then, when he was reaching into the bushes to drag out his dinghy, he got whacked from behind.

Now he was naked, lying on his back and locked in some kind of strange cage. It was in a clearing, and to his right was a bed of coals, glowing orange. Prendick had no illusions what those coals were for. He checked the other side, and could see his clothes in a pile just a few feet away on his left.

Was my gun in the pile as well?

He couldn't tell, and couldn't reach. The cage gave him no freedom to move, the bars crisscrossing his chest and back. It was sort of like being the meat in an iron sandwich.

Pendrick knew it was the ferals. It had to be. But he didn't see any of them around so he was able to control his panic. This cage had to have some kind of locking mechanism, something that didn't involve any kind of key, because those cannibals wouldn't have keys. That meant a crossbar, or some sort of lever set-up. He began to explore the bars with his fingers, seeking out the hinges. They were covered with a thick layer of charred grease.

"Hello, Prendick."

Someone was standing over him, but Prendick couldn't crane his neck back far enough to see who it was.

"Who is it? Christ, you gotta help me. Those goddamn savages are going to roast me alive. See if there's a latch on this cage."

Movement, to his right. He looked, and saw the figure walk next to him and crouch down. His face was bathed in the soft, orange light from the coals, and Prendick sighed in relief when he recognized Martin.

"It's not a cage. It's a gridiron."

"I don't give a shit what it's called, Martin. Get me out of this thing."

Martin smiled. "Now that would be counter-productive. Who do you think put you in this thing in the first place?"

Prendick didn't think that was funny at all. He knew Martin was a killer. What else could explain the many trips Martin took to the island with a companion, only to be alone when Prendick picked him up? But he also knew Martin needed him. There weren't too many don't ask/don't tell captains on Lake Huron.

"Seriously, Martin. Let me out before those freaks come back."

"Seriously, Captain Prendick. I'm the one who hit you on the head, carried you here, and put you in the gridiron. Both Doctor Plincer and I have grown tired of your escalating prices. So we decided that I would be the supplier from now on. I'll need your boat, of course. I'm assuming it's paid for, with all the money we've given you over the years. Where's the title on that, by the way?"

Prendick read Martin's face, looking for the joke, the lie. But the man looked serious.

"I haven't bought the boat yet. Most of the money the doctor gives me goes to my mother. She has cancer, and I pay for the treatment. Seriously, you have to believe me."

Martin stared at him. Prendick felt sweat break out over his entire body, despite the cool morning air.

"Martin, if you think the cost of my services is too high, I'm happy to renegotiate. Hell, I'll even throw in some freebies. Sort of like frequent flyer miles. You've been a great customer, and I don't want to lose you."

Martin moved closer. Prendick saw a glint in his blue eyes.

"Where's the title to the boat, Captain Prendick?"

"I haven't paid it off yet. I swear."

"I see. Well, we'll find out soon enough."

Martin reached down, grabbing the bottom bar of the cage. He kept his back straight and lifted with his legs, tilting the gridiron, and Prendick, onto the side. Prendick eyed the hot coals, just a simple push away.

"Martin! Wait! We can talk this out!"

"I built this gridiron myself. Always was curious to try one, after reading about them.

While it delivers some deliciously slow and agonizing deaths, it wasn't hands-on enough for my taste. So I gave it to the ferals. They've discovered a benefit beyond its intended purpose. Cooking their food. I find the whole thing rather distasteful, really. But who am I to look down my nose at their cuisine? There isn't much else to eat on this island."

Prendick felt hysteria creeping up his spine. He fought to maintain control. "Martin, please, I'm begging you. Don't do this."

"Where's that boat title, captain?"

"If I tell you, will you promise not to push me onto those coals?"

"Of course."

"Do I have your word?"

"Cross my heart."

Prendick could feel the heat rising from the coal bed. The thought of being pressed against them, unable to pull away, was the most terrifying prospect he'd ever considered.

"Behind Goldie's tank, in the safe. The combination is my birthday, three, twenty-nine, seventy. I'll even sign the title over to you."

"How gracious of you. But that won't be necessary. I'm sure I can adequately forge your signature."

Prendick felt the gridiron shift.

"Martin!" he impotently cried. "You promised!"

"I'm a killer, Captain Prendick. Certainly you could have guessed I'm a liar as well."

Prendick screamed as the gridiron tipped over, dropping him face-first onto the burning coals.

* * *

General Alton Tope opened his eyes and shut off his alarm. He'd gotten exactly two hours of sleep. Not ideal, but it would do. He rolled out of bed and went into the toilet, still a bit wobbly from the scotch.

He brushed his teeth, shaved, combed his hair, and dressed in his uniform, perfectly timing the completion of the Windsor knot on his tie with the knock at the door.

The men he allowed into his room were under Tope's command, but the delivery they'd brought him was unofficial. In fact, records would show that both men were currently stationed at another base.

General Tope didn't like to play it this way, but his hands were tied. He'd made a mistake recently—a minor one at that—and in order to do what was right it had to be under the radar.

"Show me," Tope ordered.

One of the men placed a metal briefcase on the bed, popped the latches, and opened the lid.

Tope stared. He didn't so much as flinch, but he was shocked that something worth so much money was so small. The General told his men to leave, so entranced by what was on the bed that he wasn't even aware he'd used the word *please,* as if making a request rather than a command.

The men saluted, then turned on their heels. Tope paid them no mind as they left. There were also papers in the briefcase, but the General didn't bother checking them, knowing they were in order. He closed the lid and shook his head, marveling at what some people considered valuable.

But then, there were few things in the world that were portable, legally obtainable, easily salable, and were worth twenty-five million dollars.

General Tope didn't bother checking his watch because he already knew the time in his head. His plane would be leaving a little over two hours, enough time for him to carry out the legitimate orders he'd been given for the day.

He picked up the briefcase and headed out, confident that he was about to take the first step in changing the future of the USA, and by extension, the future of the world.

. . .

Laneesha opened her eyes. But she couldn't see anything, only feel a sharp yet empty throb.

That was because her eyeballs were gone.

. . .

Sara closed her eyes. She wasn't a religious person. She understood the social and psychological needs that religion sated. Apart from a few late night college gab fests with fellow psych majors fueled by wine and pot, she'd managed to avoid having to justify her godless convictions.

But locked in the trunk, relieving the biggest horror of her past and waiting to experience one that would be even worse, knowing she'd lost her kids, her husband, her son, Sara gave herself over to a higher power and prayed for death.

She prayed hard, with all she had, chanting the phrase over and over in her head until *please God let me die* became one long, infinite word, ends running into beginnings running into ends.

She tried to help God along, hyperventilating to the point of dizziness, trying to suck up the last bit of oxygen in the trunk.

letmediepleasegodletmedieplease...

When that didn't work, possibly because the trunk wasn't air tight, Sara tried holding her breath, willing her body to give up, picturing her brain cells dying and bodily functions ceasing through the sheer force of determination.

That didn't work either. Sara sobbed for a while, alternately being assaulted by terrifying memories of the past, self-hatred at her own naïveté for loving and trusting and being married to a monster, and the despair of what would happen to the rest of her kids, of what had probably happened to Jack, and the horror of the tortures yet to come. The darkness nipped away at her soul, the heat and cramps making the claustrophobia even worse than when Timmy locked her in the trunk all those years ago. The feeling of helplessness was so encompassing, so powerful, she lost all sense of anything else.

The shift was gradual. The sobbing abated, mostly out of exhaustion. The darkness remained, but became a tiny bit more bearable. Anger snuck into the mix, jockeying for position against fear and guilt. It built slowly, and Sara embraced it, fed off of it, and added a fuel she didn't have when she was nine years old; responsibility.

This wasn't just her life on the line. There were children involved. Children she'd pledged to help and protect.

And Jack had to be alive. He *had* to. As monstrous as Martin was, he wouldn't kill his son.

She had to escape.

Sara stretched out a crick in her neck, shifted her weight, and began to test her bonds. The rope was thin, nylon, the same type the ferals had used to string up Martin.

Should have let the bastard hang there.

She let the anger carry her forward, twisting her arms, trying to get some play in the rope to slip out. Her wrists became slick, first with sweat, then with blood, but the knots were simply too tight.

Then she remembered the nail clippers that she'd shoved into her back pocket while at the campsite. Were they still there, or had Martin taken them?

Sara shifted again, bending her knees to give her hands more room to work. Her fingers dug into her pocket and touched the small metal object.

Small, but packed full of hope.

They weren't the best tool for the job, and Sara couldn't see what she was doing, but she opened up the clippers and began to slowly nip away at the rope binding her left wrist.

It was slow going, and involved intense concentration. The clippers were slippery, and the repetitive motion made her fingers cramp and throb. But she kept at it, clipping a few nylon threads at a time, and after five minutes of exhausting work she was through the rope.

It freed her left arm, which was one of the greatest feelings Sara had ever experienced. But her right wrist was still tied to her legs, the multiple knots Martin had used still holding tight. Sara attacked the rope again, using her left hand. But it lacked the control, and strength, of her right, and after ten minutes she'd only gotten halfway through.

Self-doubt returned. Martin could come back any minute. He might even be in the room right now. Maybe he left her the nail clippers on purpose, seeing if she'd try to escape, waiting for her to come out. He'd fooled Sara for years without her suspecting a thing. Clearly he was capable of anything.

The darkness pressed down on Sara, getting into her nose and mouth and ears, reminding her what was going to happen.

Keep cool. Stay focused. You can do this.

She doubled her effort, fighting the cramps, imagining the clippers were a tiny alligator, relentless, tenacious, biting, biting, biting—

I'm free.

Sara didn't bother with her ankles. She turned onto her back, pressed her feet against the top of the trunk, and pushed like she was doing the mother of all leg-presses.

The trunk lid creaked, then popped open, drenching Sara in beautiful, majestic light.

She did a sit-up, looking around the room, nail clippers clenched in her hand to poke in Martin's eye if he were anywhere close.

He wasn't. The room was empty.

Sara pulled herself out of the trunk, rolling over the edge and closing the lid behind her. She inch-wormed over to the table with the tools. There, on the top, was the survival knife.

She recoiled. Martin had found a match for Timmy's knife, the one that haunted Sara's imagination. It was horrible looking, with a seven inch blade, and a serrated back that seemed capable of sawing through wood.

Even though it would have made a good weapon, Sara couldn't bring herself to touch it. Instead she took a utility knife—one with a retractable razor blade—and quickly freed her wrists and ankles. Then she grabbed Jack's sling, winding it over her shoulder.

Now to go get my kids.

Sara went to the door and carefully checked the hallway. Clear. Not knowing which way to go, she chose left, creeping alongside the wall, listening for any sounds.

One came from behind her. A toilet flush.

Sara hurried into the nearest room. It looked a lot like Martin's, with a bed and a table piled high with gore-stained tools. Along the wall were dozens of pictures, taped there. Pictures of people. Of victims. Some of them kids from the Center. Alongside the wall was a large wooden crate.

Footsteps, from the hall. Getting closer.

The table was too small to fit beneath. The bed had no dust ruffle and she'd be easily spotted. There weren't any other doors.

That left the crate. Sara rushed to it, put a leg over the side, and climbed in, pressing her belly down onto a pile of hay.

The smell hit her first, reminding her of a dog kennel.

Then she realized there was something in the crate with her.

"Uuuuuuhhhhnnnn," it said.

Sara clamped a hand over her mouth so she didn't scream. It was only a foot away from her, buried beneath the filthy straw. The thing undulated, and Sara saw a glimpse of white skin.

"Uuuuuuuhhhhhnn."

The footsteps came into the room. Sara heard them walk over to a dresser, heard the drawer open.

The thing wiggled. "Uhhhhhnnnnnn."

"Lester will clean the crate soon," said the man who belonged to the footsteps. "Lester promises."

More hay fell away, and Sara stared at something that used to be human. The eyes were gone, the limbs were gone, the face horribly scarred and yet somehow...

Familiar.

"Uhhhhhhhhhhnnn."

The torso turned toward Sara, sniffing her, squirming closer, and Sara realized who she was looking at.

My god. It's Martin's brother, Joe.

"Lester will change the bedding later. Be quiet, or Lester will get angry."

Joe opened his mouth, getting ready to wail again. With a mixture of revulsion and sadness, Sara reached over and put her hand over his mouth to keep him quiet.

It didn't keep Joe quiet. When Joe was touched, he screamed. Sara recoiled, pushing back against the side of the crate, trying to bury herself in the soiled straw as Lester's footsteps drew closer.

"The pet wants hay," Lester said. "Lester will get some hay. Along with the stick."

The crate shook—Lester giving it a kick. Then Sara heard him walk out of the room.

Sara moved fast, getting to her knees, swinging a leg over the side, and then stopping.

She looked back down at Joe's torso, pale and scarred. She couldn't leave him like this. There didn't seem to be any of Joe left in this body. The funny, outgoing man she once knew was now a pathetic, sub-human creature.

"I'm sorry, Joe," she whispered.

The utility knife parted his neck with a whisper, and Sara hopped out as the blood began to gush.

Sara ran to the hallway, focusing on the task ahead rather than dwelling on what she'd just done. Seeing Lester disappear around a corner, Sara went in the opposite direction, finding another door.

Dark in the room. Dark and quiet.

She squinted in the darkness, making out a square shape in the corner.

Another crate? Jesus... another trunk?

Sara wanted out of the room, but she knew she had to check it out. She inched closer, grasping the bloody utility knife, letting her eyes adjust to the dim.

No, not a trunk.

A crib.

She rushed toward it, still frightened but needing to know. Hands on the railing, she stared down at the tangle of blankets, hoping against all hope...

Jack's eyes were closed, his little chest moving up and down as he slept.

Crying silently, Sara pressed her son to her chest, kissing his head, inhaling his beautiful baby smell. She tucked him into his sling on her belly, adjusted the straps and belt, and crept back into the hallway, heading for the stairs.

Sara froze, hearing the footsteps echoing up at her, drawing closer. She went the other way, down the long corridor, which dead-ended at a door. A large, iron door, with a slot in the center and a bar across it.

"Here comes Lester, and Lester is angry."

Sara looked through the slot, seeing an antechamber with another door, also with a slot. She didn't like the looks of it, but she heard Lester's footsteps echoing closer and had no place else to go.

She removed the bar and went inside, closing the door gently behind her. On the floor were two empty plates and glasses. Sara approached the second door cautiously, placing an ear against it.

There was nothing to hear.

Sara bent down, putting her face close to the slot, trying to peer inside. She could make out a room, awash in dim, flickering light. There was also a smell. A sickly sweet, coppery smell.

"NOOOOOOOOOOO!"

Lester must have discovered Joe. Sara had no options left. She opened the second door and went inside.

The lighting effect was from candles, set up all around the room. But rather than evoke a peaceful, church-like setting, it was more akin to a medieval dungeon. The stone walls looked damp, and the floor was covered with brown stains that made Sara's shoes stick.

She looked around. There was a large bureau, an umbrella stand, a workbench, and a table and chair with salt and pepper shakers and a roll of paper towels. There was also a bed, and for a bad moment it looked like there was someone in it.

No; it was just pillows and shadows. But beneath the bed might make a good place to hide. With the low light in here, it would be tough to see under it.

Sara also wondered if she could hide in the bureau, which seemed big enough, when she noticed another door in the corner of the room.

A bathroom? A closet?

The door was wooden, slightly ajar. Sara didn't want to see what was behind it but knew she had no real choice.

She was heading for the door when she heard a squeaking sound.

It's coming from the bureau.

She paused, moving closer, her arms wrapped protectively around Jack.

The bureau rattled.

That's when Sara realized it wasn't a bureau at all. It was something else. Something horrible.

And someone was inside.

.   .   .

After only a few minutes, Martin tired of Captain Prendick's screams. The gridiron was as he'd remembered; hands-off and boring. There was nothing for him to do but watch, and Prendick was face-down so he couldn't even see the man's expressions.

Martin said a goodbye that probably wasn't even heard, then took off. He was anxious to get started on Sara. He also needed another Vicodin—his cheeks *really* stung.

Gun cocked and eyes scanning the trees for ferals, Martin headed back to the prison.

.   .   .

Tom hurt. His finger felt like it was being crushed, burned, and sawed-off, all at the same time. Then that freakazoid Lester poked him over and over with that frickin' nail, and each one was worse than a bullet wound combined with a snake bite, which was a guess on Tom's part because he'd never actually been shot or bitten. But they hurt like frickin' hell.

To make the whole thing even worse, he was thirsty, he was forced to watch Tyrone and that skank Cindy hold hands and make lovey-dovey eyes at each other, and he still had a little piece of Meadow stuck in his teeth that he couldn't get out.

Tom wondered, obliquely, when someone was going to come and rescue him. Every time he'd ever gotten into trouble, there was always somebody there to bail him out. No matter how often he screwed up, it always could have been worse.

But this situation didn't seem like it could get any worse. Plus, none of this was even his fault, except for going a little hyper with the gun, and getting that stringy thing wedged between his back molars. But Tom didn't blame himself for what he ate. Sure, it wasn't his food, but how was he supposed to know it was a person? Tom did, however, wish he'd taken smaller bites and chewed more carefully, because every time he touched that stringy bit with his tongue he felt like ralphing again.

"Tom. Tom, you awake, dog?"

Tom ignored Tyrone. If that guy minded his own damn business, Tom would have still had the gun, and he wouldn't be in this frickin' cell.

"Tom, man, I see something on the floor, near your cell. A few feet in front of your door."

Tom refused to look. *Screw that guy, and his skank.*

"Tommy boy, I think it's a key."

Now Tom looked. Sure enough, sitting on the concrete like a brown dog turd, was one of those rusty old skeleton keys.

"Can you reach it?"

"I got handcuffs on, brainiac. How'm I supposed to reach it?"

"Try your legs, man."

Tom decided to try his legs. The bars were close together, but he was thin, and he forced his right foot through the gap. Then he scooted closer. His knee was a little too big. He pushed hard, but it wouldn't go in.

"Try turning on an angle, Tom."

"No duh."

Tom turned on an angle, bending his knee slightly, and it slipped between the bars. He inched closer, trying to touch the key with his toe.

"Careful, Tom."

"I know what I'm doing, Tyrone."

Tom shifted again, reaching a bit more, and accidentally kicked the key a few inches further.

"Shut up," he said, even though Tyrone hadn't said anything.

Tom laid down on his back, shimmying closer to the bars, pushing his thigh through almost up to his crotch. He felt around with his heel, listening for the tinkling sound of metal.

Then the lights came on.

"Tommy. Someone's coming."

Tom heard the tinkle, felt the bump under his foot.

"I found it."

Footsteps echoed closer. Tom didn't dare to look. He tried to focus all of his attention on getting that key.

"Just forget it, man," Tyrone ordered. "Get your leg back in."

But Tom wasn't going to forget it. No frickin' way. His concentration was razor sharp, rock solid. He carefully bent his leg, dragging the key closer, and closer, tuning out the oncoming footsteps, tuning out Tyrone's pleas to quit.

See? I can focus when I have to.

"Hello, Tom. What is this?"

Frick. Martin.

Martin grabbed Tom's ankle and lifted it up, revealing the key.

"Whoa. Someone made a mistake here. If you guys had gotten this, you would have probably all escaped."

Martin crouched down, picking up the key and pocketing it. Then he yanked Tom's leg. The action was sudden and violent, bouncing Tom's groin against the iron bar. The pain was like a gong being rung; sudden strike… building up… and then resonating, lingering.

Tom howled, sitting up. Martin leaned forward and frowned, feigning concern.

"I sense a bit of distress, Tom."

He jerked Tom's leg once again, repeating the move.

"Would you like to talk about how you're feeling?" Martin asked. "You know I'm here for you."

It hurt so bad Tom couldn't even inhale. His vision was peppered by swirling red and gold specks.

"Leave him alone," Tyrone said.

"We'll get to you in a moment, Tyrone. Right now it's Tom's time to talk."

"You think you all badass? Why don' you come over here, step in this cell wit' me."

Martin let go of his ankle, and thank God, because Tom didn't think he could handle anymore. He pulled his leg back and brought his knees to his chest, curing up fetal on his side, staring as Martin walked over to Tyrone.

"Do you know what you are Tyrone? Sticking your chest out, trying to act tough? You're a stereotype. Poor African American kid, no father, grows up on the mean streets and joins a gang. Would you like to know why you never hear any stories about gangbangers who grow up to be happy, productive members of society? Because there aren't any."

"You wouldn't last two minutes in my hood."

"That's because I wouldn't ever go to your hood, Tyrone. It's full of losers. That's what you are. Born a loser, die a loser. You're a statistic, Tyrone. And you know what else? You're not tough at all. When we're finished with you, you're going to be crying like a little baby."

"Hells no."

"*Hells yeah,*" Martin mocked.

Martin spread out his hands, as if welcoming a big group of people.

"You still don't know why I brought you here. Of course, why should you? You're not the best and brightest of our nation's youth. You're not even in the top ninety-eight percent. So I'm going to be a nice guy and tell you what's going to happen. A man is coming to the island. A very important man, who is going to change the world. But he's going to need to be convinced. So you're going to help convince him."

Martin smiled, and it scared Tom to his core.

"He's going to tell us what to do to you, and we're going to do it. Happily, I might add. Painful things. Bloody things."

Tom couldn't help it. He started to cry.

"No tears yet, Tom. Save them for later. Besides, you three should actually feel pretty good about yourselves. You've defied all expectations, and done something productive with your lives. Something useful. Society always figured you would amount to nothing, but you're the final pieces in this wonderful puzzle. Every ritual needs sacrificial lambs."

Martin's eyes drilled into Tom, and the man who counseled him, mentored him, taught him, and pretended to actually give a shit about him, winked.

"Now if you kids will excuse me, I have to go upstairs and torture my wife."

•　　•　　•

The bureau was Sara's height. It was black, which made the dark red sketch on the front hard to see, but as Sara got closer, she could make it out.

A human outline.

Scrawled on the side, in chalk, were the words:

Taylor's Magic Box

In fact, it looked like one of those magician's cabinets, the kind where a woman went in and then was pierced with swords and cut into thirds.

It also had the same little doors on the front, so the audience could see different parts of the woman's body, to prove she was still in there.

But Sara didn't think this was an illusion. And a sickening sinking feeling in her gut told her who was probably inside.

She reached for the top door, the one that would expose the face, but she stopped inches from touching it.

All across the surface of the cabinet were round black knobs. Dozens of them. They were also on the sides, and the back, from top to bottom. Sara touched one, gently.

Someone inside the box screamed, making Sara flinch.

What the hell were these things?

She looked around, stared down at the umbrella stand next to the cabinet.

But it wasn't filled with umbrellas. It was filled with long things that ended in black knobs.

Suddenly understanding what they were, Sara grabbed the end of a knob in the middle of the cabinet and pulled.

Just like the magician's trick, Sara removed a six inch metal skewer from the box.

Unlike the magician's trick, this skewer was slick with blood.

"Oh, Jesus. Laneesha."

Sara knew Lester was coming. Martin would be back soon, too. She and Jack had to get out of there. But she wasn't going to leave Laneesha here with these monsters.

That posed a problem. There were dozens—perhaps over a hundred—of these skewers sticking in the cabinet. Did Sara even have time to remove all of them? And if she did, would Laneesha bleed to death?

She looked around for an answer, and saw two things on the floor that made her stomach churn. A car battery with jumper cables, and a handheld blowtorch.

She *had* to get Laneesha out of there.

"Laneesha, honey, it's Sara. I'm going to help you, okay? I need to get these things out of your face first. Jesus, I'm sorry, I'm so, so sorry…"

Sara lifted her hands, hesitated, reached closer, hesitated, and then pulled the six skewers out of the outline of the head as fast as she could, Laneesha's cries of pain scarring her soul. Then she opened the door to view Laneesha's face.

"Kill me," Laneesha croaked.

Sara recoiled in horror. The blood. The damage. The agony the girl must be in.

That's when Sara sensed someone behind her.

She didn't hear it. She sensed it. Like feeling a glance from across a room. Since the door Sara came through hadn't opened, the person must have come from the other door in the room.

Not Lester. Not Martin. This was the one who had done this to Laneesha. This had to be Taylor, the owner of the Magic Box.

Sara spun around, tugging the utility knife out of her jeans, ready to stab.

It was a man. A fat, scarred man, naked except a black rubber apron that stretched from his chest to his thighs. He'd come out of the door—the bathroom door—Sara had been about to open. His greasy hair was shoulder-length. His pocked cheeks glistened with sweat over several days' worth of stubble. His patchwork skin was lined with long, parallel scabs, like stripes, some of them still bleeding.

And in his crippled right hand he was clenching a meat hook.

.   .   .

Lester's rage was a diesel engine in his chest, pumping and burning and threatening to blow. The pet was special to Lester. He came to the island with Martin, and Lester had bitten off some of his sensitive parts, but left him mostly untouched. He liked the funny *uhhhnnnnn* sound the pet made. But he didn't care for the begging, or the attempts to get away. So Doctor fixed him for Lester. Fixed his brain so he stopped talking. Fixed his arms and legs so he couldn't run or fight back.

For years, Lester had taken good care of the pet. He was Lester's friend.

But now someone had killed him.

The doctor was in the lab. Martin was out. The stairs were the only way up to Lester's room, and he didn't pass anyone while bringing the hay.

That left one person. The only other person on the second floor.

Subject 33.

Lester looked around for a weapon, wrapping his large hand around a filet knife. Razor sharp. Perfect for detail work.

He stormed out his room, heading down the corridor.

·　　·　　·

When Marshal Otis Taylor was a little boy, he wanted to kill people when he grew up. If his parents had known any abnormal psychology, they would have noted little Taylor wet the bed, started fires, and liked to hurt animals. These behaviors were documented precursors to psychopathy.

But they were too busy physically and sexually abusing Taylor to notice that he might be a little off-kilter.

Perhaps they should have paid more attention, because when Taylor turned twelve he turned on the gas stove, blew out the flame, and waited in the back yard while the carbon monoxide filled the house and poisoned them to death.

It was deemed an accident, and the neighbors corroborated that Taylor was a handful and his parents sometimes made him sleep outside.

Taylor did the foster home shuffle for several years, eventually running away at fifteen and joining a travelling carnival. He learned how to be charming there, and how charm was the key to deception. He was taught street magic, and the art of the hustle, and may other carny tricks. He also learned how to drive the double-clutch eighteen-wheelers used for hauling equipment from town to town.

By age nineteen his boyish good looks had bloomed into masculinity, and he'd saved and swindled enough money to buy his own truck.

The truck-stop hookers thought he was so cute, they often gave him freebies.

He killed his first one in Wisconsin. His second in Nebraska.

Over the years, Taylor's route, and his hunting ground, encompassed the entire lower forty-eight. He killed one in every state, and after that lost count.

When they finally caught him, he was only charged with twenty murders, which wasn't even a third of them.

Taylor received the death sentence, and he had memories of being strapped to the table, the prison doctor hooking up the IV that contained the lethal injection.

Then his memories got fuzzy.

He remembered snippets of things. Some sort of military training. A special forces unit. Foreign countries. Missions that involved even more killing. Screaming people. Lots and lots of screaming people.

And coyotes. Taylor remembered the coyotes, eating him alive while he was unable to fight back.

Then somehow, well over a year ago, sewn back together like a crazy-quilt, Taylor had wound up here.

He wasn't even sure where *here* was.

His good looks were ruined. His body didn't work like it should have, due to muscle loss, his voice was gone, and his fingers jutted out at odd angles and were barely functional. The insane doctor who kept him here—Doctor Plincer—had tinkered with Taylor's brain.

Before the tinkering, Taylor had enjoyed causing others pain.

After the tinkering, causing pain was the only think Taylor lived for.

It was an addiction, stronger than any drug.

And the doctor fed his addiction, for the most part, supplying him with a steady stream of victims.

Of course, the one victim Taylor longed for most was the doctor himself.

He just *had* to get the bastard in his Magic Box.

The box was based on months of testing and experimenting. Every skewer positioned and angled so it wouldn't hit anything vital. Taylor's biggest wish was to get the doctor in there, and make him suffer for weeks.

But until that day came, he had other victims to play with.

Like this tender little morsel clutching a baby.

The woman was cute. Cute ones were so sexy when they screamed.

But the baby...

Taylor had never done a baby before.

It sounded like a lot of fun.

.   .   .

Sara was paralyzed with fear. A tiny part of her brain recognized what a cliché that was. But it was true. She was so terrified, so overwhelmed by dread, she couldn't move.

Taylor stared at her. Through her. Sara knew he could read her thoughts, sense her helplessness.

He lowered the meat hook and gave her a lopsided grin. Then he limped slowly to Sara's left, his gait wobbly and twisted, like he had a degenerative muscle disease. But Sara noticed it wasn't a disease—beneath his scarred skin, some of his muscles were simply *gone.*

Taylor stopped at a dresser, his bloodshot gaze drilling into her.

Run! Sara yelled at herself. *Get out of there!*

But her feet remained planted, her veins felt filled with cement. She couldn't even turn her head, staring at her abductor out of the corner of her eyes, watching as he slowly pulled open a drawer. He put his hand inside, grinning, obviously enjoying himself, and then removed a rope.

No! Don't let him tie you up, Sara! You have to move!

That's when the door burst open.

The sound was enough to break Sara out of her frozen state. In one smooth motion she yanked Jack from his sling and dove sideways, keeping him off the floor, and scooted lengthwise under the bed. She placed her baby on his belly, tucked against her side, and felt him kick against her as he woke up.

"You! You killed my pet!"

Lester's presence seemed to fill the room. He looked twice as big as the last time Sara saw him, and his eyes were wide and lips pulled back to bare his revolting teeth. He was pointing, accusingly, his hand ending in a knife that glinted orange in the candlelight.

But he wasn't looking at Sara. He was looking at Taylor.

"The pet is dead. Now Lester will kill Subject 33's pet."

Lester took two quick steps toward Laneesha's cabinet, and Sara watched aghast as he flung open the large middle door without removing the skewers.

Laneesha's insides came out, spilling onto the ground, some of them sliding under the bed and onto Sara and Jack. She shoved her knuckles into her mouth and bit down to keep from screaming. When she looked down at Jack, Sara saw his eyes were open and he was making that pinched, unhappy face he would always make before he started to cry.

Sara shoved her finger in his mouth. He made a tiny little whine of protest.

Lester turned toward Taylor, raising the knife.

"Now Lester will kill Subject 33."

Taylor held up one hand in supplication as he shook his head. His other hand was gesturing wildly.

Pointing right at Sara.

But Lester wasn't following the man's finger, and though Taylor's lips were moving, no sounds were coming out.

Lester lunged.

For a limping, pudgy man, Taylor moved pretty fast. He danced away from the blade and came up on Lester's side, the meat hook raised. Taylor swung, cutting through empty air with a *whir*.

Jack let out a soft cry. Sara massaged his gums with her fingertip. He began to suck.

Lester lunged again, nicking Taylor on the shoulder. Taylor again swung and missed. The taller man's reach was too long, and he easily kept Taylor at a distance.

When Lester cut Taylor's other shoulder, she could see the futility on Taylor's face. He knew he was going to die. That's when he stared Sara dead in the eyes, and then ran right at her.

Sara shrank back, tugging Jack with her, but it wouldn't help. This was a cheap bed, light and flimsy. Taylor would be able to upend it with one hand, exposing them both to Lester.

But Lester acted fast, sticking out a foot, tripping Taylor so he fell near the edge of the bed. The fat man flopped onto his belly, momentum making him slide across the gore toward Sara.

The meathook clanged to the floor and bounced away, and Sara locked eyes with the fallen killer, less than two feet between them. Up close, Taylor's face looked like it had been sculpted by a preschooler, all disfigured and missing parts. He opened his ruined mouth and let out a wheeze, his bloodshot eyes wide with panic.

Then Taylor stretched his hands under the bed and grabbed Jack's arm.

Martin was feeling pretty good. The drugs had taken the edge off his injuries, the children were all accounted for, and he was about to spend some quality time with the missus. Plus, he was now the owner of a pretty sweet boat. Which, unfortunately, he was going to have to sink.

Martin had told Captain Prendick the truth about his prices being too high, and Martin was fully prepared to takeover Plincer's supply needs. But the real reason he killed Prendick was because he needed the boat for his plan to work.

A noted psychologist, a ship's captain, and six teenagers couldn't just disappear while Martin walked away scot-free. So Martin was going to use Prendick's GPS navigation system to find the deepest part of the lake; Huron went down 750 feet in some parts. Then he was going to set the boat on fire and sink it, putting in a last minute call to the Coast Guard just as he jumped overboard.

"There was some kind of horrible explosion," he would tell the authorities. "I must have been thrown clear. Damn lucky thing I had my life jacket on. Oh, my poor now-dead wife. My poor son. Those poor, underprivileged, blown-up children. What a terrible and tragic freak accident."

He'd work on the story, and his delivery. A few burn marks on his life preserver would lend credence, as would his outstanding reputation in the field of social work.

The best part? Sara was insured for half a million dollars. Enough to buy a nice, new boat. Joe had been right about that one thing; boating life was the way to go.

Martin got to the top of the stairs and wondered if he should drop in on brother Joe, maybe give him a dog bone for old time's sake. But the growing tension in his groin told him to wait until later. He wanted to get in some husband and wife bonding first.

He walked to his room, smiling when he saw the trunk in the corner. Martin could picture Sara in there, tied up and terrified. He thought of all those countless, wasted nights, holding her in bed because she was frightened, pretending to care.

Payback was a bitch.

Martin snuck over, raising his palm to give the chest a good whack and scare the crap out of her, when he heard Lester yell something down the hall.

Odd. Lester never yelled. Not in the years Martin had known him. Something must be happening.

He left Sara to her personal hell and went into the corridor.

Another yell from Lester.

It seemed to be coming from Subject 33's room.

Martin headed that way.

.   .   .

Whatever grip fear had over Sara since her youth disappeared when this ghoul grabbed her baby.

Instead, her fear was replaced by rage.

Taylor gripped Jack's little arm, his bloodshot eyes huge with panic, trying to drag her son from her grasp.

No way in hell that was going to happen.

Sara still held the utility knife, and she used it without hesitation, slashing at his knuckles, his hands, his arms. Digging deep and twisting the triangular blade.

Taylor released Jack, his soundless lips flapping as Lester tugged him away from the bed. Taylor's arms scoured the floor, trying to grab onto something, finding only bits of Laneesha.

Sara watched, awestruck, as Lester placed a huge foot on Taylor's flabby backside, leaned down, and plunged the knife into his back. Taylor flopped around for a bit, like a fish on a pier, his mouth wide in a silent scream.

Then, all at once, he stopped moving, a sail that ran out of wind.

She stared, knowing Lester wasn't going to stop there. While part of her said she should turn away, another part wanted to watch as Lester cut Laneesha's killer into a million little pieces. Indeed, Lester tugged out the knife and raised it again. But his plans were interrupted when the door opened.

"Lester? Aw, shit, Lester! What did you do?"

Sara felt herself grow very cold. Martin had walked into the room.

Jack heard his father's voice and cooed happily. Sara felt around and stuck her finger back into his mouth.

Lester squinted at the knife like he didn't know how it got there. Then he looked at Martin.

"Subject 33 killed the pet. So Lester killed Subject 33."

"Dammit, Lester, you can always get a new pet. Plincer's going to be pissed at you."

Martin knelt down, felt Taylor's neck. Though Sara thought nothing could shock her any more, Martin's callous disregard for his brother's death made him even more horrible.

"He's still alive. Help me get him to the lab."

They each grabbed a leg, and dragged Taylor across the bloody floor, out the door.

Sara waited. She needed to figure out what to do next. She still had four kids left. The three in the cells, and Georgia, wherever she was being held. But those cells were solid. She would need tools to get in. A saw, or a pry bar.

Or a drill.

There was a drill in Martin's room, on his tool bench.

Sara slowly slid out from underneath the bed, avoiding the blood on the floor and refusing to look in Laneesha's direction. She tucked Jack back into his sling and was halfway to the door when she realized Laneesha deserved better than that. Taking a deep breath, she forced herself to face the cabinet.

"I'm sorry," Sara whispered, feeling the words stick in her throat. "I know you believed we go someplace, after we die. If you're right, and you can hear me, I'm making you a promise. If… no…*when* I get out of here, I'll make sure your daughter finds a good home, and knows how brave her mother was. I'm so sorry."

Sara closed her eyes but could still picture the ruined, bloody thing before her.

"I also promise, even if I die trying, to get every one of those fuckers who did this."

Sara snuck out into the antechamber, and then peeked around the corner before committing to the hallway. Once she deemed it clear she moved quickly, on the balls of her feet, pausing by Martin's doorway. She heard voices, from the spiral staircase ahead of her.

"…sick of dragging this heavy bastard. The wheelchair is in my room. I'll go get it."

Martin.

Sara hurried into his room, frantically looking for a hiding place. It was too well lit in here to hide under the bed. But there wasn't any place else. Except…

Can I do this?

She gaped at the trunk, her legs feeling weak. The alternative was facing Martin with the utility knife—which had too small a blade to do any serious damage. Plus Martin attended the same judo class as she did. Sara had more experience, but he was stronger and outweighed her by sixty pounds. She silently cursed herself for making him take classes with her.

His footsteps reverberated through the stone corridor, getting closer.

I can do this.

Utility knife clenched in a death-grip, Sara cautiously lifted the trunk lid.

It's so dark in there.

She cradled Jack's head and climbed in anyway, forcing herself to squat down, the pain in her leg making her wince.

But she couldn't get herself to close the lid.

Martin's footsteps drew closer, practically outside the room.

Dammit, Sara. Look what Laneesha went through. You can do this.

Sara eased the lid down, watching her light get smaller until it was a thick line… a thinner line… just a speck…

And then the darkness.

It assaulted her like a freezing wind, making her want to scream while also taking her breath away. A minute ago, a second ago, she'd been empowered, a woman on a mission. But the dark reduced her to jelly. She wasn't even sure if she could keep hold of the utility knife.

Sara strained to hear outside the trunk. Was Martin in the room yet? What was he doing? Would he notice the lock on the trunk was broken? What if he opened the lid? Would she even be able to defend herself while holding her baby?

Then there was a huge banging noise and the trunk shook and Sara screamed and dropped the knife, the darkness swallowing it, and her.

*   *   *

Martin slapped the top of the trunk and was rewarded with a cry of absolute terror from the woman he exchanged vows with.

"You okay in there, honey? I don't want you thinking I've forgotten about you."

Sara's crying continued, and it was so infantile it almost sounded like a baby.

Martin went to the wheelchair, parked next to the tool bench. It had shackles on it, and was useful for moving people around.

An elevator would have been more useful, but Lester was pretty strong and there weren't many people he couldn't lift by himself.

Subject 33, however, had to weigh three hundred and fifty pounds. He'd really let himself go since Plincer locked him in that room. Martin made a mental note to bring him a Nordic Track or something on his next visit. If the fat bastard pulled through.

He wheeled the chair to the doorway and then abruptly stopped.

Something was wrong. He felt it.

Martin turned around, scanning the room. Work bench. Dresser. Peg board. Bed. Trunk.

There, by the trunk.

"Trying to get away? You naughty girl."

Martin walked over, bending at the waist to pick up the object on the floor. Chereese's tanned hide was lying in a pile, like a dropped leather jacket. Martin had put all of his skins away, but somehow had overlooked her. He lifted her up, brushing a piece of rock salt out of her hair, and reverently put her back in the dresser.

Then Martin left the room. He had to walk backwards down the stairs, lest the wheelchair get away from him. Lester hadn't waited, and had pulled Subject 33 by himself halfway across the cell area. Martin rolled up to him, and they hefted the fat man into the chair.

The lab was on the other side of the cells, through a doorway and at the end of the hall, between Plincer's bedroom and the kitchen. As expected, the doctor was in the lab, fussing with some test tubes.

"What happened now?"

Martin frowned. "He and Lester had a disagreement. So Lester stabbed him in the back."

Plincer came over, peering close. "So how did he get so fat?"

"Eating too much and lack of exercise."

Subject 33 groaned.

"Oh dear, we don't want this one waking up on us. Hold him down."

Lester placed his hands on Subject 33's shoulders and leaned on him. Martin stared at Doctor Plincer, clucking like a mother hen while he searched his cabinets for some succinocholine, and wondered how a man so brilliant could be such a space cadet at the same time.

The doctor found the bottle and filled a syringe. By now Subject 33's eyes were open. He stared up at Lester, projecting hate. Lester projected hate right back. Plincer gave the fat man a shot in the thigh.

"Okay, let's try to get him up on the table. Face down."

The three of them heaved, sweated, grunted, and strained, and eventually managed to beach the whale on the stainless steel operating table.

"We've got a knife wound four inches right of the L2 vertebra." Plincer placed his ear to Subject 33's back. "There's a pneumothorax. How long was the knife?"

Lester held his fingers apart.

"Possible liver puncture as well. Did you do all of these other cuts as well?" Plincer spread out his hands, indicating the dozens of slices on the fat man's body.

"Subject 33 was like that when Lester stabbed him."

"Self-inflicted? Fascinating." Plincer peered over his glasses at Lester. "You weren't trying to kill him, were you?"

"Not right away," Lester said.

"But for heaven's sake, why try at all?"

"Subject 33 killed the pet."

"How did he get out of his room?"

Lester shrugged. So did Martin.

"Did you, perhaps, stop and think that maybe someone let him out?"

Martin dug into his pocket. "Lurch here dropped a key in the cell area," he said, holding it up.

"Not Lurch," Lester said. "Lester did it."

Plincer rolled his eyes. "The meeting is in less than an hour. Make sure that everyone is where they're supposed to be. Including Georgia."

Martin and Lester both turned to leave.

"Hold it, hold it please. I'm going to need some help re-inflating his lung and sewing him up. Lester, you stay here with me, since you're the one that did this. Martin, are you sure your wife is contained?"

"I'm sure."

"Double-check. And as for you, old friend." Plincer patted Subject 33's head. "I'm afraid I don't have time to properly sedate you. You're going to feel this, but that's what you get for messing around with another man's property."

Lester smiled. Martin sighed, heading back to his room. He was annoyed, and tense.

But he had complete faith that a few minutes with Sara would help relax him.

. . .

Sara listened, as hard as she could, but Jack's crying flooded her ears. Had Martin left? Or was he still there, silently waiting, ready to grab her when she opened the trunk?

She tried rubbing Jack's gums again, but the noise of his father banging on the trunk had scared him too much. His wailing increased in volume. Even more than the suffocating darkness, Sara feared Martin would hear him, figure out what was going on.

Adjusting her body, she stuck Jack up under her shirt, pulling down her bra.

He latched onto her breast and began to nurse.

Sara sighed, stroking his scalp. For a precious minute, she and Jack were the only two people in the universe. He suckled lazily, and then she felt him release her, his body relaxing in sleep.

The smothering dark returned.

I'll count to a fifty. Then I'll come out.

Sara made it to seventeen, then popped out and gasped for air like she'd been underwater, swinging the knife around in case Martin was close.

He wasn't. The room was empty. But the sudden movement woke up Jack, and he began to cry again.

Sara climbed out of the trunk on shaky legs. She closed the lid, standing still for a few seconds, trying to get her hyperventilating under control. Now wasn't a good time to pass out.

Jack's volume increased. She tried her breast again, but he turned away from it.

Overtired? Bored? Wet?

She stuck a finger in his diaper. Dry.

"Shush," she told him.

He didn't shush.

Sara had to get out of there, fast. But first, she needed tools. Sara made her way to the work table and picked up the cordless drill. The bit was thick, four inches long. She squeezed the trigger and it whirred to life.

Jack stopped crying, reaching a tiny hand out to touch the drill.

"Do you like the drill? Yes you do like the drill."

She kept up the baby-talk patter and let it whir for another few seconds. Then she noticed something potentially more important.

On the table, in an ashtray, was a key.

It didn't look like it would open the cells. This was a new key, and those were over a hundred years old, with locks to match. But it couldn't hurt to hold on to.

Sara took it, and closed the utility knife, sticking both into her pocket. She also took from the bench an ice pick, a hammer, and a hacksaw. She then put down the saw, unable to carry everything at once, and rushed into the hallway, heading for the stairs.

When she was almost there she put on the brakes, noticing another door.

It looked out of place in the castle-type environment, made of silver metal with a bright new doorknob.

Keep going. Save the kids.

But what if there's some other poor victim in there? What if it's Georgia?

Sara reached for the doorknob hesitantly, as if she were about to touch a hot stove. She paused.

Yes or no?

Sara palmed the knob and gave it a deft turn.

Locked.

"Hello? Who's there?"

That was Georgia's voice.

Sara moved her mouth closer to the door. "Georgia? Are you in there?"

"Sara? Is that you?"

Sara put her hand on the door, leaning against it. "It's me. Are you okay?"

"I'm scared, Sara." Georgia's voice got louder. "Please get me out of here."

"I'm going to try. Don't worry. I won't leave you."

It was a no-brainer what to try first. The key. She set down the drill and the hammer and fished out the key, fitting it into the lock easily. Sara tried to twist.

No good. The key wouldn't turn.

Sara gave it the standard key-jiggle, bumped the door with her shoulder to loosen up the bolt, and tried again.

It worked. Sara pocketed the key and pushed the door open, keeping a protective hand on Jack as she looked around. The room was well-lit, but there didn't seem to be anyone around. Sara saw a bed, a dresser, but no Georgia.

Sara studied the door, and noticed the pneumatic arm at the top. She bent down and jammed the ice pick under the rail so it wouldn't close automatically, and then stepped inside.

"Georgia?"

Sara glanced behind the door and was met with the shocking image of a Georgia standing there, nude and covered in blood.

"Georgia! Are you okay?"

"I'm fine, now that you're here."

Georgia smiled, oddly incongruous with her appearance. Then Sara noticed the bloody scissors in Georgia's hand.

"Georgia?"

The pudgy girl launched herself at Sara, stabbing downward with the scissors.

Instinct took over, Sara sidestepped to the right, ducking under the arc of Georgia's swing and driving an elbow into the teen's back.

Georgia smacked into the dresser and Sara turned to face her, planting her feet apart and stepping on something squishy. She took a quick look at the floor.

It was covered with blood. Blood and animal parts.

Georgia spun, raising the scissors again. Her expression was gleefully manic.

"It's me, Georgia," Sara pleaded, cradling Jack against her chest. "It's Sara."

"I know who you are, bitch."

The girl lunged again, but this time she feinted before the swing, throwing Sara off balance. Sara back-pedaled, the scissors passing inches in front of Jack's head. Her ass hit a desk, and Georgia slid and fell onto one knee.

Sara looked to her right. The bed was in the corner of the room, at least ten feet away. Then looked down at her son, and at the crazed face of Georgia.

Without second-guessing herself, Sara yanked Jack from his sling and tossed him through the air, at the center of the bed, aiming so he hit back-first. Before she could tell if she hit her target, Georgia had recovered and plowed into her, doubling Sara over and knocking her onto her back.

Jack didn't make a sound, and Sara couldn't see him.

Georgia fought like a rabid dog. Sara fought to push the girl off, but Georgia had straddled her, making the older woman cry out when she ground her knee into Sara's leg wound. Sara strained against her, but Georgia was strong and fierce and weighed more.

Georgia used that weight, leaning onto the scissors, bringing the blades closer and closer to Sara's throat until they poked into her chin.

.   .   .

Georgia was more than just excited. She was aroused. The scissors pricked at Sara's face, making little blood freckles, and Georgia was loving it.

The rat had been fun, but this was a hundred times better. Georgia had never tried any drugs, never had friends who attempted to share any with her. But she imagined this is what they must feel like. Each drop of blood that bloomed on Sara's face was like another spike of ecstasy. Heroin and sex and cocaine and sky-diving all mixed up in one gigantic, pleasurable rush.

Then Georgia's fingers were being bent back, and she had to turn her body with the rotation so they didn't break.

She rolled off of Sara, no longer holding the scissors. The intense pleasure was gone, like a faucet that had been shut off. Not even an afterglow.

Georgia looked up at Sara and snarled.

"We can get you help," Sara said, wiping red off her chin. "You have to trust me."

"I don't want help."

Georgia scrambled onto all fours and then tackled Sara, wanting, needing, to bite the bitch's face off.

.   .   .

Martin reached the top of the stairs and immediately noticed a power drill and hammer next to Georgia's door. He ran to them, saw the door was open, and saw a naked Georgia wrestling with...

Sara. How the hell did she get free?

He rushed into the room, blood boiling, yanking Georgia out of the way and cocking back a fist guaranteed to break his wife's jaw.

.   .   .

Georgia was there one second, gone the next, replaced by Martin. Sara had been trying to control Georgia without seriously hurting her, but with Martin she had no such compunction. She kicked him with everything she had, right between the legs, and then threw a right cross that broke the bastard's nose.

Martin went down.

Then Sara was running for the bed. She panicked when she didn't see Jack—

Did I miss the mattress? Did he bounce off?

—then saw him behind a bunched-up blanket.

Sara scooped Jack up with one hand, pressing him to her chest, and took a quick look over her shoulder.

Martin was getting up, turning her way.

Georgia was on the floor, reaching for Sara's ankle.

Sara vaulted over Georgia's hand, toward the doorway. Then she was reaching for the ice pick and yanking it free, pulling the door shut behind her. After confirming the door was locked, she stuck the pick in her pocket and checked Jack over.

He smiled at her. This had to be the least-fussy, best-behaved child on the planet. She kissed his forehead and tucked him into his sling, then scooped up the hammer and drill, and limped down the stone stairs. They came to an end at the cell room, which was brighter with the lights on, but not by much. She gingerly touched her leg wounds and noted they were bleeding again.

Wouldn't it be funny if I lived through this and then died of an infection?

She ignored the pain, scurrying over to the kids' cells. They each had their hands cuffed behind their backs, and Tom was curled up in a ball.

"Sara!"

"Shh," she told Cindy. "I'm going to try to get the doors open. You all need to watch the stairs and the door over there, make sure no one is coming. What happened to Tom?"

"Lester and Martin," Tyrone said. "Beat him up pretty good. Why'd you marry that guy anyway?"

"The man I fell in love with was a good man," Sara said, squinting at the lock on Cindy's prison door. "He was turned into something else."

Sara knew the key for Georgia's room wouldn't fit, but she tried it anyway. No suck luck. Then she stuck the ice pick in the keyhole. Sara had no idea how lock mechanisms worked, other than something needed to be turned. She poked around for a minute without getting anywhere.

"Tyrone, can you pick locks?"

"Why, 'cause I'm black?"

"No, Tyrone. Because you're a criminal."

"Hells no. Only thing I ever needed to bust a lock was my foot, or a gat."

Sara tucked the ice pick away and wielded the drill.

"That might work, too," Tyrone said.

She placed the bit inside the keyhole and pushed while pressing the trigger. The bit was stronger than the old iron, and it immediately began to dig in.

Then the drill whined, and slowly petered to a stop. Sara pressed the trigger a few more times.

The battery was dead.

.　　.　　.

"Lester, did you hear that?" Dr. Plincer asked.

Lester hadn't been paying attention. While Doctor was busy sewing Subject 33 up, Lester had been clandestinely squeezing the paralyzed man's testicles. Lester got pleasure from the act, as he did whenever he was hurting someone, but was unhappy that Subject 33 couldn't scream or cry. Pain without screams was like ice cream without chocolate sauce.

Lester would wait for the drug to wear off. Then he'd do much worse things.

"It sounds like a machine of some sort," Doctor said. "In the cell room."

Lester listened, hearing a faint buzzing noise that faded out.

"Go check it, please, Lester, if you would be so kind."

Lester gave Subject 33 one more big squeeze and then headed for the door.

·　　·　　·

Martin sprinted at the metal security door for the third time, slamming his shoulder against it. His nose was bleeding over his mouth, down his neck, but he didn't pay it any mind. His only goal was to get through this door and get that bitch he married.

"Don't you have a key?" Georgia asked.

Martin sneered at her. "If I had a key, would I be trying to bust it down?"

The girl rolled her eyes. "You always were an asshole, Martin. How's your nose? Looks painful."

Georgia chewed on her lower lip and gave his nose a stiff poke.

Martin lashed out with a backhand, knocking the little brat across the room. "Don't touch me ever again. And put on some goddamn clothes."

He stared at his nemesis, the door, once more. Solid metal. Set in a stone wall. Calling for help was an option, but he didn't think his voice would carry all the way to the lab. Kicking wouldn't it be any more useful than ramming it, especially since the door opened inward.

Wait a sec. The hinges are on the inside.

Martin looked around on the floor, found the bloody metal shears. There were three hinges on the door, each with a pin holding the two parts of the shaft together. He knelt down and pried the bottom pin up, like pulling a nail. It took a bit of effort, but he was able to get it out.

The middle pin was more difficult, probably because the door's weight was no longer evenly distributed. Martin took off his hiking boot, placed the tip of the scissors under the pin's head, and beat on the end until it came free.

He used the same hammering technique on the last pin, which was the toughest of all. The sucker simply didn't want to budge. But Martin was ferocious in his determination, and millimeter by millimeter the pin eased out of the shaft until it finally popped out the top and clanged onto the floor.

Now hingeless, Martin could pry the door open. It fell behind him with a crash that made Georgia jump. Martin put his boot back on, stuck the scissors in his back pocket, and wiped his bleeding nose on his sleeve.

Punch me? Let's see how you punch when I cut your fingers off, Sara.

Sara didn't bother to curse the universe. Even though it was probably warranted, she didn't have the time. She tried unplugging the battery and plugging it back in, but it did nothing. The drill was useless.

That left the hammer and the ice pick. She stuck the pick back in the lock and gripped it tight, ready to give the base a whack.

"Sara!" Cindy's voice had gone up an octave. "Lester's coming!"

Sara didn't bother to look. She continued to beat on the ice pick.

"Shit," Tyrone sounded scared. "Martin just came down the stairs. You gotta run, Sara."

Sara whacked the pick again. "I'm not leaving you here."

Cindy said, "Lester's coming this way."

"So is Martin," Tyrone said. "Sara, you gotta *go*."

She shook her head, not daring to look up. "No. I'm getting you out."

"Sara," Cindy was leaning against the bars. "Go to the gridiron. I dropped a gun in the bushes right next to it. It's bright out now. You can find it, then come back and save us."

Sara hit the pick once more. The tip broke in half. She felt like crying.

"Sara, please. Go."

Now Sara did look up. Her husband and Lester were heading toward her, and then Martin pointed.

"There you are!"

Sara stared hard at Cindy. "I'll be back for you." Their fingers touched.

Then Sara ran. She ran to the big steel door, turned the lock, and pushed.

Nothing happened.

She pushed harder, leaning into it, and the door squealed and inched open.

"Sara!" Cindy yelled.

Sara didn't want to look, but she did. Martin and Lester were twenty yards away at most, both of them running. Sara only had a few seconds.

She strained against the heavy door, putting all of her weight into it, her injured leg trembling and feeling like it was about to burst.

The door opened to a foot wide, maybe an inch or two less. Sara crammed Jack through the crack, holding him by the back of his onesie. Then she tried to wedge herself into the space, sand-wiched between the door and the frame, fitting her head through sideways. But her body wouldn't follow suit, her chest was too big.

I'm stuck.

Sara could hear Martin and Lester almost upon her. She strained, but the door was too heavy, squeezing her too tight.

Incredibly, her subconscious latched on to a solution, a logic problem she liked to tell her kids. A truck, fifteen feet tall, gets struck under an overpass that is only fourteen feet, ten inches high. What's the easiest way to free the truck?

Let the air out of the tires.

Sara exhaled forcefully, blowing out her cheeks, emptying her lungs.

Someone grabbed her. But Sara had compressed her ribcage just enough, and she slipped through the door and pulled away and ran outside and into the woods and ran around trees and through shrubs and ran and ran and ran.

Eventually, her bad leg just stopped supporting her, and Sara had to lean against an elm and rub out the cramp that had formed around the fork wounds. Her jeans were soaked with blood, and she realized she was still holding on to the hammer.

While she tried to catch her breath, Sara listened to the woods, to see if she was being followed. She didn't hear the sounds of pursuit, but she did hear another sound.

Sara glanced overhead, and watched a low-flying helicopter skirt the tree canopy, heading toward the prison.

．　＊　．

Dr. Plincer tied off his last suture, then used his stethoscope to make sure Subject 33's lungs were inflated. They both sounded fine. Plincer hooked up an IV filled with antibiotics, then peeled off his latex gloves. Subject 33 would be paralyzed for several more hours, so there was no need to get him locked up right away. Besides, the guests would be arriving in just a few minutes.

Plincer left the lab and strolled down the hallway, into his bedroom. He checked his facial putty in the mirror and judged the scar coverage to be adequate. There were some spatters of blood on his lab coat, but he didn't see how that would do anything to hurt the negotiations.

In the top drawer of his dresser were a detailed account of his procedure, an ingredient list of his serum, and various notes, charts, and graphs supporting his findings. He also picked up a plastic bag filled with items Captain Prendick had acquired for him at some sex store.

Plincer returned to the lab, where he grabbed a sealed test tube sample of the serum used in the procedure. This was the latest version, the kind that was apparently successful with Georgia.

Then he went into the cell room, to prepare the volunteers. The three children looked suitably cowed. The white one also looked like someone had used him as the board in a game of darts.

The doctor reached into the sex bag and pulled out a ball gag. Red rubber, with a strap that wound around the head to hold it in the mouth.

"You, young man, if you'd be so kind I need you to put your back against the bars so I can put this on you."

"Hells no. You can stick that thing up yo ass, old dude."

"It's just a simple ball gag. Surely you don't want to annoy our special guests with your screaming."

"Ain' no way you gettin' that thing in my mouth."

Plincer nodded. "I do admire a man with convictions. But I must mention the alternative. If you won't allow me to gag you, I'll have to sew your lips together."

The black boy paused, then put his back to the bars and opened his mouth. Plincer made sure the buckle was on tight, then put the next one on the girl in the same fashion. The white boy was difficult—his injuries seemed to limit his range of motion. Plincer managed to coerce him into rolling over to the bars, and put the gag on him as he was lying down.

Doctor Plincer had something else they each needed to wear, also from the sex store, but chose to wait for Lester and Martin to assist, because they'd no doubt balk at the sight of them.

As though God was reading Plincer's thoughts, Martin suddenly burst in through the outside door. He was pinching his nose, his shirt tie-dyed with blood. Lester strolled in behind him, a large frown creasing his face.

"Sara got away," Martin said by way of explanation. "With the baby."

"She has no place to run. You can find her after the company leaves. And make sure the baby lives. You know I want him for my next enhancement." Plincer glanced up at Lester. "And why, might I ask, are you sulking?"

"Martin told Lester that the Sara woman killed the pet, not Subject 33. Lester wants to bite off the Sara woman's fingers."

"I'm sure you'll have the chance later, Lester. Martin, you'd better go get cleaned up. Also make sure Georgia is presentable, and please find a tool belt for her with all the standard equipment, if you'd be so kind. Lester, please help me put these on the children. I believe they're going to object."

Plincer reached into the bag once again, withdrawing three black leather dog collars.

PART V
REAPING

General Tope waited for the engine to cut off before he removed the protective hearing muffs from his ears. The chopper ride had been loud and bumpy, and passing over the trees had reminded him of the last time he'd taken a bird into the field. Vietnam, more than thirty years ago.

All for God and country, Tope thought.

It didn't matter to the General that his country had no idea he was here. The US Military needed this. Whether they wanted it or not didn't matter.

With reserves, the US military boasted over two and a half million personnel. But India and Russia each had just as many. China and North Korea each had even more. Turkey, Brazil, Pakistan, and Egypt combined for another four million.

The United Stated of America was outnumbered and outgunned.

Nukes didn't mean a thing anymore. Tope knew they'd never be used in battle, and their deterrent power ended with the Cold War.

He reflected back on the old times, and how much things have changed. These days, wars were fought with intelligence and technology. But they never ended. They dragged on, troops dying in vain, with no discernable progress. When was the last time the US won a war?

But throughout history, wars *had* been won. And not by tech. It was ruthlessness that decided the victor.

Ghengis Khan. Trajan. Napoleon. Atilla the Hun. Marius. Alexander the Great. Julius Caesar. There was no mercy on the field of battle for these great leaders.

An army with no mercy was a fearsome force.

But an army with a thirst for blood—that was an unstoppable force.

General Tope had plans for making his army unstoppable. Plans that involved the serum and procedure Dr. Plincer had developed to enhance a subject's aggression.

If Plincer could actually turn a normal person into a bloodthirsty sadist, the US would have the most powerful weapon ever created.

Imagine a thousand such psychopaths unleashed on a city. Imagine ten thousand let loose in Iran, or North Korea.

Such an army would be cost-free. It would have no need for weapons or training. It wouldn't require food or shelter. It could use the transportation already available in the country it had infiltrated. Such an army wouldn't even need orders, having the order to kill already programmed into its collective brain.

Just like the infomercial said. *You could just set it, and forget it.*

And General Tope could have it all for just twenty-five million dollars. A pittance. And the ATACMS missiles and launcher he sold to Hamas to cover the cost were "officially" considered obsolete surplus and destroyed, so they wouldn't be missed.

Tope unbuckled his seat belt and grabbed his metal suitcase, waiting for the rotor blades to stop turning before he exited the chopper. The pilot, a First Lieutenant named Crouch, would stay with the helicopter. A burly Sergeant named Benson would accompany Tope to the meeting and act as muscle if needed. Both were doing this off the clock, and not out of patriotism—Tope had paid them well.

Intel reported that Plincer lived alone, except for his enhanced subjects and the wild people who didn't respond well to the procedure. As of this morning, the Orbiting Strand Satellite Telescope readings had placed the diminishing number of people on the island at twenty-four. Tope hoped these weren't the volunteers Plincer had been planning to use in his demonstration. He didn't want to waste time having his men hunt down one of the ferals to use.

The clearing they'd landed in was surrounded by woods, the prison building less than fifty yards away. Tope walked briskly, and Benson matched his pace, sidearm in hand and scanning the treeline for trouble.

General Tope didn't need to look at his watch, but he did so anyway. Nine o'clock precisely. He allowed himself a measure of satisfaction at being on time, then rapped strongly on the iron door.

Almost immediately it creaked opened, but so slowly that Tope ordered Benson to assist.

Dr. Plincer was balder, older, and uglier than in his press clippings from a decade ago.

"Good morning, General Tope. Welcome to my island."

Tope noted the fresh blood on the doctor's smock and was grateful Plincer didn't attempt to shake hands.

"Good morning, Dr. Plincer." He didn't bother introducing Benson.

"Allow me to take you around to the back of the prison. We've decided to stage our demonstration outside. No need to worry about cleaning up afterward."

He led them around the side of the building, to a small courtyard where six people were waiting.

One was an unusually tall man in overalls. He was flanked on either side by a chubby girl in jeans and a sweater, and a man in khakis and a button-down shirt.

Ten yards away from them were three teenagers. They stood with their hands behind their backs, each in front of a large, wooden pole. Tope noted their necks were tethered to the poles.

Good. No need to waste time hunting ferals.

"This area was used for the firing squad, during the Civil War. You're familiar with the war between the states, I take it?"

General Tope nodded. He was familiar with every war in modern history.

"If you're a collector, you might keep your eyes peeled for souvenirs. It's pretty easy to spot old bullets and cartridges with the naked eye. See? There's one right there. Might even be some Confederate DNA still on it."

Plincer pointed at the ground.

This man is out of his goddamn mind, Tope thought.

"Can we get to it, Doctor? I have a meeting this afternoon."

"Yes, yes. Of course."

They approached the tall man and his companions.

"General Tope, these are three of my biggest successes. High level functioning, perfectly rational."

"But totally psychotic," Tope said.

"We prefer to use the term *enhanced*. The procedure enhances the brain's aggression centers, triggering the neurotransmitter dopamine during violent acts. In layman's terms, killing is an addiction. Causing harm gets them high."

Tope frowned, simply because frowning made people try harder to please him.

"Do they follow orders?"

"But of course. Anything you'd like for them to do to our volunteers over there, they'd be happy to do. But first, I'd like to see the item I requested from you."

Tope gestured for Benson to hold the metal briefcase while he opened it.

"Wonderful," Plincer said, eyes twinkling. "The papers are in order?"

"Yes. Complete with bill of sale. I take it you're an aficionado?"

The doctor shook his head. "No, not at all. I just have a healthy distrust of banks. And twenty-five million dollars, even in large bills, is a bit cumbersome."

General Tope couldn't care less. "Where are the notes and the serum?"

"Inside. I assumed you'd want to see the demonstration first."

He nodded, closing the briefcase. "You may proceed, Doctor."

"Certainly. Pick one of the enhanced and tell them what to do."

"What are they capable of doing?"

"Whatever you'd like."

Tope raised an eyebrow. He was getting more interested. "Torture? Mutilation? Rape? Murder?"

"Any and all of the above, if you wish."

"Not to be rude, Doctor," General Tope said, knowing he was being rude, "but I could order my bodyguard here to do any of those things, and he'd also obey."

That probably wasn't true. Tope knew that most men had their limits, and only a special few could commit atrocities without being affected.

"I have no doubt, General. But he wouldn't enjoy it as much as they do. And he wouldn't do it on his own if given the chance."

"Fine," Tope said. "The girl. Have her disembowel..." Tope studied at the three victims, then pointed. "That one."

.   .   .

Sara was torn. Maybe the helicopter was sent by the authorities. Or maybe it was part of all the other bad things happening on this island.

So do I follow it, or search for the gun?

She hoped, *needed*, for the helicopter to be the good guys, coming to the rescue. Even if she had a weapon, what was she going to do? Kill Martin, Plincer, Lester, and Taylor? Sara had never fired a gun, but she knew most held six bullets, and some people could be shot multiple times without dying. And from recent experience on the beach, Sara knew guns were really loud. Firing one next to Jack's fragile little ears would probably cause permanent hearing loss.

Perhaps she could use the gun to keep them at bay and save the kids, but they'd still be stuck on the island. Could she force Plincer to call Captain Prendick, and then force him to take them back to safety? It was sounding more and more far-fetched.

Or maybe she could save the kids and force the *helicopter* to take them to safety.

That made better sense. Get the gun. Take Plincer as a hostage. Then fly the hell out of here.

Now all Sara had to do was find a lone gun in two miles of forest.

She still had the compass, but realized it didn't matter because she didn't know which way to go. The cliff was north. The beach was east. But where was the gridiron?

That's when another sense took over. Sara's sense of smell. *Someone is cooking meat.*

But Sara knew it wasn't meat. It was something else. Her stomach threatened to tie itself into a knot.

Still, she had to follow it, because the smell would probably lead to her destination.

Tracking by smell wasn't easy. Sara would take ten steps in a particular direction, lose the scent, and have to go back. The breeze was strong enough to mix and twist the odor, but not so strong she could simply follow it upwind.

But eventually Sara came upon something better than scent alone. Smoke.

Smoke could be followed. The thicker it got, the closer she got, and whenever the trees thinned out Sara could see the gray cloud climbing into the sky, the X marking the spot.

When she got closer, her mouth began to water, and she hated herself and her body for betraying her.

When she got really close, she saw that she wasn't the only one drawn to the cookout.

At the sight of the first feral, Sara ducked behind an ash tree. She was still a good twenty yards away from the fire, and from Cindy's earlier description, the girl had been only a few feet away when she lost the gun. Sara chanced another look, doing a head count.

It was tough to be accurate because of the bushes and tree cover, but she estimated there were between fifteen and twenty cannibals.

Sara didn't like those odds. She had a bad leg and didn't know the territory, plus it was daylight and much easier for them to see her. A chase would end in her being caught, and if she was caught...

Her stomach grumbled, and she cursed herself.

I'd just better make damn sure they don't see me.

Sara moved slow and low, alternating her attention between the ferals and her footing. She didn't want to step on a twig and make a sound, or worse, trip. The task absorbed her full concentration. Never before had she tried to be so precise in her movement, and never before was so much riding on her.

Halfway there and the sweat was running down Sara's cheeks, stinging the cuts Georgia had made with the scissors.

Two-thirds of the way there and she had to stop and crouch lower when one of the ferals turned his head in her direction. Sara waited, still as a deer, her injured leg beginning to cramp up, then shake.

The cannibal didn't see her, and she continued forward.

Three quarters of the way there, she could finally see the gridiron. It was an awful thing, like a giant outdoor grill. She tried not to look at Meadow, caught in the middle. She tried not to look at the parts the people were eating.

She looked anyway.

It was nightmarish, a warped combination of familiarity and obscenity.

It also wasn't Meadow in the fire. Though charred, and partially devoured, Sara saw enough of the body to tell it was Captain
Prendick.

Which meant his boat was still here. If the helicopter route
didn't work, maybe they could sail off this godforsaken rock.
Maybe they could all actually live through—

That's when Jack began to cry.

She immediately shoved a finger in his mouth. He showed no
interest in sucking, batting her hand away.

"Shhhh," she whispered. "Please."

He filled his lungs, his eyes squeezing shut, his tiny mouth
stretching open, preparing to shout out to the whole world that
he was there—

And Sara covered his mouth, muffling the howl.

Quiet, Jack. You have to be quiet.

Jack clenched his fist and his little arms shook in rage. Sara
removed her hand, and the tail end of his cry echoed throughout
the woods.

Sara took a quick peek at the ferals. No one had noticed her
yet, but any second they would hear Jack's cries. She scurried
backward, retreating, and then noticed another group of the wild
people, passing through the forest. Heading her way.

We're surrounded.

Jack drew in another breath. He was getting ready for the biggest howl yet. Sara hunkered down, grabbing her son roughly by
the arms, giving him a little shake.

He needed to stop crying. He needed to stop crying *right now*.
The past twelve hours had been the most horrible of Sara's entire
life, and she was exhausted and hurt and hungry and scared and
completely overwhelmed.

Stop crying.

Stop fucking crying.

Sara felt a swell of rage toward her innocent child, and prepared to shake him even harder. If this little bastard didn't shut up
they were both going to die.

Stop crying, damn you! STOP IT!

Her rage only lasted a millisecond. But it scared her almost as much as the cannibals did.

Sara choked back a sob, then gently touched Jack's cheek, her whole hand shaking with tremors.

He screamed, but it was one of those screams that was so strong, so high-pitched, that the only real sound that came out was air.

Sara knew the tantrum would be coming next, Jack getting so worked up that it would take him forever to calm down.

Behind her, the ferals ventured closer.

Sara wiped a tear off of Jack's face with her thumb, then re-flexively stuck her finger in his diaper.

Wet. He's wet! That's why he's crying.

She had his onesie and diaper off in five seconds, a consummate pro at this. In the sling pocket was a fresh diaper, and with cannibals less than five yards away she fastened it onto his little butt, shoved him back in the sling, shoved her breast in his mouth, and rocked him back and forth, hoping for a miracle.

And then she felt one. Jack sucked in a huge breath, then latched on to her nipple.

She dropped down onto her side, cradling Jack in her arms as he nursed, pressing her back into a bush as the feral party walked past and joined the feast.

Jack's fingers grasped onto her belly, giving her a squeeze.

Maybe they'd live through this after all. But first she had to find...

The gun.

It was only a few feet away, right at the roots of a dogwood bush. Even better, it wasn't a revolver. It was one of those guns that had the bullets in a clip, which meant it probably held more than just six.

Sara carefully got to her feet, staying in a crouch. She took one careful step toward the gun, and then she felt her ears get hot, like her body could sense that a person was staring at her.

She looked up.

A person was staring.

In fact, all eighteen of them were.

. . .

Georgia tingled all over. She felt deliciously alive, and though she wasn't prone to smiling she couldn't get the smile off her face.

In one hand, she gripped the bloody filet knife.

In the other, she gripped something even more exciting.

She strolled up to the man in the uniform, the one called Tope, the muffled screams in the air almost musical in how they conveyed pain.

Then, abruptly, she stopped, her arm jerking back.

She tugged a bit harder, but it was no use.

Tom's intestines wouldn't stretch any farther.

. . .

Cindy had her eyes squeezed shut, and wished she could squeeze her ears shut as well. Of all the horrors of the past day, nothing could compare to when Georgia walked over with that knife. She was humming, *actually humming*, like this was some sort of game.

Then, without a word, she cut Tom open.

It got really bad after that.

In a perverse way, Cindy was grateful for the mouth gags. If she'd been forced to hear Tom beg, or scream at full throttle, Cindy was sure she would have lost her mind.

She peeked at Tyrone, who was also closing his eyes.

This wasn't how it was supposed to end. Cindy was finally straightening out her life. She finally found a good guy to be her boyfriend. She'd kicked drugs and her sentence was almost up and she was excited to become a waitress, of all stupid things, because that's what regular teenagers did and she so wanted to be regular.

Cindy tried to picture her parents, when they used to look at her with love instead of suspicion, tried to hear their voices rather than the voice of that horrible General giving Georgia orders.

"Now do his eyes."

Cindy wondered if her body would ever be found. If her mom and dad would ever know what happened to her. She wondered if they would care. She wondered, absurdly, if there was some way for an autopsy to be done, and it could show her parents, her family, her old friends, the whole world, that Cindy Welp died clean and sober, not a trace of meth in her system.

"Now do his genitals."

Cindy wished she could say goodbye to them. To tell them how sorry she was, but even more than that. To thank them, for all they've given her. To make them understand that *she* could finally understand. To say *I love you* one last time.

"Now do his scalp."

Cindy chanced another peek at Tyrone, and he was peeking at her. All the potential, all the possibility, they shared it in that one long look. Cindy had a brief, intense fantasy, something far beyond becoming a waitress. She stared at him and saw herself through his eyes, in ways she never dreamed of. As a wife. A mother. A grandmother. Someone who was important to other people. Someone needed. Someone loved.

A tear rolled down Tyrone's face. Cindy realized she was crying too.

"Now do the girl."

*   *   *

Taylor blinked. The pain he was in defied imagination. Surgery without anesthesia was agonizing enough, but Lester had hurt him even worse with his squeezing.

He blinked again.

They would suffer. Lester, and the doctor. Taylor would take his time with them. Keep them alive for months. Feed them through a stomach tube if he had to.

He blinked once more, and then twitched his fingers.

Taylor tried to remember the procedure, those many months ago. He'd been awake for that, too. But it took him all night before he was able to move again. Yet now he was already able to blink and twitch.

He concentrated, really hard, and jerked his left foot.

Maybe the procedure had done something to him, to make the paralytic wear off quicker. Or maybe the doctor had given him an incorrect dose, not accounting for all the weight he'd gained.

Taylor didn't care about the reason why. He embraced it.

The sooner he could move, the sooner he could pay them back, tenfold.

The man known as Subject 33 blinked, then forced his lips into a smile.

.   .   .

Tom kept waiting for the white light, waiting for the angel choir. But as his blood and breath and life leaked out of his ruined body, he realized there was nothing. Absolutely nothing.

His gramma had been frickin' right all along.

.   .   .

At first, no one moved. The scene seemed frozen in time. Sara, bending down for the gun. Almost twenty feral people, watching her with a mixture of curiosity and hostility.

Then one of them said, "More… food."

That broke the spell. Sara snatched up the gun and ran.

The adrenalin spiking through Sara's system made her leg injury all but disappear. She moved fast and fleet-footed, dodging around trees, hurdling thicket, zig-zagging sharply to throw her attackers off.

Jack popped off her breast and began to cry again, and she let him, holding him tight, refusing to stop for anything.

I didn't come this far to die now. Not now.

The sounds of pursuit clung to Sara's heels. It was as if the forest had come alive around her, foliage shaking, blurry figures weaving in and out peripherally, whoops and hollers used to tighten the circle around her, to cinch the noose.

Sara had no idea where she was going, no idea how she was going to get away. Eventually she would tire, or hit the island's edge. There were too many of them, and they were coordinating their hunt. She was tired and hurt and had never fired a gun before. This was futile.

But then Sara got lucky.

Ahead, tied to a tree trunk, was an orange ribbon.

Orange ribbons led to the prison.

A tiny beacon of hope flashed in Sara's mind. Maybe she wasn't going to die now after all. She poured on the speed, finding a second ribbon, and a third, distancing herself from her pursuers now that she had a goal.

Then the trees parted, the sun shining on the giant gray mounds of the bone yard. Sara ran into it, the piles taller than she was, darting left, then right, then right again, cradling Jack in her arms like he was a football and she was dodging defensive linemen, catching a glimpse of the prison and heading toward it in a roundabout, serpentine way.

There, on the side of the prison, tied to poles...

Cindy. Tyrone. Tom.

Sara didn't think she had any reserves left, but the sight of her kids prompted a burst of speed and she sprinted toward them like she was running on air.

. . .

As Tyrone watched Georgia work the knife, he remembered a conversation he had with his moms, who told him if he kept up his gangbanging he was going to be dead in an alley with two bullets in him by the time he was eighteen.

Tyrone hadn't believed her, but he had recognized the possibility of it happening.

Neither he nor his moms could have predicted he was going to be done in by a crazy white chick on some cannibal island next to a secret Civil War prison.

"Can I burn her?" Georgia asked the General. She was looking at Cindy when she said it.

"Yes," he replied.

Georgia, hands red with poor Tom's blood, reached into a pouch on her tool belt. Lester and Martin also had tool belts, with various items dangling from them. Tyrone figured they weren't going to use them to build anything.

Georgia removed a plastic baggie, filled with powder.

"I made this myself, back at the Center. I've been itching to try it."

With her other hand, Georgia pulled a cylinder from her belt, the size of a soda bottle. It said PROPANE and a torch was fitted onto the top.

Cindy's eyes got wide. Tyrone knew she was afraid of fire. Knew there wasn't anything worse for her.

He couldn't let her go out like that.

Tyrone screamed, loud as he could, kicking out at Georgia even though she was out of reach. He pulled against the dog collar until his vision went red, thrashing and moaning, knowing he wasn't going to stop her.

But this display wasn't for Georgia.

"The boy seems to want to go first," Tope said. "Give him his wish."

Tyrone relaxed. Mission accomplished. He could feel Cindy's eyes on him, but he didn't trust that he could look at her without completely breaking down.

Then he realized, *fuck it.*

Thug life was all about frontin', and representin', and bein' some bullshit stereotype just like Martin said. Tyrone wasn't a thug no more. He was just a man. Men didn't need to be strong 24/7. Not in front of the woman they loved.

So as Georgia approached him with the torch, he dropped his guard and let Cindy look at him as he really was. And in her eyes—the last thing he was ever going to see before he burned to death—Tyrone Morrow found acceptance.

Then a gunshot broke the silence, like the handclap of an angry god.

"Back the fuck away, Georgia."

Tyrone turned.

Sara.

General Alton Tope wasn't easily impressed, but the chubby girl's zeal in mutilating the boy was something to behold. According to the doctor, the serum would be relatively cheap and easy to produce, the procedure simple to teach. Tope doubted he'd get any sort of green light from Washington, but it wouldn't be the first time the military experiments on troops without anyone's knowledge or consent.

Worst case scenario, Tope could scour the prisons for lifers and death row garbage. He'd done so in the past. Putting together a team of several hundred men and women wouldn't be too difficult.

And two hundred people with the enthusiasm of this girl would be a formidable unit indeed.

They would need to do some testing first. Perhaps enhance fifty troops and unleash them on a small town in Mexico. Or even someplace secluded in the US. It was easier to cover-up than one might think.

Then some other woman ran up to the children and fired a gun into the air, breaking Tope's reverie.

What an interesting turn of events.

Benson raised his sidearm, but General Tope held up a finger, stopping him. This new woman was obviously not a threat. She was haggard and bleeding and out of breath, and she held the gun like it was a snake she wished to throw away, and she had something—*an infant*—in a sling across her belly. Tope wanted to see how this played out. Wanted to see how the chubby girl reacted to this new threat.

The chubby girl fulfilled Tope's expectations. She lunged at the woman.

The woman twisted to the side and kicked her in the face, knocking her onto the ground.

A pity. All that sadistic rage, but no skill.

"I apologize for this," Dr. Plincer said. "I'll have Lester and Martin take care of it."

Plincer nodded at his men. They advanced on the woman.

Fascinating.

The woman was armed. The men only had hand weapons. But they approached her without fear.

Tope was liking this serum more and more.

Rather than try to shoot them like she should have, the woman instead ducked around the boy's pole. There was another shot, and then the boy's hands were free.

Stupid. She should have taken care of the threat first, then released the children. This woman was no soldier. She was an idiot.

The men closed the gap on her, and she wasted even more time freeing the girl by firing at her bonds.

Then a handful of wild people rushed out of the woods. *The ferals.* They threw themselves at Lester and Martin, snarling and slobbering and brandishing... *was that silverware?*

What the ferals lacked in technique, they apparently made up for in savagery. Tope became concerned.

Lester and Martin had much better skills than the pudgy girl. They dispatched several of those wild people with precise, almost eloquent, strokes of their knives.

But when a dozen more ferals came screaming into the area, Lester and Martin fled. So did Dr. Plincer.

Benson had his gun out, shooting two of the wild people who ran at him. They fell, but were quickly followed by five more.

That's when Tope's concern became fear.

He ran, briefcase in hand, back the way he'd come. Benson fired twice more, and it sounded like the woman was shooting as well.

Then a man cried out, "Help me!"

Benson, whom Tope had hired to protect him, was calling for help. General Tope found no amusement in the irony, and he certainly didn't offer assistance of any kind. Tope didn't even turn around to see what had happened. He was too intent on running for the helicopter.

Tope rounded the corner and saw the chopper in the distance. He hoped the pilot, Crouch, was paying attention and about to start the engine, because Tope could sense he had several feral people chasing him. He chanced a look.

More than several. Five or six.

Tope wasn't in the best shape, and wasn't a fast runner, but terror was the ultimate motivator. He reached the helicopter before the savages, yanking on the door handle.

Locked.

The turbine engine whined to life, the rotors beginning to spin. That idiot Crouch was staring over Tope's shoulder at the oncoming horde, his eyes big as duck eggs.

General Tope banged on the door. Once he got inside he was going to strangle that fool. Revise that; after he got inside *and* was taken to safety, he would strangle him.

Then the unthinkable happened. General Alton Tope, the man who was going to make sure the US military maintained world supremacy, was dragged away from the helicopter in utter disbelief.

The suitcase was ripped from his hand, but these people had no interest in its contents. They seemed interested in him, wrestling him to the ground, pinning him down.

But why? What could these ferals possibly want?

The first jolt of pain was in Tope's leg. It was followed swiftly by an equal pain in his arm.

They're biting me.

Typical Army fuck-up. A multi-billion dollar spy telescope, plus a decade of clandestine intel, and no one had known the ferals were maneaters.

Tope screamed, and a savage stuck his ugly face in Tope's, flecks of flesh and blood in his filthy beard, mouth open and drooling, his lips moving closer and closer.

Tope was more revolted by this man's kiss than by those who were chewing on him.

But it turned out this man wanted to chew as well.

General Tope was tangentially aware of a strong wind, the helicopter taking off, as more and more of his body was gripped in the mouths of these cannibals. He began to choke, blood running down his windpipe from the bleeding hole where his nose used to be.

The helicopter's speaker system crackled and came to life. The last human voice Tope ever heard was that bastard, Crouch.

"Sorry, General. You didn't pay me enough to die here."

Tope exposed his neck, praying to be bitten there, praying for someone to pierce his jugular or carotid and end his suffering.

He had no takers.

Apparently the ferals liked their meals alive and kicking.

·　　·　　·

This was unfortunate. Most unfortunate indeed. Dr. Plincer had been so close to sealing the deal. Who could have guessed the ferals would have showed up?

Well, actually, he should have guessed it. He was the one who made them that way in the first place.

But Plincer hadn't known there were so many. He also hadn't known they'd been able to organize their group, almost like some primitive tribe. It was fascinating, from a scientific standpoint, but a huge disaster from a financial one.

Hopefully, General Tope would get away, and they'd be able to try again at a later date. If not, perhaps the military would send another representative. The Russians were also a possibility.

Plincer had even been contacted by a former member of the KGB. This situation was just a slight delay—a hiccup—in the overall game plan.

Plincer hurried through the big iron door into the prison, but before he got a chance to lock it someone grabbed him from behind, pinning his arm up behind his back.

Subject 33.

"Well, you recovered quickly," Plincer said. "It's good to see you up and about."

Subject 33 twisted upwards, popping Plincer's shoulder out of its socket and taking the doctor's breath away.

After that it got bad.

Very bad.

.   .   .

They didn't run. They hid. Cindy couldn't believe how wonderful it was to get this second chance. She promised herself she wouldn't waste it.

Right after Sara freed her and fired a few times at the oncoming wild people, the four of them ducked into the trees and jumped into a shallow ditch.

Tyrone had his arm around her, and it felt better than the biggest hit of meth she'd ever taken. She helped him take the dog collar off, and then removed hers. After being unable to use her hands for so long, the freedom to move them again was fantastic, though the cuffs were still pinching her wrists—Sara had only shot the chain between them. Even the throb from the bite wound seemed to hurt less.

Now all they needed to do was keep away from the psychos, the cannibals, those army guys, and the mad doctor. The army guys seemed to have left, their helicopter flying off overhead.

"Help me!"

Cindy turned in the direction of the plea. It came from nearby. A woman.

Georgia.

Sara stood up. She looked strong and sure and every bit Cindy's hero.

"You two stay here," Sara said.

Cindy shook her head. "Don't."

"I have to help her."

"She killed Tom."

"Plincer did something to her brain. It's not her fault. Maybe it can be fixed."

Cindy reached out, grabbed Sara's arm. "You didn't see it, Sara. She's a monster."

Sara's eyes got glassy. She placed her hand on Cindy's. "I wouldn't give up on you. Or Tyrone. I've... lost... I just... I can't give up on Georgia either."

Cindy understood. "We're coming with you, then."

Sara kissed the crying Jack on the head, and nodded.

"Please help!"

They crept over the ditch, so close to each other they looked like a single six-legged creature. Georgia was lying on her back in the clearing, twenty yards away from the bone yard. Her face was a mask of bright red blood, but her chest was moving up and down. One of her hands was clenched in a fist. The other still held the cylindrical propane torch. Cindy could see the blue flame coming out of it, scorching the earth it touched black.

Cindy didn't want to get any closer. Though Georgia looked seriously injured, she had a weapon in her hand. A terrible weapon, one she'd tried to use on her and Tyrone. If Cindy lived to a hundred and never saw another flame again, she'd be fine with that.

But they did get closer. So close that if Georgia so much as flinched Cindy would have wet her pants in fright.

"Sara!"

Tyrone pointed to the right. Cindy glanced in that direction, saw Sara turn and raise the gun and aim at two cannibals rushing at them, but then Cindy turned back to Georgia, not trusting the insane girl, feeling something wasn't right.

There. On the ground. Small and white and plastic.

A ketchup wrapper.

Sara fired the gun, the shots so loud they made Cindy's head ache.

Georgia sat up and her eyes popped open, boring into Cindy. She smiled, licked some ketchup off her upper lip—ketchup she'd shown Cindy last night, the stuff she was going to scare the boys with.

"Burn, bitch."

Georgia's lips formed the words, but Cindy's ears were ringing so she couldn't hear them, and then Georgia was raising her clenched fist—it was filled with that powder she had in the baggy—and Sara fired another shot, and Cindy decided she was not going to burn, not now and not ever, and she lashed out and slapped Georgia's hand, the powder forming a cloud in the air.

Georgia's face went from surprise to anger as the cloud settled around her. Then it went from anger to surprise as she turned her attention at the open flame she was holding.

There was a huge *whump*, and Cindy felt like she'd been hit with a thousand hairdryers at once as the cloud around Georgia exploded.

Cindy jumped backward, feeling her eyebrows singe, quickly patting out the tiny fire that had started on her shirt.

Georgia also tried to pat herself out, with less effective results. She was completely on fire. Her hair. Her clothes. Her shoes. Even her skin.

Sara stepped in front of Cindy, thrusting a yowling Jack into her arms, tugging her own shirt up over her head and swatting at Georgia. But that only fanned the flames, making them bigger.

Georgia may have tried to scream, but she'd apparently inhaled some of that powder, because the only thing that came out of her mouth was flames.

Cindy turned away, saw two cannibals dead on the grass—the ones that Sara had shot—and then Tyrone was holding her and patting her back and Cindy wondered if this nightmare would ever be over, if they'd ever be safe.

That's when she saw Lester walking toward them.

*　　*　　*

Every nerve ending in Georgia's body was firing at once. All she cared about, her entire world, was centered on when the pain would end.

She remembered, inexorably, an old saying—a star that shines twice as bright burns half as long—and hoped it was true, hoped this would be over soon.

It wasn't.

Georgia burned bright, that was for sure. But she also burned for a very long time.

.   .   .

Lester Paks watched the Sara woman standing over Georgia girl. First the pet. Now his girlfriend. Lester was so angry his teeth were clenched, something he tried to avoid because their sharp points made his gums bleed. His gums were bleeding so badly his cheeks began to bulge.

The Sara woman needed to die. And the boy and the girl with the Sara woman needed to die.

And the baby?

Lester liked the baby. It would make a nice, new pet, once he chewed off its arms and legs.

Lester walked after them, barely glancing at the still burning, still twitching Georgia girl. When the three began to run, Lester ran too. Lester had long legs, and strong muscles. He would catch them.

They went into the area where the helicopter landed. The helicopter wasn't there anymore. But the General was still there.

At least, most of him was.

The feral people were squatting around his body. The Sara woman and the children jogged past, but the boy broke away, heading for something; the metal suitcase Tope had been carrying. The boy picked it up and rejoined the two women.

The ferals paid the boy no attention. But when they saw Lester, they scattered. The ferals were scared of Lester. They had reason to be. Usually, Martin would bring Lester playmates. Sometimes boats would come to the island, and Lester could get his own playmates. But if Lester didn't have any playmates, Lester would take a feral person. They were smelly and dirty, but they screamed as well as anyone else.

The Sara woman and the children ran north, probably not knowing why. This pleased Lester. The lake was to the north. Very close. And the shore was high up, more than thirty feet above the water. When they reached the ledge, there would be no place left to go.

Lester ran faster, closing the distance between them.

The clearing ended, and the forest began. The woods were thick here, blocking out most of the sun. Sometimes Lester lost sight of them. But they were easy to hear, clomping through the woods, breathing heavy, yelling encouraging words at each other. Lester spit out a stream of blood, and his cheeks began to fill again.

"There's nowhere to go," said the Sara woman. "We're trapped."

That made Lester smile. He had many items on his tool belt. He decided to use the mallet first. He would break all of their knees, so they couldn't run away. Then he could take his time.

The trees thinned, and Lester saw Lake Huron, spreading out into the distance. He stopped several yards before the edge. It was a long drop down, and there were sharp rocks among the waves.

Lester looked left, and then right. He saw the girl on the ground next to a big tree, the baby in her lap. She was holding her leg and crying. The girl must have hurt herself. Lester took out the mallet, happy to make it hurt even worse.

"Lester needs a new girlfriend," he said, raising the weapon.

But something went wrong. Lester's head jerked back, and he stumbled sideways. He reached up and touched his face.

Six of Lester's teeth fell into his large palm.

My teeth! My teeth! My beautiful teeth!

He looked up in time to see the boy swing the metal suitcase a second time. The boy had been hiding behind the tree. He and the girl had tricked Lester.

Lester backed up, staying out of range. He had dropped the mallet when the boy hit him, so he reached for his tool belt, seeking the hatchet. The boy swung again, but this time he let go of the suitcase. It hit Lester in the chin. More of Lester's beautiful teeth left his mouth, arcing through the air, going over the edge of the cliff.

That's when he saw the Sara woman, already running at him, leaping in a flying kick.

She connected with Lester's chest. He'd been bracing himself, but it still made him stagger backward two steps.

Unfortunately, the second step was a long one.

One moment Lester was on land. The next moment he wasn't.

He managed to twist around as he fell, so he could see the rocks coming up at him at a blinding speed.

Maybe I will see Georgia girl in hel—

The thought ended with an abrupt crunch.

．　．　．

Dr. Plincer had to give Subject 33 credit. The man could inflict pain like a maestro conducted an orchestra. He'd even managed to top Plincer's time with Lester so long ago.

He wasn't sure how long he'd been in Subject 33's box, but it seemed like hours. Plincer could understand why so many people screamed for so long. He would have as well, if it hadn't been for the skewers in his tongue.

At least Plincer's curiosity had been satisfied. He'd always wondered about the machine Subject 33 had built. Really an ingenious device. Plincer just wished he wasn't forced to have firsthand knowledge.

A tiny, still coherent part of him wondered why he hadn't passed out yet. After all, it couldn't possibly get worse.

Then Subject 33 hooked up the car battery, and it got worse.

But unconsciousness still didn't come.

．　．　．

Their bellies were full, but their appetite for drawing blood had only been whetted. The few that were still alive grouped together, forming a hunting party. They went in search of more people to kill. The woman and the children had gotten away. But the island was small. They would find them.

They ran alongside the prison, looking for the woman, and one of them stopped.

The others looked.

The prison door. It was open.

They snarled and hooted and ran inside.

* * *

Sara looked over the edge. Lester was gone, though she could make out the blood stain where he'd hit the rock.

"I thought the plan was to lead him north to the ledge and then shoot his ass, not go all Jackie Chan," Tyrone said.

Sara shrugged. "No bullets left."

Cindy walked over with Jack, holding Sara's wrist as she peeked downward. "Is he dead?"

"Yes."

"You sure he's not going to come back, try to kill us again?"

Sara pointed at the body floating out into the big water. "I'm sure."

They watched him for a while, bobbing in the waves. Sara tried to figure out how many men she'd killed this camping trip, and realized she'd lost count.

There'll be time for therapy later. Now we need to find Captain Prendick's boat.

She checked the compass, located east.

"Come on, guys. Let's go."

"Hold on a sec. Let's see what's in this briefcase, first. Gotta be somethin' valuable."

Tyrone set it on the ground, and they all gathered to look when he opened the lid.

"Great," he said. "Some ugly ho."

Actually, it was a painting of an ugly ho. In three-quarter profile, sandwiched between two thick pieces of Plexiglas. She had bulgy eyes and a gold cross around her neck and a blue dress, and the style was oddly familiar.

"Think it's worth somethin'?" Tyrone asked.

Sara lifted the painting. Under it was a bill of sale, from the Van Gogh Museum in Amsterdam, for just under 20 million Euro. Sara shook her head, amazed.

"It's Vincent Van Gogh's *Portrait of Woman in Blue*, and the bill of sale looks real."

"Twenty million Euro?" Cindy said. "Is that like pesos, meaning it's only worth a few hundred bucks?"

"The Euro is stronger than the dollar, Cindy." Sara said, suddenly nervous to be holding it. "This painting is worth about twenty-five million dollars."

"That's one pricey ho." Tyrone whistled. "Guess when I go to college I ain' gotta worry about no student loans."

"Tyrone, you couldn't get into college, even if you lived long enough to try."

Sara jerked in the direction of the voice.

Martin.

*   *   *

Taylor tried to stay calm. He hurt all over, and he wanted to make the doctor pay. But he didn't want the doctor to die. Not for a long time. So he had to show restraint.

Taylor knew there were painkillers in the lab, but he didn't know which drugs he should take. If he was able to talk, he would have asked the doctor. But he couldn't talk, and when he tried to write what he wanted on paper, the doctor just screamed and babbled incoherently. So Taylor was forced to suffer.

The doctor would suffer with him.

Taylor was deciding where to stick the fiftieth skewer when he heard a noise behind him. He jumped away, fearing it to be Lester.

But it wasn't Lester. It was a dirty, bearded man with ripped clothes.

Taylor walked toward him. Though he was injured, it would still be easy to subdue this skinny little man. Taylor could take his wrath out on him, keeping the doctor alive to enjoy later.

He stopped in mid-step when another dirty man came in. Then another followed. And another. And another.

They had weapons. Rusty knives. Tree branches. One had a fork.

Taylor backed away, his lips flapping, his hands raised in supplication.

The dirty people attacked. Taylor felt like he was in a barbed wire tornado, being ripped apart on all sides. Poking, stabbing, hitting, biting, gouging, bit by agonizing bit.

Stop! I don't handle pain well!

Taylor fell to his knees, covering his face, screaming soundlessly and enduring quite a lot of pain for quite a long time as they tore him to pieces.

⸱　　⸱　　⸱

Martin was through fooling around. When the ferals attacked and the craziness started, he went straight for Tope's bodyguard. A quick poke in the stomach with a hunting knife, and the man graciously gave up his gun. Martin then waited in the woods for things to settle down and Sara to appear.

She did, dragging Jack and her precious kids with her. Pathetic, really. The dumb bitch even tried to save Georgia. Probably hoping to help her.

She would have had better luck teaching an alligator to fetch.

When Lester joined the fun, Martin tagged along.

There was a bad moment, after Martin followed them into the woods, when he worried Lester would kill his wife before he got there. But, incredibly, they'd managed to take out the big guy.

Which was fine. Martin didn't like to share anyway.

"This is how it's going to work, Sara," he said, basking in the fear he knew his words caused her. "We're all going to march back to the prison like a big happy family. Then you're going back into the trunk, and you'll get to listen while I have some playtime with the meth whore. Tyrone, buddy, you're allowed to watch. To make it more fun, every time Cindy screams, I'll cut off one of your fingers."

"No," Sara said.

Martin's grin slipped a notch. "Excuse me? You see I'm holding a gun, right?"

"Cindy, Tyrone, get behind me. When I say so, take Jack and run into the woods.

The children listened to their surrogate mother, who then held the painting at waist-level.

Martin sneered. "What, I'm not going to shoot you because you've got some ugly chick?"

"It's a Van Gogh, Martin. Worth twenty five million dollars. You're an art lover. You wouldn't do anything to ruin it. And you won't shoot me in the chest or head, because you don't want me to die that easily."

Martin laughed, full and genuine. "You're kidding me, right?"

He aimed right at the ugly chick's head. When the bullet passed through the painting, it would shatter Sara's hip.

How terribly painful, being curled up in a trunk with a broken femur.

"Put down the gun, Martin, and I'll give you the painting."

"You're out of your mind," he said.

"You won't shoot. I know you."

"The hell I won't."

Then he fired.

*   *   *

The impact of the bullet slammed the painting into Sara's pelvis, but she had anticipated it and was already moving forward, rushing at him.

Martin fired again, clearly surprised, and the painting vibrated in her hands. She felt pain, her leg giving out, but momentum took her the next few steps, and then she was angling the portrait upward, swinging the sharp corner against Martin's hand, knocking the gun away.

"Run!" Sara yelled.

She thrust the painting at him again, aiming for his head, but now Martin was backpedaling, pulling something from his tool belt.

The survival knife. That awful, horrifying survival knife.

He slashed.

Sara blocked with the painting.

He thrust.

Sara blocked with the painting.

He roared, throwing himself at her, driving Sara onto her back with the painting sandwiched between them. He brought the terrible knife up to her face.

I can see my reflection in the blade.

"I'm going to cut your fucking tongue out and lock you in that fucking trunk for a week," Martin screamed, spittle flecking out of his mouth.

But Sara wasn't afraid anymore. She was done being afraid.

Sara grabbed the knife blade as it came up, feeling it slice into her fingers, all the way to the bone. But she wouldn't let go. She wouldn't back down. Never. Again.

As Martin's face creased with astonishment, Sara used the momentum of her grab and the leverage of her grip to force the tip of the blade around, driving it right into the son of a bitch's eye.

Martin flinched backward, dropping the knife, pressing both hands to his face, and then Sara saw Tyrone standing over them, once again holding the metal suitcase.

He swung like Sammy Sosa, cracking Martin square in the nose, knocking him off Sara and onto the ground.

"That tough enough for ya, asshole?" Tyrone said, staring down at him.

Martin was clearly disoriented, but he managed to get onto all fours. He shook his head like a wet dog, spraying blood everywhere.

Tyrone raised the suitcase again.

"No," Sara ordered.

Tyrone looked at her. So did Martin.

That's when Sara held up the gun Martin had dropped and blew the top of her husband's head off.

.　　.　　.

Dr. Plincer watched the ferals tear Subject 33 apart, crying with relief that they would no doubt attack him next. Plincer wanted to die more than he'd ever wanted anything in his life. The pain was too unbearable.

Kill me. Kill me quickly. My life's work will remain. Someone will find my notes, my serum. I can die, because my work will live on.

In a brief flash of lucidity, Plincer reflected on his legacy, and came to a startling, ironic conclusion. He'd thought the only way to create pure evil was by enhancing that portion of the brain. But he'd been deceiving himself.

Anyone who wanted to create pure evil had to, by extension, be pure evil himself.

Imagine that. I'm the worst one of all, and have been all along.

Plincer lamented not being able to study his own brain before the ferals killed him.

But the ferals didn't kill Plincer. They looked at him closely, gave each other brief nods, and then left him there in the box, helpless and agonized and alone and wondering how long car batteries lasted before they ran out of juice.

Seven hours, it turned out. But Plincer succumbed to a heart attack after enduring only six.

.　　.　　.

The cut on her hand was bad, and Sara wondered if she would lose her fingers. But even if she did, it was a small price to pay for surviving.

The five of them, including the *Woman in Blue*, walked along the beach until they found Captain Prendick's dinghy, hidden behind some rocks. As Sara had guessed, the bullets and Martin's knife had barely made a dent in the painting's Plexiglas frame. When something was worth twenty-five mil, it was a good bet it was going to be well-protected. Of course the glass was bulletproof. A master like Van Gogh didn't deserve any less.

Cindy was the only one with two good hands, so she had to start the dinghy's outboard motor and steer it out to Prendick's boat. She was awkward at first, but quickly got the hang of it.

Once they were all in the dinghy, Sara spent a minute checking Jack for any injuries. Then, above the din of the motor, Sara whistled in Jack's left ear, then the right one, relieved that he turned his head toward the sounds. She'd done her best to keep the pistol away from his ears, and was grateful her shooting hadn't damaged his hearing.

"He okay?" Tyrone yelled to her.

"Just a poopy diaper!" she yelled back. "He needs to be changed!"

"Me too!" Tyrone said, a big grin on his face.

That's when Lester jumped out of the water, heaving his upper body onto the side of the boat and wrapping his arm around Tyrone's neck.

Cindy screamed, turning the dinghy too hard, threatening to flip it. Sara pitched forward, dropping Jack onto the flat rubber bottom of the boat, and then a wave hit, knocking her back into Cindy.

The engine sputtered, and died.

Tyrone and Lester wrestled on the boat's port side, raising up the starboard side with their weight until Cindy and Sara were several feet up in the air.

Jack began to slide toward the edge. He bumped into the inflatable side, only a foot from where Tyrone fought for his life. Sara reached for him, but her weight made the boat even more lopsided, threatening to flip it.

"Back!" Sara yelled at Cindy. They leaned starboard, and the dinghy leveled off. But Sara couldn't get to Jack, and she couldn't help Tyrone, who had both hands locked onto Lester's wrist.

Lester's hand was locked onto a hatchet.

Then, abruptly, both Tyrone and Lester fell overboard.

The sudden redistribution of weight caused the boat to tilt up toward Sara's side, launching Jack into the air in a high arc over Sara's head.

Her balance lost, Sara reached up, her fingers barely touching Jack's foot as she went ass over head and into Lake Huron.

The water was a shock, like falling into an ice chest. Sara held her breath, her eyes wide open, searching for her lost baby.

The water was dark, murky, the overhead sun not penetrating more than a few feet. Sara let out some of her air so she was neutrally buoyant, then methodically began to scan the depths.

No Jack in front of her.

No Jack on the left.

No Jack behind her.

No Jack on the right.

Jesus, where was—

Below her—she glimpsed the white of Jack's onesie, sinking fast.

Sara dove, getting to him in two strokes, grabbing his little leg, spinning around and kicking to the surface, thrusting Jack up out of the water...

"Cindy!"

Cindy reached for the baby, pulling him back in the boat. Sara hung onto the edge, waiting for Jack to move, desperately trying to remember the baby CPR class she took during the first trimester.

And then the little guy coughed and started to cry.

Sara spun around, looking for Tyrone and Lester. The waves were strong, but not so high she couldn't see over them. There was no one on her side.

"Cindy! Do you see Tyrone?"

"I don't see him!" Cindy said, her head swiveling all around. "I don't see him, Sara!"

Then Sara felt the boat jerk. It jerked again, the inflatable edge bumping her in the face.

They were beneath it.

Sara took a deep breath and went under. She saw them immediately, Lester biting Tyrone's arm as the boy tried to gouge out the giant's eyes.

Sara swam to them, adding her good hand to Tyrone's efforts, digging her thumbnail into Lester's socket.

Lester released Tyrone...

...and grabbed her.

Sara planted her feet on his chest, trying to get away, while his head drew closer and his bloody mouth opened, aiming for her neck.

Unable to break his grip, Sara again clawed at the monster's face, hooking a finger into his nostril and ripping.

But Lester still wouldn't let go. And Sara was almost out of air.

Spots appeared before her eyes—oxygen deprivation—and the urge to breathe was becoming overwhelming. Sara would be forced to inhale any second, even if it meant taking lake water into her lungs. As a last ditch effort she went completely limp, trying to play dead, hoping Lester would let her go.

Sara heard the boat motor start, but it sounded very far away. A small part of her mind—the part not crazed with a lust for air—hoped Tyrone had gotten away and that he and Cindy could get Jack to Plincer's boat.

Then, incredibly, she was free.

Sara kicked frantically for the surface, her mouth open and sucking air the moment her face broke the surface. She wheezed, coughed, and then caught something in her peripheral vision.

Lester. His hatched raised high up out of the water, poised to come down on her skull.

She caught the handle with both hands, screaming as the cuts on her fingers reopened.

Then, her absolute worst fears were realized. She looked in the direction of the approaching sound.

Rather than escape with her baby, Cindy and Tyrone were coming back.

Sara wanted to yell for them to get away, to save themselves. But she had nothing left. Lester shook off her grip and reared the ax back, about to take the killing blow.

That's when the boat hit him.

But instead of running into him head-on, it had *backed* into him instead.

Lester screamed like a high-pitched tornado siren, his entire body shaking as the motor propeller ripped into his back.

Cindy gunned the throttle, revving the engine, and Sara stared, horrified, as the prop blades rode up his shoulders and separated most of his head from his spine.

The giant's bloodshot eyes rolled up into his head, and his chin touched his chest, a geyser of blood spraying out of the stump like a Fourth of July roman candle. Then the engine stalled out and Lester Pak's dead body sank into Huron.

. . .

The remainder of the trip back to Captain Prendick's boat was uneventful. Except for shivering, they were all okay. Once on board, Cindy found a stack of thick beach towels and a hairdryer, and they all dried off.

Jack fell asleep naked, wrapped in a sheet and nestled in the center of a life preserver.

Sara located Prendick's radio, and called the Coast Guard. The *real* Coast Guard. And just to be sure, she spoke with ten other boats currently on Lake Huron and asked them for help too.

She was exhausted, but she refused to so much as sit down until they were safe.

"So what we gonna do," Tyrone said. "Put the ho up on eBay?"

For all the tossing and tumbling on the dinghy, the *Woman in Blue* hadn't gotten so much as splashed.

"I don't think the Van Gogh Museum willingly sells their paintings," Sara said, figuring the military must have unlawfully persuaded them. "I'm sure they'll be happy to buy it back."

"For twenty-five million?"

"I don't know, Tyrone."

"You not gonna keep all the money, on account of me being a minor, are you?"

Sara allowed herself a small smile. "I think a three way split is fair, don't you both?"

Tyrone nodded. "That's eight million, three hundred thirty three thousand, three hundred thirty three dollars each."

Cindy gave him a playful punch in the shoulder. "How'd you figure that out so quick?"

"Girl, you got yourself involved with a society's worst nightmare. An intelligent black man."

"And I thought I was only interested in your body and your money."

"You really interested in my body?"

They kissed, and Sara gave them their privacy.

She went onto the deck. Lake Huron was a giant blue mirror, stretching out as far as Sara could see. She closed her eyes. Even with all the pain she was in, the sun felt glorious on her face.

Then, to her left, she heard a soft thump.

Sara's heart didn't race. Her palms didn't sweat. Her mouth didn't go dry. She didn't so much as flinch.

It's nothing. But even if it is something, I can handle it. I can handle anything.

Languidly, Sara opened her eyes. A seagull stood on the deck, a few feet away from her. It cocked its tiny head, did a little hop, and then spread its wings, flying past Sara. She watched it glide off across the big water, beautiful and free and marvelously alive, changing directions to avoid hitting the Coast Guard cutter heading their way.

*   *   *

Most of them were dead. Martin was dead. Lester was dead. Subject 33 was dead. Doctor Plincer was dead. The island was quiet, almost peaceful.

There would be authorities coming soon. They would stay for a while, try to make sense of it all. Search the prison, and discover the lab, and the serum, and take all of it away.

It didn't matter how hard they searched. They wouldn't be able to search everywhere.

There were many places to hide on the island.

There would be hoopla for a while. Media. News and TV. Not only because of Dr. Plincer and the deaths of the children. But because there was a previously unknown historical discovery on this island. A secret prison, piled high with the bones of dead Confederate soldiers.

Rock Island—Plincer's Island—would soon become a landmark.

Landmarks meant visitors. Lots of visitors.

All the seven surviving ferals had to do was be patient.

They would hunt again.

Soon.

ABOUT THE AUTHOR

Joe Konrath is the author of more than twenty novels and dozens of shorter works in the mystery, thriller, horror, and science fiction genres. He's sold over three million books worldwide, and besides Jude Hrdin he's collaborated with bestsellers Blake Crouch, Ann Voss Peterson, Henry Perez, Tom Schreck, Jeff Strand, Tracy Sharp, Bernard Schaffer, Barry Eisler, Ken Lindsey, Garth Perry, Iain Rob Wright, and F. Paul Wilson. He likes beer, pinball machines, and playing pinball when drinking beer.

Visit him at www.jakonrath.com

Joe Konrath's
COMPLETE BIBLIOGRAPHY

JACK DANIELS THRILLERS

WHISKEY SOUR

BLOODY MARY

RUSTY NAIL

DIRTY MARTINI

FUZZY NAVEL

CHERRY BOMB

SHAKEN

STIRRED *with Blake Crouch*

RUM RUNNER

LAST CALL

SHOT OF TEQUILA

SERIAL KILLERS UNCUT *with Blake Crouch*

LADY 52 *with Jude Hardin*

65 PROOF *short stories*

FLOATERS *short with Henry Perez*

BURNERS *short with Henry Perez*

SUCKERS *short with Jeff Strand*

FLOATERS short with Henry Perez

BURNERS *short with Henry Perez*

JACKED UP! *short with Tracy Sharp*

STRAIGHT UP *short with Iain Rob Wright*

CHEESE WRESTLING *short with Bernard Schaffer*

ABDUCTIONS *short with Garth Perry*

BEAT DOWN *short with Garth Perry*

BABYSITTING MONEY *short with Ken Lindsey*

OCTOBER DARK *short with Joshua Simcox*

RACKED *short with Jude Hardin*

BABE ON BOARD *short with Ann Voss Peterson*

BANANA HAMMOCK

CODENAME: CHANDLER SERIES

EXPOSED *with Ann Voss Peterson*

HIT *with Ann Voss Peterson*

NAUGHTY *with Ann Voss Peterson*

FLEE *with Ann Voss Peterson*

SPREE *with Ann Voss Peterson*

THREE *with Ann Voss Peterson*

FIX *with F. Paul Wilson and Ann Voss Peterson*

RESCUE

THE KONRATH/KILBORN HORROR COLLECTIVE

ORIGIN

THE LIST

DISTURB

AFRAID

TRAPPED

ENDURANCE

HAUNTED HOUSE

WEBCAM

DRACULAS *with Blake Crouch, Jeff Strand, and F. Paul Wilson*

HOLES IN THE GROUND *with Iain Rob Wright*

THE GREYS

SECOND COMING

THE NINE

GRANDMA? *with Talon Konrath*

WILD NIGHT IS CALLING *short with Ann Voss Peterson*

TIMECASTER SERIES

TIMECASTER

TIMECASTER SUPERSYMMETRY

TIMECASTER STEAMPUNK

BYTER

EROTICA
(WRITING AS MELINDA DUCHAMP)

FIFTY SHADES OF ALICE IN WONDERLAND

FIFTY SHADES OF ALICE THROUGH THE LOOKING GLASS

FIFTY SHADES OF ALICE AT THE HELLFIRE CLUB

WANT IT BAD

FIFTY SHADES OF JEZEBEL AND THE BEANSTALK

FIFTY SHADES OF PUSS IN BOOTS

FIFTY SHADES OF GOLDILOCKS

THE SEXPERTS – FIFTY GRADES OF SHAY

THE SEXPERTS – THE GIRL WITH THE PEARL NECKLACE

THE SEXPERTS – LOVING THE ALIEN

ORIGIN

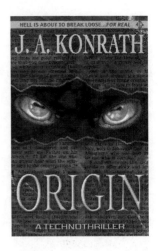

There are six books in the Konrath/Kilborn Collective. ORIGIN, THE LIST, AFRAID, TRAPPED, *and* ENDURANCE *are the first five, and can be read in any order. The sixth,* HAUNTED HOUSE, *contains characters from each of the previous books.*

Thriller writer J.A. Konrath, author of the Lt. Jack Daniels series, digs into the vaults and unearths a technohorror tale from the depths of hell…

1906–Something is discovered by workers digging the Panama Canal. Something dormant. Sinister. Very much alive.

2009–Project Samhain. A secret underground government installation begun 103 years ago in New Mexico. The best minds in the world have been recruited to study the most amazing discovery in the history of mankind. But the century of peaceful research is about to end.

Because it just woke up.

When linguist Andrew Dennison is yanked from his bed by the Secret Service and taken to a top secret facility in the desert , he has no idea he's been brought there to translate the words of an ancient demon.

He joins pretty but cold veterinarian Sun Jones, eccentric molecular biologist Dr. Frank Belgium, and a hodge-podge of religious, military, and science personnel to try and figure out if the creature is, indeed, Satan.

But things quickly go bad, and very soon Andy isn't just fighting for his life, but the lives of everyone on earth…

ORIGIN by J.A. Konrath

All hell is about to break loose. For real.

FLEE

J.A. Konrath and Ann Voss Peterson

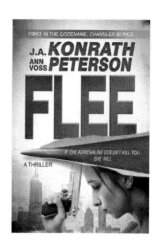

CODENAME: CHANDLER

She's an elite spy, working for an agency so secret only three people know it exists. Trained by the best of the best, she has honed her body, her instincts, and her intellect to become the perfect weapon.

FLEE

Then her cover is explosively blown, and she becomes a walking bulls-eye, stalked by assassins who want the secrets she holds, and those who'd prefer she die before talking.

Chandler now has twenty-four hours to thwart a kidnapping, stop a murderous psychopath, uncover the mystery of her past, retire five highly-trained contract killers, and save the world from nuclear annihilation, all while dodging 10,000 bullets and a tenacious cop named Jack Daniels.

Buckle up. It's going to be one helluva ride.

DISTURB

A medical investigator tormented by secret guilt.

A beautiful doctor with an illicit desire.

A millionaire businessman indulging a passion for murder.

And a human guinea pig who has been awake for seven straight weeks.

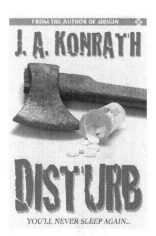

Sign up for the J.A. Konrath newsletter. A few times a year I pick random people to give free stuff to. It could be you.

http://www.jakonrath.com/mailing-list.php

I won't spam you or give your information out without your permission!

Made in the USA
San Bernardino, CA
08 December 2016